LONGS PEAK

JOE REGENBOGEN

MILFORD
HOUSE
an imprint of Sunbury Press, Inc.
Mechanicsburg, PA USA

MILFORD HOUSE

an imprint of Sunbury Press, Inc.
Mechanicsburg, PA USA

For information about special discounts for bulk purchases, please contact Sunbury Press Orders Dept. at (855) 338-8359 or orders@sunburypress.com.

To request one of our authors for speaking engagements or book signings, please contact Sunbury Press Publicity Dept. at publicity@sunburypress.com.

FIRST MILFORD HOUSE PRESS EDITION: January 2022

Set in Adobe Garamond Pro | Interior design by Crystal Devine | Cover by Lawrence Knorr | Edited by Sarah Peachey.

Publisher's Cataloging-in-Publication Data
Names: Regenbogen, Joe, author.
Title: Longs Peak / Joe Regenbogen.
Description: First trade paperback edition. | Mechanicsburg, PA : Milford House Press, 2022.
Summary: The shadow of one tragic night haunts Gordon's life. He has separated from his family and sleepwalks through his lessons as a high school history teacher. After Ben, an old college friend invites Gordon to join him in the Colorado Rockies, the two friends decide to relive the dodgy climb to the top of Longs Peak. Standing on the mountain's crest, Gordon finally finds the strength to confront his past.
Identifiers: ISBN : 978-1-62006-764-2 (softcover).
Subjects: FICTION / Family Life / Marriage & Divorce | FICTION / Friendship | FICTION / Nature & the Environment.

Product of the United States of America
0 1 1 2 3 5 8 13 21 34 55

Continue the Enlightenment!

To Julie and Jack,
    no father has ever been so proud.

"Life can only be understood backwards;
but it must be lived forwards."

—Soren Kierkegaard

"Just as a snake sheds its skin,
we must shed our past over and over again."

—Gautama Buddha

CHAPTER

1

Gordon grimaced at the dead eyes gazing back in his rearview mirror. He looked away from his reflection, searching for visual stimulation in the idled traffic. To his right, a woman driving a tomato-red SUV was applying eyeliner with the precision of a surgeon. On his left, a man with a dark beard was studying his phone, possibly checking the latest Dow Jones numbers. His black Porsche was undoubtedly a testament to his recent success in the market. Gordon inched his dinged-up ten-year-old Corolla a few feet. Glancing to his right, he saw a green pickup truck with "Deacon Roofing" on the side panel. The driver was in his mid-fifties, judging from the gray ponytail poking out from the back of his greasy cap. He turned and made eye contact, smiling to acknowledge a connection. Gordon quickly turned away.

It was a Thursday morning in late May, and Gordon would soon complete his sixteenth year as a high school history teacher. He'd celebrated his thirty-eighth birthday the night before with a six-pack and now paid the price. The long commute from St. Charles County on the western edge of the sprawling St. Louis metropolitan area had become a time-consuming part of his day. After six months, this still seemed like a novelty. St. Charles County was the fastest growing in the state, but it felt like the other side of the moon to Gordon. Farmland had turned into apartment complexes, flashy strip malls, and rambling subdivisions. It represented urban sprawl at its most extreme. Squeezed into the confluence of the nation's two longest rivers and then expanding in a westward direction, St. Charles County had played a leading role in transforming Missouri from a political bellwether into a solidly red state.

Gordon had lived with his wife, Elaine, and his two children in a small ranch half a mile from Beachwood North High School, the home of the BNH Vikings. Gordon had lucked into a teaching position in the heart of St. Louis County fresh out of college and never taught anywhere else. East of the Missouri River, St. Louis County arched around the city of St. Louis, pressing the original metropolis up against the Mississippi River. Continuing a trend begun in the 1950s, the county was now more than three times the city's population. For almost sixteen years, Gordon had lived on a quiet, tree-shaded street in the center of St. Louis County, where he'd been able to walk to his job, at least on pleasant days.

Now he wrestled with rush hour traffic. Gordon had experimented with other routes, but there was no quicker course than I-64, the main artery linking downtown St. Louis to its burgeoning western suburbs. Many people still referred to the thoroughfare by its U.S. Highway designation, "highway forty," or as its older residents like to say, "highway farty." On most mornings, traffic backed up several miles like a blocked artery. Gordon had tried leaving earlier to avoid the rush hour traffic, but rolling out of bed before sunrise was an anathema to his system. What used to be a ten-minute stroll or a two-minute drive had become an hour-long commute.

Today's traffic was even worse than usual. Gordon's phone told him an accident on the shoulder just before the Clarkson exit was the reason, but when he finally crept past the scene of the collision, the tow trucks had already departed. For the next few miles, traffic accelerated to between ten and fifteen miles per hour. The highway along this stretch rose and dropped sharply into choppy little hills resembling the transitory roller coasters found at county fairs. Even worse, Gordon's easterly route took him directly into the rising sun. He fumbled for his sunglasses in the glove compartment, but as he closed the lid, the glasses tumbled onto the floor, just out of reach. Now there was no choice. Gordon would have to squint and look away as much as possible until he turned north onto the 270 beltway.

The interstate snaked through a canyon of office buildings, hospitals, and religious structures. The crowning tower on the left was the St. Louis Missouri Temple, the majestic cathedral constructed by the Mormon

Church twenty-five years ago. Gordon thought of how the planners had been wise to surround the highway with these massive nonresidential buildings. They insulated the posh homes and manors from the sound of screeching brakes, thunderous motorcycles, and blasting horns. To Gordon, navigating through this corridor was mind-numbing.

Gordon had undoubtedly descended into a rut. He coaxed himself to peek into the rearview mirror and briefly studied his reflection. There was a roadmap of wrinkles appearing on his forehead, and a few gray hairs had sprouted in what had previously been one of his proudest physical assets. For a moment, Gordon could see the sharper features and the penetrating eyes of a boy staring back, but then this visage sank into the weathered shell of a thirty-eight-year-old man prematurely approaching middle age.

Gordon reached up and patted down his dark mane, hoping to disperse the gray into the black. Then he glanced back at his face. His eyes were bloodshot. Hopefully, his students wouldn't notice, or if they did, he prayed they had the good graces not to comment. Another evening had stretched a six-pack into the late-night talk shows.

Gordon peered down into his lap. He couldn't see his foot on the accelerator because of the round mass obstructing his view. At six foot two, Gordon had been a wide receiver on his high school football team. He'd worked out with weights and jogged at least twenty miles a week through college and for several years beyond. That seemed long ago. Now he was approaching three hundred pounds and looked more like a guard blocking for the team's running back. He patted his pumpkin belly, frowned, and shook his head.

It had been six months since Gordon hastily filled a couple of travel bags, loaded up the aging Toyota, and moved in with his seventy-four-year-old father. Dad was happy to have the company since Gordon's mom died of cancer five years earlier. He was long retired, but like Gordon, Dad had also been a high school teacher, although his certification area was science.

Gordon's parents had moved to a small two-bedroom spread in the southern part of St. Charles County shortly after retiring. They did this to flee the stairs in their older two-story home and to exchange the county's congestion for what appeared to be a country cottage. It was a charming little abode with red bricks and white shutters, located in a hilly rural section just north of the tiny hamlet of Defiance. Of course, with all the new subdivisions now springing up like dandelions, the house was part of the same sprawl Gordon's parents had tried to escape.

Now, Dad was Gordon's roommate. They rose at roughly the same time each morning, shared breakfast, and drained a pot of coffee. If time allowed and the weather cooperated, Gordon would step out onto the back deck for a cigarette before starting his long commute. He'd recently resumed the smoking habit he first began in high school, but Gordon told himself that by not smoking inside Dad's house and, of course, on school grounds, he'd keep his nasty habit to under half a pack a day.

Gordon had always maintained an even relationship with his father. Although Gordon didn't always have much to say, Dad was a good listener. His father never pushed any unwanted advice about his disintegrating marriage. Talk, when it occurred, was usually about the weather, the St. Louis Cardinals, and the latest political news. Gordon had inherited a keen interest in politics from both parents, so on most mornings, when Dad scanned the paper to grumble about the latest headlines, the dialogue between father and son grew increasingly energized as they traded their observations and jokes. For Gordon, this was often the best part of the day.

In most respects, Gordon revered his father. The fact that both pursued careers as high school educators was no coincidence. Dad had recognized Gordon's intellectual potential from a young age and encouraged his son to read, play chess, and pursue high school extracurriculars, like debate and mock trial competitions. After an explosive growth spurt, Gordon first broached the subject of athletics in the summer before ninth grade. Dad had suggested cross country running. When Gordon said he preferred to play football, Dad had recommended becoming a kicker. Nevertheless, when Gordon won the starting wide receiver position, Dad attended every game. He cringed whenever his son took a potentially concussive blow, and he leaped up in delight whenever Gordon caught a pass.

For a couple of minutes, the traffic slowly accelerated. Then Gordon saw red brake lights up ahead, sparkling like they were attached to a single filament. He was already running late; judging by the new problem, he'd never make it before the school's first bell. Gordon lit up his second cigarette of the day, touched a name on his list of favorite contacts, and waited for an answer.

"Jim?"

"Gordon? Where are you? Are you in the building? Why are you calling my cell number?"

"Because I'm stuck in traffic, and it looks like I may be here a while." Gordon paused and exhaled a gray cloud of smoke through the open window. "There was an accident this morning, and no one's moving. It looks like I'll miss the start of first period."

Silence. The hush reeked of exasperation. Jim had been Gordon's best friend since they were kids, but now that he was an assistant principal, their friendship was sometimes tested, particularly at moments like this.

"You know, buddy," Jim finally stated in a tone more sardonic than joking, "this wouldn't be an issue except that lately, it happens more than it should. If we weren't friends and you were just another teacher, I'd be kind of pissed right now."

"I get it," replied Gordon. "But look, the school year's almost over, and I'll figure out a better way to handle this bullshit traffic next year. That, or maybe I'll find a place closer to school. Anyhow, can you help me out?"

Gordon heard a loud sigh. Finally, Jim responded in a surprisingly friendly tone.

"Okay, the usual, right? Open up your room and take roll?"

"Yeah," Gordon replied, sounding as conciliatory as possible. "Except this time, since I might be a bit later than before, could you turn on the projector and start a PowerPoint? It's labeled 'World War Two,' and it's sitting on my computer's desktop. Just open it up to the first slide. There's a kid named Monica who's pretty reliable—sits towards the front—ask her to advance the slides at a pace that'll allow the students to take notes."

"World War Two? I've never taught history, Gordon, but it's kind of late in the year to only be on World War Two. I mean, will your kids ever learn about what's happened *since* World War Two?"

"Granted, I didn't do the best job pacing myself this year. It's not like I'm the only one. I'll get in some quick lessons over the recent past before finals begin."

"All right, I got it," Jim replied. "You owe me, though, and your debt's continuing to rise. We'll have to settle up one of these days."

"You're right. I owe you big. Then again, you and I've been friends a *long* time. I don't mean this as an excuse. You know better than anyone that I've been going through a rough time."

"Yeah, *I* know."

"And it's gotten even worse since I moved out to my Dad's six months ago."

"Yeah, *I know.* Maybe that's something we could talk about?"

Gordon tried to sound like he wasn't blowing off the question, but he couldn't help it, especially while sitting in traffic moving slower than a parade of slugs. "No offense, buddy, but there are some things I'd prefer to keep to myself." Realizing how snarky that sounded, Gordon added, "Actually, Jim, there are just some things I haven't been able to share yet with *anyone.*"

"Well, that in itself may be part of the problem." Wanting to change the subject, Jim added, "By the way, I have a quick question to ask you about summer school."

Gordon heard the rising volume of chatter in the background. He realized Jim was making his way through a congested hallway towards his classroom.

"What's on your mind?"

"I can schedule you to teach two sections of remedial U.S. history, but you know how lengthy the periods are. That'll make for a long day. *Or,* I can put you down for one section of remedial and one section of an enrichment class. It's not too late to add that Supreme Court course you taught years ago. Do you know the one? Where the kids presented arguments to each other like they were pleading actual cases before the Supreme Court?"

"Uh-huh." Gordon paused as though he was giving the question some thought. "Nah, I don't think so. I'll take the two sections of remedial history. It may make for a longer day, but to be frank, I don't have the juice for the other option."

"All right," replied Jim, drawing out the second syllable. "I just wanted to give you a choice. Don't complain to me when you're leaving at the end of the day in a stupor."

"Okay, I promise. Hey, I'd better get going. The cars are finally starting to move."

In reality, the cars around him had frozen. Gordon wanted to end the conversation and use the bottleneck as an opportunity to mull over a few things. If nothing else, the mindlessness of standstill traffic afforded him a chance for some serious reflection. Gordon let his mind drift to other subjects.

Up until two years ago, he'd been the envy of his friends. They saw the passion he brought every day into the classroom, the romantic flame that continued to blaze years after he'd married Elaine, and the satisfaction that followed the birth of his two children. What had happened? Gordon had been asking himself that question every day, especially over the last six months. Usually, it sprang into his mind in the morning while shaving. The befuddled expression on his face staring back in the mirror usually triggered the question, but today, it didn't arise until he was driving.

Thinking about the question at this moment was especially troubling as Gordon approached the interchange between I-64 and 270. Every morning since last December, he drove up this ramp that climbed high into the sky as it curved to the left, shifting the eastbound traffic into a trajectory heading north. The interchange consisted of only one lane with narrow shoulders on both sides. At one point in the bend, Gordon could see nothing but the sky. Today, it was an azure blue, framed only by wispy contrails left by commercial airliners crisscrossing the flyover parts of the nation. To Gordon, it looked like a gate entering heaven.

At this moment, a thought compulsively flew into his head. Over the past few months, the same idea frequently materialized at this same spot in his long drive to school. It was crazy, but like so many other parts of his life where self-control was withering, he couldn't keep it out. To make the ninety-degree turn required careful control of the steering wheel, calibrated to keep his car between the parallel white lines that guided traffic from one highway onto the other. What if he steered the car in a straight alignment rather than curving to the left? And what if, at just that moment, he accelerated rather than maintaining the more prudent speed required to traverse the bend?

Gordon visualized his beat-up Toyota crashing through the guard-rail and going airborne. With enough momentum, maybe he could fly into the vast medical complex built around Missouri Baptist Hospital. Sometimes, Gordon smiled at the irony of his car landing squarely in the middle of the offices of the Psych Care Consultants. Picturing the flight sent a shiver up his spine, the same exhilaration that drove him onto the most thrilling rides at Six Flags when he was a kid. And the land-ing? Gordon could envision the wreck that would ensue—the twisted metal, the jagged glass, the potential fireball that would ascend above the thunderous explosion.

The carnage that followed would be immaterial. Someone else would have to clean up the mess. First responders would extinguish the blaze, a tow truck would dispose of the remnants of the Corolla, and a funeral home would attend to Gordon's remains. He thought about Epicurus, the Hellenistic philosopher he taught about every year in his world history classes. What did Epicurus say about death? *Death is nothing to us. When we exist, death is not; and when death exists, we are not. All sensation and consciousness ends with death.*

Within seconds he'd crash through the concrete barrier and embark upon a flight where the balding tires of his Corolla would no longer touch the ground. A descent into a permanent state of unconsciousness would follow the few seconds of ecstasy. Gordon would be enveloped by darkness as though someone had suddenly turned off the lights. He had an uncle who once said that death was nothing to be feared. It was like going to sleep and never waking up.

For most of his life, sleep had never been a problem. When he was a small child, his parents took turns reading stories to him as he lay with his head on a soft pillow bathed in the cozy light of his bedside lamp. After both parents kissed him and turned off the lights, Gordon would quickly drift into the warm embrace of sleep. It was only recently that he tossed and turned with insomnia.

Falling into a deep sleep while driving on this glorious morning in late May had a magnetic allure. True, he'd never wake. But as Epicurus had said, Gordon wouldn't be aware of his demise. Others might miss him. There'd probably be speculation about whether he was the victim of an accident or the pilot of his death. His children would grow up without a father, but they were still young enough to heal. Elaine could avoid the stress of filing for divorce, and as long as his death didn't look too much like suicide, she'd benefit from his life insurance. There were friends and other family members, but most had recently drifted away. His students would probably welcome the news that there wouldn't be a final exam in history.

Then there was Dad. Gordon imagined the scene where state troopers would arrive at the small cottage amid the sparkling new subdivisions. They'd climb out of their car, slowly ascend the front steps, and ring the doorbell. Gordon could visualize the troubled look in his father's eyes as he opened the door and saw the severe expressions on the faces of the uniformed men. He could see the raised eyebrows and clenched lips on Dad's weathered face. Gordon caught the tears streaming down his father's wrinkled cheeks after the troopers gave him the news. Finally, Dad would crumble into a heap.

After suffering two tragic losses over the past five years, this would be the final crushing blow. It would plunge an emotional dagger into the center of his heart. At that reflection, Gordon once again turned the steering wheel to follow the concave ramp taking him to another day of teaching at Beachwood North High School rather than choosing the other path into the dark void.

CHAPTER

2

Gordon glanced at his watch as he bounded up the front steps, taking two at a time. If he skipped checking his mailbox in the faculty lounge and headed directly to his classroom, he wouldn't be tardy by more than ten minutes. Thanks to Jim, his tenth graders would already be taking notes from the presentation he'd created years ago. Gordon could then step in and teach the rest of the period from the slides that contained an assortment of bullet points, maps, and other visuals. Some pictures linked to video clips, but he no longer remembered what the videos were or where to find them. In the past, he would've taken time to reacquaint himself with the substance of the PowerPoint, and in his earliest years, he would have updated the content and added several new eye-catching illustrations. Not today. Gordon would have to fly by the seat of his pants. It was getting easier since it had become increasingly common over the past two years.

Jim's chiseled face was the only one to glance up and smile when Gordon walked into the classroom. He sat at the more considerable teacher desk in the back of the room. Most of the students either fixated on the glowing screen in front or busily scribbled notes. A couple on the opposite side of the room buried their heads within the cradle of their arms. None seemed to notice Mr. Goldman's entry. Jim stood up, nodded towards Gordon, and unobtrusively slipped out of the room.

Fluorescent lights hummed as they cast an artificial glow in the back half of the windowless room. The lack of natural light was thanks to some genius architects from the 1970s, who thought the outside world might distract students from their lessons. Years ago, Gordon tried to compensate for this by plastering the painted cinder block walls with enlarged photographs from road trips he'd taken with Elaine during those unbridled years before kids came along. Some were national monuments. He'd taken others at military battlefields. His favorites consisted of a collection of sunrise and sunset photos from national parks out west: The Grand Canyon, the Narrows in Zion, Yosemite Falls, Longs Peak in the Colorado Rockies. Since he never bothered to place them under framed glass, many developed a yellowish pall as though afflicted with jaundice.

There were thirty student desks in the room arranged in regimented rows. In his first years of teaching, Gordon had experimented with placing desks in a circular or U-shaped arrangement to facilitate face-to-face interaction amongst the students. As his instruction wilted into a more traditional, teacher-centered model, the layout of his classroom reflected this reversion. Now all students faced the front of the room, focusing on the SmartBoard, the mammoth world map, and Mr. Gordon Goldman.

Gordon gazed around the room. Seeing three empty seats, he surmised that one student was absent, a pain-in-the-ass kid named Andre. Gordon knew he could still slip in late, so he resisted the urge to feel a sense of relief. Students stared at a picture of Japanese airplanes sporting big red circles and dropping bombs on American warships in Pearl Harbor. Gordon held a clicker in his left hand, ready to advance the PowerPoint slides. He walked to the front of the room, cleared his throat, and waited.

"Ladies and gentlemen, I apologize for being a little late this morning, but we can begin as soon as you're ready."

Inside his head, Gordon slowly counted. Usually, by the time he reached ten, the students would attentively face forward. On this day, it took another ten seconds before the sleeping beauties off to the side lifted their heads and opened their notebooks. Even though the students at Beachwood were issued Chromebooks at the start of the year, Gordon's "old school" approach still required they take notes by hand.

"Okay, everyone should be ready." After a brief pause, Gordon continued, "Can someone tell me what's going on in this picture?"

Monica's hand shot up like a rocket. As sure as the sun rose every morning, she'd always be the first volunteer to answer the questions he posed. Gordon, who by this point propped himself up on a stool with his arms folded across his chest, looked down on Monica, waving like she was hailing a cab.

"Monica, while I greatly appreciate your helping out this morning, let's give someone else a chance."

Gordon saw Monica's exaggerated puppy dog look of disappointment, with her upper lip hidden by her pouty lower lip. Everyone by now was accustomed to this daily ritual. It was common knowledge Monica was the best student in the class and perhaps the only one who enjoyed Mr. G's lectures. Monica's blond ponytail whipped around as she turned to face her classmates, almost daring one to answer the question. Gordon peered over her head to see if anyone else had raised a hand.

"It's the attack on Pearl Harbor, Mr. G."

Gordon looked at the back corner of the room from where he heard the voice. He couldn't conceal a frown.

"Andre?" he moaned. "When did you arrive? *Man*, I thought you were absent."

"I was a little late," he responded. "But then again, Mr. G, I walked in behind *you*. Maybe you didn't notice."

"I don't suppose you have a pass?"

Gordon scowled as he glided over to his computer to update the attendance. He already knew the answer, but posing the question was a stalling tactic intended to buy enough time to change Andre's absence on the school's digital roll book to another tardy.

"Nope," Andre answered. After a couple of seconds, he added, "Do you?"

Gordon ignored the question and returned to the front of the room. He leaned back onto his stool and, for a moment, with his lips clenched together, glared at Andre. The students waited to see which gunslinger would draw first. Andre stared back while lowering his wiry body to assume the most disrespectful slouch possible. His chin almost rested on top of his chest, the visor of his St. Louis Blues cap overshadowed the upper half of his face, and his bony knees rose to make room for his slight frame. Gordon finally broke the impasse.

"See me at the end of class," Gordon said calmly. Andre nodded, cocked his head, and touched the cap's visor in a mock salute. He made no effort, however, to sit up straight.

Inside, Gordon was seething. There was something about Andre that went beyond the one annoying student who always took up space in every class. He was seldom absent but frequently tardy. He did well on tests, better than most, but his essays were sloppy and poorly developed. He participated in class, and his answers and insights were always spot on, but no matter what Gordon said, he refused to raise his hand. It was almost a game to Andre to see what kind of reaction he could extract from Mr. G.

Gordon had sent an email to Andre's parents at the start of the school year, but there'd been no response. Finally, when the situation deteriorated further, he called Andre's mother one evening and managed to get her on the phone. The conversation had been civil, even friendly at times, but in the end, the only accomplishment was that Gordon picked up a few crumbs of background information. He learned that Andre's father had disappeared years ago and that his mom worked two jobs to support three children. He also discovered that Andre lived in the Section 8 apartment complexes recently constructed in the southern end of the Beachwood North attendance area.

Gordon had described his frustration as plainly as possible. He told Mrs. Roberts that her son was one of the brightest students in the class and also one of the laziest. He explained that Andre had unlimited potential, but the enormous chip on his shoulder was a significant hindrance. She listened empathetically, but in the end, she confessed she didn't know what to do with her son. Andre's mother reminded Gordon that while he might have to put up with Andre for fifty-five minutes a day, she was responsible for him when he wasn't in school. Her greatest triumph was that most of the time, she'd kept him off the streets. Otherwise, she was at her wit's end. She concluded the conversation by saying that Andre needed a male role model in his life more than anything. Gordon thought about that for a day or two but then dismissed its implications.

For the remaining forty minutes, Gordon taught from his Power-Point presentation. He covered events steadily, from America's entry into the war, up through the D-Day invasion. Gordon had always found this subject enthralling as a kid, and he'd started to assume his students should feel the same way. If not, it was *their* problem. Gordon thought he'd honed his story-telling skills over the years and was now simply playing to one of his strengths. Besides, time flew by whenever he lectured. If forced, Gordon might concede that many kids *didn't* share his interest in history. But like so many other matters lately, he'd developed the habit of repressing unpleasant thoughts.

Towards the end of the period, Gordon spoke a little louder to magnify the excitement of the Allied invasion of Europe, intending this to be the climactic end to the day's lesson. Build to a crescendo and then leave them on the edge of their seats. Or so he hoped. Shortly before the bell rang, Gordon concluded the lesson, turned on the front lights, and scanned the room for a moment.

Moving from face to face, it was like the classroom scene from *Ferris Bueller's Day Off.* Some students had their heads down, a few in the back focused on their phones, and several were mesmerized by the clock above Gordon's head. Some were writing in their notebooks, but Gordon was pretty sure they were doodling, not finishing their history notes. None were looking up at him. Then Gordon locked eyes with one student in the back. Andre. He was still slouching down in his desk, and it was difficult to see his eyes beneath the brim of his cap, but Andre had been paying attention. It also looked like he might be smiling.

As students packed their bookbags, Gordon slowly ventured from the front of the room, maneuvering around its peripheral edge and falling into the cushioned chair behind his paper-strewn desk. As he stared down into his clasped hands, the bell rang, and the students boisterously exited the room. The following period was planning time for Gordon, so his classroom would be empty for the next hour. He continued to stare at the random papers beneath his forearms. Then his desk darkened. Someone was standing in front of him, blocking out the overhead light.

"Andre?" Gordon uttered in surprise. "Oh hell, I forgot I asked you to stick around."

Andre looked away for a moment and then turned his gaze downward. A frown monopolized the bottom half of his face, the part beneath his cap. Gordon looked up at the sixteen-year-old, who appeared to be at least six feet tall and was now towering intimidatingly above.

"Andre, as I recall, you have math next, right?"

Andre nodded. He could be chatty in class, but now he was mute.

"In that case," Gordon responded, "pull up a seat and let's talk. I'll write you a pass when we've finished."

Gordon observed a smirk on Andre's face. While he knew his wayward student probably didn't look forward to another private conversation with his history teacher, he also knew Andre was just as happy to miss the start of his math class as he was to come in late for history. Andre grabbed one of the student desks, pulled it up to face his teacher, and gracefully sat down. Gordon was relieved to look him directly in the eye.

"Would you mind taking off your hat?" Gordon requested. "I'd like to see your face while we talk."

Andre looked away for a moment while considering the request. Then he snapped off his hat, revealing the start of dreadlocks that randomly exploded in every direction.

"Okay. I've lost count of how many times we've had these conversations. By now, your math teacher must be pretty upset with me. What's more, they've never made a difference. But don't worry, I'll spare you the lecture this time. You won't hear anything about tardiness or rude behavior. Not today. The year's almost done, so what's the point?"

Andre faintly lifted his eyebrows but didn't respond.

"Andre, you've got *so* much potential. You're one of the smartest people in this class."

"Excuse me, Mr. G., but this sounds like the start of another lecture, and I've heard this one before."

"Fair enough," Gordon responded with a slight grin. "But you've got to give me a chance to introduce what I want to say. Andre, I think you've hit a real fork in the road. You know what I mean?"

"Yeah, I know what you mean. But so what? Like you already said, Mr. G., the school year's almost done."

"I want you to look at the bigger picture for a moment," Gordon replied. "I want you to look into your *distant* future."

Gordon noticed Andre's eyes roll up, but since there was no other reaction, he continued.

"You're almost halfway through high school, and I've seen your grades. A two-point GPA means you're probably headed to a minimum wage job after you graduate high school. Man, don't you want *more*?"

Gordon surprised himself. Talking to a student after class had always been part of his classroom management arsenal. It was also better to defer confrontations to later when cooler heads could prevail, and no one would feel the need to perform in front of a live audience. This time, though, he'd steered the conversation in an unexpected direction. Gordon had chosen an extemporaneous route instead of following the usual script. While Andre looked away again, hopefully, to process his question, Gordon decided to forge ahead.

"What if after the summer, you chose a different path? What if you returned in August *determined* to be a good student? If you could combine a solid work ethic with your talent, there's no limit to what you could do. College? Grad school? Hell, knowing the way you think, what about law school?"

Andre looked up with an even broader smirk on his face.

"What?" Gordon asked. "I say something funny?"

Andre wiped under his lower lip and began to laugh.

"*Man,*" Andre cackled while shaking his head, "I *never* heard this one before."

Gordon glanced away momentarily. He tried to maintain a serious demeanor, but Andre's laughter made it impossible.

"I don't know," answered Gordon. "I'm kind of winging it here as we go along." After a brief pause, he added, "that doesn't make it untrue, though. I *meant* every word. Why *not* use this summer to grow up? I don't mean that to be insulting or anything, but if you matured some and lost that huge chip on your shoulder, there's no limit to how far you might go."

For a moment, there was silence as teacher and student stared at each other quizzically. Finally, Gordon said, "Look, I've got an idea."

He purposefully hesitated to pique his student's interest. After Andre gave an almost imperceptible nod, Gordon continued.

"Why don't you change your schedule for next year? Rather than taking U.S. History, switch into the AP course."

Andre leaned back with his arms crossed behind his head and raised a dubious eyebrow.

"Man, now I *know* you're tripping. I don't even come close to meeting the requirements for *that* class."

"That's true," Gordon replied. "But exceptions can be made. Let me talk to your counselor. I can explain the circumstances and tell her we'd like to do a trial for the first six weeks. Worst case scenario? You can always drop back into the American history class."

Andre brought his hands onto the student desk and twiddled his thumbs. For a moment, it looked like he'd hypnotized himself. Then a grin slowly crept across his face.

"That'd mean a second year with you, wouldn't it, Mr. G?"

"Yeah? Is that so bad? I think you *like* history. And unlike a lot of students, you always stay awake in my class."

Andre continued to look down at his entangled fingers.

"Nah, you're not wrong," Andre mumbled. "I like it enough. It's just that . . ."

"What?" Gordon asked.

Andre looked up. This time, the smirk was gone entirely. For a moment, Gordon could see the adult he would soon become.

"Mr. G," Andre replied, "Do you remember a student named Robin Jones?"

"The name's familiar. Why do you ask?"

"My mother works with Mrs. Jones. I met her the other day, and when I told her where I went to school, she asked if I knew you. I told her you were my world history teacher, and you know what she said?" Without waiting for an answer, Andre continued. "She said I was *lucky*. Mrs. Jones must have seen the look of surprise on my face—no offense—so she went on to explain. She said she'd been in your class ten years ago, and you'd been her *favorite* teacher. Not just for that year, but for *all* time."

"Keep going," Gordon stated as he rocked back, clinched the fingers behind his head, and raised the corners of his mouth. "It's been a *while* since I've heard something like this."

"Well," Andre said, and then he paused. "I asked her *why* she liked you so much. Mrs. Jones said it was all the cool stuff she did in your class. She talked about these seminars where you'd put students in a circle and just let them talk. She mentioned debates, games, and mock trials. Mrs. Jones said you even took her class on a trip to Washington, D.C. The way she spoke, *man*, it sounded like a *cool* class. She said she learned so much from you, and she still remembers most of it."

Gordon stared down at the papers scattered across his desk. He tried to picture Robin Jones. While the image of her face was lost, he could still remember the class. Teaching was different back then. It was challenging and exhausting, but at the same time, fulfilling and joyful. It was like high-stakes poker, where immense losses balanced against even greater wins. This type of education required a higher octane. It was the supreme roller coaster ride. Gordon would butt heads with an older, tradition-bound teacher in the lounge. Ten minutes later, students would exuberantly burst into his classroom, anxious to continue the discussions from the day before. At a parent conference, a complaint of too much bias would come after a compliment about turning a teenager's life around.

But that was all a lifetime ago, and now Gordon was a different man. Even on his best days, that teaching style was exhausting. Gordon's family paid the price. Then, two years ago, his personal life collapsed. Something had to give. Gordon's day-to-day survival meant accepting compromises and concessions.

Droplets of moisture had collected on Gordon's forehead. When he finally looked up, he was surprised to see compassion in Andre's eyes.

CHAPTER

3

Gordon hardly recognized the image staring back in the mirror. The eyes were tired and bloodshot, the skin below sallow and puffy. A streetlight on the edge of the parking lot cast a brilliant halo around his head, highlighting random tufts of hair. He studied the car key in his hand for a moment and then fumbled to fit it into the Corolla's ignition. Gordon sat paralyzed for a moment, lost in a web of indecision. Should he drive home or call a cab? The tavern where he'd spent the last few hours was on Highway 94, so it was a straight shot south to Dad's house. Gordon grimaced and slammed the stick into reverse.

Repeating the mantra that he must be prudent, Gordon turned onto the highway and cautiously accelerated. At this hour, there was little traffic. He set the cruise control to maintain a speed well under the limit and told himself to calm down. After exhaling a deep breath, Gordon concluded it might be a mistake to become too relaxed. Falling asleep at the wheel with a questionable blood alcohol level would be disastrous. He needed something to galvanize his mind for the ride home.

Why not mentally review the last several hours? Gordon thought back to the end of the school day when he'd walked into the teacher's lounge to make one final check of his mailbox.

Spinning around to leave, he almost crashed head-on into Jim. The morning's stressful events were already forgotten, surpassed by a friendship dating back to the second grade. Jim had thrown the passes to Gordon on their high school football team, and he'd been the best man at Gordon's wedding. Even though Jim had chosen to teach math rather than social studies, many facets of their lives had run parallel, like steel rails bearing a locomotive.

Jim had pale blue eyes and an alluring smile. He'd recently begun sporting a pair of reading glasses draped down his chest like a necklace. His sandy-colored hair was thinning a bit, but there was no bald spot so far. Jim wasn't particularly tall. He used to stand on his toes to better spot receivers down the field. He liked to joke that his style was reminiscent of Drew Brees, the New Orleans Saints quarterback who'd enjoyed a spectacular career despite his undersized stature. While Jim didn't possess Brees' athleticism, he was just as much a natural leader on and off the gridiron. He maintained his composure under any circumstance. Jim was naturally calm, relaxed, and reflective. More and more, he'd become a steadying influence for Gordon, an anchor in a churning sea.

One glance at Gordon elicited concern from Jim. He had honed his radar over the years to spot even the subtlest clues.

"Whoa, Gordon!" he exclaimed. "Take it easy. You *okay?*"

Gordon cast his eyes downward and took a step back. He knew better than to invent a response since Jim would suspect anything but the truth.

"It's the same old thing. I've got a lot on my mind." Looking up, he added, "That's all. There's no reason to be concerned."

Jim momentarily turned away and peered through the floor-to-ceiling window towards the parking lot below. He'd just come up from supervising the daily departure from the north side of the building. The last yellow school bus was pulling out, trailed by a caravan of teachers' SUVs and minivans.

"Look," Jim said. "I've got some paperwork piled on my desk, but it can wait. Why don't you give me a few minutes, and I'll meet you at The Post for a beer?"

"You sure?" Gordon asked. He felt the saliva saturating his tongue at the thought of a cold Bud. "I mean, you've had a *long* day, right?"

"Yes, I'm sure. It isn't a chore. Besides, as you know, it's on my way home."

Gordon nodded. "Okay then, I'll see you there in about forty-five minutes?"

"Sounds good," Jim replied.

Thirty minutes later, Gordon again found himself jammed in traffic. It was too early to encounter so much volume making its way into St.

Charles County, so he assumed there must be another accident. Sure enough, shortly before reaching the bridge over the Missouri River, a green pickup truck with "Deacon Roofing" on the door panel had slammed into a black Porsche. Gordon couldn't make out the drivers, but he wondered if these were the identical vehicles he'd encountered that morning. Two police cars and a tow truck flanked the crash site. Their swirling bubblegum lights cast a spellbinding show, but unfortunately, they also blocked two lanes of traffic. If Jim had taken a different route, he'd be waiting a while for Gordon to show up.

"Where've you been?" Jim asked as Gordon plopped onto a barstool.

"Accident. You didn't see it?'

"No, what accident?" Jim asked. "Where?"

"Just east of the bridge. Backed traffic up to 141."

A bartender with tattoos on both forearms approached, and before he could say a word, Gordon asked for a Bud. Jim was still nursing his first and waved off the request for a second.

"So, before we get to other stuff," Jim said, "I want to double-check something." After a sip of beer, he continued. "Are you sure about summer school? I just think teaching two remedial classes back-to-back, especially when each is two and a half hours long, is going to make for a hell of a long summer."

The bartender dropped a frosted mug in front of Gordon, who reached for it as though he'd just crossed the Sahara on foot. The two men then clinked their glasses without bothering to make a toast.

"Yeah, that's probably true," Gordon mused. "But I need the money, and at this point, I don't have enough energy to teach that Supreme Court class."

Gordon took a long sip of beer, wiped the foam from his upper lip, and swallowed. After a brief pause, he continued. "Look. I'm not too excited about teaching this summer. Five hours a day with students who flunked a subject they never liked doesn't exactly get my blood flowing. But, I need the money, and I don't want to have to work too hard to earn it."

"I get it," Jim replied. He shook his head and then tilted it back to drain the rest of his beer. Finally, he added, "Okay, I'll put you down for two sections of remedial history."

"*You Can't Always Get What You Want*" by the Rolling Stones began to play on speakers wedged into the room's upper corners. Gordon looked straight ahead and locked eyes with Jim's reflection in the mirror behind the bar. There was unabashed concern on his friend's face.

"Gordon, I'm starting to worry about you. How long have you been at your Dad's now? Five months, six?"

"About that," Gordon replied. Then, to deflect what was coming, Gordon asked, "I'm starting to worry about you too, buddy. How long have you been living in that little bachelor pad of yours? Five years, six?"

Settling down had been an ongoing topic of conversation since their college graduation. While Gordon had married Elaine shortly after landing his teaching job, Jim played the field for a *long* time. Every year brought a new girlfriend, but none ever lasted. Gordon wondered if his best friend had a severe case of "failure to commit."

"No need to be concerned about me," Jim replied. "I've been dating plenty, and I'll settle down soon enough. I've recently gone out a few times with a woman named Amy. I'll tell you about her later. For now, I want to get back to *you*."

Gordon slowly turned to look at his friend. Jim stared back, exhibiting the patience to wait for a response. Feeling like a witness about to face cross-examination, Gordon downed the rest of his beer and pushed the empty mug forward, hoping to catch the bartender's eye.

"Okay," Gordon muttered after letting out a deep sigh. "What do you want to know?"

"I think you know," Jim replied. "I've been asking the same question since the holidays."

Gordon looked down at the bar for a moment and focused on the fine grain of the wood. He slid his hand across, enjoying the silkiness of the polished veneer. When he finally glanced up, Gordon caught the bartender's attention and pointed at his empty mug. "You know it's been pretty tough these past two years, and you *know* why."

"I do," Jim replied. "What I don't get is why you moved out of your *house*. Why did you leave Elaine and your kids?"

Hearing his wife's name triggered a sudden jolt, like when the weighted rubber hammer strikes the knee. He briefly shut his eyes and thought to himself that so far, he hadn't shared the details of this story with *anyone*, not even his father. On the surface, the actions leading to his exile from home were embarrassing. Gordon instinctively knew there was also something else going on, something he didn't want to consider.

"I didn't leave Elaine," he finally responded. "She kicked me out."

"*What*? Why?"

Gordon took a long sip from his recently refilled beer stein, swished the amber liquid around his mouth for a few seconds before swallowing, and finally turned towards Jim. "To answer that," he finally said, "I'll need to go back about six months . . ."

Do you remember that stretch of wacky warm weather we had back between Christmas and New Year's? One day, the temperature hit sixty-five degrees. It was sunny too. Elaine said we should take advantage and get the kids out of the house. She suggested we do a picnic at Creve Coeur Park. Do you know that area by the waterfall? That's always been one of our favorite places to hang out, even before we got married. There's a shelter nearby and some picnic tables. Elaine packed the cooler, grabbed some games, and dressed the kids so they wouldn't get too chilly.

To be frank, I didn't want to go. *Hell*, if I'm honest, I didn't feel like doing anything over that holiday break. It was enough to get out of bed before noon. Anyhow, I finally caved, and before we left, I grabbed a six-pack and squeezed it into the cooler. I thought it might fortify me enough to get through the day.

It was all right when we first got there. I'm always amazed there's such a pretty spot in the middle of the West County suburbs. It'd been a lot colder previously, so there was still ice draped over parts of the falls. The sky was a deep shade of blue that afternoon, and there wasn't a cloud anywhere in sight. The sun was sparkling on the chunks of ice polished by the flowing water.

When we first arrived, I opened a blanket and tried to play some games with David and Annie while Elaine spread some food out on a picnic table. It was hard since David was already eight and Annie had just celebrated her fourth birthday. I mean, what games can you play with kids that far apart in age?

I feel bad saying this now, but the kids started to get on my nerves pretty soon. Annie's so damn adventurous, which is probably a good thing in the long run, but out there, it meant that Elaine was constantly distracted by her. And David's *so* sensitive. If I just looked at him cross-eyed, he'd go off and sulk. I quickly gave up trying to be the good father. I pulled out a folding recliner from the trunk, yanked a beer out of the cooler, and plugged in some headphones so I could lose myself in some classic Springsteen.

A couple of times, I peeked over at Elaine, who'd taken my place on the blanket. She was doing a good job keeping the kids entertained, mainly by reading books to them. Her blonde hair hung down like drapes shielding her eyes as she leaned over a book with a kid flanked on each side. Elaine's always doing that. Once or twice, she glanced up, and I could see what looked like a blend of resentment and concern in her green eyes.

For two years, she'd been understanding, at least most of the time. Elaine had been putting up with a lot of my bullshit. I didn't get angry too often, but I was trapped in a crappy mood twenty-four hours a day. By this point, I think it was starting to wear thin. Lately, she'd been complaining that I cared more for my students than I did my two children, which isn't saying much. More and more, I was staying at school longer than necessary, and I think she was starting to catch on to what I was doing.

There's another thing I should probably admit. I've always preferred to be around older kids. That's why I like teaching high school, especially the upper grades, not elementary. I mean, can you see me teaching second graders? When David was born, I used to find *any* reason I could to stay late at school. I'd come back after a long weekend proclaiming, "TGIM, thank God it's Monday!" Remember? It all got a little better after the kids no longer wore diapers, but I still wasn't a candidate for father-of-the-year. And that was *before* things went south.

On that afternoon in late December, I spent the next hour or two alternating between short naps and downing cans of beer. Elaine tried a few times to include me. At one point, she took the kids for a long walk on that pitiful excuse for a beach. I could see off in the distance they'd each found sticks and were drawing images in the dirty sand. I thought about joining them, but I couldn't find the juice.

Finally, when it was clear the kids were getting tired, Elaine said we should pack up and go. There was a scowl on her face when she looked at me—what a contrast. Years earlier, we'd walked in this same area, arm-in-arm, blissfully talking about our future. I don't know if you remember, but that's the spot where I proposed to Elaine. Now, we were both wondering what'd happened.

When I stood up and tried to fold the recliner, a wave of nausea swept over me. I was maybe a little drunk, and Elaine could tell. She forced me to hand over the car keys so she could drive us home. The next thing I remember was waking up in the passenger seat inside the garage. It must have been around dusk because only a little bit of natural light was streaming in through the backdoor window. I'd fallen asleep on the way home, and no one woke me.

When I stumbled inside, there was a plate of food on the kitchen table. A hot dog, I think, and some chips. I could see dirty dishes piled in the sink, so Elaine and the kids had already eaten. My movement was still slow, but otherwise, I felt better. After eating dinner, I even washed the dishes. Down in the basement, I could hear the sounds of a Disney film filtering up the steps. Elaine was watching *Frozen* with David and Annie for the eighteenth time.

Since I'd screwed up the day so badly, I looked around for something productive that might salvage the evening. One option was to head downstairs and watch the rest of the movie with my family. Hell, I probably should've made popcorn to bring down as a peace offering. I just couldn't do it. Then I peered into the dining room and saw my briefcase. I knew that I still needed to grade a stack of essays from my AP class.

In the old days, I would've graded and returned those papers within a day or two. I used to hate having that chore hanging over my head. But things were different now. Those essays had been in my briefcase for at least a week, and there'd be no excuse for not getting them done by the end of winter break. Since I now had more energy, I pulled them out and started to grade. I figured if I got them done that night, it would be a positive way to cap off what had otherwise been a crappy day. It probably didn't help, though, when I also broke out another six-pack to lubricate the experience.

An hour later, I heard the thunder of six legs marching up the steps. I glanced over and saw Elaine turn off the downstairs light. She guided the kids through the kitchen, and I heard her tell them to get ready for bed. Then she glanced in my direction. A furrowed brow and a clenched jaw had replaced the usual smile and look of compassion. Elaine shook her head before turning away.

As I took another sip of beer, it hit me that today was a turning point. I loved my wife so much because of her bottomless patience and understanding. Now I could see there was a bottom after all. I looked at the can in my hand and studied the vintage label. Then I swigged another large sip and swirled it around like mouthwash. I was on a steep descent. It's like when you trip and begin to fall, and you know the only way to stop is to hit the ground and hope it won't hurt too much.

I looked down at the stack of papers. There were still several more to grade, and I wasn't feeling good about the ones I'd finished. The marks were probably too low and the written comments too negative. No teacher should ever evaluate papers in a foul mood, but if I always followed that maxim, my students' essays would *never* get graded.

Then I looked up towards the kitchen. David was walking in, holding a full cup of grape juice. I'd never liked this little bedtime ritual since it usually meant he'd be up using the bathroom in the middle of the night. Nevertheless, it had grown into a longstanding tradition, and one day, David would probably down a full glass of grape juice each night before going to sleep in his nursing home. Since I was seated at the dining room table, we were level in height, and I could see that his eyes reflected my diminishing conscience. When David took a sip of his juice, I reached over for a swig of my beer.

There was sorrow beneath his mop of auburn hair. He looked so much like his mother, especially with that piercing gaze. David had come in to tell me goodnight, but his eyes pleaded for so much more. What should I say? Two years earlier, I would've walked him into his room, laid down next to him, and read him a goodnight story. Since he especially loved those kids' books that focused on historical figures, this had become a mutual pleasure. So much had changed since back then. David was two years older, and I was a different man.

"Good night Daddy," he murmured.

He stood there in his dinosaur pajamas, waiting for a response. His right hand reached up to touch my shoulder while his left still held the cup filled with grape juice. I struggled over what to say. Was there any way to make up for my absence that evening or my cold indifference at the park? Was there any way to explain the past two years? My mind was empty.

Just when I was about to tell him goodnight, a whirling dervish flashed out of the kitchen. It was Annie. Seeing David standing next to me, she rushed in to join us. Elaine had probably just brushed her blond hair, but already, it was in disarray. She had her mother's angular features and was tall for her age. A bundle of energy, Annie slammed into her brother's back. A chain reaction began, which ended with grape juice spilling on the ungraded papers. Behind her, I could see Elaine coming to retrieve both kids. It was too late.

When I looked down at the papers drenched in purple, something arose I couldn't control. It's the same feeling you get when you start to wretch, and there's no way to hold it down. In this case, it was anger, even rage. Since David was the one standing the closest, and his grape juice splattered all over my students' papers, he became the target. Without thought, my left hand whipped out in his direction. It was more a push than a smack, but it still sent him reeling backward. Frankly, I think yelling his name provoked more reaction than physical contact. He instantly started to cry. Then he turned and fled.

With my left hand still elevated, I looked over at Annie. Her mouth was a big "O," like The Scream painting by Edvard Munch. For a moment, she stood there in shock. Then she also turned and fled. That just left Elaine. I scrutinized her face, searching for tears or anger or signs of disgust. Instead, there was nothing but steely resolve.

"That's it," she said in a measured monotone. "I want you out."

I looked at Elaine. For a moment, she held her gaze, unflinching. There was no visible anger or passion. She meant business. When it became clear she was expecting a response, I calmly nodded my head. That was it. She left the dining room in search of David and Annie. I gathered the essays, including those unscathed by the juice, and pitched them in the kitchen waste can. After the winter break, I told the students I'd accidentally lost their essays. To mollify them, I said they'd all get perfect grades for this one assignment.

I put away the rest of the beer and straightened up the dining room and kitchen, and then I made my way down into the basement and slept that night on the couch. I packed some bags and headed out to Dad's place in Defiance the following day. You know the rest.

For a moment, the two friends stared at each other. Gordon waited for a response, but it was clear Jim was still processing everything he'd heard. Finally, Jim broke the silence. He patted Gordon on the shoulder, sighed, and then turned to stare at his empty beer stein, still painted with dried foam along the rim. The bartender had left the hollow mug even though Jim had declined several offers for a refill.

"Granted," Jim finally said, "it wasn't your finest hour. But you're human, my friend, and it could've been worse." After a brief pause, he inquired, "Have you had much contact with Elaine since that night?"

"Not right away," Gordon replied. "Over time, though, we had to talk about things like money, the kids, you know, life's little details. We set up a schedule where I'd pick up the kids and spend time with them on Saturdays."

"How's that been working out?"

"For now, it's working. I still hope this doesn't last forever, but for now, it's working."

Jim reached for his wallet and threw a twenty on the counter. Then he turned to face his friend.

"You'll get past this, Gordon. You still don't want to talk to a professional?"

Gordon shook his head.

"Well, you know what they say," Jim added. "Time heals all wounds. Try to hang in there. Also . . ."

"Yeah?"

Jim stood up, reached over, and placed his hands on Gordon's shoulders.

"Gordon, you know you've got *friends*, right? You don't have to be in this all alone."

"Yeah, I know." Gordon attempted to smile.

"Okay then, I'm going to head home. I still got more work to do. It never ends. You're going to stick around for a while?"

Gordon nodded. He gave Jim a little wave while turning back to the bartender for a refill. A few hours later, he pulled into his father's driveway. A Cardinals' game on the tavern's TV combined with more beer, a plate of toasted ravioli, and some friendly banter had extended Gordon's evening much later than anticipated.

Gordon found his father fast asleep when he finally entered the living room, sprawled on a leather recliner with age-spotted hands in his lap. Dad then awoke, flashed an appreciative smile upon seeing that his son was home safe, and then slowly stood up to go to bed. His arthritic knees gave off a loud crack as he rose out of the chair. Gordon noticed the TV was still playing the Cardinals' postgame show. While his father slowly trudged up the steps, Gordon headed into the kitchen, looking for a nightcap.

CHAPTER
4

Gordon was distressed when he glanced in his rearview mirror. There was a large SUV with tinted windows closing in fast. He was driving east into the city on I-64 and had briefly entered the left lane to pass a cluster of trucks. Although Gordon had increased his speed well above the limit, the clown behind him was clearly in a hurry. There couldn't have been more than five feet separating his front bumper from the Corolla's rear end. Gordon could see the Cadillac crest and wreath emblem riding high on the SUV's hood. He remembered how his dad said Cadillac owners drove like they owned the road. At the time, Gordon argued the comment was a classic stereotype, and there were numerous exceptions. Since then, the evidence suggested his father may have been right. The monstrous image in his mirror was Exhibit A.

After overtaking the knot of trucks, Gordon put on his signal and slid back into the center lane. The SUV exploded past him and disappeared over the crest of an upcoming hill. Gordon inhaled a deep breath and casually glanced around to see if the kids had noticed any of the NASCAR action taking place around them. David sat comatose in the front seat, staring at the slower traffic in the right lane. Suddenly, as they approached a mammoth eighteen-wheeler, he came to life by opening his side window, sticking out his skinny right arm, and pumping his fist so the truck might reward him with a loud blast. The driver was too high up to see him, so David dolefully closed his window and peered over at his father.

Gordon then peeked into his review mirror to check on Annie. Strapped into her car seat, she was oblivious to the whole world beyond her furry Big Bird hand puppet. Soft babbling sounds suggested she was engaged in a conversation with Big Bird. Even though Gordon only saw Annie on Saturdays, he knew Big Bird had become her closest friend. Wherever she went, Big Bird tagged along. Gordon noticed that Elaine must have recently painted new black circles to replace those that had worn off Big Bird's bulbous eyes.

As they approached the inner suburbs, traffic slowed to a crawl. Why? It was late morning on a Saturday. There shouldn't be so much traffic on the weekend. Then Gordon remembered. The Cardinals were playing the Cubs in a game that started in just under an hour. There would be over forty-five thousand ebullient fans, many in blue as well as red, packed into Busch Stadium. Gordon thought back to Jim's call late last night. Somehow, he'd gotten his hands on a couple of tickets right behind the visitor's dugout. Gordon could be sitting next to his best friend right now, driving towards the perfect day—aquamarine skies unblemished by clouds, a high temperature in the mid-seventies, and a parade of brats, peanuts, and of course, cold Buds. Gordon salivated at the thought.

He scanned around the car again and tried to swallow the bitter taste building in his mouth. Gordon needed a diversion. As traffic inched past the small sign marking the city's western edge, he peeked back at Annie. Sustaining a conversation with her was challenging even when she wasn't seated directly behind. Having Big Bird for competition made it even trickier. That left David. Gordon cleared his throat and turned to address his son.

"So, David," Gordon asked with manufactured interest. "How's school?"

Gordon knew David was nearing the end of third grade, but that was about all he knew. David woke from his hypnotic trance and turned to face his Dad. There was an awkward moment while he rummaged for an answer. Finally, David responded.

"It's going okay, I guess."

"Just okay? The school year is almost over, right?" After a pause, Gordon added, "What were some of the highlights of this past year?"

David wiped under his nose while vacuuming air up into his nostrils. Gordon noticed this had recently become a nervous habit.

"Well, I liked Mrs. Harrison," David said with mounting confidence. "She told us a lot of great stories about her dogs and cats, and I loved her art lessons."

Gordon thought back to the open house last fall when he and Elaine had been favorably impressed by Mrs. Harrison. While she was young and possibly a little naïve, she more than made up for this with passion and sincerity.

"So, overall," Gordon asked, "would you say it was a good year?"

David looked down at his white sneakers that still didn't reach the floorboards. Once again, there was hesitation. Seeing this, Gordon awkwardly reached over to rub the back of his son's neck. David slowly rotated his head to look up at his father. Gordon saw sadness in his eyes.

"What is it, son?"

Once again, David wiped under his nose, and Gordon could hear the sniffling.

After a lengthy pause, he said, "There are some boys in my class. They're bigger. They say they're just teasing, but almost every day, they say or do things."

"Like what?" Gordon asked, feeling his temperature starting to rise.

"They come up from behind and snap my ears. They call me names like squirrel face or Elmo. At recess, one will sneak up behind and get down on his hands and knees while the other pushes me backward to fall over him. They do something almost *every* day, and most of the time, they do it in front of others to make everyone laugh."

Gordon studied the Volkswagen directly ahead to gather his thoughts. On the one hand, he was pleased David was finally opening up to him. Gordon couldn't remember the last time his son had strung together so many uninterrupted words. On the other hand, no father likes to hear his son is getting bullied.

"Do you think that's their goal?" Gordon asked. "To see how much they can make the others laugh?"

David nodded while turning to gaze at his dusty sneakers, which were tapping nervously.

"Did you say anything to Mrs. Harrison?"

"Yeah," David replied robotically while continuing to study his shoes. "She talked to them plenty of times. I think she even called their parents. It helped for a while, but it never lasted. Lately, they've been doing it again."

"Have you told your mom about this?" Gordon inquired.

"A long time ago. Mom said I should keep telling Mrs. Harrison whenever it happens."

Gordon looked down at his son with exasperation written in the wrinkles of his furrowed brow.

"Is that all she said?" Gordon asked. "That isn't working anymore, is it?"

"She says that's all I can do," David responded.

Gordon noticed the traffic had started to move, and they would soon be at the Hampton exit. He would need to concentrate on finding a parking place at the zoo, and with the crowds that would be out on a gorgeous day like this, that would be a challenge. Gordon raised his volume to wrap up the conversation temporarily.

"David, you may have some other options. Mom was right to tell you to go through your teacher, but you may need to handle things yourself at this point. We'll talk some more inside the zoo, okay?"

Twenty minutes later, Gordon and David walked side-by-side behind Annie, who leisurely led them past the bear pits. He noticed his daughter seemed more interested in the humans. Affable by nature, she scanned around, observing the people as they gawked at the animals. Annie hardly paid attention to the bears behind their moats. When Gordon saw this, it put a smile on his face.

Then he peered down at David. The polar bears had enchanted David so much that Gordon had to gently nudge him when it was time to move on to the grizzlies. David didn't notice the physical contact, but Gordon was still self-conscious whenever he touched his son in an unaffectionate manner. After making their way to the Lakeside Café, both children took a table within sight while Gordon stood in line to order lunch.

He thought over the conversation in the car about the bullies. There had recently been a workshop at school about bullying, which was as endemic in high school as it was in the lower grades. A thought leaped into his head. Gordon found that he was excited about the chance to steer his son through this third-grade crisis.

"So, David, here's a thought," Gordon pronounced as he plunked down a plastic tray on the table crowded with wrapped hot dogs, cardboard platters bursting with salty fries, and paper cups overflowing with iced soda. Randomly scattered throughout were the condiment packets. David looked up inquisitively.

"What if the next time those kids in school do or say something mean, you get in one of their faces, and then loudly and firmly yell, '*stop it!*'" He pronounced these last two words with a higher dose of intensity.

David frowned. Gordon continued.

"Those boys are classic bullies. They won't expect someone to stand up to them. They usually target the kids who *won't* stand up to them. Therefore, if you tell them in a strong and confident voice to stop, it might work."

David's frown changed into a downward glance as he skeptically raised his eyebrows. Gordon continued.

"Bullies often choose a victim they think won't object to what they're doing. David, don't be *that* victim. Make sure those boys know they can't walk over you. Telling your teacher's a good approach, but she can't always be there to protect you, right? If you make it clear you won't put up with bullies, then you *won't* be bullied."

"Did you ever do this when you were a kid?" David asked.

Gordon suppressed a smile. When he was younger, his larger size shielded him from bullies. He was never the victim.

"No, I just recently learned about this approach," Gordon responded. "But I've been told it works. I like how it makes you use your *words* to stand up for yourself. *Never* fists, you understand? Just words."

David nodded, and while he kept his lips together, the corners of his mouth began to rise. Gordon reached over to rub the back of his son's neck, and this time it felt more natural. Then he turned to face his daughter. Gordon asked to see Big Bird for a moment, and she reluctantly handed over the fuzzy puppet. When he pretended to feed Big Bird some fries, Annie laughed with delight and soon joined the game.

After lunch, the threesome headed towards the children's zoo, which lay on the other side of a small lake. This time, Gordon and David led the way with Annie dawdling behind. A violent shriek abruptly shattered the moment. Gordon spun around to see Annie peeking over the stone railing of a small arched bridge that crossed a narrow isthmus. She was up on her toes, looking in horror at the murky water below. Annie turned to face Gordon. A cloudburst of tears swiftly supplanted the wide-eyed shock.

"*What*! What is it, sweetheart?"

Gordon rushed towards his daughter. He grabbed her by both shoulders, looking for a cut or some other injury. There was nothing.

"Sweetheart, what happened? Did you hurt yourself?"

Annie stood motionless while tears flooded her cheeks. Then the wailing stopped, replaced by a silent scream. After a moment or two of panic-stricken breathing, more howling erupted, this time sounding like an air-raid siren. Annie turned back towards the lake and extended her arm. She was pointing towards an object floating in the water. Something fluffy and yellow. It was Big Bird.

Gordon didn't see what'd happened, but he surmised that Annie had been leaning over the bridge's railing to watch a flock of ducks. Or maybe, knowing her, she was captivated by people feeding the ducks. Either way, she must not have been paying attention to her best friend as he slipped from her grasp. Now the puppet was lying face down in the tranquil lake, like a drowned corpse.

Gordon once again worked hard to repress a smile. He knelt to her level, placed his hands on her shoulders, and gently turned his daughter so they would be face-to-face.

"Sweetheart, look at me. I want you to calm down, okay? I promise we'll get him back."

Gordon's words were like an elixir. The crying instantly stopped as Annie reached up to wipe away tears. Seeing that his daughter was at least temporarily pacified, Gordon looked around for a stick. At first, there was nothing. Then, off in the distance, he spotted what looked like a tree branch beneath a large oak. It was crooked and a bit rotten, but it would have to do. With luck, it would extend his reach by two or three feet. If Gordon stood at the right spot along the shore, he might reach Big Bird.

Unfortunately, a clump of lily pads immobilized the furry puppet, pausing its glacial movement towards the shore. The branch helped some, but there were still two or three feet to cover. Now, Gordon looked around and realized he was running out of ideas. David and Annie stood above him on the bridge, providing an attentive audience.

Gordon sucked in a deep breath, acknowledging what he'd have to do. Since the temperature had been cooler in the morning when he'd first dressed, Gordon had thrown on a pair of old jeans rather than the usual shorts. Now he kicked off his sandals and rolled up his jeans just above his ankles. Then Gordon tentatively stepped into the water, hoping the shadowy surface hid a bottom only a few inches below. No such luck. His first step landed about three inches beneath the surface but then sank at least three more into the slimy muck. Gordon silently cursed while extending the stick toward the intransigent bird. Still too far. He looked up at the kids and focused on Annie's face. She looked like a baseball fan praying for a miracle comeback in the bottom of the ninth inning.

Gordon looked down. Already, the stagnant water had soaked one leg of his jeans. What was the point in keeping the other dry? He took another step closer towards Big Bird. This time, the bottom was at least a foot beneath the surface, and again, he sank further into the shadowy gloom. As he started to tilt forward, Gordon lifted his back foot out of its muddy tomb and took a step to restore his balance. Now the water came up to mid-thigh on both legs. After securing his foothold, Gordon took another deep breath and reached for the elusive puppet with the bent stick. This time, it worked. Gordon maneuvered Big Bird to a spot where he could grab him with his hand. When he pulled the dripping hand puppet out of the black soup, Gordon looked up at Annie. A huge grin exploded across her face. Behind them, a small crowd that had gathered broke out into applause.

Three hours later, Gordon backed his Corolla out of a parking spot at the Steak 'n Shake a few blocks south of the zoo. He'd splurged by ordering two chocolate shakes to accompany their steakburgers, one for David and another he shared with Annie. Gordon had initially planned to take the kids out for a nice Italian meal on the Hill, but the moldy smell of his damp jeans eliminated that option. It didn't matter to David and Annie since Steak 'n Shake was one of their favorite restaurants, but he missed the plate of lasagna along with an order of toasted ravioli.

A quick glimpse in the rearview mirror revealed that Annie had already fallen asleep in her car seat. It was a bit of a cliché, but the best word Gordon could think of to describe his sleeping daughter was "angelic." He turned onto the entrance ramp of I-64, heading west into a brilliant sun. Once he'd caught up to speed with the gushing river of traffic, Gordon stole a glimpse to his right. Racing vehicles all-around had once again lulled David into a daze. Gordon secured both hands at the top of the steering wheel, leaned back with his head against the backrest, and smiled to himself. It'd been a good day.

Reflecting over the last few hours, Gordon suddenly remembered the baseball game he'd missed. He turned the dial to KMOX just in time to catch the end of the postgame show. The Cardinals had won nine to three, but since most of the scoring had taken place in the early innings, Gordon assumed the game had been a bit dull. Maybe he was rationalizing, but looking back over the day, he knew he'd made the right choice. Most baseball games quickly get lost in a hazy fog, but Gordon knew he'd remember this day for a long time.

He reached over to put on his sunglasses. The journey back to the western suburbs required protection from the fiery glare, but Gordon knew wearing them would darken the glorious tapestry unfolding up ahead. Cirrus clouds on the horizon filtered the dazzling rays into an Impressionistic painting. Almost by instinct, Gordon reached over again to rub the back of David's neck tenderly. When he looked over at his son, a warm smile was his reward.

At that moment, Gordon had an epiphany. He loved his children. Not just in the way family members routinely say they love each other; no, he *loved* his children. His paternal heart had never been empty, but something had always been missing. Gordon had heard other fathers say that witnessing the birth of their children was the most transformative moment of their lives. He'd been present to see both of his kids enter the world, yet Gordon hadn't felt the expected euphoria. Was something wrong with him? Driving Elaine and baby David home from the hospital had left him feeling more anxiety than joy. Was that normal?

By the time he passed the Lindbergh exit, the sun had set low enough for Gordon to remove his shades. He turned on the car's headlights and then scanned around once more to see the blackening shadows of his children. Gordon didn't understand why it had taken so long, but he was finally overwhelmed by adoration for his children. A day at the zoo had become a potentially life-altering experience, and now he thought things might never be the same. As he entered the 270-north ramp, Gordon reached a decision.

Ten minutes later, he carried his sleeping daughter up to the front porch of what still felt like his house. David trailed sleepily behind. As Gordon walked towards the entranceway, the front door opened, and there stood Elaine, framed by the glow from a floor lamp guarding the living room. It was difficult to discern the expression on her face in the shadows. The first words out of her mouth, though, expressed concern.

"Is everything okay?" she asked. "It's getting late. I was starting to worry."

Elaine stepped back to clear a path so Gordon could carry his princess to her bedroom. Gordon gently deposited Annie on her bed, noting that Elaine had pulled back the covers. He bent down, kissed her cheek, and then raised the rail to prevent her from falling. When he turned around, Gordon could see the bewilderment on his wife's face.

"Let's step out," he whispered. "I'd like to discuss something."

Elaine trailed Gordon back into the living room, where they found David standing in the foyer like he was waiting for an invitation to make himself comfortable. Gordon told him to get ready for bed, and David started to shuffle towards his room robotically. Gordon reached for David's shoulder almost as an afterthought, and his son immediately spun around to hug his Dad's waist.

After David left, Gordon collapsed into the recliner next to the front door while Elaine planted herself on the leather couch behind the wooden coffee table. He noticed her face was a bit ashen for late spring. Even under a large Cardinals' T-shirt, Elaine's shapely form brought back good memories. While patiently waiting for Gordon to speak, she pulled back her dark blonde hair into a ponytail, revealing high cheekbones above her dimples.

Gordon glanced around the room, territory that was both familiar and foreign. He cleared his throat while attempting to gather his thoughts.

"First," he finally said, "I'd like to apologize. We had a good time at the zoo today, although we had one little adventure. We ended up staying later than planned."

Elaine nodded to indicate that Gordon should continue.

"I should've called," he said, "but the battery in my phone was dead. I guess it's getting old. I even looked around for a payphone, but nowadays, I guess you can only find those in museums. Anyhow, I'm sorry we're late, and I'm sorry if you were worried."

Gordon's tone was conciliatory; at least, he hoped that's how it sounded. He was sorry. Besides, the last thing he wanted was to upset Elaine before broaching the next subject.

"It's all right," Elaine responded. "Not a big deal. Tell me about the zoo."

"It was a good day," Gordon answered. "We've been there so many times before, and it was the same old animals. The penguins were lively, and the gorillas put on a show. But it wasn't that. It was *something* about the kids."

"The *kids*?" Elaine inquired. "What happened today with the kids?"

"Oh, they're fine," Gordon answered. "But I heard all about the two bullies in David's class, and he opened up enough so we could *talk*. It felt good. And then there was the Big Bird incident."

"Big Bird? Go on," Elaine said with a chuckle. "This ought to be interesting."

"Somehow, Big Bird dove into the lake. Annie howled and then went into shock."

"Oh my!" Elaine said, covering her gaping smile with both hands.

"I found a stick to fish it out, but I still ended up halfway in the lake. That's some pretty disgusting water, by the way. "

"I guess that explains the funky smell," Elaine replied while staring down at Gordon's jeans.

"Yeah," Gordon mumbled. "Still, Annie's been giving me goo-goo eyes ever since. I think I've become her new hero."

Elaine leaned back on the couch and grinned. "Nice, *well done,* Gordon. By the way, where's the yellow furry victim you saved from drowning? I hope it didn't need CPR."

"Still in the backseat," Gordon replied. "She insisted on keeping him nearby despite the foul aroma. I'll fetch him before I leave. You'll want to let him spend some time in the washer and dryer."

"*No doubt.*"

The grin on Gordon's face slowly dissolved. He clasped his hands together between his knees and stared down at the carpeted floor.

"Elaine," Gordon said cautiously, "I was thinking during the drive home that today was fun. I mean, *really* fun. For the first time in a while, I enjoyed being with the kids. Elaine, I'd like to have them more than just one day a week."

Gordon looked up to see the response on his wife's face. Sure enough, her smile had melted away, replaced by tightened lips. She looked down, refusing to make eye contact.

"Oh?" she finally inquired. "So, you're finally *enjoying* your children?"

She looked up, revealing a sardonic smile beneath a piercing glare. Gordon immediately realized he'd chosen the wrong words.

"Well, yes," Gordon responded. He was suddenly startled by the roar of a motorcycle blasting down what was usually a quiet street. Then he turned back and stared directly into Elaine's penetrating eyes. The conversation wasn't going as planned. Gordon was so far off the script that the only thing he could think to do now was to double down and hope for the best.

"I was thinking," he continued, "it isn't just the kids I'm missing. Elaine, I miss *you.* I miss our life. I'd like to see the kids, and I'd like to see you, *and* not just once or twice a week."

Elaine squeezed her lips together and looked up at the dark shadow hovering in a dark corner above Gordon's head. Silence descended into the open space between them. When she finally looked back at her husband, Gordon could see a tear inching down her cheek.

"Are you willing to see someone?" Elaine inquired. "A therapist or some other kind of professional?"

Gordon knew what Elaine was asking, although this was the first time she'd directly raised the question. His first thought was the standard response. He didn't feel the need. Yes, he was still wrestling with the same demons that had haunted him for the past two years, but this didn't require professional help. It would be highly uncomfortable to share his thoughts and memories with a stranger. He could handle this—he *was* handling this—and with a little more time, he'd be able to shove it back into his past. It was also a matter of pride. Like his father, he preferred to resolve his problems on his own.

"I'm getting there," Gordon responded. "I don't feel the need to pay for professional advice. I've been working on some things. And today . . ." Gordon hesitated. "Today was a good day. I think I may have turned a corner."

Elaine wiped her cheek and reached for a Kleenex. After blowing her nose, she slowly began to shake her head side-to-side.

"I'm sorry, Gordon, but I'm afraid that's not good enough. It's one thing to have fun with the kids at the zoo, but I need to know that if you're home alone with them, you're not drinking, and you won't do them *any* harm."

Gordon tightened his jaw, and now he began to shake his head.

"I promise, Elaine, I can give up drinking *right* now. This very minute. Just let me come home. I can pack up my bags tomorrow morning and be home in time to take you and the kids out for Sunday brunch. Come on," Gordon said pleadingly. "*Please*, let me come home."

Elaine dabbed her cheeks, but it was no longer necessary.

"No, Gordon. It's easy to say those words at the end of one good day, but putting them into practice is a different story. Especially if you're not willing to accept outside help."

"I don't need to see anyone," Gordon responded. "I know what's eating away at me. We both do. But it has *nothing* to do with how I feel about you and the kids."

"Gordon, I recently spoke to a friend who's also a family therapist. You know who I'm talking about."

Gordon couldn't conceal the frown on his face. Even though Elaine may have had good intentions, she had no right to share their personal life with *any* of her friends.

"It was just a brief conversation, nothing formal. But my friend said that until you get some outside help, I should minimize the time you spend alone with the kids. I'm not worried about you taking them to places in public, but being with them twenty-four hours a day, seven days a week, is *not* an option. Not right now."

Gordon lowered his hands between his knees, rested his forearms on his thighs, and looked up. There was both anger and sorrow in his eyes. Now, he felt a tear seeping down his cheek. Seeing this, Elaine paused and then continued.

"For now, I'd prefer to hold to our current arrangement. You can call the children every day if you'd like, but for now, let's stick with seeing them on Saturdays."

"But I'm not just talking about the children, Elaine. I want to move back home and be your husband again. Even if you're worried about me being around David and Annie every day, you'd be around too. We could go back to being a family."

Gordon could see a thought jump into Elaine's head. It wasn't a good thought. She glanced away for a moment like she was looking for guidance from someone off to the side.

"Even if I did agree to let you see the kids more than once a week, I'm not ready for you to move home. *I'm* not ready. Do you understand? It's been almost six months since you moved out. *Six months.* That's a long time, Gordon. At this point, I'm pretty confused. I don't know how I feel anymore. I don't know how I feel . . . about *you.*"

Gordon noticed that Elaine's tone had hardened. Her tears had dried, and she voiced her last remarks as though she had rehearsed them. Gordon slowly began to rise.

"Okay," he said while turning towards the front door. "I get it; I *do.*" After a deep sigh, he added, "I guess I'd better get going. Oh, let me go grab Big Bird."

Gordon walked outside. Cool fresh air descended on him as though he'd just stepped under a waterfall. He glanced towards the horizon to see a full beige moon climbing in the darkening skies to the east. It cleared his head. He walked over to the Corolla parked in what he still thought of as his driveway and retrieved the damp hand puppet from the back seat. Gordon felt like a slashed tire with the air still escaping as he made his way to the porch. The good feelings that had overtaken him during the drive home were gone. He also admitted that distant memories were still overpowering the fresher ones.

Gordon handed over the damp puppet to Elaine, who stood at the front door. His face was purposefully expressionless.

"Next Saturday?" Gordon asked in a monotone. "I'll take the kids out to Chuck E. Cheese for pizza?"

Elaine nodded.

"Three o'clock okay?" he asked.

"That'll work. I'll have the children ready." Elaine smiled, trying to restore a sense of normalcy.

"Okay," Gordon said. "I'll see you then."

Gordon spun on his heels and walked to the car without waiting for a response. Five minutes later, he turned into his familiar QuikTrip, where he glided past the empty gas pumps and parked directly in front of the store entrance. After another ten minutes, Gordon lit up a recently purchased cigarette with the car lighter. Then he glanced over at the passenger seat that just an hour ago had been occupied by David. Now, his passenger was a six-pack.

CHAPTER

5

Gordon struggled to focus on his reflection in the bathroom mirror. He wiped out the accumulated eye gunk and leaned in closer for a better look. Gordon barely recognized the man staring back. It had been months since his last haircut, so tufts jetted out in all directions, overshadowing his ears. Wrinkles creased his forehead, and crow's feet exploded from the outer corners of his eyes, like fireworks in a night sky. Gordon was even grayer than he'd remembered. Ashy patches had invaded the whiskers on his face. He searched in vain to find remnants of the striking man who had greeted him every morning just a few years ago. The effort only further addled his aching head.

After downing three aspirin, Gordon meticulously brushed his teeth, hoping the vigorous scrubbing of each tooth might dispel the foul taste in his mouth. After a full minute, he glanced up in the mirror and saw what looked like a rabid dog. Gordon spit, rinsed, and then spent another thirty seconds gargling mouth wash. Despite his best efforts, he couldn't shake the fetid taste from the night before.

This particular Sunday morning in late May had been the cradle of good memories in previous years. Two days earlier was the last day of school and the official start of summer. Gordon recalled the joke he'd heard when he first decided to become a teacher. What are the three biggest reasons to teach? June, July, and August. Even though he'd taught summer school the past few years, there was always a week off before he had to return to teaching. Since Gordon and Elaine were both teachers, they'd always enjoyed a celebratory Sunday morning brunch to kick off the start of this glorious week. Today was different. Instead of enjoying a brunch with his wife, he suffered a hangover with his dad.

Gordon's only hope was coffee. He staggered into the kitchen wearing aged pajama bottoms and the rumpled T-shirt he'd worn the day before. As he approached the table, Dad, who had been scouring the sports section of the *St. Louis Post-Dispatch,* laid out in front of him like a giant placemat, greeted him with a look of trepidation.

"Coffee?" asked Gordon trying to conceal his desperation.

"No thanks," Dad replied. "I've already got a full cup." His father chuckled at his little joke. Gordon frowned at his dad as he lurched over to the counter and then sighed with relief when he saw the pot was still mostly full. He filled a mug to the brim, then joined his father at the table. Gordon squinted at the sunlight flooding through the kitchen window, illuminating dust particles above Dad's head.

Feigning a tone of normalcy, Gordon stated, "I saw the Cardinals lost again."

"Yep, that makes five in a row. I think it's the relief pitching. Even when the Cardinals have a lead, they never seem to hold it."

Gordon shook his head to acknowledge his father's disgust and then reached across for the front page. He was beginning to feel a little better and wanted to establish a typical Sunday morning.

"So, what's going on with you?" Dad suddenly asked. "You look *awful.*"

Gordon peered up from the front page where he'd started to read the caption beneath an unflattering picture of Donald Trump. He scratched his head and looked directly at his father. Dad still had a full head of snowy gray hair he kept clipped and combed. His face was a palette of wrinkles, blemishes, and age spots, but compassion still filled his crystal blue eyes. There was no point in trying to conceal what had occurred the day before.

"I took the kids to Chuck E. Cheese yesterday," Gordon stated matter-of-factly. "In retrospect, it may have been a mistake."

"Oh?" Dad replied. "Was there a problem?"

"No, not exactly. It's just I *hate* that place. It's so loud, and it's phony and commercial."

Dad raised a bewildered eyebrow. "What do you mean?"

"You know me," Gordon continued. "I prefer nature and natural beauty, not the manufactured forms of entertainment designed to *suck* money out of my wallet. That's why I was never a fan of Disney World for kids or Vegas for adults."

"So, why'd you take them there?"

"Good question. I guess I thought the kids might enjoy singing robotic animals. Also, I've never met a pizza I didn't like."

"Did David and Annie like the place?"

"They didn't complain," Gordon responded. "But they didn't seem happy either. David was mostly quiet. I think he was overwhelmed by all the noise, the crowds, and the commotion. Annie looked like the singing animals hypnotized her. She didn't smile much. There were moments when she looked like she was in a coma."

"Hmm, how long did you guys stay?"

"Long enough to eat our pizza, which by the way, disproved my theory that there's no such thing as a bad pizza. Unlike the week before, I shocked Elaine when I got the kids home early."

"So, this is why you look like something the cat dragged in?"

"No," Gordon replied. "But it didn't help. You know, I'd had such a *good* time with the kids the week before. Yesterday was a *huge* disappointment, for them, I think, as well as for me. I felt pretty down when I dropped them off. Then just as I was leaving Elaine's, Jim called and asked if I wanted to join him and some other teachers at Buffalo Wild Wings. It was still early, and they were watching the Cards and celebrating the end of school, so I decided to join them."

"How'd *that* go?" asked Dad, who was now guiding Gordon through his story like a cop interrogating a suspect.

"It's hard to say; I'm still trying to remember. The way the Cards lost didn't help, and I was already in a crappy mood. I don't think I said nearly as much as I drank. The pitchers of beer kept coming, and I kept drinking. Finally, Jim woke me up. I must have rested my head on the table for a minute and then fallen asleep. They let me sleep, which is kind of embarrassing now that I think about it."

"You didn't drive home, did you?" Dad asked with mounting concern. He glanced out the window and breathed a sigh of relief when he didn't see Gordon's car parked in the driveway.

"No, they wouldn't let me. I guess Jim was the designated driver. I don't think I'm the only one he drove home."

"You want a ride later today to get your car?" Dad offered.

Gordon nodded, but before he could say more, "Here Comes the King," the Budweiser theme song, could be heard playing from the living room.

"That's my phone," Gordon said as he tried to stand. Moving in slow motion, he answered just before the caller hung up. He switched to speakerphone, as was his custom, so he wouldn't have to keep the flat face of the smartphone plastered against his ear.

"Hello," Gordon said, trying to catch his breath.

"Gordon?"

"Yeah."

"You recognize my voice?"

There was a moment of awkward silence.

"Come on, buddy, I know it's been a long time, but I didn't think you'd ever forget me." He enunciated the words slowly to make it easier for his voice to be recognized.

Gordon glanced at the display on his phone but couldn't identify the number. Even the 424 area code was a mystery. Gordon dropped down on the couch, scratched his forehead, and stared blankly at his cell phone. He was unaware that his father was listening from the kitchen, curious to know who had called.

"Uh, give me a second," Gordon said, trying to buy a little time. He was in no mood for guessing games, but the voice had a reassuring familiarity. Somewhere deep in his brain, Gordon connected the sound with pleasant memories from the past. "Holy shit, Ben? Is that *you?*"

"Yeah, man. I'm glad to see you haven't *entirely* forgotten me."

"Well, you've got to cut me some slack," Gordon responded. "I haven't completely woken up yet. Also, what's it been? Four or five years? I don't remember the last time I've heard from you."

"Fair enough," replied Ben. "Until recently, I've been super busy. But that's no excuse. Then again, I don't remember the last time I've heard from *you* either."

Gordon peered out the front window trying to think of a response. The single-lane highway was quiet, but that was typical for a Sunday morning. The only movement was the shaking of the lower limbs of the towering elm tree overshadowing the front yard when a fat gray squirrel leaped acrobatically from one branch to another.

"I guess that's fair," Gordon finally responded. "I've been pretty distracted myself over the past couple of years. But as you say, that's no excuse."

"Well, better late than never. You got some time to catch up?"

"Sure, this is a good time," replied Gordon.

"I've been trying to think," Ben pronounced, attempting to jumpstart a conversation, "when's the last time we *saw* each other? I bet it's been at least ten years."

Gordon tried to picture his old friend. Ben was shorter, barely over five foot eight, but surprisingly athletic. He wore rimless glasses back in college and kept his dark hair short and well-groomed. His defining trait was the dimple in each cheek that magnetically attracted coeds like bees to spring flowers. A boisterous sense of humor and unlimited energy were sometimes distracting when Gordon wanted to study, but otherwise, Ben had been the ideal college roommate. Even more, during his four years at Mizzou, he'd been Gordon's best friend.

Ben and Gordon had something else in common that semester. When others were suffering through the silly hazing rituals required to enter a fraternity, particularly Zeta Beta Tau, the largest Jewish fraternity on campus, the two roommates decided to resist the peer pressure. They joked about not following the lemmings off the cliff. Eventually, they joined Alpha Phil Omega, a service fraternity open to everyone.

By the start of their junior year, they rented a large house off-campus with eight bedrooms. Then they convinced other members of APO, both male and female, to join them there. This way, they combined the social advantages of Greek life with the community service of APO. In addition, there were no Greek letters on the side of the house. There also wasn't any hazing, and most importantly, there was none of the elitism associated with the fraternity and sorority practice of blackballing. Gordon and Ben shared these same values, but they also connected by splitting the leadership experience. They were proud to have cleared their path rather than following others over the cliff.

"When was your wedding?" Gordon asked. "That's the last time we saw each other."

"Then I'm right," Ben replied. "Kathy and I celebrated our tenth anniversary in January, so it's been over ten years since we've seen each other."

"You know, you're the only person I've ever known who planned a wedding for January."

"You didn't seem to mind," Ben replied flippantly. "As I recall, you and Elaine were delighted to take a break from the frigid wasteland of St. Louis for a few days in Malibu."

Gordon chuckled and then added, "Well, congratulations on making it ten years, buddy. I'm proud of you."

"Don't be too proud," Ben replied. "I don't think we're going to make it to eleven."

There was a drawn-out pause. Ben waited for a reaction while Gordon struggled for the right words. In the kitchen, Dad was also taken aback by Ben's news. He sipped the last of his coffee, anxiously waiting for the phone conversation to continue.

"Man, I'm *so* sorry," Gordon responded. "What happened? I know it's been a while, but at your wedding, you and Kathy looked so happy!"

"We *were*, but as you said, it's been a while. Things have grown pretty complicated since then."

Gordon could hear a loud sigh. He patiently waited for his old college roommate to collect his thoughts.

"This may be a gross oversimplification," Ben finally declared, "but I think I'm going through an early midlife crisis. It isn't just my marriage. I've also left my job. In fact, for now, I've left *everything*." After a brief pause, he added, "Gordon, I didn't like myself very much in southern California. The money was good, but everything else had grown hollow. Pretension is the rule in L.A., and I was no better than anyone else there. I needed to get away."

More silence. Before Gordon could respond, Ben continued.

"I'm sorry, Gordon, it was never my intent to dump this on you over the phone. I just wanted to catch up." After a few more seconds, he changed the subject by adding, "How have you been? I hope you're doing better than me."

Gordon began to laugh. He tried to regain his composure, but as he replayed Ben's last comment, he strangely found it to be funny. Around the corner, Dad flinched at his son's untimely laughter. Ben finally interrupted by posing another question.

"So, is it safe to say you're *not* doing any better?"

"I don't know," Gordon responded. "But if we're holding a contest to see whose life sucks the most right now, I think my chances would be pretty good."

Before Gordon could continue, Ben interrupted. "Hey, I'm going to jump ahead to the real reason behind this call. I called you to extend an invitation. Since it seems like we've got a lot of stuff to catch up on, let's not do it over the phone. Let's do it in *person*."

"What?" Gordon asked. "You're still out in California, aren't you?"

"Actually, no," Ben replied. "I'm at my parents' cabin in Grand Lake. Remember that place? We had some *good* times here back in college."

Gordon's head was swimming. One moment, Ben was talking about his "early midlife crisis." Before that even ended, Gordon was wrestling with how much to share about his issues. Then suddenly, Ben was suggesting a possible reunion in the Colorado Rockies? The conversation was moving too fast. He needed to slow it down to process everything. Gordon recalled this was similar to many of the discussions he'd had with Ben twenty years ago.

"Yeah, *of course,* I remember the cabin in Grand Lake," Gordon stated, purposefully speaking at a more deliberate pace. "We spent two months there back in college. I remember hiking and climbing every day. We even made it up Longs Peak. That was the toughest thing I *ever* did. And at night, I recall sitting around fires drinking, getting high, and talking about all the shit that seemed so important back in college."

"Well, I'm back here now," Ben replied enthusiastically. "Why don't you come out and join me? We can catch up and relive some of those good times. Who knows? Maybe we can even take turns practicing therapy on each other."

Gordon thought back to that summer before his junior year at Mizzou. Ben and Gordon had explored every trail west of the Continental

Divide using the cabin as a home base. Before starting, they purchased some gear in Columbia, including packs with water bladders, several topo maps, and durable hiking boots. During the long drive across the Kansas prairie, they decided to make Longs Peak the highlight of their summer. That mountain, the highest in the northern Rockies, involved a fifteen-mile roundtrip hike and a climb of more than five thousand feet. Gordon still got shivers remembering the view from the narrow ledge where he could look straight down for more than half a mile.

Over the years, just thinking about Colorado put a smile on Gordon's face. When he crossed the teacher's lounge, making his way to the men's room, he'd sometimes escape by envisioning a herd of elk grazing next to a splashing stream. Behind were peaks crowned by glacial snow. For Gordon, crossing the Continental Divide was like traversing the border into another world, a better place. The air was thinner but crisp and cleansing; Gordon always found it easier to breathe in the mountains.

He used to walk along the edge of Grand Lake early in the morning. Brilliant rays from the rising sun would spotlight the wooded and granite faces on the western shore. The frozen reflection of mountains mirrored on the lake's polished surface created a canvas that was both soothing and enthralling. The water was so clear Gordon could see trout dancing along the sandy bottom. He never understood why he rose so early in Colorado and slept so late in Missouri.

Back in college, hiking in the Rockies was a religious experience. Since quitting Sunday School after the eighth grade, Gordon had only sporadically entered a synagogue and then just for someone's bar mitzvah or funeral. He had serious doubts about the existence of God, but the only time he'd ever sensed the presence of a deity was along the wooded paths of Colorado's western slope. To Gordon, Grand Lake was the epicenter of the West, and the West was a place that had always attracted people looking for a better life.

Every year in his history classes, Gordon looked forward to teaching about the Turner Thesis. He agreed with Frederick Jackson Turner, the historian who once said the West had molded the American character, forming a restless people that idolized the individual. People began anew in the West, from the early explorers until the dawn of the Twentieth Century. Like millions of pioneers who'd crossed the plains seeking not just a better life but a renewed spirit, Gordon felt the irresistible pull of the West.

He closed his eyes and pictured the blue columbines peering over the edge of Emerald Lake. Gordon visualized the bull moose grazing along the banks of a cascading stream. And, nowhere else had he ever seen such a panorama of stars ornamenting a moonless night. Despite the discussion about whose life had taken the turn for the worst, Gordon now had an unrestrained smile splashed across his face.

"Those were good times," Gordon finally responded, "but why are you in Grand Lake *now*?"

"I drove up from L.A. a couple of weeks ago. I took a sabbatical from my accounting firm, withdrew some cash from our savings, and headed straight to Grand Lake. As you can probably understand, there's *no* better place in the world to clear your head."

Dad looked up from his newspaper. Gordon stared at his phone and nodded.

"So, here's what I'm thinking," Ben stated as he cleared his throat. "I could try to fill you in *right now* on all my misery, or I could just tell you about it *in person. Here.* In Grand Lake. I'm planning to hang around at least until the end of July. As I recall, you're a teacher with a summer that's about to start, right? Why don't you come out and join me?"

Taking the silence as a sign his pitch was working, Ben decided to close the sale.

"When I asked how *you* were doing after mentioning my problems, your only response was laughter. Can I assume you've also got some issues of your own? *Come on,* Gordon, join me out West. Let's relive some of our best memories. We can catch up on the past decade *in person*, not through a long-distance phone call."

"I don't know," Gordon responded. At the moment, his mind was empty.

"All right," said Ben. "Think of it this way. If you *don't* come, we'll talk for another hour or so, and then pretty soon, we'll forget most of what we said. Then it'll be another decade or so before we talk again. Gordon, *man*, there was once a time when I considered you my best friend. What happened? How'd you go from being the best man in my wedding to being a hazy memory?"

"I don't know," Gordon replied. "That's a *good* question. I guess that's how life is sometimes. One moment, you're sharing a dorm room in college, and the next, your best friend's an accountant two thousand miles away. Over the years, you drift apart. Higher priority goes to wives, families, careers. Pretty soon, your college friend is so far on a backburner he drifts out of your life. But you're right, Ben. We *should* have done a better job staying in touch."

Gordon stood up and paced. While talking about why they had drifted apart, he mulled over the invitation to Grand Lake. Around the corner in the sun-drenched kitchen, Dad was folding up his newspaper and quietly uttering a little prayer his son would say yes to Ben's offer.

"That's true, Gordon. We should agree to talk more often. But a friendship also needs to be nourished now and then by face-to-face contact, *not* just phone calls. So, come on, Gordon. Drive out and join me at Grand Lake. You'll have a rent-free bedroom, and I promise to keep the fridge stocked with beer."

Dad frowned a little upon hearing those words.

"That sounds *very* tempting," Gordon responded. Then he shifted his thinking from Grand Lake to St. Louis.

Gordon thought about Elaine. A couple of months away from her wouldn't help his chances of resurrecting their marriage. Then again, a reconciliation with his wife didn't look promising. And what about David and Annie? How could he be away from them for so long? He couldn't; he just couldn't. Besides, he'd agreed to teach summer school. Jim was currently his best friend, and he'd committed to him. True, some younger teachers needed the money and would be happy to fill in, but Gordon also needed the money. He let out a sigh so loud it put a frown on his father's expectant face.

"No," Gordon slowly replied. "I can't do it. It's tempting. Believe me, Ben, it's *so* tempting. But I've got commitments here. I have some family issues to resolve, and I've also committed to teaching summer school. And frankly, Ben, I need the dough. If I came out to Colorado this summer, I'd be spending money, not earning it."

Gordon could hear his friend exhale from almost a thousand miles away.

"You sure, Gordon?"

"Yeah, I'm sure. It looks like we'll just have to use the next hour or so to catch up over the phone."

"Wait a minute, boys!" Dad hollered from the kitchen. Gordon looked up in shock, forgetting his father had been within easy listening distance the whole time. He peered up towards the kitchen just as Dad came loping into the room. His father donned a broad smile with a gleam in his deep blue eyes.

"Ben," Dad bellowed, "I'm sorry to intrude into your conversation, but I've just overheard the generous offer you've made to my son. Can Gordon call you back in a few minutes? I've got a proposal for him that might change everything."

CHAPTER
6

Gordon tentatively touched his phone to terminate the call. He leaned back on the couch, preparing for a conversation he suspected would be fruitless. Outside, a rare eighteen-wheeler roared up the highway, temporarily distracting him and his father, both of whom reflexively spun their heads to gaze out the front window. They missed the truck, but Gordon took notice of the shadowy web on the front lawn cast by the branches of the giant elm tree.

"It's not too late for breakfast," Dad casually commented. "Should we head back to the kitchen, and I'll make us an omelet?"

Gordon raised a suspicious eyebrow. He knew this invitation was part of his father's technique—employ a mellow tone backed by comforting food to soften up an obstinate subject. Gordon had grown up seeing his dad use this approach countless times with other family members. He'd also been a victim himself during his teenage years.

"That sounds good," Gordon replied, "but I'll take a pass for now. I'd like to continue my conversation with Ben, so let's hear your idea."

"Okay," Dad said with hesitation. He navigated around the coffee table and joined Gordon on the opposite end of the couch. For a moment, father and son eyed each other like two boxers waiting for the other to throw the first punch. Then Dad cracked a warm smile, instantly melting the frozen expression on Gordon's face.

"For starters," Dad said at last, "I think you should *go* to Colorado, and the sooner, the better. Now, before you say anything, hear me out, *okay?*"

Gordon nodded.

"It'll be good for you to get away," he continued. "And you *love* the West; you've *always* loved the West. We took all those summer road trips when you were a kid, and you hated coming back, didn't you?"

Once again, Gordon nodded.

"Remember the trip to the Smokies? Shenandoah? Acadia? You had a good time in those eastern parks, but not like you did out West—Glacier, the Cascades, the Tetons—I don't know why, but you were happier when there was snow on top of the mountains. When we went on hikes out West, you'd race ahead, find a remarkable rock formation, and start to climb. You made your mother *so* nervous, but you knew what you were doing. Frankly, I worried more about you spontaneously exploding from all your energy than I did about a climbing accident. I wish we could've sent you out West for college, but since we had to be prepared to pay double tuition in those days, we needed to keep you in-state."

Dad paused to catch his breath. When he did, Gordon jumped into the breach.

"Okay, Dad, I'm convinced. Yes, I *love* the West. That's never been a secret. And yes, I would love to have gone to college in Boulder or Laramie, but I understood the money. As it turns out, though, that's still the critical issue. I need to earn some cash this summer. As you know, Elaine's home with the kids, and David's going to a pricey day camp. They're counting on my summer paychecks."

Dad held up his hand like a crossing guard to interrupt his son.

"I know, I understand about the money. I'm getting to that. Remember, you agreed to hear me out."

Gordon fell silent.

"All right," Dad continued with renewed vigor. "I've got a ten-thousand-dollar CD coming due, and I don't need the money. I want you to have it. Use it in place of your summer school income and to pay for your trip out West."

Gordon was about to object, but Dad cut him off. "I'm not done, Gordon, so sit back and relax."

For a moment, it struck Gordon how he could be a thirty-eight-year-old man and the father of two children, and yet at times like this, he still felt like a kid. He leaned back and motioned for his father to continue.

"Son, I want you to have this money. I *want* you to have it, understand? It's part of *my* savings, and it's how I want to use this money. One day when you're my age, you can pay it forward to David or Annie, but for now, you *need* this trip out West, and I want you to go."

Not hearing an objection, Dad continued.

"What's more, I want you to take the *long* way out to Colorado. Go up into the Dakotas and come down through Wyoming. Do a little camping. There are places in that part of the country you've never seen: The Badlands, Theodore Roosevelt National Park, Devil's Tower. And there aren't many people in those places, just a lot of open roads."

Dad paused to wipe moisture from his mouth. He was growing increasingly animated. Even though Gordon tried to resist, he absorbed his father's enthusiasm.

"This would be a great way to clear your head, Gordon. As much as possible, drive the backroads, not the interstates. And when you get to Grand Lake, go on long hikes every day and spend each night with your college buddy. Sit by warm fires in his cabin or out on that back deck and have some *good* heart-to-hearts. I heard what Ben was saying. You guys *need* each other right now."

"Can I ask a question?" Gordon inquired. Dad scowled a little at the interruption. "Let's say I agree. What about my family? How do I just pick up and leave *them*?"

Dad looked away momentarily. He'd always been an avid chess player and had taught his kids how to play a good game when they were little. Now he had to utilize those same thinking skills, and there wasn't much time to formulate a plan.

"Ah, I knew that was coming. Here's your plan, Gordon. Drop by school tomorrow and talk to Jim. Tell him the reason why you're backing out of summer school. I'll bet it's not too late for him to find a replacement. Aren't there other teachers who need the money? Besides, Jim's a good friend, he'll understand. Then go by your house and meet with Elaine and the kids. They *love* you, Gordon, and they'll understand too. Besides, you'll be a better father once you come back, so that'll make it worth the time you're apart. Think of it as making a long-term investment. Then in the afternoon, purchase some camping gear and load up your car. Finally, get up early Tuesday morning and hit the road. Gordon, it's *that* simple!"

Silence filled the room. A self-congratulatory grin crept across Dad's face.

"What about you?" Gordon finally inquired.

"What about me?"

"I'm just supposed to desert *you*?"

"Oh my God, Gordon, you're *right*! How the hell will I ever survive without you?"

"You know what I mean. Don't be such a smartass."

"Look, Gordon, since your mom died, I've gotten pretty used to being alone. I have my friends and volunteer work, and I've got a well-established routine. I'll be *fine*. Besides, while it's been nice to have you around, frankly, you haven't been the best roomie lately. You know what I mean?"

Gordon glanced down at the coffee table and sighed. He nodded to indicate his understanding but didn't reply. Seeing the gloom on his son's face, Dad leaned forward, clasped his hands together, and rested his elbows on his knees.

"Look, Gordon, let me tell you something I learned the hard way. It took me a *long* time to figure this out. When a man decides to have children and wants to be a good father, there's only one thing that matters. You know what that is?"

Gordon looked directly at his father. Acknowledging the gravity of the moment, he tightened his lips and swallowed. Then he slowly shook his head back and forth.

"*Happiness.* I'm not talking about your happiness, Gordon. I mean the happiness of your children. That's it; that's *all* that matters. You want your kids to be *happy*. Good grades, a successful career, a loving marriage, all those things that parents are always fretting over; they're just the means to an end. When you go to sleep at night, you want to be able to lay your head down on your pillow with a smile on your face, knowing your kids are *happy*. If you haven't figured that out yet with David and Annie, Gordon, you will. I guarantee it. And . . ."

There was a pause as Gordon absorbed everything he'd heard. Dad looked away so his son wouldn't observe him wiping away a tear that rolled down his cheek.

"Dad, what is it?"

"Nothing, it's nothing, Gordon. Let's just say I haven't always been able to go to sleep every night with that smile on my face."

Dad turned back towards his son, and this time he made no effort to conceal the moisture beneath his eyes. Gordon instantly reached over and took his father's hand. They looked directly at each other and exchanged smiles. Then Gordon surprised himself. He slid down the couch, reached out for his father, and pulled him in for a tight bear hug. Glancing over his shoulder through the front window, Gordon watched as a breeze stirred the silver maples across the highway. Finally, Gordon drew in a deep breath, closed his eyes, and then uttered the words that would put a massive grin on his dad's face.

"Man, I'd *love* to spend this summer in the mountains."

"Then *do* it," Dad exclaimed. He gently pulled back to look up into his son's face.

"Well, if my happiness is so necessary for *you* to be happy, I guess there's no other choice, is there?"

"Oh, thank you, Gordon, thank you *so* much. Thank you for making the sacrifice."

"My pleasure," Gordon stated. After a brief pause, he added, "Dad, I love you."

A few minutes later, he called Ben with the news. Then Gordon gobbled down a bacon omelet and asked for seconds. After picking up his car, he spent the afternoon with his father watching the Cards beat the Pirates, although Gordon didn't focus on the action in Busch Stadium. A little later, he and his father went out for pizza. They shared a pitcher of Diet Pepsi. Later that evening, they watched *Field of Dreams*, with Dad slung back on his leather recliner and Gordon sprawled out on the couch. Even though they had seen the film several times, it never grew old.

Finally, when Dad stood to go to bed, Gordon also rose. His father looked a little stunned since Gordon usually would be on the couch for another couple of hours nursing a six-pack and watching Sports Center and other ESPN programs. After the day's second hug, the two men retired to their bedrooms. That night, they slept with smiles on their faces.

The next day, Gordon rose early. He'd set the alarm for seven in the morning but was showered and shaved by six-thirty. Knowing he had time to kill, Gordon enjoyed a leisurely breakfast with Dad, where they shared the *Post-Dispatch* and drained an entire pot of coffee. By seven-thirty, Gordon inched his way towards the climbing sun on I-64. The traffic was thick, but at least there were no accidents.

Shortly after eight-thirty, Gordon bounded up the school's front steps. It was a glorious day, not a cloud in the sky. He noticed the pink and white colors that had dominated the bushes, and small trees adorning the school's façade had turned to emerald green. Spring was over, and summer had begun. Gordon wore khaki shorts and a white Blues T-shirt, dressed more like a student than a teacher.

When Gordon entered Jim's office, his friend was on the phone. Jim had already loosened his tie and rolled his long sleeves up to the elbow. He motioned for Gordon to take a seat and held up a finger, indicating he'd be available in a minute. As soon as he hung up, the phone rang again, and Jim answered. He was inundated with calls about summer school registration. Sensing this might take a long time, Gordon pulled out his phone, typed out a text message, and hit send.

> I'm sorry, Jim, but I can't teach this summer. A buddy from college invited me out to his cabin in Colorado for a couple of months. Other history teachers would be happy to take my place. Sorry about the inconvenience, but I NEED to take this trip. I hope you understand.

Jim heard the ding come from his pocket. He pulled out his cell phone while continuing the conversation with the distraught parent on his office phone. Jim stared at the text longer than it should've taken to read. His eyes enlarged, and he began to shake his head vigorously. Anticipating this, Gordon quickly thumbed out a second text.

I called Julie, Scott, and Bob last night.
They ALL said they could use the money
and would be happy to take my place.
Jim, I have to take this trip. PLEASE
understand.

When Jim looked up from reading the second text, the expression on his face softened. The corners of his mouth rose, his eyes widened, and he began to nod his head slowly. Gordon mouthed the words "thank you" and stood. At that exact moment, Jim asked the parent to hold for a minute. He stood up, circled his desk, and reached out to hug Gordon.

"You have a safe trip," Jim whispered. "Text me pictures and updates when you can."

Gordon nodded. As he walked towards the office door, Jim called after him.

"Buddy, heal yourself."

Gordon smiled and nodded. As he turned into the hallway, he could hear Jim's voice guaranteeing that he would fix the scheduling snafu posthaste. He hadn't taken more than ten steps towards the stairwell before he was startled by a different voice.

"Mr. G!"

Gordon turned to see a tall, skinny kid. He was wearing a dingy baseball cap sheltering a toothy smile.

"Andre!" Gordon exclaimed. "How are you? What're you doing here?"

"Signing up for summer school. *Man*, I flunked math, and now they're making me take a second course too because they said everyone has to have *two* classes. Something to do with transportation."

"Yeah, that's true," responded Gordon. "There're no buses to take students home after the first class. Hey, I hear good things about an enrichment class called Hollywood History. You mostly watch films about the past and then research their accuracy. It's the kind of class you'd like, and I think you'd do well."

"That's the one I was planning to take." Andre paused and then added, "So, Mr. G, what're *you* doing here? Are you teaching this summer? You look like you're going to the beach."

"I'm headed to the mountains. I *was* supposed to teach this summer, but I just got out of it. I'm planning to hit the road tomorrow."

Andre glanced out the huge picture window to the stadium below. A jogger on the track attempted to navigate his way through a gaggle of older women engaged in animated conversation. Gordon followed Andre's gaze and smiled at the image of the older people making use of the school's track.

"Well," Gordon added in a subdued tone, "I better get going. I've got a lot of packing to do. You take care of yourself, Andre, and be sure to pass that math class. I hope you didn't fail because of too many tardies, if you know what I mean."

"Nah, I flunked cuz I hated the class. But don't worry, I'll pass it this summer. Afterward, I don't *ever* want to hear the word 'geometry' again. Oh, by the way, Mr. G., my counselor put me in your AP class for the fall. Thought I'd give it a try."

"Yeah, I heard," Gordon responded with a grin on his face. "I told her about our plan, and she said she'd talk to you. On the last day of school, she told me you agreed. You can always change your schedule if you want up through October, but I think you'll do all right."

"I think so too," responded Andre, "but it's not me I'm worried about."

"What are you talking about?"

Andre yanked off his cap and turned to face Gordon directly. "Let's just say I hope you have a good trip, Mr. G., cuz this time, I have an assignment for *you*. Remember Robin Jones and what she said about your class?"

Gordon nodded.

"Come back *that* teacher. No offense, Mr. G, but I want Robin's teacher in three months, not the one I had this past year. Think you can do that?"

Gordon's chest heaved as he sucked in a deep breath. He looked down for a moment at the swirling patterns on the hideous hallway carpeting, dark shades of purple to mask the dirt tracked in by thousands of adolescent feet every day. Then he looked up, chuckled a little, and finally saluted to acknowledge his summer assignment.

Ten minutes later, Gordon turned his Corolla into the same driveway he'd pulled into thousands of times before. He noticed the lawn had just been mowed and enjoyed the fresh airy smell of grass clippings. Gordon looked over in admiration at the landscaping that encircled the front porch. Between each of the blooming azalea bushes was a rainbow of sprouting tulips. Elaine always did a magnificent job maintaining their household, both inside and out.

Hearing the drone of a lawnmower, Gordon circled to the backyard. For a moment, he stood motionless, studying his wife from behind as she guided the self-propelled mower. Elaine had tied her blond hair up in a ponytail that stuck out from the back of a red Cardinals cap. She wore a white T-shirt tied up to reveal the lower part of her back and some gray athletic shorts accentuating her lower curves. Gordon knew Elaine purposefully intended the outfit to keep her as cool as possible on a warm day, but he couldn't help but admire what he saw.

When Elaine turned and marched towards him, Gordon noticed the air buds pointed down from both ears like a pair of sleek, white earrings. She cast her eyes down in front of her, and he saw her lips moving, singing along with the music coming from the phone stuffed deep inside the front pocket of her shorts. For a brief moment, Gordon had second thoughts about leaving town for the summer.

As she came closer, Elaine spotted Gordon. There was a startled look on her face, one that grew uneasy as she cut off the mower and removed the air buds.

"What are you doing here?" she asked. "Everything okay?"

"I was in the neighborhood," responded Gordon. "I thought I'd drop by and say hello. Also, I need to discuss something."

"You in a rush? If not, why don't you go inside and say hi to the kids while I finish the backyard."

"Sounds good, thanks," Gordon replied.

Gordon found Annie enraptured by *Sesame Street* in the den. Grover and Big Bird were engaged in silly but educational dialogue. Annie finally looked up and saw her dad. For a moment, her expression was blank, like she was staring at a stranger. Then a grin exploded across her face.

"Daddy!" she bellowed. "What are you doing here?'

"Hey, sweetheart. I just dropped by for a quick visit."

Gordon looked around the room. It was incredibly tidy, considering both kids owned their fair share of toys and games. Before he could say anything else, David loped in from the kitchen. A half-eaten bowl of cereal drenched in milk was on the table behind him.

"Hi, Dad," exclaimed David. "I didn't expect to see you today."

"Well, it's just for a few minutes," replied Gordon. "There's something I want to go over with you."

Gordon asked both kids to sit on the couch while he muted the TV. He reached for the iPad sitting on the end table that generally was used by the children to play games. Annie and David sat next to each other with their backs pressed to the rear cushions of the beige leather sofa, their short legs sticking straight out in front of them. They had eager smiles on their faces. Gordon handed the iPad to David.

"You know how to use FaceTime on this?"

"I'm not sure how to call someone, but I know how to answer," replied David.

"Good, excellent! I'm going into the living room to call you on Face-Time. When it rings, just answer. Okay?"

David nodded.

A few seconds later, Gordon was staring at David's alert face on his iPhone.

"Okay," stated Gordon. "You see the little square in the corner, the one that has your face in it?"

He could see David nod his head.

"Now," Gordon added, "hold the iPad so you can see your face *and* Annie's face in that little square. Got it?"

Once again, David nodded, and this time, Annie's beaming face came into view.

"Remember, David, what you see in the small square is what I see on my phone. Whenever you talk to someone through FaceTime, remember this, okay?"

David nodded again, but this time, his smile faded.

"Why are we doing this?" David inquired.

Gordon hung up his phone as he reentered the den.

"Because I want you and Annie to see that talking to me on FaceTime is like seeing me in person."

Gordon hesitated while both kids waited for him to say more.

"I'm planning to take a trip, guys, and I'll be gone for at least a month, maybe two. Since I won't take you out on Saturdays for a while, I thought we could talk on FaceTime. And not just once a week, either, at least every other day."

Over his shoulder, Gordon noticed movement in his peripheral vision. It was Elaine, standing in the doorway with her arms folded. The FaceTime demonstration had so preoccupied Gordon that he didn't notice the quiet that ensued after Elaine had shut down the mower. He didn't even hear Elaine slip in from the garage on the far side of the kitchen.

"Gordon," Elaine said, almost in a whisper, "can I see you in the living room?"

Gordon raised his eyebrows and smiled in embarrassment. He felt like the teacher had just busted him and was taking him into the hallway for a private conversation. Gordon held up an index finger to indicate he would return soon, unmuted the TV, and then slowly exited the den. Elaine followed on his heels.

Gordon flopped onto his well-known recliner next to the front door. His wife sat across in her familiar spot on the living room sofa. Elaine looked exasperated, like she was dealing with one of her recalcitrant second graders.

"A trip?" Elaine asked with muted edginess. "Where're you going?"

"I got a call from Ben yesterday. Remember him?"

"Of *course*," Elaine responded. "I know it's been a while, but you think I could ever forget Ben? You were the best man at his wedding."

"Yes, of course. Anyhow, a lot is going on in his life. He's also going through some kind of separation or divorce, and he's left his job. Elaine, Ben's in some kind of trouble. He drove from L.A. to his folks' cabin in Grand Lake. He's there now. When he realized I'm not doing so well either, Ben invited me to join him in Colorado."

"For how long?" asked Elaine. "You need to be back by next Monday for summer school."

"A month, maybe two," responded Gordon. He spoke calmly, knowing how this troubled his wife.

"What about summer school?" asked Elaine with mounting alarm.

"I just left school," Gordon replied. "I met with Jim and told him there's a line of people anxious to take my place. He understood."

"Good for the two of you," Elaine said, her volume beginning to rise. "I don't know if *I* can be so understanding. Gordon, we need the money from your summer school teaching. How else do we pay for David's camp?"

Gordon reached into his pocket and handed over a slip of paper.

"What's this?" Elaine asked. "Five thousand dollars?"

"Yes, Dad made out the check to you last night. It's a long story, but he wouldn't take no for an answer. I originally turned Ben down *because* of the money. That's when Dad stepped in. He offered to pay for my trip and make up my summer school salary."

Elaine stared at the check. She removed her baseball cap and wiped the side of her face. Gordon couldn't tell if Elaine was mopping away sweat or tears. Finally, she looked up and intensity burned in her eyes.

"Your dad's a *good* man," Elaine said somberly.

Gordon kept silent but nodded in agreement.

"So are you, Gordon," she added. "You're just like your dad, or at least you used to be." "Well, I guess that's a big reason for taking this trip. Maybe it'll do me some good." Then after a pause, Gordon added, "So, I've got your blessing?"

Elaine bit down on her lower lip. From behind, she could hear the beguiling laughter of her children coming from the den. Blending in was the gruff voice of Oscar the Grouch.

"Yes, you have my blessing. *But* with some ground rules."

"Yeah?" Gordon asked as a smile creased his face.

"First, you try to FaceTime with your kids whenever you can, around supper time."

"Check!" Gordon responded. "I was already planning on that one."

"Second, don't take *any* risks. I mean none. Everything you do, driving, hiking, camping, I mean *everything*, do it with the understanding that you have two children back home that worship you and expect you to come *home*."

Gordon stayed quiet with this condition but nodded gravely.

"Just one more, Gordon. I want you to search high and low, and I want you to find the man I first married. You've refused to see a professional, so I guess Ben or Mother Nature will have to do. Whatever it takes, Gordon, find *that* man."

Gordon sighed. He couldn't guarantee this last ground rule; they both knew that. Something had disappeared two years earlier, and it may have been irreplaceable, like an arm or maybe even a beating heart. He clasped his hands between his legs and met Elaine's gaze head-on. For a moment, they locked eyes. For now, this was the best he could offer.

Before leaving, Gordon called the kids in to say goodbye. He bent down to hug them, and his arms squeezed a little tighter and remained a little longer, knowing he wouldn't see them for a month or two. Behind his back, David and Annie each looked up with practically identical expressions of bewilderment. Seeing this, Elaine smiled and winked to signify everything was okay.

Gordon turned to leave. Elaine moved towards her husband and wrapped her arms around his neck. For the first time in several months, they embraced.

"Does this mean there's still hope?" Gordon whispered as they pulled back.

Elaine smiled. "You come home safe," she responded. "No promises, okay? But yes, there's always been hope."

Two hours later, after a pricey trip to REI, Gordon drove west to his Dad's home in St. Charles County, his trunk filled with a tent, a sleeping bag, and other camping gear. When he pressed the button on the Corolla's radio for KSHE, he heard the pounding rhythm of his favorite song, Bruce Springsteen's "Born to Run." Gordon glanced into the rearview mirror and, for the first time since he could remember, liked the face he saw staring back.

CHAPTER

7

Gordon's Toyota climbed the ramp from the outer beltway and curved to the west on I-70, advancing towards the Missouri River. He found himself surrounded by vehicles of all kinds, many of which towered above him. The eighteen-wheelers formed an impenetrable wall on his right, and massive SUVs and pickups roared past on the left. It was disconcerting. He couldn't wait to reach Columbia in the middle of the state, where he'd exit the interstate and continue his trek to Omaha via less traveled highways. For now, he'd have to bear the same two-hour route he'd traversed dozens of times back in college.

The sun's rays reached over his shoulders in the early morning. Gordon had chosen a classic selection of music to launch his foray into the West, starting with a CD of Aaron Copland hits. Blasting the score from *Billy the Kid* sent a chill down his spine as he visualized some of the sites he'd soon see. Gordon engaged in a mental exercise he frequently used on long trips to distract him from the traffic. He'd visualize the surrounding terrain as it looked in the distant past.

Gordon understood why St. Louis was called the Gateway to the West. He imagined Lewis and Clark starting their keelboat journey on the river he'd just crossed. He could make out early pioneers like Daniel Boone, who'd constructed his final home just to the south, and Joseph Smith, who'd led his Mormon congregation to western Missouri before moving back east to build the community of Nauvoo in Illinois. Gordon's favorite vision was the assortment of settlers who'd made their way across Missouri to Westport, where they joined the overland caravans rolling west on the Oregon Trail. Then there were the Bushwhackers and the Jayhawkers who'd waged their bloody civil war throughout the state. Finally, Gordon loved to think about how Missouri's hinterland had nourished a young Harry Truman.

Ghosts from the past populated everything Gordon saw for the next several hours. He hesitated to share these wandering thoughts with others out of fear of being labeled a history nerd. Still, he loved to tour battlefields, graveyards, and other historical sites. When visiting a new place, how could one not appreciate what had occurred there in the past? Gordon knew others possessed this sixth sense; he wasn't the only one. It was a key reason he loved to travel, and he most certainly intended to explore several historical locales on his arching path towards Colorado.

Because of the slower state highways after reaching Columbia, it was mid-afternoon when Gordon arrived in Omaha. Not knowing much about the city, he drove directly to the zoo. Others had told him it was one of the "must-see" spots in eastern Nebraska, but it proved to be a bit of a letdown. Gordon knew there'd soon be opportunities to view a wide range of wildlife in their natural habitat, so it was disheartening to see them in enclosed spaces. Besides, David and Annie weren't with him to share the experience. Gordon took a few pictures to text for Elaine to share with the kids.

The weather was uncomfortably warm, so Gordon decided to postpone the camping experience and check into a Holiday Inn Express on the north side of town. After returning with fast food, he unlocked his second-floor room, plopped down on the spongy bed, and pulled out his phone to FaceTime with the kids. The call ended ten minutes later. David was sullen, and while Annie smiled during most of their brief exchange, she had little to say. Elaine remained on the sidelines, primarily out of the picture and conversation.

Gordon glanced at his watch and saw it was only seven-thirty, too soon to think about going to sleep even though he wanted an early start the following day. He wandered next door to a sports bar and was delighted to see the Cardinals battling the Cubs on their primary screen. The game was at Wrigley, but Gordon smiled when he saw almost as much red in the crowd as blue. He settled into the next three hours like an exhausted man laying his head onto a soft pillow at the end of a hard day. A bowl of peanuts, a pitcher of beer, and a narrow Cardinals' victory capped off what had otherwise been a forgettable day.

As he staggered back to the hotel, Gordon thought it was a good thing he didn't have to drive. Nevertheless, his head ached, and he felt a pang of regret. Gordon didn't want to begin his expedition into the West like this. He stared at his reflection in the bathroom mirror long after he'd finished brushing his teeth. He had dark bags beneath his eyes and a fleshy innertube around his waist. Gordon sucked in his stomach, but it didn't help.

Throughout the night, Gordon made several trips to the bathroom. The pitcher of beer was the apparent cause, but other factors disrupted his sleep. When he was younger, Gordon could easily ignore unfamiliar surroundings. But now, the light filtering in from the parking lot combined with intermittent hallway noises made it impossible to plunge into long periods of serenity. Each time he got up, Gordon could briefly recall his dreams, but they were unsettling, and fortunately, they quickly vanished from memory.

Gordon woke long before the alarm on his phone could rouse him. Like a machine, he hastily downed some hotel coffee, brushed his teeth, and threw on a fresh T-shirt to go with the cargo shorts he'd worn the day before. By the time the sun climbed on his right, Gordon was already cruising on single-lane highways up the eastern rim of Nebraska. Open fields of corn, wheat, and soybeans provided a sense of solitude that gradually lifted his spirits.

Gordon drove across an invisible boundary by mid-morning and observed rock formations, prairie dog towns, and cerulean skies. It was starting to look like the American West. He'd already decided to forgo the more popular destinations like Mount Rushmore, and he intended to skip the tacky Wall Drug, whose signs he'd regularly seen for the last few hundred miles. Besides, Gordon had visited those sites years before on a road trip to Mount Rushmore. Today, Wounded Knee was his target.

Gordon taught about this spot in the southwest corner of South Dakota every year. Its significance, as he explained, was that thirty years of brutal warfare had ended on this site. The Plains Indians had won their most significant victory fourteen years earlier when they annihilated

Custer's forces at Little Big Horn. Unfortunately, this was a classic example of winning a battle but losing the war. In the long run, the Sioux had no chance, and when they became increasingly desperate, they'd turned to visions inspired by the Ghost Dance.

Gordon taught that the growing popularity of this spiritual movement had unnerved troops stationed in the upper plains. Killing Sitting Bull when they attempted to arrest him on a North Dakota reservation made the situation even tenser. At the end of December in 1890, the 7th Cavalry surrounded a Sioux encampment along the banks of Wounded Knee Creek. When the troops attempted to disarm the Indians, a scuffle turned into a full-fledged battle. Gordon always taught that by finally putting an end to Native resistance, Wounded Knee was the nation's final victory in "winning the West."

It was one thing to teach about a historical event in the classroom but quite another to roam over the hallowed ground where it occurred. When Gordon arrived at the site, its eerie emptiness left him in a state of awe. He hadn't seen a car in at least thirty minutes. As Gordon idled up the road, he scanned in every direction. There was *no one* around. A place he'd emphasized so much in his history classes was far off the beaten path and evidently of little interest to passing tourists.

Gordon pulled over, climbed out of his Corolla, and stood with both hands on his hips. Slowly, he spun around to peer in every direction. It looked like a scene from *Dances with Wolves*. The rolling plains and small hills extended as far as the eye could see. Just above were azure skies decorated by splashes of powdery cirrus clouds. A solitary tree occasionally punctuated the open space.

Gordon next noticed a weathered monument in front of a small cemetery. A low chain-link fence surrounded the century-old headstones with a kaleidoscope of attached ribbons flapping in the wind. Gordon strolled in that direction. As he climbed a gentle slope, a warm breeze careened over his shoulders. It was exceedingly dry, unlike any wind he'd felt in Missouri.

As Gordon read the large red sign summarizing the events at Wounded Knee, the wind picked up. He spun around, thinking he heard a whisper, and then smiled to himself. It was just the breeze flattening the open ocean of prairie grass. Gordon looked around again, but there was still no one in sight. It was an isolated locale that could have been on the far side of the moon. Three hundred Miniconjou Lakota had been massacred at this site. Now, Mr. Gordon Goldman, who'd taught the textbook version of what had occurred here one hundred and thirty years ago, looked over the grounds, completely alone.

Gordon suddenly realized he wasn't alone when he looked from the hill that gave him a panoramic view. Further up the road from where he'd pulled over, there was an intersection, and on the far corner, beneath a cottonwood tree, he could see an older woman sitting behind a folding table. Laid out in front of her was a selection of pottery, woven baskets, and other curiosities. Gordon studied the scene for a moment, baffled that he'd failed to notice her before.

Despite the warm afternoon sun, there was a black shawl draped over her shoulders. A broad-brimmed hat sheltered her face, but Gordon could still see gray woven pigtails hanging down her back. She sat motionless, like a sculpture, hands clasped in front of her, staring hypnotically at the wares spread out on her table. The woman hadn't seen Gordon gazing down from atop his little peak. For a moment or two, he simply absorbed the authenticity of the scene. Gordon surmised the woman lived at the nearby Pine Ridge Indian Reservation and probably came here on days like this to peddle her goods to the few tourists who might stumble across this historical oasis.

Slowly, Gordon made his way down the gentle slope in the woman's direction and her table of goods. It occurred to him this might be a unique opportunity to enter a wormhole into the past. Gordon wanted to strike up a conversation but didn't know how to start. The obvious tactic was to look over the items scattered across her table and possibly make a purchase. If nothing else, maybe he could find something for David or Annie.

When Gordon neared the woman, she unexpectedly jolted, startled by the shadow now blanketing the items on her table. Shielding her eyes from the sun that cast a corona around Gordon's head, she craned her neck back to see the stranger towering above.

"Hanska?" she screeched in a high-pitched voice.

Sensing the woman had confused him with someone else, Gordon pulled off his red Cardinals cap and removed his sunglasses.

"No, no," Gordon replied with hands up like he was surrendering. "I just came to see what you've got for sale."

Silence.

"For sale? These goods for sale? Yes? Understand?"

Gordon realized he was speaking slower and louder, as though the woman had just stepped off a spaceship from a distant galaxy.

"Yes," the woman finally replied. "Everything for sale." She had leaped from thinking this was Hanska to realizing she had a potential customer.

Believing he made a connection, Gordon decided to press on. The clarity of her English words encouraged him.

"Do you live over on the Pine Ridge Reservation?"

The woman nodded. Deep wrinkles reached across her sun-roasted cheeks like the surface of a glacier. If Gordon had to guess her age, it could be anywhere between seventy and one hundred.

"Have you always lived on the reservation?"

Again, she nodded.

Gordon realized he should buy something if he wanted to extend the conversation. He looked down to study the merchandise on display. Two items immediately caught his attention. The first was a figurine resembling the Kachina dolls he'd seen as a kid on a family road trip to the southwest. The other was a circular netted item with gray and blue feathers attached. Annie would probably like the figurine, and the netted piece would look nice on the wall above David's bed. He pointed to both, inquiring about their price. Suddenly, it was Gordon's turn to be startled by a shadow darkening his right shoulder.

"Getting ready to negotiate with my grandmother?" a deep but gentle voice asked from behind. "Good luck with that. It's always fun to watch this part."

Gordon twisted around to stare directly at the chin and puffy lips of a giant. He'd come out of nowhere. For a big man, he moved like a ghost. The giant's lips parted into a wide grin, revealing two rows of teeth as white as bleached bones. His face was hairless, the skin reddish in color and unblemished like the surface of a pearl. Dark sunglasses hid the giant's eyes, and a straw hat with a wide brim and red feather dangling in the back covered his head. Jet black hair cascaded down his shoulders. He looked a little like the "Chief" from *One Flew Over the Cuckoo's Nest*.

"Yes," Gordon finally responded. "I was trying to ask her the price of these two items." After a brief moment, he added, "Also, I was hoping to learn some things about her background."

"Good luck with that. She speaks some English, but most of the time, my grandmother's very quiet."

Gordon stepped back to better appraise the giant, whom he assumed was Hanska. The man must have been close to seven feet tall. His shoulders were broad, and he was big-boned. There was no discernable body fat, although it was difficult to tell beneath his 4XL football jersey. Hanska could probably be a starting offensive lineman with the Denver Broncos if he put on a few pounds.

"How about you?" asked Gordon. "Would you answer a few questions from a nosey tourist?"

"Sure, ask away."

"Okay, great! So, what's your name?" Gordon realized he'd been silently calling him Hanska, but this may not be correct.

"Officially, it's Tatanka Ptecila, which means Little Bull. Ironic, huh?"

Gordon nodded and laughed.

"Most people just call me Hanska, which simply means tall. And this is my *nookamis*, my grandmother. Her birth name is Black Shawl, but she also goes by Tasina. These were the names of Crazy Horse's wife. She's very proud of these names."

Delighted to have finally broken the ice, Gordon reached out to offer his hand.

"Nice to meet you, Hanska. My name's Gordon. I'm from St. Louis."

Gordon almost lost his hand inside Hanska's giant grip. Black Shawl continued to stare down at her table, dwarfed by the two goliaths hovering above.

"So," continued Gordon, "you also live on the reservation?"

"Yes, I teach at one of the schools. When the weather's nice, I also bring my grandmother out here to sell her goods. I was just picking her up. Now, mind if I watch the bargaining?"

Gordon grinned, turned back towards the table, and pointed at the two items he'd spotted earlier.

"How much?" he asked.

"Twenty dollars." After a brief pause, she added, "each."

From behind, Gordon heard a chuckle.

"Your move," Hanska uttered. "I warn you. She's a negotiating wizard."

The way Hanska's words flowed naturally off his tongue, smooth but with gentle inflections, was like small waves lapping at a sandy beach.

Glancing back, Gordon stated, "No, that's a fair price."

He pulled out two twenties from his wallet and handed them to Black Shawl. She took the cash and, from nowhere, pulled out a brown paper bag for the two items.

Hanska chuckled. "White Man's Guilt, huh?"

Gordon turned back towards Hanska. "Yeah, maybe," he stated. Then he added, "You say you're a teacher? What do you teach?"

"History," replied Hanska. "Well, middle school social studies," he added with a shrug.

"You're *kidding*," Gordon's face burst into a huge grin. "That's what I teach too—high school history."

"Yeah, I kind of figured," Hanska replied. "History teachers are about the only people who travel this far out of their way to visit this place."

For a moment, the only sounds were the crinkling noise of the paper bag when Black Shawl handed it over and the wind whistling through the wisps of prairie grass. Finally, Hanska decided to challenge the history teacher.

"Let me ask you a question, Gordon. Do you teach your students about Wounded Knee? If so, how do *you* describe what happened here?"

"Yeah, of course, I teach about this place every year. I explain it was the final battle in the Indian wars."

"Battle? A battle? Have you ever seen the casualty figures from this so-called *battle*? The army indeed lost twenty-five dead, but most of these resulted from friendly fire. When this *battle* ended, the army loaded only fifty-one survivors from Big Foot's group that originally numbered more than three hundred and fifty. The bodies of the others were scattered around here to freeze into blocks of ice." Hanska slowly swept his arm around to indicate the battle that occurred in this little valley where they stood. "Nearly half of them were women and children. That's a battle? No offense, Gordon, but you should teach the truth. Wounded Knee wasn't a battle. It was a *massacre*."

There was a steady rhythm and pace in the pronunciation of each word. Hanska was the younger man, but he spoke with the authority of a venerable scholar. Gordon's eyebrows arched upward, and his lips squeezed tightly together. He looked a little like a scolded puppy. Gordon wiped away the droplets of sweat that gathered on his upper brow and slowly shook his head.

"You're right," he stated solemnly. "I didn't know those numbers." After a pause, Gordon inquired like a schoolboy on a field trip, "How were most of the Sioux killed?"

Hanska again raised his mammoth hand to point.

"You see over there? And there? And up there? And up that way?"

Gordon nodded as Hanska pointed to four small hills surrounding the little basin where they stood.

"That's where General Miles positioned his four rapid-fire Hotchkiss guns. These were a combination of machine guns and cannons. The Hotchkiss guns fired fifty two-pound shells per minute. Some of the warriors with Big Foot *were* armed, but there was *no* way they could battle against these weapons, not to mention the five hundred troops surrounding them."

Gordon was speechless. Looking down while shifting his weight back and forth, he unknowingly pinched the brown paper bag holding the gifts for his children.

"I'm sorry, Gordon, I didn't mean to be so dramatic. It's just you said you were a history teacher. I couldn't help myself. I get pretty worked up about Wounded Knee." Hanska reached over and patted Gordon on his shoulder.

"No problem," Gordon responded. "I'd say I understand, but that wouldn't be true. These were *your* people, and it was my ancestors who fired those awful guns."

Hanska smiled and nodded, acknowledging Gordon's attempt to show empathy. Then he squared his mammoth shoulders and sucked in a deep breath.

"If you don't mind me asking," Hanska inquired, "when you teach this period of American history, do you refer to it as 'the Indian Wars?'"

"Well yeah, I do." After a brief pause, Gordon added, "I emphasize, though, that many of the tribes, like the Sioux, the Cheyenne, the Nez Perce, the Comanche, and especially the Apache were fierce warriors who fought with great courage."

"Gordon, I hope this doesn't seem like one of those workshops they probably force you to attend each year, but if you don't mind, I'd like to ask a few more questions about what you teach."

Gordon nodded without saying a word. He wore the expression of a child about to be disciplined.

"Do you also teach about the Bear River Massacre of 1863?"

"No. Never heard of it."

"The army killed two hundred and fifty Shoshone. How about Sand Creek?"

"Heard of it," replied Gordon, "but I don't know much about it."

"Colorado, 1864. Up to five hundred Arapaho and Cheyenne were killed and mutilated. About two-thirds were women and children. How about the Marias Massacre?"

Looking dumbfounded, Gordon slowly shook his head.

"Montana, 1870. Two hundred Blackfeet killed. Most were women, children, and older men. I could keep going, Gordon; the list is incredibly long. But I don't want this to turn into a lecture; that's not the point. I just want to know if you *truly* understand."

"I think I'm beginning to," replied Gordon.

Hanska peered over Gordon's head and then slowly looked to his left and right, taking in the panorama. With his lips tightly locked, he exhaled loudly through his nostrils. Finally, Hanska looked down at Gordon, ready to drive home his point.

"Gordon, I know you've been teaching history longer than me. But I've come to understand something I'd like to share. What we teach isn't like math or science, where there's usually one right answer. History is fluid; it's always changing. It's a mistake to say history is what happened in the past. It's what we *believe* happened, and that's always shifting like the sandy bottom of a fast-moving stream."

Hanska paused. Gordon nodded, encouraging him to continue.

"Much of that perception is shaped by the bias of those writing the history. You've probably heard that it's the winners who write about the past, right? And that's especially true with the history of the American West. Gordon, what you see all around you *isn't* the site of the final battle of the Indian Wars. It's the place where a horrible massacre occurred— one of *many*. And while there are plenty of examples where native people fought back with great courage, they *never* had a chance against disease, slavery, ethnic cleansing, and *massacres*. Entire tribal cultures completely disappeared. When Dee Brown wrote his history of the American West through the eyes of its native victims, there's a reason he called it *Bury My Heart at Wounded Knee*."

Gordon nodded again, but this time, Hanska's lips parted into a smile.

"I'm sorry, Gordon, there I go again. I'll get off my soapbox and stop trying to tell you how to teach."

Gordon briefly glanced downward. When he looked back up, his smile mirrored the one still beaming on Hanska's face. The two men simultaneously laughed.

"Please don't apologize," Gordon pronounced. "You've given me *so* much to consider. I have to admit that after sixteen years, my lessons have grown stale. I should probably renovate my whole approach to how I teach history."

Hanska continued to look down with a kind smile chiseled on his face. Finally, Gordon stuck out his hand. This time, the handshake was firmer, prolonged, and reinforced with the other hand. Looking to move on to a different subject, Gordon pulled the net-like piece of art out of his bag and held it up for Hanska.

"Can you tell me about this? I was planning to give it to my son."

Hanska laughed. "You don't know about dream catchers? They sell them on practically every reservation out West. People believe good dreams will come along if you hang a dream catcher above your bed."

Suddenly, Black Shawl murmured a short monologue. To Gordon, the language was foreign, but Hanska gazed down, intently following his grandmother's words. Finally, Black Shawl looked up at Gordon, waiting for his reaction as Hanska translated.

"Gordon, my grandmother, believes you carry a . . . ," he paused, searching for the right words. "My friend, she believes you're carrying a troubled spirit."

Gordon stepped back. His eyes enlarged, and his lips parted. A dry breeze unexpectedly raked through his dark hair.

"She thinks your heartache stems from family. She didn't give details, but I know Black Shawl believes family shapes our inner core. It defines our place in the universe. She wanted me to tell you that her family's soul rests here in this place. It's sacred, Gordon. Her grandfather was killed right here at Wounded Knee. She doesn't share that with most people, but she wanted *you* to know."

Gordon turned, wiping away moisture beneath his eyes. When he circled back, he reached for his wallet and pulled out another twenty. Gordon then handed it to Black Shawl while pointing at another dream catcher.

"This one's for *my* bedroom." Then he turned back to face Hanska. "It's been such a pleasure talking to you today."

Hanska nodded and smiled. After exchanging handshakes one more time, Gordon took the second dream catcher and slid it into his crumpled paper bag. Black Shawl didn't extend her hand, but her mouth unlocked a toothless grin for the first time. Gordon smiled back and then spun around to begin the short hike back to his car.

CHAPTER

8

The ninety-minute drive to Rapid City was a blur. Under ordinary circumstances, Gordon might have slowed down to appreciate the unique rock formations near Badlands National Park. More than a million years ago, sheets of multicolored sedimentary rock were deposited like layers of cake, and since then, erosion shaped them into a collection of abstract sculptures. Hurling through the blend of earthy colors, mainly orange, gray, and beige, all drenched in the late afternoon sunlight, was like driving through a primordial landscape. For a moment, Gordon smiled at the irony of calling such lush scenery "Badlands." Then he remembered how dry and impossible this land was to farm or ranch. After his time spent with Hanska, Gordon understood why the government chose this acreage for a Sioux reservation.

For the moment, Gordon wanted to reach a more populated area with a strong enough signal for his cell phone. The plan was to FaceTime David and Annie, grab some fast food burgers or tacos for dinner, and then drive the sixty miles back to Badlands National Park to set up his tent for the night. Ideally, Gordon needed to do this before sunset to put up his camp without fumbling around in the dark.

Finding a Wendy's east of town off I-90 was a good first step. He pulled into an empty area in the back of the parking lot, opened his windows, and launched the call. David was at first lackadaisical when his father held up the dreamcatcher. Then his spirits seemed to rise when Gordon told him about its "magical" power to provide pleasant dreams when hung over his bed. For the first time since leaving St. Louis, Gordon saw a smile break out on the tiny image of his son's face. Annie was easier to please. She squealed with delight upon seeing the figurine, though Gordon suspected she might have thought it was bigger than it was because of the way he'd positioned the doll on the screen.

As Gordon prepared to wrap up the call, he tried to think of something to say to Elaine. It was a good day, and he needed to share more details. Before he could open his mouth, Elaine jumped in to compliment Gordon on his purchases, told him to drive safe, and then concluded their call. Gordon mumbled a goodbye and then, for a full minute, sat staring at the charcoal screen of his phone. He was stunned. While he understood this had become the state of their marriage, part of him hoped for more.

He still had a long way to go, but Gordon realized that "healing" meant he'd also have to deal with missing his wife and kids. During most of the drive from Wounded Knee, he'd meditated over images from his marriage: first dates, first love-making sessions, the first birth of children, first road trips. There were many good times. Gordon mostly missed coming home to tell Elaine about his day. The better the details, the more he wanted to share them. Elaine had been an empathetic listener, and when the occasion called for it, she always had the right advice.

Gordon heard his stomach growl like a grizzly. He smiled to himself, inhaled a deep breath, and climbed out of the car. Gordon ordered a couple of Dave's singles along with a bowl of chili and finished off with a chocolate frosty. Then, while enjoying one of his favorite fast-food meals, he hashed out an email to Elaine on his phone.

Dear Elaine,

The FaceTime plan seems to be working with the kids, but I'd prefer to exchange emails as a better way to communicate between the two of us. Sorry about the formal tone of this introduction, but maybe formal is what we need right now. I'll understand if you would prefer not to reply, but at least, I hope you'll read over the emails I send.

I know you've been after me to see a professional for some time. Maybe you're right. For now, this road trip is the next best thing. Today at Wounded Knee, I ran into a couple of people who live on the nearby reservation. It's hard to describe, but somehow, we made a connection. In addition, I learned

some hard truths about what occurred there 130 years ago. I'll use this to
improve my unit on the American West, but some of what I learned struck
me on a deeper level.

The main thing I wanted to say is I miss you. This has been an incredible day,
and I wanted to share it with my wife. In the past, we would've been here
together. Since that isn't possible, I'd like to communicate through emails. I
hope you don't mind. Like I said, even if you choose not to reply, maybe you
can read my emails and consider what I have to say. I plan to write you after
each FaceTime call with the kids.

Thanks for your understanding about my need to take this trip. I love you,

G.

After sending the email, Gordon trekked to a campsite in Badlands
National Park. He climbed into his tent two hours later and squirmed
into a puffy sleeping bag. Then it started to rain. Hard. The temperature
tumbled into the mid-forties, and Gordon huddled beneath several layers of clothing. Perhaps because it'd been years since he'd last experienced
the discomforts of camping, he couldn't fall asleep.

Random thoughts raced through his head, fluctuating from images
of Lakota children running in terror as shells exploded, to the joyful smile
on Black Shawl's face. Gordon also reviewed a montage of memories
from his past, including recent outings with his children and intimate
moments spent with Elaine. There was no pattern to his thoughts. He
wasn't sure he was awake at times since he couldn't distinguish between
those visions and the recurring dreams that visited him at night.

Somewhere around two in the morning, Gordon unzipped the front
flap of his tent and climbed out to pee. He knew from the ghostly quiet
that the rain had stopped, but when he gazed up, the parade of stars
marching across the moonless sky paralyzed Gordon. One stood out and
drifted at a steady pace from east to west. He knew it had to be a satellite.
Thousands of dimmer flashpoints filled out the rest of the inky canvas
like embers floating above a campfire. Gordon walked across the wet,
sandy ground to a rock outcropping that formed a natural bench. He sat
down at a spot where he could lean back to take in the show. The air was

clear, unblemished by the light pollution he was accustomed to at home. For several minutes, he studied the sky, unaware of the gaping grin on his face.

Four hours later, Gordon climbed out of his sleeping bag like a butterfly emerging from a cocoon. Despite the broken sleep, he felt refreshed. With the energy of a child excited to see his friends at recess, Gordon broke camp, loaded up his car, and drove to a trailhead for an early morning hike. His goal was to complete the ten-mile Castle Trail, the longest and reputably the most spectacular in the park. Knowing he wasn't in condition for such a marathon, he nevertheless figured it'd be worth the price he'd later have to pay.

Over the next four hours, Gordon spotted a herd of bison grazing on a distant prairie, startled a couple of mule deer, photographed a small herd of pronghorn, and discovered a quilt of flowers that must've blossomed overnight. The morning was chillier than expected, but Gordon had shed his outer layers by noon, wrapping his sweatshirt around his khaki cargo shorts. A couple of times, he stumbled across other hikers. One of them smiled and pronounced "Go Cards!" upon seeing Gordon's red cap bearing the curvy white "S" superimposed over the small "T" and the larger "L." As predicted, the hike's distance was grueling, and in the final hour, he rationed out the water remaining in his camel pack. By the end, Gordon was pleased with his first hike.

By midafternoon, he was back in Rapid City. Gordon conducted his FaceTime call with the kids over a bison burger at Thirsty's pub, where he sat in an empty outdoor patio, his achy legs stretched out beneath the table. Since Gordon had already texted the day's wildlife photos, most of the conversation was about the bison and pronghorn. Before hanging up, Elaine took back the iPad from the kids to say she appreciated Gordon's email. That was it. She told him he should feel free to write whenever he wanted, but since her life was uneventful at the moment, she probably wouldn't reply.

Gordon was disappointed. It would make for a long drive to his next destination, Theodore Roosevelt National Park in North Dakota. What should have been an easy four-hour drive felt twice as long. The scenery was agreeable, and a series of Bruce Springsteen CDs helped keep his head above water. Gordon resolved to keep sending emails to Elaine "whenever he wanted," even if she never responded. It'd taken a long time to descend into this crevasse, and he knew it might take even longer to climb out.

During his driving daydreams, Gordon thought about the story behind the park's name. He planned to share it with Elaine in an email, hoping she might connect it with their current situation. He'd tell her that on Valentine's Day in 1884, Teddy Roosevelt's mother and wife both died within hours of each other. Naturally, TR was devastated. Roosevelt came to North Dakota to find inner peace, where he spent hours, even entire days, riding alone among the canyons and buttes. There was something restorative about this land.

Camping that night was uneventful. The weather was still chilly, but the sky remained clear, and Gordon fell asleep almost immediately after laying his head on a pillowcase stuffed with soft T-shirts. He awoke the following day feeling stiff and achy. The previous day's ten-mile hike had been relatively flat, but Gordon was seriously out of shape. The beer, cigarettes, and fatty meals had taken their toll. In the morning, he decided to take it easy by touring the park from his car and making frequent stops for pictures.

Gordon noticed a teardrop Coleman camper parked on the site next to his tent as he returned from the campground bathroom. In front was a beige Ford SUV. Had it been there the night before? The door abruptly opened, and a tall, slim man with a blue Cubs baseball cap stepped down and walked towards Gordon. The gray stubble on his cheeks indicated he must have been in his sixties or seventies, but there were few lines on his face, so maybe he was younger. Seeing Gordon's red cap, the man smiled and tipped his hat in a friendly salute. Gordon made a mental note that perhaps this evening, he might want to introduce himself to his baseball rival.

By the middle of the day, Gordon grew restless. Driving was no way to see a national park, so he motored over to the trailhead of a four-mile hike known as the Caprock Coulee Loop. A mile into the hike, Gordon spotted a prairie dog town. He pulled off his pack, found a comfortable viewing perch, and grazed on some trail mix. The show was spectacular.

For about five minutes, the little critters popped up and down like the stars of a whack-a-mole game. Their squeaking noises reminded Gordon of a childhood memory. Dad had dressed as a clown on Halloween, and he invited his boys to squeeze his round red nose. It made the same shrill sound now coming from the prairie dogs. Gordon took a series of pictures, knowing how much David loved their exhibit at the St. Louis Zoo.

After taking a minute to review his photos, Gordon looked up and noticed the scene had petrified. Only a few of the critters were still visible, standing erect on their hind legs like frozen statuettes. Danger was lurking. Off in a patch of high prairie grass, Gordon spotted a coyote hunched low, stealthily moving towards the edge of the dog town, each foot falling in slow motion. Gordon switched the camera on his phone to video mode and began to shoot.

Suddenly, the coyote flashed towards the closest prairie dog. The others instantly vanished, but the one targeted by the coyote wasn't so lucky. The prairie dog was facing the other way, so by the time he could see the danger, it was too late. For a moment, Gordon saw the coyote's head disappear inside the hole where the prairie dog attempted to leap. When it reemerged, the coyote clenched a downy carcass smeared in blood. After it proudly marched off with its prey, Gordon saw dozens of prairie dogs reemerge from their underground refuge. They sat upon their haunches, and some leaped wildly off the ground issuing fanatical screeching noises. Was this a celebration because they'd survived? Was it some kind of memorial to the recently lost member of their community? Or was it simply an all-clear signal?

Gordon reviewed the video. He'd have to warn Elaine about its graphic content and trust her judgment about whether to show it to the kids. David might be able to handle it, but certainly not Annie. Either way, Gordon was thrilled. The video was a bit amateurish—a professional would have used a more powerful zoom and a tripod to reduce the shakiness. Nevertheless, this was a keeper, and Gordon would never forget what he'd witnessed.

Towards the end of his hike, Gordon stumbled across another extraordinary sight. Just as he was about to veer off towards the parking lot, he spotted horses crossing the trail in front of him. The pack wasn't a quiet herd grazing inside a fenced pasture; they were wild horses moving with unfettered freedom. Once again, Gordon yanked out his phone and took pictures and a video. He knew feral herds of wild horses had been roaming the West since their introduction by the Spanish five centuries before. Gordon never thought he'd see one in person.

For half an hour, the spectacle of horses feasting on prairie grass growing high along the banks of a small creek riveted Gordon. Some of the stallions were a solid, chocolate brown, a few were a light tan, and others were a rich blend of deep orange and white. There were a few ponies scattered amongst the mares. None had *ever* worn a saddle. When they finally moved on, Gordon noticed the sun had descended towards the jagged horizon. Its remaining rays streaked through creamy cumulus clouds, emitting lush shades of orange, yellow, and red. Gordon admired the day's closing scene behind his darkened sunglasses.

As he strolled towards the trailhead, Gordon thought about his day. Between the prairie dogs, the coyote, the horses, and the sunset, he must have taken a hundred pictures on his phone. Reviewing and editing these photos would keep him busy until bedtime. Elaine and the kids already knew not to expect a call this evening because of the park's remote location. Still, he couldn't wait until he reached a strong enough signal to send pictures, video, and another email back to St. Louis.

Driving back to his campsite, Gordon passed a park store. Since it was just about dark, he decided to grab a sandwich for dinner. Gordon saw they also sold ice cream, and to his astonishment, they listed licorice as one of the flavors. Licorice was his favorite ice cream, but he could never find it back home. Now, in the last place he'd expect to find licorice ice cream, Gordon would have the perfect dessert to follow his roast beef sandwich. What an excellent way to wrap up the day!

Gordon exited the store five minutes later, juggling a sandwich, a cardboard bowl filled with jet black ice cream, and a Diet Coke. He glanced around for a place to sit, realizing there wouldn't be time to take his dinner back to the campsite before the ice cream turned into soup. There were three picnic tables on the store's wrap-around porch, and they were all occupied. Then Gordon saw the blue baseball cap fronted by the big red C. Mr. Chicago Cubs was sitting at one of the tables by himself, with a reddish-brown Irish Setter sleeping near his feet. Gordon approached, hoping to share the table.

"Okay, if a Cardinals fan joins you?"

Mr. Cubs looked up, initially a little startled. The fluorescent lighting on the ceiling above the porch flicked on, casting a pasty aura around his almond-shaped eyes. Then his thin lips parted into a broad smile.

"Yes, *yes*! By all means, join me!" He pulled off his Cubs cap, revealing a full head of shaggy gray hair. "Tell you what, let's call a truce to the rivalry, at least for now."

Gordon swung one leg over the bench like he was mounting a horse. Straddling the seat, he swung the other leg over, placed his tray on the table, and removed his Cardinals cap.

"Sounds good," Gordon replied. "Who's your buddy under the table?"

"That's Phil," the man answered while glancing down at the setter lying next to his feet. "I've had him a couple of months now. He's been a *wonderful* travel companion." After a brief pause, he added, "And my name's Dylan."

"Dylan? Nice to meet you." The two men shook hands. "I'm Gordon." Then he added, "I'm a bit envious. It must be nice to have a travel buddy like Phil."

The Irish Setter stood upon hearing his name, walked around the table, and placed his muzzle on Gordon's leg. He looked up, his black eyes beckoning for food, love, or both.

"Looks like you've made a friend," Dylan said.

"Okay to share a little of my sandwich?"

Dylan nodded. "Of course. Understand that after you do, though, his head won't move until you've finished eating."

"No problem. I'm happy to share."

Gordon tore off a small piece of roast beef from his sandwich and offered it to Phil, who gently inhaled it without bothering to chew. The setter scored several more helpings before Gordon finished his sandwich.

"So," Gordon stated while continuing to focus on Phil, "I notice you're sleeping in that Coleman camper next to where I set up my tent. Is it just you and Phil?"

"Yep," Dylan responded. He glanced away into the darkening void for a moment before continuing. "I guess you could say I'm pursuing a life-long fantasy."

Gordon looked up from feeding the setter, encouraging Dylan to continue.

"You see, I've always wanted to hitch a camper to my car and take a road trip. It's been a dream for as long as I can remember. Unplanned, you know? Just go wherever the spirit took me. Absolute, *total* freedom. Set up camp someplace pretty and stay as long as I liked. Then, when it was time to move on, I'd pull out the map and figure out where to go next."

"When you say it's been a life-long fantasy, does that mean you've never done this before?"

Dylan raised his eyebrows and inhaled deeply as though he'd crossed the Rubicon, and there was no turning back. "That's what I'm saying. Phil and I left Chicago three weeks ago, and so far, we've spent most of our time in Wisconsin and Minnesota. We just arrived here yesterday. I think we'll explore the Dakotas for a while and then push on to Montana and Wyoming. Nothing's planned. We just need to be further south before the snow comes."

Gordon tried to think of the best way to respond. He wavered between disbelief and envy. In the end, there was no concealing a covetous smile.

"If you don't mind me asking," Gordon finally responded, "why are you doing this *now*? I mean, what kept you from pursuing this fantasy earlier?"

Dylan turned towards the darkened hills off in the distance as if they held the answer. He tightened his lips and then swiveled back to face Gordon squarely.

"Emma," Dylan stated definitively. After a pause, he added, "Emma was my wife. For almost sixty-two years. I know it's a bit cliché, but she was the love of my life. Lots of people say that, but in our case, it was true."

Gordon gave the last piece of roast beef to Phil, grabbed a plastic spoon, and began to attack his mushy ice cream. Sensing a good story, he nodded for Dylan to continue.

"We went out on our first date in the final month of our senior year at the University of Illinois. I was planning to stick around another three years for law school, but since Emma was about to complete her degree in elementary education, she had a teaching job lined up in Chicago. We both knew after one date, though, that we'd magically stumbled across something rare, something most people *never* experience. There wasn't *any* hesitation. We saw each other every day after that first date, got married in August, and then Emma lucked into a teaching job in Urbana shortly after I began my legal studies."

"And then you lived happily ever after, huh?"

"No. Well, yeah, overall, it was truly a loving marriage, but not every day was perfect. We had our ups and downs. Doesn't everyone?"

"Isn't *that* the truth," Gordon agreed.

"But overall," Dylan continued, "no complaints. We raised some terrific kids. My oldest son also grew up to be a lawyer. He lives in Seattle. I plan to spend some time with him and his family on this trip. And my daughter's a teacher, just like her mom. Teaches high school English in Dallas."

"Wait a minute," Gordon interjected. "You said you were married sixty-two years, right? If you got married right before law school, you'd have to be at least what, eighty-four?"

"Yep, very good! I turn eighty-five in November."

"I thought you were about seventy, maybe *younger*."

"Yeah, I get that from people. I've been lucky. I never had any major health problems. I built up a successful legal practice, and as I said, I got to marry my dream girl. I suppose a happy life will keep you looking younger."

Gordon saw a brilliant cobweb streak across the sky on the dark horizon. The lightning must have been far away since there was no follow-up thunder. When Gordon turned back, he saw Dylan staring at his tightly clenched hands. He looked troubled, like a child bothered by a guilty conscience.

"Gordon, I left out an important piece of the story."

He looked up and waited patiently to reestablish eye contact before continuing.

"My life wasn't completely perfect. We had a third child, a son who died in high school. David was his name, and he was a *great* kid; smart, funny, a good athlete, and although Emma would never admit it, I think he was her favorite."

Dylan glanced down for a moment and hastily wiped something from his cheek.

"David asked to go on a float trip in Wisconsin with some older friends. He was only fifteen, and Emma tried to veto the idea. I was the one who pushed to let him go. I figured it would be a good growing experience."

Dylan looked up pleadingly like he was seeking some sort of affirmation.

"Maybe it's a generational thing, but I'd grown up with a *lot* of freedom, and I figured it'd made me more independent. Sure, there's some risk, but there's risk in everything you do, right? I mean, if you're always avoiding risk, you're not fully living your life."

After a brief pause, Dylan continued. "Anyhow, something happened that day on the river. The water was high from recent downpours, and they went through a rough area. David was bringing up the rear, so no one ever saw what happened to him. When they finally came to a calmer spot, the other kids found his innertube. David was *gone*. They found his body downstream the following day."

"Ah, Dylan, I'm *so* sorry! *Man*, that's rough."

For a moment, Dylan buried his face in hands propped up by his elbows. There was no sound except for the breeze starting to blow harder from a coal-black sky. Dylan finally looked up with surprisingly dry eyes.

"Yeah, it was rough. It took years to get past that day. It affected *everything*. My law practice, my marriage, the other two kids. For years, I just wasn't the same."

A tear finally squeezed out of one eye, and this time, Dylan ignored the pearl as it streaked down through the stubble on his cheek.

"Gordon, they say the toughest thing in the world is getting over the death of a child. But you know what made this even worse?"

Gordon looked up, patiently waiting for the answer. He pushed aside the empty cup of ice cream as though he didn't want any obstacles between himself and Dylan.

"It was *guilt*. I blamed myself. I never should've let David go on that trip. I should've listened to Emma since she always had the better instinct. Even now, I'm *still* blaming myself."

Gordon swallowed hard. He looked beyond Dylan just in time to see another crack of lightning, this one like jagged lines in the shell of a broken egg. A growl of thunder followed shortly afterward. Gordon briefly considered telling Dylan they each had a son by the same name but then realized this wasn't the time. After a moment, he cleared his throat and squeaked out a question.

"Dylan, how'd you finally manage to get on with your life?"

"The strength didn't come from me. It was *Emma*. She was always the stronger one. And you know what? I almost drove her away. She held on, though. She wouldn't let go. She understood something better than I did."

"What was that?" Gordon asked intently.

"She knew we were better together than we'd ever been apart. She knew as long as we had our marriage, we could pull through *anything*." After another pause, Dylan added, "You know, Gordon, this would've ended a *lot* of marriages. After all, Emma could've held me responsible. But she didn't. She knew we still had two other kids and that we had to get on with our lives. She was the glue that kept our family together."

Gordon nodded in understanding. "You're a lucky man, Dylan." Then a thought occurred to him. "Did you ever see any kind of therapist?"

"No, probably should've, but you know, too much pride and all. Looking back with hindsight, a counselor probably would've sped up the healing process, but Emma and I managed to find our way."

For a moment, there was silence. Then came more deep rumbling. It was like someone had turned up the volume. When Gordon looked back at Dylan, he saw wet cheeks hovering over an incandescent smile.

"I'm sorry, Gordon. I didn't mean to monopolize so much of the conversation. Tell me about *yourself*. You're from St. Louis, right? What on earth brought you up here?"

Instantly, Gordon knew he wanted to avoid the spotlight. He wasn't ready to share his story.

"Oh, it's pretty simple. I'm a high school history teacher with a passion for the American West. I'm off for the summer, and my wife gave me the green light to take this trip. My destination's Grand Lake, Colorado, where I'm supposed to meet up with an old college buddy. Just taking the scenic way to get there." Gordon smiled at this last point.

"Sounds like you've got a good one too," replied Dylan. "Wife, I mean. It sounds like she's kind and patient and understands your needs. You realize how lucky you are?"

Gordon laughed, primarily to himself. Then he and Dylan glanced up as heavy beads of water started to crash down on the cars in the parking lot. The rat-a-tat-tat created by the pounding rain on the tin roof steadily increased in volume. Phil, who by now had stretched out underneath Dylan's feet, raised his head and whined.

"I hope it's all right to ask this," Gordon inquired in a solemn tone, "but how did you lose Emma?"

Dylan calmly shook his head while transfixed by the curtain of cascading water. His face lacked expression, and his voice was surprisingly serene.

"Emma died three months ago. It was leukemia. She went fast, Gordon. There wasn't much pain."

More silence. The only sound came from the hammering rain. Finally, Dylan turned to face Gordon directly.

"That's why I'm taking this trip."

Gordon's inquisitive expression begged for details.

"Oh, we'd *always* traveled," Dylan added. "*Plenty*. There were cruises and excursions all over the world. But Emma didn't like long road trips, and she'd *never* sleep in a camper. Something about claustrophobia. Emma was also allergic to dogs."

Dylan glanced down at his feet with that last comment. Then, as suddenly as it'd begun, the rain stopped. It was like someone had turned off a faucet.

"I get it," Gordon stated. "Now you're finally taking the one trip of your dreams. Sort of like Teddy Roosevelt when he first came to this area. The change of scenery also helped him to get over the wife and mother he'd just lost."

Dylan nodded and turned to stare back into the inky blackness.

"Yes, I know why Roosevelt came out here, and of all things, it turned him into a *cowboy*." A smile creased his face with this last comment.

Then, in a graver tone, he added, "You know, Gordon, I'd give anything for one more day with Emma. This trip's helping, but it's not the same. It'll *never* be the same. Everything good in my life came from that woman— *everything*. And you know what? Emma knew it too. She understood. She knew I'd be a lost child without her. So, you know what she did?"

Gordon tightened his lips and slowly shook his head, patiently waiting for the answer. Inside, he felt like a dam was about to burst, one holding back a rising flood.

"When I returned from the funeral, there was a Coleman camper sitting in the driveway. Emma had arranged this with the kids. When I opened the door, this little critter came running out, wagging his tail as though we'd always been best friends."

Dylan glanced down at Phil and smiled. Then he drew in a deep breath giving him the fortitude to finish the story.

"Inside on the camper's table, there was a note."

Hearing a tremor in Dylan's voice, Gordon waited. Then he finally asked, "What'd the note say?"

For a little while, there was only silence. The breeze had died down, and the only sound was the high-pitched chirping of crickets. Gordon again waited patiently.

"It was short," Dylan stated, pausing to wipe away another droplet from his cheek. "I remember *every* word. It said, 'I know you feel lost right now. As soon as you can, I want you to take this camper and this dog and go find the man I first married.'"

The dam finally broke. Gordon dropped his face inside his crossed arms on the table and cried softly. He'd tried to keep it under control. After all, Gordon barely knew Dylan. But those final words, about finding "the man I first married," had pulled the trigger. His shoulders began to convulse.

Dylan was mystified. As the sobbing continued, he grew alarmed. He looked around and saw they were alone. The camp store had closed, and the glass window behind Gordon had turned into a darkened mirror.

"Gordon, are you all right? What is it? Did I say something?"

Finally, Gordon straightened up and briskly wiped away his tears. An embarrassing smile exploded across his face.

"I'm *so* sorry," Gordon said, pausing to catch his breath. "I don't know why I reacted that way. It's just that Emma's note sounded so familiar. It hit a nerve."

A moment passed while the two men smiled at each other. Then Dylan chuckled. It became infectious. Both men were soon giggling like children.

"What?" Gordon finally managed to ask. "Why are we laughing? What's so funny?"

"You should see your teeth." Dylan motioned for Gordon to spin around to see himself in the reflection of the darkened window. "They're so black you almost look toothless."

Gordon turned around, opened his mouth, and studied the image.

"Oh!" exclaimed Gordon. "That must be from the licorice ice cream."

After a pause, Dylan patted his thighs, slowly stood, and reached for Phil's leash.

"Well, young man, now that it's stopped raining, I better head back to that camper. Planning on a big hike in the morning. It's been a real pleasure spending time with a Cardinals fan and not having to put up with all that constant bragging."

"Oh, I see, that's how it is, huh?" Gordon joked. "The truce's over. Well, you guys got a taste of victory in 2016. Too bad it'll probably take another century for it to happen again."

Dylan placed the blue cap on his head and circled the table to face Gordon. Then he spread out his arms, and the two men embraced.

CHAPTER
9

Two EMTs lifted the gurney and pulled it out of the rear of their ambulance. They had turned off the siren, but the spinning red lights cast sinister shapes and shadows on the canopy ceiling guarding the emergency room entrance. The EMTs, both young men sporting grave expressions, roused Gordon out of his stupor. As they wheeled him through the electric doors at Campbell County Memorial Hospital, Gordon caught a glimpse of his reflection in the plate-glass window. There was a fat bandage wrapped around his head, snow-white except for a large red splotch. Gordon looked like an extra in a zombie movie.

The clock above the admitting station showed it was almost half-past eleven. Gordon glanced around, and although his vision was hazy, the lobby appeared to be empty. This was probably the norm on a Thursday night in Gillette, Wyoming. The admitting nurse instructed the EMTs to wheel Gordon into an examination room and transfer him onto a hospital gurney. A second nurse followed from behind to supervise. Once Gordon was settled, the EMTs left, leaving the nurse to perform a cursory examination and fill out the blank forms on her clipboard.

Peeking beneath the bandage, the nurse frowned, sucked in a deep breath, and momentarily pinched her eyes shut. She'd seen some ghastly injuries in the ER, but jagged cuts like this one, running horizontally from the corner of Gordon's eye to his ear lobe, still made her squirm. The patient would need several stitches, but the more immediate concern was permanent vision loss. Despite her best efforts, she'd never developed the acting skills necessary to remain nonchalant when confronted by such a violent wound. Still, she'd learned to be a realistic truth-teller while maintaining a reassuring demeanor.

"That's a nasty little cut," she exclaimed. "We're talking about at least a dozen stitches so you won't spend the rest of your life looking like Frankenstein's monster. Are there other injuries I should know about?"

The nurse expertly checked his vitals, including blood pressure, as he prepared to answer. Gordon already knew he didn't want to spend the night, so he'd need to conceal any symptoms of a concussion. He might have a cracked rib or two, but hopefully, that wouldn't earn him an overnight stay. Gordon smiled to himself upon hearing the reference to Frankenstein's monster. Most people thought the beast *was* Frankenstein. Gordon was impressed the nurse knew the monster had been Dr. Frankenstein's creation.

"Yeah, I got a little beat up around my stomach and chest," replied Gordon. He squirmed in his prone position to lift his T-shirt.

"Yep," the nurse replied. "You've got some pretty good bruises around those ribs. They should heal okay, but we should still do an x-ray to see if any are broken."

For the first time, Gordon focused on the nurse's face. She had dark hair parted down the middle, turquoise eyes, and flawless skin. Gordon glanced at her name tag. Emma. He thought about Dylan's wife.

"What are you grinning about?" the nurse inquired. "You must be thinking about how much worse the other guy looks right now, huh?"

Gordon started to laugh but abruptly stopped when it sent a jolt of pain up his spine.

"I wish," Gordon said. "They deserve far worse, but I'm afraid they got in the first punches, and I never had a chance."

"I was just kidding. I see your name's Gordon. Mine's Emma. Okay, here's the plan. First, I need to get some information from you, including your health history. Second, I'll take you down for x-rays, and then finally, I'll be here to assist the doc when it's time to get your stitches. And seriously, Gordon, don't worry. There're some tricks to help with the pain. Also, at some point, Margie will stop by for some health insurance information."

"That's no problem," Gordon responded. "I've got a card here in my wallet. I get insurance through my school district."

"Oh? Are you a teacher?"

Gordon was hoping she'd ask. He took pride in talking about his profession. While it may not sound as impressive as saying doctor or lawyer, it still reflected the value he placed on making a difference in the lives of others. Everyone knew teachers weren't well-paid. In Gordon's mind, that made his career choice even more honorable.

"Yes, I teach high school history."

"Oh, I always *hated* history in high school. It was *so* boring. I regret it now, though. There's much about the world I don't understand, and the older I get, the more important it all seems."

"Yeah, it's occurred to me that history's wasted on teenagers," responded Gordon. "It would be far easier to teach it to adults like yourself."

"That's what makes your job so challenging," Emma countered. "You've got to find a way to make it appealing to people who only have a thirty-second attention span. My history teachers just liked to hear themselves talk." After a pause, she added, "Of course, I'm sure your classes are much more interesting."

Gordon momentarily glanced away. He made a mental note that when there was time for self-reflection in the car or on a long hike, he'd give this one more thought, to find a way to rejuvenate his teaching or get the *hell* out of the classroom. Gordon was becoming a parody of the stereotypical history teacher. The way things were going, pretty soon, he'd be the subject of a *Saturday Night Live* skit.

It only took a few minutes to answer Emma's questions about his health history. Gordon didn't have any allergies, was currently under no medication, and had always been in relatively good shape. He admitted to drinking more beer than he probably should and even owned up to the recent renewal of his smoking habit. There was also no hiding his noticeable weight.

Along the way for x-rays, Gordon confirmed he was the ER's only patient. The hallways were deathly quiet except for the low humming of fluorescent lights unnaturally luminescent for such a late hour. The x-rays revealed a couple of bruised ribs, but none broken. Emma then escorted Gordon back into the examination room to await the doctor's visit. After closing the door, she gently peeled off Gordon's bandage and prepared a tray with needles, sutures, and other items necessary for the stitching.

"In a big-city hospital, you'd probably have this done by a plastic surgeon. That's the *best* way to ensure there won't be a visible scar."

"And what if I just have the stitching done here?" inquired Gordon.

"There shouldn't be much of a scar after everything heals, but *no* guarantees."

"It'll add some character," Gordon pronounced. "Besides, I'd like to be done with this whole mess. It wasn't one of my prouder moments."

Gordon observed Emma repeatedly peeking towards the door as though she was waiting for the doctor to make a grand entrance.

"The doctor's probably still on her midnight dinner break," Emma said.

"She?"

"Is that a *problem*?" Emma asked, making no effort to conceal the scowl on her face.

"No. *No*, not at all!" Gordon protested. He kicked himself for his chauvinistic faux pas. He was sure he didn't have a concussion, but his mind wasn't firing on all cylinders.

"*She's* inside the hospital, so if needed, she can be here within seconds. While we're waiting, why don't you tell me how this happened. It's been a slow night, and I could use a good story."

Gordon recognized Emma's trick. It probably worked with adults as well as it did children. Get patients talking to distract them from thinking about what's coming. It's okay, he thought. Gordon loved to tell stories, so he was happy to play along.

"You could use a good story? Okay, then I should probably start at the very beginning. Towards the end of 1981, when President Reagan had fully recovered from the assassination attempt on his life, he had the Secret Service sneak a mystery woman into the White House. For the next several months, they carried on a torrid affair, practically right under Nancy's nose. The romance ended when this woman got pregnant with Reagan's love child. Emma, *I'm* that child, and Ronald Reagan, he's my *father*."

Emma raised an eyebrow, smiled, and began to speak. Before she could say anything, Gordon cut her off and continued.

"Now, as you probably know, Dad passed away sixteen years ago. *But*, what about Mom? To protect the former president's reputation, she'd put me up for adoption and then disappeared. *Poof!* She completely vaporized. For the past several years, I've been on this incredible quest to find her. It's been tough, as you might guess. She didn't want anyone to find her. It was as though the Feds had placed her in the witness protection program. You know what I mean?"

Emma nodded while placing a hand over her mouth to restrain a giggle. Her eyes were beaming. Gordon grew increasingly animated as he continued to spin his story. For the moment, he'd completely forgotten about bruised ribs or the open wound on the side of his head.

"*So*, I came here in pursuit of a hot lead that my mother's currently living a quiet life in Gillette, Wyoming. She'd been dodging the conspiracy theorists and the reporters from the *National Inquirer* for decades. Naturally, I was thrilled to have finally found her. When I knocked on her door just a few hours ago, my half-brothers answered. I guess they took offense at the questions I asked. They were burly guys too, kind of like if you'd cross-bred a gorilla with a cowboy. And *so*, as you can see, they ended up beating the living *crap* out of me."

Emma shook her head, laughing and gazing with astonishment.

"That's a *good* one, Gordon. You held my interest from start to finish. I'll give it to you. You've got quite the imagination." After a pause, she added, "Although I've got to tell you, Ronald Reagan's my favorite president. So, I'm a little offended."

"Really? *Really!* I was just starting to like you," Gordon responded.

"Oh . . . my . . . *god!* Please don't tell me we're about to sew up a *Democrat!*"

Gordon's smile evaporated. "Yeah, well, that's part of the reason I'm here." He turned to face Emma directly and frowned.

"So," Emma stated pointedly, "what *really* happened?"

"Well, as I said, I'm a teacher. Since I'm off for the summer, I decided to take a road trip out west. An old college buddy has a cabin down in Grand Lake, Colorado, and I've been driving the scenic way to join him. For the past week or so, I've been exploring the Dakotas."

"By yourself?"

"I've been driving on my own, but I've already met some amazing people along the way. There was a man, for example, who camped next to me in a national park up in North Dakota. Even though he's more than twice my age, we became good friends, and he and I took several long hikes together. We exchanged phone numbers at the end, although I doubt our paths will ever cross again. You know how it is. Nevertheless, I'll *never* forget him."

Suddenly, the door swung open, and a woman in her early thirties stepped into the room. She had wavy black hair tied straight back into a ponytail. The skin on her oval face was bronze and a little leathery, like she'd spent too much time in the sun. The white coat was the only evidence she was a doctor since Gordon could see tan khaki shorts and some New Balance running shoes underneath. As she turned into the small room, her gaze was fixed on a clipboard holding Gordon's chart. When she finally peered up, a dashing smile flashed across her face showing off two rows of brilliantly white teeth.

"Gordon? My name's Doctor Cohen. It's nice to meet you, although I wish it were under better circumstances."

"That makes two of us."

Gordon glanced around. With a heart monitor and a vertical stand for IVs on one side of the bed and Emma's tray on the other, not to mention three grown adults packed into the crowded room, the walls were beginning to converge. Dr. Cohen glanced down at the chart once more and then turned her attention to Gordon's x-rays. Finally, she looked up, walked over to Gordon, and placed a hand on his forehead to get a closer look at the wound.

"That's a nasty little cut," the doctor stated matter-of-factly. Gordon glanced up at Emma to acknowledge that Dr. Cohen had just echoed her exact words.

"I was just getting everything ready for you to practice your sewing skills," Emma proclaimed, "and Gordon here was getting ready to tell me the story of how he earned this little souvenir from the evening. He's been keeping me in a *lot* of suspense. I get the impression it's *quite* a story."

"*Really?* In that case, while we get you numbed up, I'd love to hear it too."

Without waiting for a response, Dr. Cohen maneuvered to the side of the gurney and traded places with her nurse. Emma adjusted something to elevate Gordon's head. Afterward, he could look directly into the faces of his eager audience. Emma bit down on her bottom lip as she stared at the side of Gordon's face. Dr. Cohen lightly applied an ointment to the area around the wound.

"Let's give it a few minutes to get you numb before I give you the real anesthetic," pronounced Dr. Cohen.

Then the young doctor and the veteran nurse stepped back and looked at Gordon expectantly, like children waiting for the start of story hour.

Gordon cleared his throat. "Okay then, here goes . . ."

This morning was magnificent. I'd been out camping for several days in Theodore Roosevelt National Park, and when I opened my tent flap, the bluest sky I've ever seen greeted me. My neighbor, an older gentleman, named Dylan who'd recently become a *good* friend, invited me to join him for coffee brewing in his camper. We sat outside in a couple of folding chairs, anticipating a miraculous day.

Dylan and I had been together for the past few days, but we both knew we'd be traveling in different directions this morning. Dylan was planning to travel due west into Montana. I needed to drive in a more southerly direction towards my final destination, Grand Lake, Colorado. Saying goodbye this morning was tough. It was one of those times when you make a friend, and then you have no idea if you'll ever see him again.

Anyhow, I planned to stop at Devil's Tower. The drive there was quiet, scenic, relaxing. Not everyone would agree since many think you have to have mountains or beaches for an area to qualify as scenic. To me, gazing at open prairie while driving the backroads is like touring through paradise. I've always hated the choking traffic back in St. Louis, so the drive this morning was exhilarating.

I assume you're both familiar with Devil's Tower since it's only about an hour from here. It's truly a remarkable place. I can see why Spielberg chose to film the pinnacle scene from *Close Encounters of the Third Kind*

on top of that butte. It rises almost nine hundred feet from nowhere. If
it were in the heart of the Rockies, it would still be a magnificent pillar,
but since it's surrounded only by a carpet of emerald-green trees, it's even
more impressive. After hiking the mile-and-a-half loop around its base,
I must have spent another half hour staring up into the pale blue sky,
following some climbers as they inched their way to the top.

By mid-afternoon, I decided what to do next. Typically, I would've
looked for a place to camp since the seven-hour drive to Grand Lake
would've required me to drive into the Rockies late at night. Then I studied Google Maps and saw your little metropolis. After spending so many
nights in my claustrophobic tent, one in a hotel sounded *luxurious*. A
spacious shower, a restaurant meal, and especially a soft mattress were the
ideal way to cap off what'd been a perfect day. I called ahead and made a
reservation at the Hampton Inn, right down the street from this hospital.

An hour later, I checked in and soon savored a warm shower. After
putting on some fresh clothes and then starting a load of laundry, I Face-
Timed with my two kids. David's eight, and little Annie's just turned
four. So far, I've been sending them pictures and videos from my phone
every day, which is part of our conversation in the evening. Their mom
has been charting my trip on a big wall map, so they've been getting more
and more excited about where I've been. My hope is I'm planting seeds
for future family road trips.

After the call ended, I wanted to find a place to eat dinner with
some local flair. Once again, I consulted my trusty Google Maps and
discovered a spot right in the heart of town called Pokeys. I know there
are about thirty thousand people here in Gillette, but I'm guessing you've
both heard of it? Pokey's looked like a cozy restaurant with a bar, some
local cuisine, and maybe a TV to catch a baseball game.

When I first pulled into the parking lot, it started to get dark. The sun
was setting, and I stopped for a moment to admire the blazing sky in the
west. I've seen some *gorgeous* sunsets on this trip, but I didn't expect to see
one from the back lot of a place called Pokeys. You guys probably take your
clear, dry air for granted, but it creates the most vibrant sunsets for me.

Upon entering the building, a hostess asked if I wanted a table. I almost
said yes, but then I noticed the television above the bar. Sure enough, my

St. Louis Cardinals were playing the Rockies at Coors Field. They were already down a couple of runs, but I still thought the game would be a good dinner companion. I asked her if I could order a steak from the end of the bar. I believe her exact answer was, "Go for it, cowboy."

I started with a Bud and then told the bartender that I'd better stick to Diet Cokes. I knew the Hampton Inn was too far to walk, and I didn't have a designated driver. Pokeys was a bit dark, but it had some local color. I'm not usually a fan of country music, but in this case, it felt right. And it wasn't all bad. A few people were scattered about at the tables, but otherwise, the place was empty. The bartender, a short woman wearing a tall cowboy hat, was friendly enough. She cheerfully took my food order: a sirloin well done, a loaded baked potato, and a salad with house dressing. So far, so good.

Twenty minutes later, two men walked in and grabbed stools around the corner of the bar from where I was sitting. The Cards had the bases loaded at the time, although they ended up blowing the opportunity, so I was pretty distracted. I didn't even notice these two men at first. It was quite a bombshell when I finally did.

Up to this point, everyone I'd encountered in Gillette had been nice and friendly, just like you'd expect in a western town. But these two? They'd been riding on Harleys, not horses. Both were wearing black leather jackets, although it was hardly cold inside Pokeys. They had thick chains around their necks and wrists, not the kind of jewelry I'd wear. They were also sporting blue jeans that looked like they had never seen the inside of a washing machine.

These two men were also *huge*! I'm six-two, but next to these guys, I felt small. One had shaggy blond hair, and I think he was the bigger of the two. This guy had two perpendicular lines tattooed just below his Adam's apple, and although I'm not certain, I'm pretty sure they were the top part of a swastika. The other goon, the one closest to me, was wearing a red hat bearing a Confederate flag. I first noticed them when their talking grew louder. I wouldn't say it was a heated argument since they seemed to be feeding off each other, but it grew increasingly garish.

I glanced around Pokeys. By this point, the other diners had left, and the bartender was in the back room. As you can see, I'm a big guy, but I was getting a little nervous. Normally, I'll shy away from a fight, but not because I'm a coward. I've always had a bit of a temper, which has gotten me into trouble at times. Also, I've been trying to learn more self-control lately, and I know it's better to walk away from a fight, even if you have to swallow some pride. In this case, though, there was still plenty of food on my plate, and the game on TV was close and undecided. With hindsight, I should have left, but at the time, I foolishly decided to stay.

Even then, everything would probably have been all right if I'd just minded my own business. These two Goliaths were having a pleasant time with each other, and for the most part, they were ignoring me. It's just I couldn't help overhearing their conversation. I imagine people out on the street could probably hear their conversation. I tried my best to block it out, but most of it was political and *highly* racist. They belonged to some kind of right-wing group; white supremacists or maybe neo-Nazis. I assume you have those here? They're like a plague back in rural Missouri.

When I heard one of them say, "fucking Jews," I couldn't control myself any longer. To my credit, I didn't jump up and start a fight. I also didn't quietly pay my bill and leave. Without thinking, I slammed my fork down on the bar to get their attention, calmly wiped my mouth with a napkin, and slid off the back of the bar stool.

"What'd you just say?" I asked, trying to maintain a natural volume.

At first, there was an eerie silence as they both turned in my direction. Since it's doubtful the combined IQ scores of these two clowns exceeded three digits, I double-downed and repeated the question.

"What did you just say about 'fucking Jews?'"

This time, I got an answer. The blond-headed Aryan glared at me, his gaze powerful enough to slice me in half. "Buddy, are you eavesdropping on a private conversation?" he snarled. "That'd be fucking rude."

"How could I not eavesdrop?" I countered. "A deaf man could hear your *private conversation*. Now, I'll ask for a third time, what did you just say about 'fucking Jews?'"

The dope beneath the red hat opted for a calmer approach. In a more conversational tone, Red Hat decided to share his thoughts. "We were talking about a *Jew* organization called ZOG. Ever heard of it? It stands for Zionist Occupation Government."

The ugly glare on his face was incompatible with his relaxed tone. I'll give him credit, though; Mr. Confederate flag had at least a middle school vocabulary. At this point, though, he reverted to sounding like an ignorant racist.

"It's about the Jews, asshole, the *fucking Jews*, and how they want to control the government in the western states."

He clenched his teeth together as he snarled the words, "fucking Jews.'"At that moment, I half expected him to leap forward and bite my throat. I recently saw a coyote do that to a prairie dog. He didn't, though; he just continued with his fascist lecture.

"We were talking about the worldwide network of *Jew* lawyers, *Jew* bankers, and *Jew* politicians. If they had their way, they'd take over our government at every level. They'd take our land, our property, our money, and our rights." After a brief pause, he added, "You agree?"

He tipped up the visor on his hat so I could better see his eyes. They were *daring* me to respond. While waiting for my response, he slid off his stool and slowly moved around the corner of the bar. His Aryan friend shifted to hover above his right shoulder. They both now squarely faced me. I noticed a half-empty bottle of Coors in the storm trooper's right hand.

Before I share what happened next, you should know some background. One reason I took this trip was to do some serious self-reflection. More than anything, I've been trying to find more discipline. Now I was being tested. It still wasn't too late to defuse the situation. I could've said something conciliatory, paid my tab, and quietly walked out. Guess I failed that test.

"That may be the most ignorant thing I've ever heard," I thundered. "You anti-Semitic sons-of-bitches! Your contemptible racism will *not* make our country great again. People like you have committed everything terrible in this nation's past—slavery, the Indian Wars, a hundred years of Jim Crow, everything ugly throughout American history."

Before I could continue their history lesson, the Aryan swung his beer bottle and cracked it against my head. At the same time, Mr. Confederate flag tore into my torso like it was a punching bag. I don't remember much after that. A few minutes later, an ambulance arrived, followed by a couple of cops. The two Klansmen were long gone.

I managed to answer a few of the cops' questions while the EMTs bandaged up my head. The cops told me to come in tomorrow if I wanted to file a formal complaint, but I got the impression it wouldn't do much good. There were no witnesses. It would just be my word against theirs. A few minutes later, they rolled me into your emergency room.

"Don't take this the wrong way," Doctor Cohen said, almost in a whisper, "but your last name is Goldman, right? Are *you* Jewish?"

Gordon nodded. By now, the doctor had applied a fresh bandage to the side of his head.

"As I said, don't be offended," the doctor continued. "My last name's Cohen. I'm one of the few Jews in this area. The closest synagogue is two hours away, down in Casper."

Gordon felt a bond beginning to emerge with the good doctor. The fact that Emma was staring at them both in bewilderment helped to cement their connection.

"Do you think they knew you were Jewish?" asked Dr. Cohen.

"No, probably not. Like I said before, those idiots weren't paying much attention to me until I spoke up."

"Do you think you'd have said anything if you *weren't* Jewish?" asked Emma.

Gordon and the doctor both turned to her and smiled.

"That's a hell of a good question," responded Gordon.

A few minutes later, he prepared to leave. Gordon's Corolla was still at Pokeys, but he said he'd pick it up in the morning. Emma offered to call him a cab, but Gordon declined. He said he felt all right, and the short walk might do him some good. Besides, he had a few things to mull over. Gordon said goodbye to his two new friends, trekked out of the emergency room, and was enveloped by a cool, fresh breeze. A half-moon dangled directly overhead.

Before going to sleep thirty minutes later, Gordon again stared at his reflection in the bathroom mirror. His head looked like he'd just climbed out of a World War One trench. Gordon leaned in closer for a better view. Gently lifting the bandage, he winced at the sight of his jagged cut stitched up like a railroad track. Gordon stepped back, grimaced, and inhaled a full breath.

Then he glanced downward, and a faint smile spread across his banged-up face. Gordon hadn't seen himself in a while, and there was noticeably less flab around his midsection. He still had a way to go, but this was encouraging. Then he took notice of the bathroom counter. There was a pack of cigarettes next to the sink, half empty. He was in a non-smoking room but had earlier stepped outside to light up after FaceTiming with the kids.

Gordon picked up the pack and held it up to the mirror. What a *stupid* thing to do. With all the information out there about the medical horrors of tobacco, why had he resumed this disgusting habit? Gordon crumbled up the package. He squeezed it so hard none of the remaining cigarettes would ever be smoked and then tossed the remnants into the waste can. Gordon made eye contact with his reflection and nodded to seal a silent covenant.

CHAPTER

10

Gordon woke with a hammering headache. He'd set a late alarm on his phone, and when it went off at ten in the morning, he rolled over and promptly went back to sleep. At noon, the cleaning staff banged on his door. Gordon managed to crawl out of bed and talk them into another hour before he'd have to check out of his room. Then he gulped a couple of aspirin from his travel bag and washed them down with a scalding cup of bitter motel coffee. The shower that followed provided a shot of adrenalin, although Gordon had to be careful to keep the bandage clinging to his head from getting wet. He also craved a cigarette. Gordon had convinced himself he was just a moderate smoker, but now he was reminded of the addictive nature of nicotine.

After climbing out of the shower, Gordon toweled off the misty droplets that blurred the bathroom mirror. He once again studied his reflection. Except for one side of his face, Gordon was impressed. If he could stick with the vows he'd recently made to himself, to stop smoking, to cut back on beer consumption, and to improve the quality of the food he was eating, Gordon might surprise some people back home. For lunch, he crossed the highway and ordered a bacon ranch grilled chicken salad at McDonald's.

Gordon felt good enough to hike back to Pokeys for his car by early afternoon. He then drove to the Gillette police station to complete the report begun the night before. The cops seemed to have only a superficial interest in Gordon's details and descriptions. At first, this aroused some suspicion, but when the police sergeant reminded him it would be virtually impossible to get a conviction, Gordon better understood. Even if they found the two ogres from the night before, there were no witnesses or video evidence. Besides, did Gordon want to return to Gillette several months later for a trial?

Gordon glanced at his watch after exiting the police station and realized a change of plan might be in order. If he left now for Grand Lake, he'd once again have to zig-zag his way through the Rocky Mountains late at night. Another evening at the Hampton Inn would give him time to relax and recuperate. Gordon could treat himself to lunch in Estes Park, the gateway town that guarded the eastern entrance to Rocky Mountain National Park, if he got an early start the following day. This plan would add some distance to the drive, but the good memories from this area would justify the extra miles.

The revised plan also meant Gordon would enter Grand Lake via the scenic Trail Ridge Road. This almost fifty-mile route traversed the park, climbed more than twelve thousand feet in elevation, and provided some of the most stunning vistas in the Rocky Mountains. Gordon could spend the afternoon wandering through the heart of the national park before descending into Grand Lake, the smaller town on the park's western edge. He quickly sent a text to Ben updating him on the change in plans.

Of course, this meant spending another night in the friendly confines of Gillette. After checking back into the Hampton Inn, Gordon noticed a Mexican restaurant directly across the street. He hoped to soak in more local flavor this evening without repeating last night's fireworks. Gordon also saw it as a test. If he could stick to something like chicken fajitas with a Diet Coke instead of a Corona or a margarita, he'd take another step in the right direction. Imagine twenty-four hours without alcohol, a cigarette, or any unhealthy food.

Before heading to dinner, Gordon stepped into the courtyard behind the hotel for his FaceTime call to the kids. Usually, this was a daily highlight, but not today. Gordon knew there was a hideous piece of gauze straddling the side of his face. His conscience allowed him to tell a little fib to the kids—he'd taken a fall last night in the shower. But with Elaine, that wouldn't fly. Gordon vowed to be copiously honest with his wife, no matter what the future held. Elaine was like a human lie detector; she always seemed to know when he wasn't truthful.

Gordon looked around before touching the pad on his cell phone. The red brick patio was surprisingly quiet, surrounded by a low wall with towering sunflowers in the background to guard the outer perimeter. Comfortable Adirondack chairs were strewn across the deck, and there was no one sitting in a single one. Gordon could sit back, enjoy the late afternoon sunshine, and conduct his call with complete privacy.

The conversation with the kids was uneventful. David expressed some initial concern when he saw the bandage and even asked if he could see the cut. Gordon said it could wait until the wound had healed a bit and then quickly changed the subject. Both children easily swallowed the yarn about falling in the shower, and then Gordon shifted the conversation by asking questions about what they'd recently been up to in St. Louis.

The conversation with Elaine didn't go as well. After taking the iPad from the kids, Gordon asked if David and Annie could leave the room. Gordon didn't hesitate to peel back the bandage when Elaine asked to see the wound. He observed how she momentarily squeezed her eyes shut and sucked in a deep breath. In record time, Gordon provided a concise summary of the events from the night before.

"I know, Elaine, I was foolish."

"Have you taken some time to think about that night?" she asked in a surprisingly calm tone.

"Yeah," Gordon responded. Slumping back in his chair, he glanced away and inhaled a deep breath that elevated his folded arms.

"Have you considered the number of times you could have avoided that fight?"

Gordon glared back at the image on the screen of his phone. He told himself to bite his tongue and choose his words carefully.

"I haven't *counted* them, but I know the fight was avoidable. It's not an excuse, Elaine, but you didn't hear the anti-Semitic filth these guys were spewing. I just kept thinking if more European Jews had stood up for themselves back in the thirties, maybe they would've saved more lives. At the very least, they could've taken some Nazis with them."

"That sounds noble," Elaine retorted sarcastically, "but this isn't Europe, this isn't the thirties, and most importantly, I thought you were trying to find some self-restraint. I don't know, Gordon; last night sounds like a setback. Judging by the look of your face, a *big* setback."

Gordon looked down at the red bricks beneath his feet. He felt like a scolded child. On the one hand, it seemed like their marriage was no longer an equitable relationship, and that pissed him off. On the other, Gordon knew losing his temper now would probably explode in his face. He noticed a dotted line of ants making their way across a brick on a mission. Gordon purposely studied their progress to buy a little time. It helped. He calmed down before speaking.

"You're right," he finally pronounced. "I've got a long drive coming up tomorrow. I plan to head down to Estes Park in the morning and then cross the Divide in the afternoon. It'll give me plenty of time to think and to do some serious soul-searching."

"That sounds good," Elaine replied.

Gordon noticed her tone had mollified. Maybe Elaine realized she'd crossed a line, that this patronizing voice wasn't appropriate with a thirty-eight-year-old man. At least that's what he hoped. Gordon wanted to say more but knew additional time was necessary to frame his thoughts. As he concluded their conversation, Gordon told himself that he'd organize his ideas and send them to Elaine in an email tomorrow.

Dinner that night was delightfully calm and quiet. As Gordon left, he headed straight back to his hotel room. A restful evening watching baseball or maybe a movie with his head propped up on a soft pillow was just what the doctor ordered. By ten, Gordon's snoring was louder than the talking heads on Sports Center. At eleven, he woke just long enough to undress, set an early alarm, and turn off the bed lamp. Brushing teeth would wait until morning.

At six in the morning, Gordon woke with a grin on his face. A few hours later, he turned his Corolla west from I-25 and traversed the unseen line from plains to mountains. This route brought back marvelous memories. Gordon was heading straight into the Rocky Mountains; their snow-capped peaks steadily expanded on the horizon as they welcomed him back into their heartfelt embrace. For Gordon, this had always been a magical moment.

To add accelerant to the blaze, Gordon had something else he'd been saving for this particular occasion. He'd recently purchased a new CD. It wasn't just an ordinary selection of songs, but Bruce Springsteen's latest, *Western Stars*. Gordon knew the entire album bore relevance to where he was going. He'd been saving this CD ever since he first purchased it along with the camping gear back in St. Louis. Now, it was to be his musical accompaniment into the Rockies.

A few clouds had gathered over the jagged peaks. That was okay; in fact, it was perfectly normal. Clear cobalt skies greeted most summer mornings in the Rockies. Patches of gray began to gather by late morning, foreshadowing the thunderstorms that punctuated most afternoons. When Gordon exited the interstate, it took a while to escape the rumbling eighteen-wheelers and the other bustling traffic. As he climbed in elevation, though, the other vehicles mysteriously vanished. His little Corolla strained as it navigated through titanic rock formations. Gordon felt like a Lilliputian entering a world of giants.

To magnify the experience, Gordon pulled out the new CD, popped it into the car's player, and opened up the front windows. With chilly, dry air refreshingly blasting into the stale interior of his car, Gordon cranked up the volume. Immediately, he felt like Dorothy stepping out of black-and-white Kansas into the technicolor land of Oz. Each song was mind-blowing. The melodies were haunting and evocative, combining country and traditional folk. But more than anything, Gordon was captivated by the poetry of the lyrics.

At first, he focused on how the words reflected Springsteen's life. Gordon had recently read the Boss's autobiography, so it wasn't hard to make connections between the words and the personal experiences of the songwriter. As his mind wandered, Gordon saw more links to his own life. One song, "The Wayfarer," expressly spoke to Gordon, and he replayed it three times. As he left the sprawling plains behind and ascended along the banks of the Big Thompson River, Gordon concentrated on one stanza:

> You start out slow in a sweet little bungalow, something two can call home
> Then rain comes fallin', the blues come callin', and you're left with a heart of stone
> Some folks are inspired sittin' by the fire, slippers tucked under the bed
> But when I go to sleep I can't count sheep for the white lines in my head

I'm a wayfarer, baby, I roam from town to town
When everyone's asleep and the midnight bells sound
My wheels are hissin' up the highway,
spinnin' 'round and 'round

Suddenly, Gordon lost his focus. Other songs on the CD continued to play, but he no longer paid attention. A thought crept into his head and swiftly expanded like a western wildfire. Yes, there was deeply-rooted pain. For the last two years, it'd found a home built on a foundation of grief and guilt. Elaine, Jim, and others had pushed Gordon to see a therapist to help detoxify the poison. He'd stubbornly and stoically resisted. Whether this would be necessary or whether Gordon could find an antidote was still an open question.

But now, a new, potentially life-altering idea cascaded into his brain. Maybe his goal shouldn't be to root out the psychological trauma to find his old self. Perhaps that man was *gone*. Or maybe Elaine never fully knew the *real* Gordon. Either way, this opened up a world of possibilities.

Gordon had always harbored doubts about the existence of God, and he was all but certain there was no hereafter. *This* life, this was the only one he'd ever get, and he needed to live it to its fullest. Is that what he was doing? Should his entire life be based on family responsibilities tied to the humdrum suburbs of a midwestern city? Or should he take advantage of his recent freedom to embrace new opportunities? Gordon thought about his new friend, Dylan. Should he wait until his mid-eighties when his children were grown and his wife was dead before buying a camper and then finally hitting the open road?

Gordon pulled into Estes Park just as his new CD ended. When he entered the east side of town, it was nice to be greeted by the old Stanley Hotel, made famous by Stephen King's, *The Shining*. Now Gordon was growing restless. The town was more beautiful than he remembered, but this was a Saturday in mid-June, and the tourists were clogging the streets. At each intersection, local police directed traffic to shepherd vast crowds of pedestrians from one side of the road to the other. Gordon crept along in bumper-to-bumper traffic. He looked around at the cheap

T-shirt shops, pizza joints, and souvenir stores, thinking this scene was reminiscent of everything he'd purposefully left behind.

Gordon planned to reach the center of town, turn south onto Moraine Avenue, and stop for lunch at Smokin' Dave's BBQ and Brew. This restaurant was a familiar haunt. He knew the food was excellent, and he hoped to get a quiet table outside with a panoramic view of the mountains. Gordon wanted to catch his breath while studying the profile of Longs Peak. He also planned to communicate with his wife. He knew just what to say; the email was already composed in his head.

It took longer than expected due to traffic. Here was the main road into Rocky Mountain National Park, and it appeared that half of Denver was arriving at the same time. When Gordon finally pulled into the restaurant's parking lot, he scowled when he saw the crowd waiting out front. Fortunately, Gordon was quickly seated at a small outdoor table since he was by himself. As he waited for food, he checked email on his iPhone. Surprisingly, and for the first time, there was a message waiting from Elaine.

Dear Gordon,

I'm sorry about our conversation last night. I was just concerned, especially when I saw the ugly gash on your head. Calling it a significant setback, however, was an overreaction on my part. I know you're trying, and I should've been more supportive.

I also wanted to update you on how the kids are doing. I've been taking Annie to the playground in Stacy Park almost every day, and she's made a new friend. His name is Scott, and they're so cute playing together. You should see them—Annie has a little boyfriend! I'll send you pictures. As for your son, David is David. What else can I say? He has his good days and his not-so-good days. I think he's missing you.

On a different note, I feel the need to disclose something that recently happened. I told you last fall about Alan Abramowitz, the new assistant principal. I've never said much to anyone at school about our current situation, but evidently, it got out that you and I had separated a few months ago. Alan and I have recently become work buddies. As you know, it doesn't hurt to have friends within your building's administration. Please understand our friendship was strictly limited to work. I've NEVER seen Alan outside of school.

The other day, Alan called my cell phone. At first, I thought it involved closing my classroom for the summer, but he didn't even mention school. We chatted for a few minutes, and then out of the blue, he asked me to meet him for drinks. I thought about it at first. It would've been so lovely to spend time with an adult my age. In the end, I told him no. I said I'm still married, and just because you were off on a long road trip didn't change that fact. Don't be upset, Gordon. He understood and instantly backed off.

I wanted to share this with you for two reasons. First, we've always been honest with each other. I didn't do anything wrong, but I figured full disclosure on my part would keep it that way. Second, it underscores the fact that we'll soon need to make some big decisions. There's a fork in the road up ahead, and at some point, we need to decide which path we're going to take.

Please don't take this as pressure. It's just when I gave "my blessing" for this trip, I didn't consider how long you'd be gone. I've tried to be patient, Gordon; I really have. At some point, though, we both need to get on with our lives.

Write back when you have a chance. Also, keep sending the videos and pictures. We're all enjoying them.

Love,

Elaine

Gordon reread her message three times. He had planned to be candid with Elaine in his next email, but he hadn't expected to hear from her. The situation with Alan was upsetting, but what could he say? It wasn't like Elaine had called him. Alan had reached out to her, and Gordon assumed there wasn't anything she said or did to encourage this call.

Nevertheless, Elaine raised a good point. Alan's call encouraged her to think more about the future, and there *were* time limits. Just because he was out west enjoying the open road, listening to Springsteen, and meeting new people didn't mean she had to put her life on hold back in St. Louis.

A waitress interrupted his thoughts when she brought him a bowl of green chili and a Caesar salad. Gordon had drained his Diet Coke, so she reached over and grabbed his glass for a refill. He looked up from his daze just in time to catch a glimpse of her smile. The waitress looked to be in her mid-twenties. Blond curls spilled from beneath a blue baseball cap sporting the restaurant's logo, framing her roundish face. Was her smile the generic type commonly used to enhance tips, or was it intentionally flirtatious? And what about the cleavage shot revealed when she leaned over to pick up his empty glass? Intentional? Gordon had been out of circulation so long it was getting harder to decipher these signals. Either way, it was gratifying to see that smile after reading about Alan's phone call.

Gordon dug into his lunch, alternating between salad and chili. Both were delicious. He looked at Elaine's email and touched the spot to launch a reply. Nothing had changed. Gordon still knew what he wanted to say, and if anything, Elaine's email provided a foundation for his thoughts. He was soon lost composing his email, so he didn't notice the waitress returning with a full glass of Diet Coke.

Dear Elaine,

Thanks for your email. I really enjoyed reading about the kids. I'm a little concerned, though, about Annie's new boyfriend. I was hoping to be the main guy in her life for a few more years. I don't know if I'm ready to be replaced by a little man named Scott.

David's another matter. Maybe in your next email, you can share more details. I'm getting worried about his rising level of anxiety. He's an intelligent kid, but his social skills are lagging. Has he made any new friends in camp? Should we be concerned?

As for Alan, I appreciate your honesty in telling me about his call. I met this guy at your school's holiday party last December, right? No offense, but if we end up "taking separate paths down the road," I think you can do a lot better.

As I read your email, I found myself contemplating similar thoughts. Alan's call may have encouraged it on your end, but believe it or not, Springsteen's new album this morning on the drive up into the mountains did the same for me. Bruce Springsteen, man, what a poet! If they can give a Nobel Prize in literature to Bob Dylan, they can certainly do the same for the Boss. Anyhow, when it comes to confronting the fork lying ahead in the road, he helped me reflect on the future.

Okay, two thoughts:

First, you might be right, Elaine; maybe I do need to see a counselor or some kind of therapist. I'm still hoping to work my problems out on this trip, but there hasn't been much progress so far. Many nights are still interrupted by bad dreams, and then it takes me a long time to fall back to sleep. If nothing changes this summer, I'll consider seeing someone in the fall.

Second, and more critical, resolving my recent issues may not be enough. What if I'm still unhappy? I apologize for sounding like the stereotypical "midlife crisis," but I've been thinking about more significant issues. Do I want to spend the rest of my life in the suburbs of St. Louis? The longer I teach at Beachwood North, the deeper my roots extend, and pretty soon, I may never be able to get out. What if I could find a teaching job out here? Or, for that matter, what if I wanted to go back to school and pursue an entirely different career? Damn, Elaine, I'm going to be forty pretty soon. Is this it? Do I want to wake up one day and find I'm a retired high school teacher spending my final years in the suburbs of St. Louis? That's where my dad is right now, and even though he's never said it, I know he harbors some regrets.

Elaine, that's my greatest worry. More than anything, I don't want to end up lying on my deathbed one day, staring up at the ceiling, and wondering about all the things I should've done with my life. You're right. We both need to do some profound thinking this summer about the paths we want to take in the fall.

As I write this email, I'm currently staring up at Longs Peak while eating my lunch in Estes Park. I'll be driving across the Divide this afternoon and will probably get some great photos above the tree line. I'll be in Grand Lake for dinner tonight. I may not get a chance to FaceTime this evening, but I'll still send some pictures, and we can talk tomorrow.

Love,

Gordon

After Gordon proofed his email, he looked up, smiled, and hit send. By now, the bill was sitting on the table next to two empty bowls. He pulled some cash out of his wallet, enough to cover the bill plus a ten-dollar tip. As he stood to leave, Gordon looked up at Longs Peak one more time. It indeed was the colossus that ruled the kingdom. At the moment, its flat, snow-capped peak, rising more than fourteen thousand feet, was crowned by dark, puffy clouds. Gordon nodded and gave it a parting wink. He'd be back.

Gordon first saw the bull moose out of the corner of his eye. He'd driven the long ascent up Trail Ridge Road to the Alpine Visitor Center. Shortly after passing the intersection with Fall River Road, the thoroughfare briefly leveled off near some beaver ponds. Gordon had pulled into a parking lot to explore the wooden walkways on the perimeter of the ponds hoping to get a picture of one of the flat-tailed critters for Annie. Instead, he almost walked into the massive bull moose. It appeared like an apparition, camouflaged beneath the limbs of an aspen tree. Gordon couldn't believe his eyes.

The moose gracefully sauntered to the grassy edge of the pond, stepped into the shallow waters, and plunged his face beneath the surface in search of tasty morsels. When his head finally reemerged, there were long strands of olive-green grass dripping from its elongated muzzle. The moose was enormous, with a web of antlers adding even more to its imposing height. For a moment, Gordon was mesmerized; the moose had put him under a spell. Never glancing away, he pulled out his cell phone and snapped photos that would shock his children.

Twenty minutes later, Gordon was still taking pictures. A small crowd had gathered by now, and the bull moose had become a local celebrity. Gordon was amazed at how people in the national parks spotted wildlife. One person, in this case, Gordon, fortuitously found the beast, and then everyone else took notice of the growing crowd. Meanwhile, the moose completely ignored his audience, nonchalantly focused on his mid-day lunch.

Gordon maneuvered into different spots to vary his camera angle. He knew a bull moose could be dangerous to an unsuspecting tourist, but the water separating him from the thousand-pound animal gave him a sense of security. Gordon smiled to himself. Without even looking over his photos, he knew there would be several to send to the kids, and he couldn't wait to hear David's reaction when they discussed the moose during their next call.

While walking back to his car, Gordon had a provocative thought. Sure, it was nice to have these photos of the bull moose, and in all likelihood, he'd probably enlarge and frame at least one. But that wasn't why he was excited. It was the *reason* behind the excitement, his anticipation over how his family would react to the photos. What did *that* mean? Family versus freedom, freedom versus family; which did he value most? The scale seemed to tip back and forth almost by the minute. Gordon understood the weight of both ideals, but framing his growing dilemma this way, even if it was a gross oversimplification, might prove helpful as he continued to wrestle with his decisions.

A half-hour later, Gordon's luck continued. At the Rainbow Curve Overlook, he spotted the profile of two bighorn sheep about fifty feet up on a rocky ledge. They were grazing on the shrubbery sprouting amid the giant boulders. Like the moose, they were indifferent to the picture-taking going on around them. For Gordon, this was a first. As much time as he'd spent in the Rockies, Gordon had never encountered these animals. They were ordinary in appearance except for their massively arched antlers. Signs pointed to the areas they tended to frequent, but Gordon had never seen them in person. Once again, he took about fifty pictures. Gordon would delete at least forty-five of them, but the ones kept would be the best. He'd come to believe that he could improve his odds of taking a quality photograph by snapping a considerable number of pictures.

Shortly afterward, the Corolla ascended into thin air above the tree line. To Gordon, this was like looking out an airplane window when it first broke free of the clouds and continued to soar into the brilliant sunlight. The pines progressively shrank in size, and when they finally disappeared, Gordon could see the distant horizon stretching dozens of miles in every direction. Jagged ridges and snow-clad peaks adorned the vast skyline. It took Gordon's breath away.

A little later, a stop near the Alpine Visitor Center *literally* took his breath away. A short hike up a nearby peak to see a panoramic view left Gordon huffing and puffing. He now stood almost two and a half miles above sea level. There was less oxygen at this elevation, and when combined with his lack of conditioning and his recently bruised ribs, Gordon struggled to reach the end of the short asphalt path. Instead of enjoying the view, he bent over with hands planted on thighs and tried to regain his breath. This feeling not only confirmed his decision to stop smoking but also convinced him of the need to begin an exercise regimen.

On the way down, Gordon observed a herd of elk in the distance. He'd hit the trifecta—a bull moose, a couple of bighorn sheep, and now a pack of elk. Using the weak zoom on his phone's camera, Gordon snapped several more pictures, giving him a whole menagerie of critters to later review with David and Annie. Before leaving, Gordon made some purchases inside the visitor center's gift shop—a small, stuffed moose for Annie and a collection of polished rocks for David, including jasper, agate, and petrified wood. While paying, he noticed some silver and turquoise earrings displayed on the counter. At the last minute, he added these for Elaine.

The drive down on the west side of the Continental Divide was the reverse of coming up. Gordon continued to negotiate extreme curves after re-entering the aspen and pine groves, descending rapidly in elevation. He frequently swallowed to clear his ears as they adjusted to the increasing air pressure. Gordon caught glimpses of a few scurrying marmots amid the rock outcroppings. They resembled beavers without the flattened tails. Gordon also saw a few mule deer along the side of the road, but these were anticlimactic compared to what he'd seen earlier.

An hour later, he pulled into the gravel drive in front of Ben's cabin. The façade was somewhat ordinary, but Gordon remembered it was more impressive in the rear since the stunning views were the primary focus of its design. It'd been a long time since he was last here, but Gordon remembered the route up the steep knoll like it was yesterday. Climbing out of his dusty Corolla, Gordon stretched and peered towards the west.

The view was more stunning than he'd remembered. Several hundred feet below and to the left, he could see the town of Grand Lake hugging the shoreline of its namesake. In the distance were larger lakes, Shadow Mountain, and Granby, although the latter hid behind a ridge of mountains. His reverie was suddenly interrupted by a loud voice from behind.

"Hey, buddy, you finally made it!"

Gordon spun around, smiled, and lifted his right arm in preparation for a handshake. Ben trotted over with a broad grin on his face and a sparkle in his eyes. As he neared, he ignored the extended hand and embraced Gordon in a tight hug. When they finally pulled back, the two old friends kept their hands on each other's shoulders, smiling and absorbing the changes that had come with age.

"You're looking good, my friend!" Gordon finally stated. "A few gray hairs, but otherwise, you haven't changed much."

"Well, you were always a nice-looking man yourself," Ben replied. "Now, there's just more of you to admire! And, *for the love of God*, what the hell happened to your face?"

"Oh, kiss my ass!" Gordon responded, and they both chuckled. "I'll show you later what's under the bandage if you want. It's a long story."

Ben nodded and then frowned as he glanced over at the Corolla with its grimy Missouri plates.

"I see you're still driving a teacher's car."

"Yep, whenever you see a Mercedes or a BMW in the school parking lot, you know it was paid for by the spouse's job. As you know, my spouse is also a teacher, so this is it."

Gordon noticed a sheepish grin on Ben's face as he nodded to his left. Looking up the drive, Gordon saw a cardinal red Mercedes-Benz CLS parked next to the cabin.

"Okay," he said, laughing, "I can see *you're* not a teacher."

Ben peered through the windows of the Corolla into the backseat.

"Let's get you unpacked and settled. Then maybe we can have a beer or two on the deck while we catch the sunset."

"Sounds good," replied Gordon. "Although I'd prefer a Diet Coke if you've got one."

Ben raised an eyebrow but didn't say anything. Working together, they brought in Gordon's luggage in a single trip.

Even though it had been over fifteen years, Gordon had a feeling of déjà vu upon entering the cabin. A mammoth stone fireplace reaching up to the twelve-foot high ceiling bisected the western wall of the great room. Enormous picture windows flanked both sides, a large exterior awning guarding against the afternoon sun. Outside was a deck that wrapped itself around the rear of the cabin. Gordon could see a large table and a fire pit encircled by a three-piece sectional dominating the center of the deck.

"This place is still amazing!" Gordon exclaimed. "But something's different."

"It's probably the furniture. My folks replaced and upgraded every-thing a few years ago."

Gordon strolled around the room for a closer examination. A flat-screen television had replaced the old dusty painting of a bison herd above the fireplace mantel. A mammoth leather couch was flanked on both sides by matching recliners. Gordon sat on one, pressed a button, and watched as his feet slowly climbed above his head. The dark leather looked expensive, probably imported from Italy, and was as soft as silk. He leaned back with hands clenched behind his head and a wide grin on his face.

"Well," Gordon stated, "this *is* nice. Your folks have done an amazing job keeping up this place." Then he turned to face his old college room-mate, who'd plopped down on the couch next to him, his head sinking into one of the matching leather pillows.

"Ben, I can't thank you enough for inviting me here. Coming out to Grand Lake is *exactly* what I need."

"You and me both, buddy! And I should be thanking you. I *love* this place, but up until now, it's been a little lonely. Thank *you* for putting your life on hold and making the long drive out here."

Ben glanced outside and observed the sun's descent between two mountains directly across the lake.

"Let's move this luggage into your room, grab some cold ones, and move out onto the deck. I like to catch the sunset whenever possible."

Ten minutes later, Gordon and Ben leaned over the deck's railing. They sported sunglasses, and Gordon again slipped out his phone to snap a few pictures. The sun's rays seeped through the mountains, casting a blend of yellow, orange, and deep red. This vision was reflected on the surface of the lake. The mirrored image of snow-covered peaks and marsh-mallow clouds, all washed in the waning light, broadened the landscape.

"You know," Ben finally said, as the sun dipped behind the peaks, "the sunset's still officially an hour away. The mountains just make it seem earlier, but we still have more daylight. What say we head into town for a steak dinner? You and I have a *lot* of catching up to do."

Ten minutes later, the two friends climbed out of the Mercedes parked diagonally along the western-style boardwalk on Cairns Street and entered the Backstreet Steakhouse. Ben insisted on treating tonight for a couple of fourteen-ounce ribeye steaks to celebrate their reunion. Gordon initially resisted, but he finally agreed, figuring he could take half home to expand his dinner into two meals.

They were seated at an outdoor table covered with white linen and lit by dancing candlelight from within a crystal chalice. The mountains' darkening images peaked over Gordon's shoulders while facing the amethyst glow in the western sky. After giving their order to an unas-suming, middle-aged waiter, Ben turned towards Gordon, clasped his hands behind his head, and inhaled a deep breath.

"A couple of weeks ago, you implied over the phone that your life had taken a turn for the worse. Tell me why. Catch me up."

Gordon did his best to review the same facts he'd recently shared with Jim. He again started with the picnic at Creve Coeur Lake that had taken place over the winter holidays and worked his way up to the present. By now, the story was getting easier to tell. He was concise and scrupulously honest. The only parts he withheld were the more recent developments, like the encounter with Dylan in North Dakota. Gordon also didn't bring up his current dilemma regarding the future.

"At this point," asked Ben, "what would you say is the status of your marriage?"

"*Good* question." Gordon turned away for a moment to gaze at the indigo still visible on the western horizon.

"A big part of me feels like a child sitting in a perpetual time-out. I fully deserved this punishment, mind you. I understand why Elaine wanted me out of the house, but I kept hoping she'd forgive me with enough atonement. Then I could eventually resume my place as husband and father."

"But," Ben said while scanning into the darkness, "you've alluded to something else that occurred a long time before, something that changed everything. Can I ask what happened?"

At that moment, the waiter approached and gingerly laid two heavy plates on the table.

"Gentlemen, would you like to cut into your steaks to be sure they're to your liking?"

Gordon and Ben dutifully complied, and both simultaneously nodded they were happy with the color of their beef. Sensing he'd intruded into their conversation, the waiter promised to check back later and sank into the shadows. Gordon cut into his steak and took a bite, buying a little time to mull over Ben's question. Finally, he looked up, a fork in one hand, a steak knife in the other, and the hint of moisture gathering around his eyes.

"Look, Ben, we haven't kept up with each other as we should've over the past few years. There's been some tragedy in my family, you know, the kind that happens to everyone given enough time. For starters, we lost Mom five years ago to cancer."

"Oh Gordon, I'm *very* sorry."

"Yeah, thanks." He paused again to draw in a deep breath.

"And there's something else that happened about two and half years ago. Ben, it's something I haven't been able to . . ."

Gordon looked down at his steak. He paused once more, this time steeling himself to continue. When he did, his voice transformed into a steady monotone.

"I haven't talked about it since, not with *anyone*. Elaine thinks I should see a professional. I just figured this was something I could work out on my own."

Gordon paused briefly and then peered directly up at Ben. "I've made some progress, at least I *think* I have. It probably would help, though, if I *did* talk to someone about that night."

He took a sip of his tea. For a moment, the clinking noise of the ice cubes filled the silence. Gordon wet his fingers from the condensation on the glass, chuckled, and then said, "Ben, maybe *you* could be my psychiatrist." After some hesitation, he added, "But *not* now. Tonight is our first evening together in a *long* time. I'm not ready to lay back on the couch and spill my guts yet. I was hoping to process some things while hiking in the mountains. Give me a little time. Hopefully, it'll all get easier to talk about."

Gordon forced a smile. Ben nodded his understanding, and for a moment, there was nothing but the background noise of other diners. Then Gordon finally broke the silence.

"Besides," he added, "I don't want all the talk tonight to be about *me*. It's your turn, buddy. Catch me up on what's been going on in *your* life."

Ben raised his eyebrows and then placed his silverware down on the table as though he was giving his utensils a rest.

"All right. I'd like to hear more about your family situation back home, but for *now*, we'll give it a break. You'll tell me when you're ready." After a pause, Ben added, "As for me, since I've been anticipating this question, I've had plenty of time to think of a response."

Ben took a long swill from his stein and swirled the beer around his mouth before swallowing. Then he inhaled a lungful of air as though he was preparing to see how long he could hold his breath.

"We've known each other since college, right? That's where I'd like to start. You know how we had to undergo a big transition between finishing school and entering the real world?"

Gordon nodded while digging into the steak he'd been ignoring. He began by slicing away the half he'd later take back to the cabin.

"And you know how some people *struggle* with that transition?"

Gordon nodded again while silently savoring the peppery flavor invading his mouth.

"Well, in my case, I never made that transition. I tried, I did. And the part where I went from school to career worked out pretty well, thanks to my dad. But I guess there's still a Peter Pan inside me because when it came to relationships, let's just say I've had some problems. You know what I mean?"

Gordon nodded encouragingly, his mouth too full to respond.

"You may know some of this already, but hear me out. I passed the CPA exam on my first try. Then I got a job with a medium-sized firm where I gained some valuable experience. After a few years, Dad offered to set me up in private practice. He loaned me some startup money, but more important, he sent several wealthy friends my way as clients. Pretty soon, I was running an office with ten other accountants working *for me*, not to mention secretaries, receptionists, and other support staff. There's a *lot* of money in L.A., especially in the film industry, and much of it spills over into the local businesses. And they're *all* looking for good accountants."

"Some of this sounds familiar," Gordon stated between bites of steak. "You told me part of this story ten years ago when we came out to California for your wedding. Remember?"

"Yeah, but what you didn't realize at the time was that I was already starting to grow unhappy. That's because I didn't know it myself, at least not yet. Misery creeps up on you slowly, my friend. It's like a rising tide you don't even notice until you're gasping for air."

"*Really*?" Gordon inquired. "You seemed happy. I expected to see nothing but smiles at a wedding, but you also told me how much you loved running your firm. You kind of rubbed it in my face. You told me that while I had to kiss the asses of principals and school administrators, you got to be your own boss. This ring a bell?"

"It's coming back," Ben replied in a rueful tone. "I was probably a little sloshed at the time, but I was still a pretty big dick, huh?" He looked squarely at Gordon. "I'm sorry. I hope I can make it up to you this summer."

Gordon hesitated and then replied, "No apology necessary. That said, hell *yeah*, you can make it up all you want!" He smiled while shoveling in another piece of steak.

"I know this is no excuse," Ben continued, "but I think acting like a dick was the symptom of a deeper problem. What's the term psychologists use, *rationalization*? When I was bragging to you about how great it was to run my firm, who was I trying to convince?"

Gordon pressed his lips together and nodded again.

"Doing the books of big restaurants and high-end clothing stores and then filing their tax returns every spring—it's quite a cash cow. But money was the *only* benefit. As the days rolled by, I was getting bored. It was the polar opposite of college. Back at Mizzou, the world was our oyster. We had good friends, there were over-the-top parties every weekend, and there was never a shortage of girls to date."

Gordon looked up and grinned. "You know, I never understood how a geek like you got laid so often." He held up his iced tea, and without a pause, Ben robotically raised his beer stein to clink it for a toast.

"And the classes? The accounting and business courses were a bit dull, but at least they were easy. Let's face it, we both could've attended more competitive schools. The workload might've been harder at a place like Wash U., but we could've gotten in, don't you think? At Mizzou, we both pulled decent grades, and we *still* had plenty of free time."

"That's probably true," Gordon exclaimed as he prepared to dive into his buttery baked potato.

"And you know the best part?" Without waiting for a response, Ben continued. "It was coming out here—this town, my folks' cabin, the long hikes, and especially climbing Longs Peak. I mean, let's face it, neither one of us was a serious climber, but when we hiked up that mountain, we did something *extraordinary*. Even now, hardly a day goes by when I don't think about it."

Gordon and Ben smiled at each other in a shared moment of silence. Then they automatically clinked their glasses in another toast.

"Look," Ben added, "I know hundreds of people hike up that mountain every day in the summer, but there are also people who've died trying."

"Yeah, I *know*," Gordon replied. "It was the perfect combination of thrill, adventure, and spectacular scenery. I was thinking about it today in Estes Park. When I was having lunch outside, I just stared up at that great big diamond."

"Well, how do you go from *all that* in college to filing tax returns every spring?"

Gordon silently nodded in understanding. Then he added, almost as an afterthought, "What about Kathy? You two seemed so happy with each other at the wedding."

"I was, man, that wasn't an act. And for a few years, Kathy made my accounting life bearable. But then came the pressure. I guess her clock was ticking. More and more, she kept after me about having kids. I didn't want any. I *never* wanted any!"

"Did you tell Kathy that *before* getting married?" Gordon inquired in a cagier tone.

"No, I guess that was part of my Peter Pan immaturity. I didn't even think about it. I knew she'd probably want children one day, but I never gave it much thought. If pushed, maybe I figured with enough income, you know, if she could be like one of those *Real Housewives of Orange County*, I'd be able to talk her out of kids."

Ben took a break long enough to carve a bite of steak and wash it down with a sip of beer. Then, as Gordon patiently waited, he finally continued.

"The *real* clash," Ben solemnly stated, "came over the use of birth control. She wanted a child so much I didn't trust her to keep taking the pill. So, I started wearing a damn condom. Man, I *hated* those things, but it was better than changing diapers. Then she finally announced she was going 'on strike,' if you know what I mean."

Gordon chuckled with a mouth full of food.

"That's right, no sex until I'd agreed to stop strapping the helmet onto my little friend. That went on for weeks. Finally, I did something I couldn't take back. I guess it made me the *real* asshole in this story. Without telling Kathy, I made an appointment for myself on a Friday afternoon. I had a friend from work pick me up since I couldn't drive home afterward."

"*No!*" Gordon uttered. "You got *snipped?*"

"Yep!" Ben replied, unable to conceal an embarrassed grin. "An hour after I told Kathy, she was packed and gone. She moved back in with her parents. At first, I thought about going after her. I figured she'd over-reacted, and maybe I could calm her down. But I just couldn't find the motivation. Her leaving shoved me in the opposite direction. Does that make sense?"

Gordon shook his head. His bewildered eyes inflated in size.

"I sort of associated Kathy with the whole Southern California lifestyle I'd come to hate. It wasn't her fault. She played her role as the loving wife, but it didn't leave us much in common if you removed all the materialistic bullshit from our lives. And guess what? After she left, I discovered something else. I didn't miss her that much."

"*Oh*," Gordon replied, staring down at his plate. He was at a loss for words.

"Then, with my newfound freedom, I went a little crazy. I was like a teenager getting his first car. I met this young woman online, and we had a brief affair. Lisa was in her mid-twenties and *drop . . . dead . . . gorgeous*! At first, it was nice having great sex practically every night without even thinking about condoms. Of course, there wasn't much to talk about afterward."

"And you were okay with all this?"

Ben grimaced and looked directly at Gordon. "No, man, I wasn't. I felt like a class-A prick." His voice turned solemn like he was entering a confessional. "One morning, when I was a bit hungover, I studied my reflection in the bathroom mirror. I barely recognized the asshole staring back. At lunch that day, I ended things with Lisa. Then I called Kathy and invited her to dinner, where I admitted everything. She wasn't too happy, as you can guess, but by that point, it didn't matter. It was *over*. Looking back, she'd always been the adult in our marriage. I was forever the child."

"And so, what brought you out here to Grand Lake?" Gordon asked, sweeping his hand towards the town.

"The day after I broke up with Lisa, it was clear I'd hit a dead end. I was *seriously* depressed. I drove to work the next morning and temporarily turned the firm's reins over to one of my senior accountants. Technically, I'm on an extended leave of absence, but I'm not sure if I'll *ever* go back. If I didn't, it wouldn't be hard to cash in and sell the firm."

Ben paused to take another bite of steak and then washed it down with a mouthful of beer. When he looked up, Gordon observed the resolute expression on his face.

"Anyhow, I called my parents about the cabin, packed up the car, and drove up here. The first few days were nice, but after a few hikes by myself, I remembered the times you and I had spent in these mountains. That's when I called."

"*Wow*," Gordon exclaimed. He thought back to Elaine's point about hitting a fork in the road. "What about your marriage? You're not divorced *yet*, right? No chance of reconciliation?"

"No, I don't think so. Look, Gordon, there was a time when Kathy and I loved each other, and in some ways, we still do. But I've come to understand we each want different things out of life."

The conversation had hit a profound moment. Gordon knew Ben wasn't his genetic clone. After all, when one college roommate goes into accounting and the other becomes a high school history teacher, there's probably a significant disparity in values. But he also understood the parallels. Ben was easy to talk to, and Gordon knew they still shared many common interests, especially their passion for the Rocky Mountains. He was starting to appreciate that their friendship was coming back to life after all these years.

Gordon looked around. The side of his face still throbbed, at least when he thought about the pain. Otherwise, Gordon felt like this was the promised land. The air was thin and cool, the dark outline of the mountains towered above, and Gordon was having dinner with a friend he'd known more than half his life. It'd been a long time since he'd felt this relaxed.

"So, then Ben, what is it *you* want from life?"

His old college roommate hesitated for a moment. He looked up at the night sky, sharing some of the tranquility.

"That's a *good* question," Ben finally responded. "Sometimes, the first step's the easiest. It's where you get to leave behind the ugly parts of your life, like a snake shedding its skin." After a few seconds, he added, "But then comes the *next* step, and that's *much* harder."

Ben picked up his knife and fork and prepared to attack the other half of his steak. He looked up at Gordon and stated with conviction, "You know, I came up here hoping to figure out what comes next. I'll admit something, though. Each night when I go to bed, I'm scared shitless. Then, when I wake up the next morning, the new day starts with a feeling of exhilaration. You understand?"

Gordon glanced up with a knowing smile. "Yeah, I get it."

The two friends stared off into the inky blackness, neither wanting to disturb the silence.

CHAPTER

12

Gordon's eyes opened slowly, appearing like narrow crescents. He couldn't focus. He reached over to turn off the alarm on his phone, but when he checked the time, it was only a quarter till six. Glancing towards the window, he saw it was still black outside. For a moment, Gordon considered rolling over, cuddling with the second pillow on his queen-sized bed, and drifting back to sleep. Then he remembered the plans he'd made with Ben the night before. The stimulating conversation, the picturesque surroundings, and the thrill of finally reaching his destination had energized Gordon. Now, ten hours later, he couldn't remember why he'd agreed to such an early hour.

After brushing his teeth, Gordon looked up to see his reflection in the bathroom mirror. The square piece of gauze taped over the side of his face was lopsided, creating the appearance of a Picasso painting. He opened the medicine cabinet and found what he was looking for—an entire box of band-aids. After gingerly removing the remaining tape that secured the dangling white square, Gordon opened three band-aids and carefully positioned them over his stitches. The pain had diminished a little overnight, and now the flesh-colored band-aids would make his war wound from three days ago a little less conspicuous.

Ten minutes later, Gordon stumbled through the great room. He was wearing cargo shorts, a T-shirt beneath a yellow Mizzou hoodie, and a red Cardinals baseball cap. Gordon had already put on two layers of socks to prevent blisters but carried his Merrell hiking boots. Ben never heard him enter the kitchen. Gordon observed that his former roommate was preoccupied with a bagel, coffee, and something on his iPad.

"For the *love of God* . . . please remind me why we're up so early . . ."

Ben startled, then looked up from his tablet and smiled. He watched as Gordon shuffled over to the counter, located a mug in the sink, gave it a quick rinse, and then flooded it with coffee.

"Well, good morning to *you,* princess," Ben replied. Putting aside the iPad, he added, "We've got a big day ahead of us. In addition to a fairly long hike, there're some things I'd like to show you this afternoon. I guarantee you'll like these places. Toasted bagel?"

Gordon shook his head. He sat across from Ben and spooned some cream and sugar into his coffee.

"I thought we were just doing a regular hike today. You said something about the Colorado River Trail, right? The one we did years ago?"

"Yeah, that was the plan, but . . . I was thinking. You've already done some longer hikes in the Dakotas, right?"

Gordon nodded as he blew into the coffee, frustrated he could still see a cloud of steam. He was desperately craving caffeine.

"Let's go *further* this time," Ben said, talking with excitement. "There's a lot more to see, not just scenery but other things from the area's past. I've done some homework, and I think as a history teacher, you'll find this interesting."

A fissure opened up on Gordon's granite face, and it wasn't only from the caffeine. His lips parted into a slight grin. It'd been many years, but some things still hadn't changed.

An hour later, Ben pulled his Mercedes into the trailhead parking lot. Gordon jumped out to retrieve his backpack from the trunk and spun around to sling it over his shoulders. Glancing up, he saw two dark eyes staring back, completely frozen. At first, Gordon thought he'd come face-to-face with someone's little dog, but then he remembered where he was. This creature was reddish-orange and white, with a white-tipped tail and black ears and feet. Reaching into the side pocket of his cargo shorts, Gordon effortlessly pulled out his phone, opened the camera app, pointed, and began to shoot. He zoomed in closer and took several more pictures. David and Annie will *love* this little fellow.

"That's a red fox," Ben whispered.

As Gordon turned, the downy animal disappeared like a magician. The two friends gazed at each other in amazement.

"Let's see your pictures."

Ben and Gordon leaned over the tiny screen for a couple of minutes and silently studied the photos. Every few seconds, Gordon swiped the screen from right to left.

"You've got some good ones," Ben finally commented. "But why so *many*? You must've taken fifteen or twenty in less than a minute."

"Well, I was constantly adjusting the zoom and the angle, so each picture should be a little different. I'll delete most of them, but the ones I keep should be pretty good. And with those, I can edit them further by making all kinds of adjustments, especially with their framing."

"I guess that makes sense."

"When I was a kid, my dad used to go through dozens of expensive rolls of film and then pay even more to have the pictures developed. He still only ended up keeping *maybe* ten percent. It's mind-blowing how many things have been changed by the digital revolution."

"You were always the photographer in our excursions, and I don't see any reason to change that now," Ben stated matter-of-factly. "But I'm glad it's gotten *easier* for you."

Gordon glanced over and smiled. "So, where are we headed?"

"Back in college, we only went a mile or two up this trail. Remember? It wasn't scenic, and I was feeling hungover. We gave up on it pretty early."

"Yeah, I recall," Gordon responded. "We caught a few glimpses of the Colorado River, which up here looked more like a little stream. Otherwise, it was just a nice walk in the woods."

"Well, as I said, this time, we'll go further."

They commenced their hike a few minutes later, with Ben taking the lead. Gordon was happy to follow in his wake. He was still half asleep, and the gentle rhythm of their steps on the spongy ground was soothing and hypnotic. After the first mile or so, Gordon was more focused. He compelled himself to think through some of the topics he'd been saving for just this moment.

Gordon organized his thoughts into two separate spheres. First, there was that *one night* two and half years ago. It still weighed on him like an anchor tied to his leg while attempting to tread water. That night still polluted his dreams, still darkened those everyday moments that otherwise should have filled his life with joy. Most important, memories from that night still poisoned his soul. They kept him from being the man he wanted to see staring back in the mirror. Gordon knew he had to exorcise the demons from that night, possibly by fleshing them out with someone, but every time he tried, it was like placing his hand over an open flame.

Ben had asked him about that night, but was he the right person with whom to confide? They had a long history and knew each other well. On the other hand, he hadn't seen much of his old college roommate for ten years, and Ben didn't exactly have a background in psychology. Gordon looked up the trail where Ben jauntily navigated around the roots, rocks, and other impediments lying ahead on the path. Even with the cloudless blue heavens hovering over this rugged landscape, Gordon still wasn't ready to discuss the events of that night.

The subject matter in the second sphere was easier to address. Gordon knew he had a wife and two beautiful kids back in St. Louis. His marriage had unquestionably stumbled into a quagmire, but wasn't that true with many couples? This problem wasn't necessarily insurmountable. Besides, how would a divorce affect David and Annie? They were *his* children too; shouldn't their needs always come first? As a teacher, Gordon could always spot the students from broken homes. He understood that kids were *sometimes* better off living with one parent rather than two who hated each other. But that *wasn't* the case with Elaine. The flame may have recently dimmed, but there was still fire.

Gordon caught a glimpse of the tiny Colorado River, its crystal waters kneading through a maze of boulders and stones. The scene was pastoral, bookended by aspen trees with soft white bark reaching up to silver leaves quaking in the breeze. What if he could see this *every* day? What if Gordon could find a teaching job at a high school up here in the Rockies? This land had permeated his spirit years ago. Out here, he could start over, redefine himself. No one would ever have to know about that night two and half years ago. Besides, if we get only one life to live, and Gordon was nearing the first half of his, shouldn't he make the most out of every remaining day? Just thinking about the freedom that would enable him to hike through these mountains sent a chill up his spine.

Gordon shook his head and smiled to himself. So far, he'd done a decent job defining the essence of both issues. Making decisions and establishing closure would take more time. Multiple forks were lying ahead in the road, and Gordon could only hope that he'd eventually gain the insight to choose the best path.

"Here it is," said Ben as he dropped back to walk beside his friend. Gordon realized they had stepped into a clearing. "This is Lulu City," Ben added, speaking like a tour guide.

Gordon snickered.

"What? What's so funny?"

"City?" Gordon asked, slowly spinning around. "Do you *see* a city?"

"Use your imagination, Gordon. You know—what did you call it?—that sixth sense where you're able to envision a certain place from the past. This was once the site of a thriving city."

"I see," Gordon responded in a more somber tone. "Is this part of your research? All right, tell me what you've learned."

"You'll need to cut me a little slack; after all, I'm not a history teacher, but here's what I learned. From 1879 to 1884, Lulu City had a population of about two hundred people. There was a hotel, a post office, a courthouse, and some timber mills. But mostly, it was a mining town. You know, gold, lead, and *especially* silver. The ore turned out to be low quality, though, so the town only lasted a few years."

Ben walked towards the river, more like a creek than the raging torrent most people imagine. He nodded for Gordon to follow.

"Over here, you can see foundations of some of the town's buildings." Then he added hesitantly, "Look, I know there isn't much to see now, but once upon a time, this place was linked to the town of Grand Lake."

Gordon nodded for him to continue.

"You see, back then, there was a feud raging over which town should be the county seat. It might sound trivial today, but make no mistake, one hundred and forty years ago, they were *dead* serious. It mostly involved the fine folks of Grand Lake versus the upstanding citizens of Sulphur Springs, a town just to the west. In Lulu City, these people sided with the commissioners from Grand Lake. Back then, the people populating the shore of the lake were mostly miners. You know that Grand Lake—the lake itself, I mean—has always been here, right? It's the biggest and deepest natural lake in the state. Anyhow, the *real* fight primarily involved the mining interests of Lulu City allied with Grand Lake on one side versus the ranching interests down by the Springs. You got this?"

Gordon pulled off his red Cardinals cap, wiped his brow, and smiled.

"Oh, and there's *more*," Ben said, sounding like the host of a game show. "You haven't even heard the best part. But . . . that's for later."

"Okay," Gordon replied, feigning a disappointed tone, "then where are we headed next?"

"We just keep going, at least another three miles. That means six miles one-way, more than twelve total. You up for it?"

Gordon put his cap back on, glanced around, and inhaled deeply. "Sure, let's go!" There was some trepidation in his voice.

Over the next two hours, Ben and Gordon gradually climbed in elevation. Dense forests, mostly aspens and pine, still shaded several parts. Then they entered an unvegetated canyon flanked by giant rocks, colorful and jagged.

"This place is *gorgeous*," exclaimed Gordon. "It reminds me of the Grand Canyon of the Yellowstone in Wyoming. You ever been there?"

"Yeah," replied Ben. "Maybe that's why they call this place the Little Yellowstone."

Gordon stopped, threw his hands on his hips to catch his breath, and looked both left and right to probe the scenery. He then pulled out his phone, set the camera to the panoramic mode, and slowly rotated around to take a picture. It was only with some effort that Ben convinced Gordon to leave this canyon. Thirty minutes later, the trail flattened as it left the banks of the infantile river.

"This is La Poudre Pass," stated Ben. "And up ahead is La Poudre Lake. See it?"

"Yeah, it's kind of small. Although, I like how it reflects the surrounding mountains. Is there anything special about *this* place?"

"Well, yes, there is." Ben stepped next to Gordon, and a grin broke out across his face. While staring at the lake, he asked, "You've been to the Grand Canyon in Arizona, right?"

"Years ago. One of the most beautiful spots on earth."

"And looking down, you saw the Colorado River, right? Imagine the power it took for the river to carve out that awesome canyon."

"Okay," Gordon responded. "So, what's your point?"

"Ever wonder where the river officially gets its start?"

"From this little lake?" Gordon asked in an increasingly animated tone. "No *kidding*. I mean, I knew we were hiking the Colorado River Trail, but I never realized it would take us to the source of the river."

"You're *such* a nerd," Ben said, laughing. "I knew a geek like you'd get excited about seeing this spot."

"Say what you want, but this is pretty *damn* cool."

Once again, Gordon yanked out his phone and snapped pictures. In addition to panoramic shots, he took some selfies, including one with his arm flanked around Ben's shoulders. They both flashed spirited grins with the lake and the surrounding mountains offering a stately background.

After a short break for a light lunch consisting of trail mix, jerky, and raisins from their packs, Ben and Gordon began the long trek back to the trailhead. When they finally arrived, Gordon collapsed into the passenger seat, exhausted.

"Well, my friend, one more stop," Ben exclaimed. "But the good news is we can get there mostly by car, and it's on the way back into town."

Gordon's only response was a forced smile. Realizing the throbbing pain had returned to the side of his face, he reached for his pack in the backseat, pulled out a couple of aspirin, and washed them down with the remaining water in his plastic bladder. Ben fiddled with his phone to select music for the ride towards Grand Lake while Gordon leaned back and closed his eyes. Hearing John Denver's "Rocky Mountain High" on the car's stereo put a smile on Gordon's face. It was a little sentimental, but it fit the moment.

The drive down was long enough for a cat nap. Gordon woke as they pulled into a wooded area labeled Grand Lake Cemetery. It didn't look like any boneyard Gordon had ever seen before. More pines than open space, the unique headstones were the only clue it was a cemetery. They were scattered everywhere, and many weren't of the conventional variety. Some of the gravesites even had messages to the departed laid out in a chain of stones.

"This place dates back to the late 1800s," said Ben. "It's owned and operated by the town of Grand Lake, but it's one of the few cemeteries located within the boundaries of a national park."

"Cool!" Gordon replied as he anxiously climbed out of the car.

"All right, now what we're looking for are some of the oldest head-stones. Let's see if we can find names like Day, Weber, Dean, and Mills. They're all supposed to be buried here."

"Who were they?"

"Remember that feud I was telling you about up in Lulu City? Those are the names of the people who died in a bloody battle in Grand Lake on July fourth in 1883. It was an authentic, wild west shootout. Their battle rivals the more famous OK Corral fight down in Tombstone. You know, the one with Wyatt Earp and Doc Holiday? With all the books and movies, Tombstone has become incredibly famous. Somehow though, Grand Lake never became a western legend."

"*Really?*"

Beaming like an eager kid, Gordon raced around, checking each plot. While locating the stones, he completely forgot about his exhaustion from the hike and the pain on his face. The sun was starting to disappear behind the pines as they strolled back towards the car. Once they'd climbed in, Ben reviewed the story's epilogue.

"Without going into detail, since many of the facts are unknown, the guys buried here were appointed commissioners or sheriffs. Man, this *truly* was the wild west. One group ambushed the other, and there were casualties on both sides. No one knows to this day who started the shooting. By the time it ended, though, six men were dead. And this was *all* over the location of the county seat. Of course, the *real* cause was the conflicting interests of the miners in the mountains versus the ranchers in the valley."

"So where did they finally end up putting the county seat?"

As Ben turned his Mercedes towards town, he pointed straight ahead.

"Initially, Grand Lake won, but it was only the seat for a short time. Today, it's Sulphur Springs. The miners finally ended up losing to the ranchers. Many are still ranching to this day while the mines ran out a long time ago. Interestingly, though, neither town ended up as the largest in the county. Today, it's Granby. And Winter Park's probably the most famous. Ultimately, while mining lost out to ranching, ranching has more recently taken a backseat to tourism. Now, what say we stop at the cabin for a shower and then head into that *loser* town of Grand Lake for dinner?"

"You sure about eating out again? We just did that last night, and I've still got leftovers."

A grin spread across Ben's face. "After a twelve-mile hike, I think we've earned it. Don't worry, you can have your leftover steak tomorrow, and we'll stop by the grocery so you can grill us some home-cooked meals later this week."

Gordon took almost an hour to shower off the trail dust and complete his daily FaceTime ritual. Ten minutes after he ended the call, the two friends pulled up next to the curb on Grand Avenue near the town square. Since the showers gave them a second wind, they decided to walk around town before locating a restaurant. They peeked into a sporting goods store, a market, and a few gift shops. Knowing there'd be more opportunities to explore the town over the next few weeks, the purpose of this excursion was simply to reacquaint Gordon with the lay of the land. It'd been years since he'd last roamed these streets, and he observed several changes.

One store magnetically attracted their interest, so they entered to do a little shopping. It was Rocky Mountain Books. Here they parted ways. Gordon turned towards the local history section, robotically drawn like a homing missile. Ben was more interested in best-selling fiction books displayed near the front counter. After browsing longer than he'd realized, Gordon stumbled across a paperback entitled *A Quick History of Grand Lake*. This book would perfectly complement the interests Ben aroused earlier. As he sidled over to make his purchase, Gordon woke from his daze and realized Ben was actively engaged in a conversation with the woman standing behind the counter.

"Hey, Gordon, I'd like you to meet someone," Ben stated with a gleam in his eye. "This is Shannon, the owner of this fine establishment. Shannon, this is Gordon, a good friend and my former college roommate."

"It's nice to meet you, Shannon," Gordon said while extending his hand.

He immediately took note of Shannon's firm grip and inviting smile. She was probably in her late forties or early fifties; it was hard to tell. There still wasn't any gray in her closely cropped gingery hair, but a few crow's feet darted from the outside corners of her brown eyes shielded by rimless glasses. Shannon was on the short side, but her slim, erect posture helped compensate, giving her a sense of confidence and authority. She reminded Gordon of a couple of women who were the rock stars of the English Department back at Beachwood North High.

"Shannon was just telling me," Ben continued, "that she opened this store about ten years ago. Before that, there wasn't a bookstore anywhere within thirty miles of this spot."

"Well, it's a *great* store," Gordon added. "Are you originally from here?"

"No," replied Shannon. "Pueblo. I attended Colorado College years ago and then took a job as a librarian in Englewood, just south of Denver. I also married my college sweetheart. We used to come up here several times a year, especially in the summer."

"So, if you don't mind me asking," Ben said, "what brought you up here *for good?*"

"I came up after Mark, my husband, suddenly died of a heart attack. He'd been a middle school math teacher, so he'd sometimes come up here for the entire summer. I'd join him on the weekends. We both *loved* this town. After he died, I took the life insurance money and opened up Rocky Mountain Books."

Shannon spoke her last words with a mixture of sorrow and pride. She glanced away and hastily wiped the moisture from her eyes. Shannon sucked in her lower lip and then looked down at the white countertop. For a moment, there was nothing but silence. Finally, she peeked up and forced a smile.

"I can't seem to make enough from this store," Shannon said, almost as if she was apologizing. "Summer tourists like you keep my head above water, but by the end of the year, there isn't enough left to earn a living. You probably know Amazon's killing off bookstores across the nation, right? I've been wrestling with this for years, but now it looks like I've lost. I hope to get most of my money back when I put it up for sale."

She paused and tried to force another smile.

"The good news is my old librarian position in Englewood will soon open up, and they'd like me to return. And I'm also planning to keep my cabin on the outskirts of town. That way, I can still come back on weekends."

Gordon and Ben simultaneously raised their eyebrows and turned to face each other. They saw the same look of empathy reflected in each other's faces, almost as if they were gazing into a mirror.

"That's too bad," stated Gordon. "I hope you'll still find some measure of happiness."

"Thanks," responded Shannon. "There's a chance. It'll be nice to have a steady income again, and there'll be less stress. And like I said, I'll return to Grand Lake several times a year." Glancing up directly to face Ben and Gordon, she added, "I didn't mean to burden you guys with so much drama."

Gordon and Ben nodded and smiled.

"Well, I hope you find a buyer," Ben added, scanning around. "It's a *terrific* little place, and I'm sure this town would miss it."

While Gordon stepped up to make his purchase, Ben quietly roamed through the store, seemingly engaged in a conversation with himself. Shortly afterward, they both promised to return again and then made their exit.

"*Man*, that was tough to hear," Ben stated, almost in a whisper.

"You're the accountant, Ben. What do you think? Can an independent bookstore make it up here?"

"That's a *good* question," Ben replied, seemingly lost in thought. After a moment, he added, "It depends on a lot of things. Marketing strategies, websites—it'd be an interesting challenge, though."

Walking downhill to Lake Avenue, they turned to parallel the shoreline and stumbled across a restaurant with the unique name of Cork on the Water. The menu was limited, but the attraction was the location. The two friends secured a table on the outdoor deck where they could have a front-row seat to view the fading sun evaporating behind the regal mountains.

After placing an order for panini sandwiches and elk fries, they sat back and toasted the day, Ben with a cocktail, Gordon with a Diet Coke.

"When did you go on the wagon?" Ben inquired.

Gordon was gazing straight across the table, mesmerized by the reflection of the sky on the water's glassy surface. Violet clouds were a deeper purple on the lake, and the golden hue hovering above the mountains took on a darker shade of orange and red. The jagged peaks provided the perfect frame. Finally, Gordon snapped out of his trance.

"I'm sorry, yes, I'm cutting back on alcohol. An occasional beer, maybe, but that's it. Besides giving me a clearer head, it'll help with my healthier diet."

"*Diet*?" Ben replied. "Clearer head? That's quite a change from our days in college."

"I suppose a lot of things have changed since our days in college."

Gordon considered sharing more, perhaps some of his thoughts from earlier in the day. He decided to hold off. It'd be like trying to discuss the route for a long road trip before he'd consulted a map.

"What about *you*?" Gordon asked. "How have you changed since our days in college?"

Ben slurped down the rest of his cocktail and then hailed the waitress to bring another. "I figure a little more lubrication may be necessary to answer *that* one. Can you drive us back?"

Gordon grinned and then began to chuckle. "Drive a Mercedes? *Hell yeah*. How often do you think poor teachers like me get to tool around in cars like that?"

"Good, 'cause there's something I want to share with you. I got a call last night from Kathy. She told me she's already been out on a couple of *dates*. Can you believe *that*?" After a pause, he added, "Man, she didn't waste *any* time, did she?"

"Oh wow," Gordon replied. "How'd you respond?"

"Like a gentleman. We kept it all perfectly civil, no fighting. When the conversation ended, though, Kathy dropped a little bombshell. She wants a divorce."

"*Huh*! You okay with that?"

"I'm not surprised." Ben's voice took on a tone of resignation. "I know this is textbook hypocrisy, but hearing that she'd gone out with some other guys kind of touched a nerve. But you know what? I can't blame her. After all, I'm the asshole who left. And I know she's still pissed about the, uh . . ."

"Vasectomy?"

"Yeah, right, that thing. Anyhow, Kathy wants to move on with her life. I understand."

"Did you tell her that? Did you tell her that you understand?" Gordon inquired in a tone he often used with his students.

"Yes, I did. You would've been proud of me. Nevertheless, last night's call kept me up late, and it was still bothering me today when we were out hiking."

Ben picked up his glass that was still more than half full and drained it without coming up for air.

"So, did you reach any conclusions today on the trail?" asked Gordon.

"No, not yet," Ben replied. "I mostly focused on convincing myself that our marriage is over. But I think I've known that for a long time. Now I'm wrestling with another issue . . ."

Gordon gave Ben a quizzical look.

"I mean, do I return to my firm in L.A. or do I, *hell*, I don't even know my other options." After some hesitation, Ben added, "That's all right, though. With a little more time, I'll figure it out. I mean, that's why we're *here*, right?"

The two friends clinked their empty glasses.

Taking the conversation in a different direction, Gordon exclaimed, "*Hey*, I've got an idea. As I said earlier, part of my rehabilitation this summer is physical. You know, cutting back on alcohol, losing weight, getting into shape." Gordon didn't even mention his recent decision to give up smoking. "It would help to have a major goal to shoot for."

A smile creased Ben's face. "You want to do Long's Peak again, don't you?"

Gordon nodded and then added, "Don't *you*? The idea hasn't crossed your mind?"

"Weeks ago. But I wanted you to join me first, and I didn't want to push too fast. Frankly, I've been waiting for you to suggest the idea."

"Let's aim for mid-July. That'll give us a few weeks to hike at the higher elevations and get into better shape." Once again, Ben and Gordon clinked their empty glasses.

Later that night, after returning to the cabin, Gordon excused himself to get ready for bed. Even though he was thoroughly exhausted, he decided to check his email.

Dear Gordon,

I've given much thought to the predicament you described in your last email. When you mentioned midlife crisis, you put it in quotation marks as though your situation was somehow different from that of other men. Let's be honest with each other. You probably didn't need the quotation marks.

Shortly before you left, I told you to search high and low to find the man I first married. Gordon, I believe with all my heart he's still out there. You need to wrestle the demons from your past, and now you have to navigate a midlife crisis. No matter what you end up deciding, I pray you'll find peace.

As for me, I'm not going through any crisis. I know exactly what I want. I love teaching, and more importantly, I love our children. I would do ANYTHING for David and Annie. If that means you decide to remain in Colorado, I'll do everything in my power to support a strong connection between you and our kids. Even if you're a thousand miles away, we'll make full use of the internet and jet transportation to be sure you continue to play a vital role in their lives.

That said, I still believe the kids need two full-time parents. Therefore, if I have to, I'll find someone else, remarry, and be sure this man, whoever he is, will be a loving stepdad for David and Annie. Please don't take this as a threat. That's not how it's intended. And believe me, I do NOT currently have my eye on your replacement. It's just that I'm prepared to do what I have to for the welfare of my children.

One other thing. I told you back in St. Louis there was still hope. Gordon, that hasn't changed. I fell in love with you many years ago in college. The person I met at Mizzou is still the man with whom I'd prefer to spend the rest of my life.

I'll look forward to your next round of pictures and, of course, your next FaceTime call with the kids. Stay safe.

Love You,

Elaine

Gordon glanced towards the bedside lamp, the only light source in the room. Polished wood surrounded him. The floor, the ceiling, and the walls' horizontal logs were immaculately varnished, casting ghostly shadows around the room.

Gordon slowly reread Elaine's email. He was dog-tired. The side of his head was pounding, and every muscle in his body was in open rebellion. His day began before sunrise and included the longest hike he'd completed in many years. Nevertheless, he knew falling asleep would be a challenge until he wrote a reply.

Dear Elaine,

I enjoyed the FaceTime call earlier today. Annie liked the fox picture so much it made me think I should exchange the stuffed moose for a red fox if they have one. It sounds like the kids are doing pretty well. That's a testament to you. I know you're stuck in the heat and humidity of St. Louis while I'm off galivanting in the mountains. I'll always be grateful to you for giving me the green light to do this.

Your last email gave me much to consider. All I can say is I've never been so confused. I spent a lot of time this morning on a hike, lost in my thoughts. Mostly, I tried to review the situation and formulate the pros and cons of each option. As for what decision to make, I think that with enough time in Grand Lake, the best path will become clear. I hope you'll continue to be patient.

There is one other little thing I'd like to share tonight before going to sleep. At the end of each day, just after turning off the light, I always whisper something to Annie, David, and you. I know it sounds a little crazy; after all, it's not like you guys can hear me. But I find it comforting, and it helps me fall asleep. Every night, I tell each of you individually that I love you and that I miss you. I wonder what this means?

Love You Too,

Gordon

13

Gordon leaned closer towards the bathroom mirror to inspect his face. The bandages were gone, the stitches had dissolved, and the flushed remnants of a scar were slowly fading. Then he glanced beneath his nose. Gordon had skipped shaving over the past two weeks to save a little time before starting on the morning hikes. Now, it was time to decide.

Stylistically, he liked the rugged stubble and thought it fit nicely with the mountain setting. He'd also never been a fan of shaving and would love to give up this daily chore. On the flip side, the tiny freckles of gray in his beard added years to his age. Then there was the last FaceTime call with the kids when Annie clearly expressed her displeasure with the shadow creeping across Daddy's face. Ten minutes later, Gordon admired his cleanly-shaven reflection.

Next, Gordon dropped the bath towel wrapped around his waist to review the progress made from the neck down. Healthy eating and a total of at least one hundred miles of hiking over the past two weeks combined to create a noticeably leaner physique. Muscle was replacing flab, and his stomach was flattening. His face also looked a little thinner. Gordon was sure he had dropped at least twenty-five or thirty pounds since leaving St. Louis. He now needed a belt to keep his cargo shorts from drooping or sliding off. Gordon and his reflection exchanged glowing smiles.

Later in the afternoon, Gordon and Ben congratulated each other on completing their first hike above thirteen thousand feet. This achievement was a significant step towards reaching their summer goal. Longs Peak was one of the fifty-three mountains in Colorado, rising at least fourteen thousand feet above sea level. Amongst the lower forty-eight states, California comes in a distant second with twelve fourteeners, and Washington has two. Otherwise, except for Alaska, no other state has a fourteener. At 14,505 feet, Mount Whitney in California is the highest mountain in the lower forty-eight, but reaching its pinnacle simply involves a long hike. Conversely, summiting the 14,255-foot Longs Peak involves enough treacherous hand-and-foot scrambling to make it one of the toughest fourteeners in the United States to summit without equipment.

The morning began with Gordon and Ben venturing up three different mountains in the course of one nine-mile hike. The first was Mt. Chapin at twelve and a half thousand feet. From there, they scrambled up Mt. Chiquita at just over thirteen thousand feet, followed by Mt. Ypsilon, rising to a stately thirteen and a half thousand feet. Except for some elk, they didn't see any wildlife at this elevation. The clear vistas above the treeline, however, provided majestic views in every direction. This part of Rocky Mountain National Park always reminded Gordon of the opening scene from his dad's favorite movie, *The Sound of Music*, where the camera slowly zooms in on Julie Andrews, twirling and singing amid the highest peaks of the Austrian Alps.

After cleaning up, Ben and Gordon continued their daily routine by going into town. As they passed the bookstore, they noticed a "for sale" sign in the front window. They simultaneously groaned. For a moment, the two friends loitered at the front entrance trying to decide whether to enter.

"You know," Ben finally stated, "I could use something to read. I'd like to see if Shannon has anything new, maybe something by John Grisham or Stephen King. Did you want to join me?"

Gordon glanced inside and saw Shannon seated behind the counter, going over some paperwork. He felt terrible for her, especially after seeing the sign in the window. Still, the whole situation was a bit of a downer, and Gordon didn't know what to say when he saw her. Also, since he'd been so exhausted after the marathon hikes, there had been little energy to read. As a result, Gordon hadn't even finished the Grand Lake history book yet, and he still had other paperbacks he'd brought from home.

"Nah, I think I'll pass. You go in, and I'll head down to the lake for some ice cream. You can meet me down there afterward."

"*Ice cream?*"

"Yes, ice cream. Why? Are you going to give me crap about a *single* scoop of ice cream? I'm allowing myself one treat a day, and this is it. After today's hike, I think I've earned it."

"*Okay*, okay, I'll back off. Enjoy your *one* scoop. I'll see you down there in about fifteen minutes."

"Sounds good."

Forty-five minutes later, Ben still hadn't arrived. Gordon ordered praline pecan after the goofy teenage girl with the braces laughed at his request for licorice. He ate it under a gazebo near Mountain Paddlers since the daily afternoon showers had materialized out of the west. When the sun broke through the jigsaw puzzle of clouds, Ben finally descended the short hill from town, sporting a smile for no apparent reason.

"What are you grinning about?" Gordon queried. "And where's the book you went in to buy?"

"Oh, *shit*. I got so caught up in conversation, I completely forgot about buying a book. Oh well, there's always tomorrow." After a brief pause, Ben added, "Shannon told me she's going to try to stay open through the end of the summer. If she can find a buyer by then, the store won't have to close."

"I see, but that still doesn't explain your silly grin."

"Am I grinning?" Ben asked with a smirk on his face. "Well, I've been mulling over something lately. I guess I'm not even aware of it, but it must make me pretty happy."

"What were you mulling over?" Gordon inquired. "If it makes you so happy, maybe I could be thinking about it *too*."

"Nah, not yet," Ben countered. "I need to give it more thought before making any decisions. You know, Gordon, you're not the only one who needs time to process things before sharing."

Changing the subject, Gordon nodded towards the shack immediately in front of them.

"I had a thought. How would you feel about renting kayaks this afternoon?"

"I don't know," Ben answered hesitantly. "I'm not crazy about entrusting my life to a small piece of flimsy plastic. And you'll probably be so distracted by the scenery, you won't notice I've capsized and am blowing up bubbles."

"Yeah, but *I will*," said a woman's soft voice, "and I'll be out there in a jiffy to save your tush from drowning." Giggles followed.

Ben and Gordon both looked up and saw the outline of a woman lurking in the shadows of the small brown shack directly in front of them. She stood behind the counter that handles canoe and kayak rentals for Mountain Paddlers. The two friends had conducted their conversation within her domain, oblivious to her presence. Ben and Gordon concurrently stepped up for a better view, squinting to see the source of the voice. As their pupils dilated, the woman inside the shack came into focus.

"Too forward, huh?" she intoned. "I need to work on my filter."

The woman wore a Denver Broncos hat with a wavy blonde ponytail protruding from the back. Her complexion was dark, probably from spending so much time outside, and she was taller than average. Gordon thought she and Ben were about the same height. A couple of wrinkles visible beneath the cap's visor revealed she was possibly a little older than Ben and Gordon. Otherwise, her face was flawless—full lips, dimples in both cheeks, and preternaturally round eyes. The woman was still smiling, revealing a complete set of ivory that could appear in a dental whitening ad.

"So, you guys want to rent kayaks, huh?" she asked, attempting to curtail her laughter.

"*Yes*," Ben answered without hesitation.

Gordon twisted around to look at his friend, shocked by the sudden change of heart. After a moment, she asked, "Do you each want your own kayak?"

"*Yes*," replied Ben before Gordon could utter a word. "But before we do, I just want to clarify something. If I capsize, you'll *really* come out to save my tush?"

Gordon took a step back, recognizing the flirtatious tone in Ben's voice, something he hadn't heard since their college days.

"*Absolutely*. I'll keep an eye on you, I *promise*." As an afterthought, she added, "Of course, you'll probably be stone-cold dead before I can get out there."

Gordon could hear both of them chuckling. A smile broke out across his face as he watched his old roommate spring into action.

"What's your name?" Ben asked.

"Gabby. Officially, it's Gabrielle, but everyone calls me Gabby. You?"

"I'm Ben; it's a pleasure to meet you, Gabby." Almost as an afterthought, he added, "Oh, and this is Gordon. He's an old friend."

"I take it you two aren't from around here. How long will you be in the area?"

"Undetermined," Ben replied. "My folks own a cabin above the town, and I've been staying there for the past few weeks. And Gordon's my old college roommate who's joined me for the summer."

"Sounds like there's more to both of your stories," Gabby said, "But you guys didn't come here to share your stories, right? Maybe another time?"

Ben glanced over his shoulder at Gordon. There was a twinkle in his eyes, one he'd remembered seeing a long time ago at Mizzou. Whenever this happened, it was like Ben became a horse with blinders. He'd focus only on the woman directly in front of him, and everyone else faded into the background. This behavior might offend others, but Gordon found it entertaining. Witnessing these flirtatious exchanges was like watching a rom-com film.

"So, about those kayaks." Gordon finally interrupted.

The spell had temporarily broken. Gordon remembered that Ben knew the rudiments of swimming but was never confident on the water. On the other hand, Gordon knew his friend wanted to make a good impression. He could see Ben was trying to mask his anxiety. Glancing to his right, Gordon saw a solution.

"Hey, Gabby, what about those two-person kayaks at the far end?"

"They're fifteen an hour rather than ten, but since you'll only need one, it'll save you money. You want one of those?"

Ben quietly exhaled and gave Gordon a subtle nod. He reached into his back pocket, but Gordon beat him to the draw and tendered a twenty-dollar bill. Gabby handed back some change, two paddles, and a couple of lifejackets.

"You don't need to wear these, but you have to keep them on board. Now . . ." Gabby paused to glance at her watch. "It's about three-thirty.

We're not too busy thanks to the rain, so if you're in by five, we'll call it an hour."

Gordon and Ben nodded and turned towards the dock. Then Ben spun around and asked, "You'll still be here at five, right?"

Gabby, who'd just tossed a piece of gum in her mouth, smiled at Ben. "I'll be right here. We're open till six."

Over the next hour, Ben and Gordon paddled around the lake's perimeter. Sitting in the rear seat, Gordon took control of the kayak's direction and purposefully kept their route close to shore to reinforce Ben's confidence. Wilderness hugged parts of Grand Lake; homes and cabins bordered the rest. The lake's western side had the prettiest scenery since the mountains hovered in the background. Most of their conversation focused on upcoming hikes and other activities. Neither said anything about their recent exchange with Gabby.

After pulling up next to the dock, Ben jumped out and approached the rental shed. Gordon took his time securing the kayak and then stalled even longer by taking one more look at the lake. With the unique view of the translucent water at the end of the dock, Gordon decided to take some pictures, something he was too nervous to do on the kayak. First, Gordon opened up the panoramic option and carefully swept his phone from left to right, capturing the broad view of the lake and its surrounding peaks. Then he sat down and rolled onto his stomach to catch the sparkles bouncing off the lake's tiny waves. When Gordon finally strode over to drop off his life jacket and paddle, he quickly resumed the spectator's position.

"I've been here three years," Gabby was saying to Ben. "And I opened this business two years ago. There was already a boat rental place on the lake, but it focused mostly on paddle boats. He was doing a hell of a business. I thought he could use some competition."

"I've seen that outfit," Ben replied. "His prices seem a little steep, and if you ask me, paddleboats are just *too* much work. So, you're making a decent profit?" Gordon assumed he was thinking about Shannon's problems at the bookstore.

"I make enough," Gabby replied. "I supplement my income by renting cross-country ski equipment during the winter, and I keep my needs simple. I live in a small cabin just south of Shadow Mountain Lake heated by a wood-burning stove. And I don't spend much on travel. After all, I'm living in *your* vacation spot."

Once again, Gordon observed their conversation with his head oscillating back and forth like a spectator at a tennis match. When there was finally a pause, he jumped in like the kid that rushes out to retrieve the ball.

"Where are you from originally?" Gordon inquired.

"Fort Collins. My dad was a horticulture professor at Colorado State."

"So, what brought you up here?" Ben queried.

Gabby hesitated, skimming back and forth between Gordon and Ben. "Well, that's a *long* story. For now, let's just say I needed a good place to disappear."

Ben looked over at Gordon. "What? Like in a witness protection program?"

"If that's true," Gordon offered, "I'm guessing she probably wouldn't want to share that information with us."

Ben peered over at Gordon like a child about to disobey his parents.

"You know, Gordon and I are starting to get bored with the limited culinary choices in town. We've talked about cooking more, but so far, we haven't done much of that." Ben paused to glance again at Gordon. "So, how would you feel about joining us for a home-cooked meal tonight? We can grill some steaks out on the deck. It should be a nice evening," Ben added, gazing towards the western sky.

Gordon's eyes enlarged while he inhaled a deep breath. Gabby silently took notice.

"Nah, I don't want to impose," she replied. "Besides, you barely know me."

Gordon nodded imperceptibly. Part of him agreed; they had only spent about ten minutes talking to Gabby, and she was essentially a stranger. There was no wedding ring on her finger, but that didn't mean anything. At the very least, someone as charming and spirited as Gabby probably had a boyfriend. Around here, he was possibly the strapping outdoorsy type who guided rafting trips down the Colorado River.

"I know enough." Ben countered. "Look, I realize this invitation came out of left-field, but I think it'd be fun. If you don't join us, I'll have to spend another stimulating evening with Gordon over here, and we're starting to run out of topics for conversation. Come on, Gabby, take a chance. What've you got to lose?" Glancing at Gordon with a wide grin on his face, Ben added, "It's about his only talent, but my buddy Gordon here *really* knows how to grill a steak."

"That's true," added Gordon, subtly nodding to signal his approval of the plan.

"Okay, *okay*, I'm sold! What time and where's your cabin?"

"Seven okay?"

"Sounds good. I'll be there! Can I bring anything?"

"Just yourself."

While Ben wrote out an address on a slip of paper, Gordon tried to catch his breath. It had taken less than fifteen minutes to meet Gabby and then invite her to dinner. He remembered seeing Ben in operation years ago, but this may have broken a record. Still, he found himself smiling. Ben may have been right. He also had a good feeling about Gabby. Gordon might've felt like the odd man out with anyone else, but in this case, he liked their chemistry.

Ben and Gordon stopped at the Rocky Mountain Grocery to pick up steaks, potatoes, and ingredients for a salad on the way out of town. They then motored back to the cabin, cleaned up, and put on sweaters and jeans, anticipating a chilly evening. Gordon noticed a musky smell when he neared Ben in the kitchen. It must be a new cologne. Meanwhile, Gabby closed up at six, raced home for a shower, and managed to make a quick stop at Grand Lake Wine and Spirits for a bottle of pinot noir.

By nine, they had drained the bottle, and the threesome migrated from the table on the deck to the Adirondack chairs positioned around a metal fire pit. Gordon brought in the dirty dishes thinking he'd come back with some beer and a diet soda. Meanwhile, Gabby and Ben started a fire with some of the wood stacked in the corner.

On his return, Gordon noticed that Ben had turned off the exterior lamps, and the only source of light came from the kindling which had started to ignite the larger logs piled up like a teepee. The air was cool and crisp, and the lack of a moon amplified the brilliance of the stars. For a moment, the only sound was the crackle and occasional pop coming out of the fire. Ben and Gabby stared at the fiery ballet, partly out of pride in their creation and partially because the dancing flames had cast a hypnotic spell.

Gabby finally broke the silence. "So, I know a fun little game that's sort of an icebreaker. We each take something from our lives, past or present, and we highlight the best parts of it and the worst." She paused and drew in a deep breath. "Let's start with careers. The best part of my business on the lake is probably a tie between being outside all day surrounded by gorgeous scenery and meeting some *really* nice people." She smiled at that last point, glancing up at Ben and Gordon.

"What's the worst?" Gordon asked. "Or is there a worst?"

"Just the usual stress of running a business, I guess. Okay, Gordon, your turn."

Silence. Teaching was more complicated, or so it seemed to Gordon, so this would require some thought.

"You know this might surprise you, but the best part *isn't* the kids. That's what most teachers say. You know, they love working with *their* students. For me, it's the subject matter. I've developed a passion for history over the years. I'll read *anything* I can get my hands on about the past, and it's still a thrilling challenge to get kids excited about the subject."

"What if your students don't share that passion?" Gabby inquired. "Then what?"

"I suppose that's the *worst* side of my job. You're right. Most of the kids *don't* share my passion. That's the hardest part, trying to ignite some enthusiasm." Gordon gazed at the flames engulfing the log Ben placed on the fire.

"I'll admit," Gordon added, "I've lost some of my mojo lately. It's a lot of work motivating students. You have to find creative ways to engage them in the material, but lately, that's been getting harder and harder."

"Understandable," Ben said. "You've been teaching a long time. Hell, most of the teachers I remember from high school and college burned out years before. It happens to the best."

"I don't know," Gordon uttered, almost under his breath. He imperceptibly shook his head while continuing to fixate on the fire.

"How about you, Ben?" Gabby inquired. "What's the best and worst about being a big-time accountant?"

"The best is easy. It's the money. For years, it's been rolling in. Thanks to my father, we now have dozens of big clients, and *man*, each one is like a firehose when it comes to paying us for managing their wealth."

"And the downside?" asked Gordon.

"Well, there's the obvious. There's a lot of truth to that monotony stereotype attached to accounting. But that's not *my* problem. There's enough contact with clients to keep it interesting most of the time. My problem involves the questionable morality."

"What do you mean?" Gabby asked, somewhat astonished.

"Well, on the surface, it's all about money. I was making lots of it, both for my firm and clients. That often required a degree of brinkmanship, however. By that, I mean how far you can go to avoid paying taxes without stepping beyond the brink of what's legal. Then, there are the actual clients. Oh, the majority are all right, but there's a few I don't respect."

"Why?" asked Gordon and Gabby, giggling a little at their simultaneous response.

"Okay," Ben replied, "let me give you an example. I have a client who owns a chain of restaurants in southern California. The other day, when I was going over some of his expenses, I commented that his labor costs were surprisingly low. I mean, on his books, each restaurant has a manager, a host, a couple of cooks, and just two or three waiters."

"Yeah, so?" Gabby responded.

"Guys, I've seen the square footage of his restaurants. They're *huge*. There's no way he can handle all his customers with that kind of skeletal staff. So, when I inquired about it, he asked if what he said was protected by accountant-client privilege. I thought to myself, all right, *here* we go now. I probably won't want to hear the answer to my question. I told him anything he said was safe. Then he confessed that the rest of his employees—and there are plenty of them—are paid in cash and kept off the books."

"Oh, *wow*, I get it," Gabby responded like a detective solving a crime. "They're undocumented immigrants, aren't they? And he probably pays them well below minimum wage. Am I right?"

"*Yep*. Especially those who bus the tables, wash the dishes, and do all the other grunt work. No doubt, my client saves a fortune. And I don't know what's worse, the fact that he violates the law or the way he exploits some of the most vulnerable people in our society."

"*Huh*," Gordon uttered. "Of course, no one's forcing you to keep him on as a client, right?"

"True, but I also have a responsibility to my employees. If I start cutting clients just because they don't meet my moral standards, the whole firm loses money, not just me. Frankly, I'm not even sure where I'd draw the line between what's acceptable and what isn't. The whole damned business of trying to help others save money is pretty screwed up."

The threesome fell silent for a full minute. A slight breeze fanned the flames that had taken a hypnotic hold on their attention. Each was processing what they'd just shared and heard. Then Gordon observed that Ben's chair had migrated closer to Gabby's. Realizing that maybe it was time to head back into the viewing stands, Gordon leisurely stood up, stretched, and yawned.

"Guys, I think I'll call it a night," he muttered. "I didn't get a chance to FaceTime with the family today, so I should probably send an email to Elaine before going to sleep."

"Elaine?" Gabby inquired.

"Yeah," replied Ben, "Gordon's wife. That's a story for another evening and one best told by Gordon."

Gordon nodded, grabbed his empty can of Diet Coke, and sleepily stepped towards the door. Turning for a moment, he added, "Gabby, it's been a *real* pleasure. I hope we'll be seeing more of you soon." Out of the corner of his eye, Gordon saw Ben gazing at the glowing embers. There was a grin on his face, and he was nodding his head.

Dear Elaine,

Sorry I didn't get a chance to FaceTime with you and the kids today. I promise to be available tomorrow.

Our hike this morning was just under nine miles, but one of the mountains we climbed was well over thirteen thousand feet. Generally, at that elevation, every step involves heavy breathing. It surprisingly wasn't as hard as I'd expected. I've dropped some pounds lately and have been getting into better shape. If this continues, and I believe it will, I may have to buy some new shorts. My belt's the only thing keeping them up for now.

I managed to talk Ben into renting kayaks this afternoon. He wasn't crazy about the idea initially, but then he met the woman who runs the rental business. Ben continued to flirt with her like the only frat guy at a sorority party when we returned the kayaks. It was a little embarrassing but fun to watch. It took him only five minutes to invite Gabby, the woman who rented us the kayaks, to join us for grilled steaks tonight at the cabin.

I have to admit, Elaine, this time, Ben's instincts may have been on target. There's something very appealing about Gabby. I think you'd like her. She's a lovely person—attractive, personable, and most important, genuine. She reminds me of someone else I know.

In case there's any doubt, I'm referring to you. Watching Ben and Gabby tonight brought back some good memories. I hope you don't mind me saying this, but the more I observed them this evening, the more I found myself missing you.

Tell the kids I'm sorry about not calling today, but I'll make it up tomorrow. I'll talk to you then as well.

I love you,

Gordon

CHAPTER
14

Gordon woke early, threw on his hiking clothes, and softly crept into the kitchen to brew a pot of coffee. He softly tip-toed across the wooden floor with the stealth of a cat. Gordon had no idea how late Ben had stayed up with Gabby and was determined not to wake him. While waiting for the coffee to brew, Gordon grabbed a folded blanket from the couch and then inched the sliding glass door open so he could venture out onto the deck. He cast the quilt over his shoulders in anticipation of the morning cold. The smoky odor of the charred wood from last night's fire immediately greeted him. The sun hadn't risen yet, but there was already enough light in the sky to cast an aquamarine glow above the high wispy clouds. The air was crisp, and the only sound was the machine-gun fire of a downy woodpecker hidden somewhere in the pines behind the cabin.

The lake below was a smooth mirror. Delicate clouds, washed in pastel blue, gray, and pink, were part of an hourglass, observed above in the sky and reflected below on the water's surface. The surrounding mountains, blanketed by olive green with patches of snowy white, were also part of the double image. Gordon leaned on the railing to take in the view, enjoying the slight breeze in his face. He closed his eyes and inhaled deeply. For a moment, his mind was clear, empty of the memories and thoughts that had dogged him for as long as he could remember.

When Gordon finally opened his eyes, he froze. About ten yards below and off to the left stood a black bear flanked by two cubs. They were feeding on shrubbery that looked a little like a Christmas tree decorated with tiny red balls. Gordon assumed these were berries. He blindly reached for the phone in his pocket and stealthily pulled it out.

While Gordon opened up the camera app and adjusted the zoom, mama bear glanced around to protect her toddlers. For a moment, Gordon and mama locked eyes. Occupying the higher ground and standing behind the deck's railing gave Gordon a sense of security. He swiftly snapped at least two dozen pictures. Hearing the clicks of the phone's camera drew the interest of the cubs, and for about thirty seconds, the family of bears posed as if they'd paid for a family photo. These pictures would electrify Annie and David.

After a few minutes, the bears wandered off behind an aspen grove, and Gordon retreated inside the cabin. Once again, he froze. This time, he locked eyes with a woman standing next to the coffee pot, wearing nothing but an oversized football jersey. Gordon recognized the jersey. It was white with gold edging around the number ten, and he knew the name Daniel was emblazoned on the back. Gordon remembered how much his former college roommate venerated Chase Daniel, one of the greatest quarterbacks in Mizzou history. Now it was worn by a woman with wild blonde hair and widened eyes. Gordon noted the likeness between the woman's expression and that of the mama bear he had just encountered.

"Hi there."

"*Hello*," replied Gordon, unable to conceal the smile on his face.

"I thought you'd still be asleep," Gabby said. "I didn't startle you, did I?"

"Let's just say it was a pleasant surprise. Help yourself to some coffee. It should be ready by now."

Gabby nodded and reached to pull down the jersey's hem. Gordon suspected she wasn't wearing anything underneath, so he glanced away to reduce her discomfort. Keeping his eyes averted, he walked over to the sink, pulled out two mugs that had been drying since the day before, and placed them on the counter near the coffee pot. Then he shuffled over to the table, hoping Gabby would fill the mugs and bring them over.

"You want anything with your coffee?" Gabby inquired.

"Cream and sugar would be nice, thanks."

There was nothing but silence while Gabby poured and prepared their coffee. Gordon wanted to jumpstart a conversation, but at the moment, he was at a loss for words. After taking a seat, he placed his clasped hands on the table in front of him.

"*So.*"

"So," she replied, and they both giggled.

"Looks like you and Ben hit it off, huh?"

Gabby looked down at her mug, unable to conceal a sheepish grin.

"You could say that." After a brief pause, she added, "Look, Gordon, I don't want to make you uncomfortable, and the last thing I want is to come between friends."

"No, *no*, you're not making me uncomfortable, not at all. And you're certainly not coming between Ben and myself. He's been going through a rough time lately, and if you can make him a little happier, I'm all on board."

"That's sweet of you to say," Gabby replied. "He's told me all about his wife. It sounds like we met each other at the right time. I don't know what'll happen in the future, and I don't care. I just want to take one day at a time, you know? Just enjoy the present. It seems like Ben feels the same way. Frankly, I'm more concerned right now about *you.*"

"Me? Why *me?*"

"Well, I know you guys like to hike every day, and Ben told me you're trying to get in shape to tackle Longs Peak." Gabby paused to take a sip of her coffee. "Ben's already invited me to join you on a hike today, and he hinted there'll probably be more to come. I told him I couldn't go *every* day since I've got a business to run, but I also told him I have a couple of college kids that work part-time for me, and they're both eager for more hours. Ben even offered to cover some of their salaries if it gets me more free time. I don't intend to take his money, but I would like to hike with you guys whenever possible." She paused before adding, "However, *only* if it's all right with you. Gordon, I want you to be honest. I *don't* want to be in the way."

He tilted his head a little as Gabby talked and gazed directly into her eyes. He nodded slowly to signal his understanding. The more she spoke, the more Gordon raised the corners of his mouth into a closed-lip smile. When she finished, he allowed a few seconds to elapse before responding.

"I know this is sudden," Gabby interjected, attempting to fill the silence. "Our little romance blossomed overnight. It's just *crazy*, isn't it? Most people date for months or longer before reaching this stage. What can I say? Ben and I aren't kids anymore. I think we're both feeling the same thing right now and neither one of us wants to press the brakes."

More silence. Gordon continued to smile, enjoying the girlish expression on Gabby's face as she anticipated his response. She looked like a teenager waiting for her parents to give her the okay to attend her first dance. Finally, Gordon broke the tension.

"Gabby, first of all, it's *not* crazy. I think it's *wonderful*. There's no single right way to start up a relationship. You and Ben both happen to be here in Grand Lake at the same time. So, why not take it day-to-day and see where it goes? Second, I don't want to get in *your* way. I want my friend to be happy, and even though it's been less than twenty-four hours . . ."

Gordon paused when he realized he didn't even *know* Gabby yesterday morning. They simultaneously smiled at that notion.

"If you make Ben happy," he continued, "that's all that matters. As for me, under different circumstances, a third wheel might've been a problem. But I think this is different. There may be romantic magic developing between you and Ben, but I also feel like there's a nice friendship brewing between the two of us. As far as I'm concerned, Gabby, you're welcome to join us on *any* hike."

Gabby's face crumpled. Her lips squeezed tightly together into a smile while a tear sprang from one of her eyes.

"*Thank you*, Gordon," she whispered. "Last night was *so* nice."

"Yes, it was," Gordon responded, "but let's make a deal between the two of us, okay? I'll let you know if you ever become a third wheel if you let me know if I get in *your* way. Agreed?"

"*Agreed*," Gabby stated, holding out her hand to seal the deal. As an afterthought, she added, "I kind of like this threesome idea."

Gordon and Gabby broke into laughter upon hearing the unintended sexual innuendo of her last statement.

"The Three Musketeers," came a voice from behind.

Gabby and Gordon turned around to see a gaping smile on Ben's face.

"I hope you don't mind; I was eavesdropping. I *love* what I just heard."

"I don't know about musketeers," Gabby replied. "How about the Three Amigos? I think that fits us better."

Ben walked up wearing nothing but wrinkled cargo shorts. He placed his hands on the back of Gordon and Gabby's necks and then gave each a little squeeze. Gordon noted the twinkle in Ben's eyes.

Four hours later, the Three Amigos scrambled through a boulder field, looking for cairns that would lead them up the final stretch to the summit of Mt. Ida. Although just under thirteen thousand feet, the hike involved trekking five miles each way and a climb of almost twenty-five hundred feet. Gabby was in excellent condition and performed like she'd been hiking with her two friends from the start. She was happy to let Ben or Gordon set the pace and had no difficulty keeping up.

Each hiker carried a knapsack that included plenty of food, water stored in camel packs, and extra clothing should additional layers become necessary. They also wore baseball caps and dark glasses to guard against the blinding sun. Each had slathered a visible layer of sunscreen on their faces, necks, arms, and legs. Ben and Gordon sported leather boots while Gabby wore rugged hiking shoes that provided less support for her ankles but greater flexibility. It occurred to Gordon that this was Gabby's world, and she might be slowing down a bit to accommodate her flatlander friends. If so, she was a good sport.

The threesome threw off their packs at the summit, revealing large sweat stains seeping down their lower backs. Each stretched and looked around to survey the landscape. Gordon took pictures with his phone while the other two unpacked their lunch. There were other hikers off in the distance, but since Mt. Ida's peak was more of an inverted bowl than a pointy bulge, there was plenty of room to spread out.

Everywhere they looked, the scenery was breathtaking. They were well above the tree line in the heart of the Rockies. Around them were huge monoliths, abstract sculptures carved out of gray granite. Vast sheets of the snowpack topped many of the surrounding peaks. A few clouds were forming in the west, but otherwise, the sky was a vibrant shade of blue. They'd seen little wildlife since beginning the hike, but now that they'd stopped for an extended rest, marmots darted out of their rocky fissures. These giant ground squirrels, looking more like beavers without flat tails, were relatively shy, but while sitting with his lunch, Gordon took pictures of several that would later charm his daughter.

"So, Gabby," Ben pronounced as he finished downing his bag of trail mix, "maybe now's a good time to tell us your background story and how you came to live in Grand Lake?"

Gabby had just taken an enormous bite of bison jerky. Sensing the spotlight falling on her, she smiled at the awkwardness of the moment. Gabby used one hand to wipe away a drop of saliva from her lower lip while holding up the other to indicate she needed a moment. Gordon also sensed she was using this time to gather her thoughts. Finally, when she had swallowed the last of the jerky, Gabby shifted over to a more comfortable rock and turned towards Gordon and Ben like a teacher preparing to read a story to a circle of youngsters:

As Gordon discussed with me this morning, we all met for the first time yesterday. *Wow.* I feel like we've known each other much longer. I can't believe I'm about to tell two men I met just twenty-four hours ago a big part of my life story. All right, here goes.

My childhood was normal and relatively happy. Halfway through middle school, though, things changed, and I think it was mostly my fault. I went through a tough adolescence. I'm not sure why; it wasn't like I had a good reason to rebel. Back then, it was like I was a completely different person.

I used to tell myself I was born twenty-five years too late. This fact became even more apparent when I started high school. I was bored out of my mind. It was the early nineties, and I longed for the mid-sixties. Bill Clinton was the new president, and I was secretly harboring a crush on John Kennedy. While my peers listened to R.E.M. and Rage Against the Machine, I was locked in my bedroom playing albums by Bob Dylan, the Doors, and Crosby, Stills, Nash, and Young. My greatest wish was to step into a time machine to attend the "three days of peace and music" at Woodstock. I probably got my fair share of stares when walking through the hallways wearing tie-dye T-shirts every day. I even owned some bell-bottom jeans.

I remember driving my parents crazy. During the last two years of high school, I skipped at least one class a week, experimented with drugs, and had no qualms about losing my virginity. My mom and dad, who to this day are still happily married, were frustrated to no end.

Despite everything, I managed to maintain decent grades, and I stayed out of trouble for the most part. Nevertheless, my parents didn't know what to do with their only child. By the start of my senior year, my dad said he'd pay for me to go to college, but he wanted me to stay nearby under the circumstances. He said on several occasions that if I attended Colorado State and lived at home, he'd buy me a car from the money saved. I saw this for what it was, a bribe, and I figured if I lived in a dorm on a gorgeous campus somewhere far away, a car wouldn't be necessary.

I was thinking Berkeley, you know, on the "Left Coast?" Besides being one of the top schools in the nation, it'd been the epicenter of the counter-cultural movement back in the sixties. In my rebellious frame of mind, it was the *perfect* place. I managed to get accepted, but paying for it would be a different matter. Do you know they triple the tuition for students coming from out-of-state? My dad and I fought over this issue for months. It got ugly. Thanks to an inheritance, he *had* the money. I think it was just a matter of control. He wanted me to stay closer to home, and he was willing to use the money as a weapon in our power struggle.

Thanks to my mom, the ultimate peace-maker, we finally came to a compromise. Boulder was only an hour away, and we agreed that if I attended the University of Colorado, I could live in a dorm and come home when I wanted. As it turned out, CU was a pretty happening place. Boulder was also a genuine hippie town in the sixties, with student protests against the Vietnam War and visits by people like Timothy Leary, Allen Ginsberg, and the Grateful Dead. People told me they even had teach-ins, and there had been a *lot* of student activism.

It also helped that the CU campus is one of the most beautiful in the nation. Its sandstone buildings lie in the shadows of the Flatiron Mountains separating the Rockies from the Great Plains. And the town itself was *great*. We'd have a blast walking up and down Pearl Street on Saturday nights, and during the summer, we'd swim in Boulder Creek, which flowed straight out of the mountains. I quickly learned to *love* Boulder.

I still do, although nowadays, you almost have to be a billionaire to live there. The four years I spent in college turned out to be among the best in my life. I guess that's the way it's supposed to be, right?

Oh, I almost forgot something important. The summer before starting college wasn't so great. I'd had a boyfriend during my senior year of high school, and he proved to be a class-A dickhead. He was an intelligent guy who attended Dartmouth, but he was also incredibly full of himself. I dumped him in May before he could get around to breaking up with me. It came too late, though, because, in June, I found myself pregnant.

I've never had a strong desire to have kids, and when I was eighteen, giving birth to a baby was the furthest thing from my mind. Without hesitation, I sought an abortion. My best friend took me, and I never told my parents or the dickhead. At the time, it didn't seem like a big deal. In some ways, I even wore it like a badge. It meant that I'd done something revolutionary rather than just talking about rebellion or listening to rebellious music.

There were over one million abortions that year in the United States, a number I found on the Internet. Mine was just one of them. Anyhow, I quickly got over it, and by the time I started college, it was already fading into my past. I never dreamed a decision I made without batting an eye at the age of eighteen would come back to haunt me in my mid-thirties.

My rebellious flag was still flying high as I prepared to begin college. Since my dad's whole life revolved around horticulture, he'd always pushed me in the direction of science, you know, biology or chemistry. As one more defiant step, I chose to major in English with a minor in journalism. I planned to get a job as an editor with some left-wing publications and then write in my spare time. I still churn out several poems each year. I even *published* some of them.

At the start of my senior year at CU, I met Peter. He was in his final year of law school, which meant we would be graduating at the same time. I know it's cliché, but it was love at first sight for us. We instantly became a couple and managed to see each other just about every day. Peter had already completed a summer internship with a big firm in Denver, and he had a job waiting for him upon graduation. Meanwhile, I secured an editing position with an environmental magazine near the state capital building. As graduation loomed, everything was falling into place beautifully.

If I had one concern at the time, it involved Peter's career plans. Don't get me wrong, the disease of materialism had already infected me, so I was delighted when he told me about his six-figure salary. But I also knew it came at a price. He'd be working at least sixty billable hours a week at the firm. A young lawyer is like a money magnet at a firm like this. Every additional hour he works brings in several hundred dollars.

Nevertheless, Peter was like my knight in shining armor—always gentle, patient, open-minded. Initially, I insisted on getting my own place near the magazine where I worked. Peter thought it was a waste of money, especially since rent was so high and it wasn't exactly the best neighborhood, but he was patient. When I came down with mono that summer, Peter came over every night, sometimes after working twelve hours in a windowless cubicle, to cook dinner for me.

In September, I finally agreed to move in with him. Peter and I found an adorable apartment just south of Cheesman Park in Denver, only a block or so from the Botanical Gardens. We dove into our careers head-first, which at that time seemed like the natural thing to do. We were happy. Our circle of friends overlapped, and there were plenty of dinners, parties, and other social events.

I'd never lived in Denver before, so initially, the big city was a bit overwhelming with all its hustle and bustle. People were moving to the Front Range from all over the country, so traffic was getting worse every year. It took a few months to make the transition, but I learned to love the city in the end. Only a short drive away were theaters, shops, and delightful restaurants. I never tired of walking up and down the 16th Street Mall, especially on Saturday afternoons or evenings. Also, unlike most other large cities, the mountains were always within sight. In less than an hour, you could come face-to-face with an elk or throw a snowball in the middle of July.

Things got even better two years later when Peter proposed. We were out at a nice restaurant celebrating the anniversary of our first date. Peter slipped an engagement ring into his dessert, a cherry cobbler. When he literally forked it out, he pretended to wonder how it got there. Meanwhile, the room grew silent. I hadn't noticed since I was so distracted by the sparkling solitaire dripping cherry sauce. After Peter cleaned it off with a napkin dipped in his water glass, he got down on one knee and asked me to marry him. Glancing up, I saw we'd become the focal point of the whole room. I suppose it's a good thing I said yes. Once I did, everyone broke out in applause.

We got married the following summer. The ceremony took place on top of Flagstaff Mountain, with stunning views of Boulder down below. We honeymooned in the south of France. After returning to our lives in Denver, nothing changed for a long time. I got a small promotion, and Peter learned he was on the fast track to making partner. He also started coming home before seven o'clock most nights and was around more on the weekends. Since Peter had more time on his hands, he took up running and was soon finishing marathons. He was trimmer and leaner than ever before. He also let his blond hair grow longer and sported a short goatee, which in my view, made him all the more distinguished.

For the next several years, life was good. *Better* than good; it was perfect. As you can probably guess, the only piece missing from the puzzle was a baby. When the subject had come up before, I always deflected it by saying we'd get around to starting a family when the time was right. As we entered our thirties, Peter started to press the issue. He insisted the time was right. Peter grew anxious to start a family and talked more and more about biological clocks. I managed to stall for a couple of years by using my job as an excuse. I didn't want children yet, but I assumed that my maternal instincts would soon kick in.

As we live our lives, everyone has to determine the ideal balance between freedom and responsibility. In my case, I'd always leaned more towards freedom. I guess this was a relic of my rebellious years and why I was so attracted to the sixties. I told myself the world already had enough people and didn't need us to add more to the global burden. Maybe this was a rationalization, but why did I feel the need to rationalize? Peter, of course, didn't see it that way. He twisted the vise more and more.

I don't respond well to pressure. In this case, though, it was threatening our marriage. I deeply loved Peter and didn't want to lose him. If having *one* bambino would save our marriage and preserve what seemed like an idyllic life, I was willing to bend. If nothing else, I was confident my maternal instincts would emerge once the baby was born. By this time, I was already in my thirties, so I understood what Peter meant about the biological clock. One night, when we were out celebrating our tenth anniversary, we agreed to the bargain and went home immediately to start working on expanding our little family.

Over the next several months, we continued with our efforts. Don't get me wrong, trying to get pregnant wasn't exactly a chore. After several months, though, I still wasn't pregnant. Finally, after a more thorough examination, my gynecologist said she saw some scar tissue, probably a remnant of that abortion I had in a previous life. Getting pregnant now would be virtually impossible.

I'll admit that a part of me wasn't disappointed. I'd be able to keep my freedom after all. Another part, though, felt enormously frustrated. Once Peter and I had made up our minds to get pregnant, learning it couldn't happen left me angry. We'd set our minds on achieving a goal, and now a decision I made fifteen years earlier might threaten my marriage. The bottom line was that Peter and I could never biologically make a child together, which was *my* fault.

That afternoon, I did some research. By the time Peter came home, I was ready with a new plan: Adoption. Adopting newborns usually involves a long wait, anywhere between two and seven years for a healthy infant. But if you're willing to take an older child or one with a disability, the wait can be considerably shorter. Remember, I'd already rationalized that a planet struggling to support seven and half billion people didn't need more children. But raising a child trapped in the bureaucratic foster system appealed to my liberal values.

I grilled some salmon for dinner, knowing it was Peter's favorite and opened up an expensive bottle of wine. I wanted to soften the doctor's bad news. I also hoped it would reinforce the sales pitch I'd planned to deliver afterward.

From the start, it was a disaster. Peter adamantly opposed the adoption plan, and his disappointment turned into anger when I told him the truth about the abortion. I probably should've shared that news years earlier, but like I said, to me, it was never a big deal. A stressful argument deteriorated into a shouting match. I witnessed a side of Peter I'd never seen before. I guess there was a hidden conceit lurking beneath the surface, and now it poured out like magma spewing from a dormant volcano.

I told Peter there were plenty of deserving kids who were older or might have special needs, but they still needed loving parents and a good home. He only wanted his own flesh and blood. Unless he had a son or daughter that looked just like him, Peter *wasn't* interested. He said he'd been more than patient for several years, waiting for me to come around. I guess what he craved was a family of Mini-Mes. He also said if he'd known about my abortion from the start, everything might've been different.

Peter always saw everything through a legal lens, and in this case, he believed our contract was void because I'd failed to disclose vital information. I thought he was nuts. The battle raged all evening, and the grilled salmon and wine went untouched. At bedtime, Peter packed a bag and went off to stay with a friend. We'd hit an impasse, and on my side, there was nothing I could do. After all, I couldn't change the past. There was no chance I'd ever give Peter children, and he had *zero* interest in adopting a child.

While he was packing, I scraped away the uneaten food into the trashcan while managing to stay on a reasonably even keel. Once Peter left, though, I raced for the toilet to throw up. Then I took a *long* shower. I spent most of it crying. I must've been in there for at least an hour. When I finally came out, the tips of my fingers were like prunes, the bathroom mirror was all fogged up, and I'd run out of tears. I wiped the mirror with a towel and then stared at my reflection for a long, long time.

I realized that I no longer admired the person staring back. What had happened to my free spirit? Instead of a vibrant smile framed by peace symbol earrings and a rainbow-colored hat, the woman in the mirror looked tired and beaten.

At that point, it hit me that I'd slowly allowed Peter to mold me into the wife *he* wanted. I'd tried to please by agreeing to get pregnant. When that didn't work, I was even willing to adopt a child. But I was doing this primarily to accommodate Peter. I'd miss him if our marriage ended, but a big part of me relished the chance to regain my freedom.

At that moment, I did something I'll never forget, something that radically changed my life. It was like that scene from *Gone with the Wind* where Scarlett O'Hara says, "As God is my witness, I'll never be hungry again." I swore to myself right then and there that I'd resurrect the person I used to be. She was still inside me, and I'd do whatever was necessary to find her again.

We lived separately for several months, but the damage was irreparable. There was no way to win with Peter, and as time passed, I realized I didn't want him back. I liked myself more *without* him. We soon agreed to a divorce, and to his credit, he was generous in the financial settlement. We still stay in touch. Since then, Peter's remarried and is currently expecting his third child. I'm happy for him; I really am.

I hung around Denver for another year or so, but gradually it became clear I needed a change of scenery. I'd always enjoyed my job, but even that grew stale. The following summer, I used some vacation time for a road trip around the state. Places like Aspen, Vail, Breckenridge, and Telluride were all inviting, but they were too expensive and touristy. I liked Grand Junction, but it was too far west. After spending one night in Grand Lake, though, I was hooked. I think it's how the mountains encircle the largest *natural* lake in the state. Whatever it was, I fell in love with this place. It wasn't too far from my family in Fort Collins, and it's only a couple of hours from Boulder and Denver. That said, it was still far enough away for me to make a new start.

I used some of the divorce settlement to pay cash for my cabin, and for the next few months, I lived like a hermit. I read voraciously and wrote a ton of poetry. Knowing this wouldn't pay the bills, though, I took the remainder of my cash the following spring and opened the boat rental business you guys saw on the lake. The income's considerably lower than what I was used to in Denver, but that's okay. It's enough, and I've grown to like the simple life. Most importantly, I've kept that promise I made to myself that night in front of the bathroom mirror.

Gabby cocked her head, tightened her lips into a smile, and imperceptibly shrugged her shoulders. Gordon and Ben looked at each other with raised eyebrows. Without uttering a word, they both silently understood their connection with Gabby.

Later that night, Gordon was in his room preparing for bed. He thought back over the day and smiled. Then he checked the email on his phone to complete the final ritual he reserved for the end of each day.

Dear Gordon,

It sounds like your trip is continuing to go well. I wish I could say the same about the situation here. Annie's been waking up every night with bad dreams. I know this isn't good, but I've allowed her to crawl into bed with me in the middle of the night and her smiling little face greets me when I open my eyes in the morning. She's more adorable than ever throughout the day, but in the middle of the night, she becomes a haunted little soul.

The news with David is also mixed. He made a friend at camp, a nerdy little boy named Pierce. Since Pierce only lives a few blocks away, he's over here watching movies with us or playing chess with David every afternoon. Pierce is tiny and wears thick glasses, but the two boys could be twins in spirit. Unfortunately, they've both become the targets of the summer camp mafia. Who knew there were so many mean kids in the world? It's all verbal, nothing physical, but you know how wrong that saying is about "sticks and stones," right?

Sorry to dump this on you in an email, but there's no way to say it in front of the children. Gordon, this has become a long, hot summer. I even mean that literally. It's gone over a hundred degrees six days in a row, and the humidity is unbearable.

Gordon, I can survive a summer, even a long, insufferably hot summer. But when I have to go back to teaching in the fall, this will be even harder to shoulder alone. Also, I know it's taking a toll on the kids. They need a father. It's nice how you share your feelings for them every night from a thousand miles away, but ultimately, they need you here. I know this sounds like pressure, but that's not how it's intended. The sooner I know your plans, though, the sooner I can figure out how to move on with the remainder of OUR lives.

Write back when you can to let me know your thoughts.

Love,

Elaine

Gordon gazed at his phone for several minutes, not noticing when the screen went black. After rereading Elaine's words, his mind drifted back to Gabby's story. What had she said? "Everyone has to determine the ideal balance between freedom and responsibility." True, Gabby doesn't have to worry about the children she left behind, but then again, Gordon knew several divorced dads who managed to be good fathers even from out of town. So far, coming to Grand Lake had been a summer vacation, but Gordon could envision building a permanent life here, just as Gabby had done.

Gordon pressed the white button at the base of his iPhone and saw it was pushing midnight. Tomorrow would bring another long hike with Ben and Gabby. Gordon shook his head, admitting that the only thing he knew for sure at this late hour was that he was more confused than ever. His email reply to Elaine would have to wait.

CHAPTER

15

One of Gordon's favorite morning rituals was gazing at his reflection in the mirror after stepping out of the shower. Without a scale in the cabin, this was the only way to monitor his weight loss and body changes. Long hikes accompanied by healthy meals swiftly sculpted a new physique. Almost every morning, he noted another enhancement. By now, Gordon guessed he'd dropped at least thirty-five pounds, and most of it was fat. His belly was flatter, and when looking down, he could see parts that had he hadn't seen in years. He noted that his face was thinner, the musculature of his shoulders more pronounced, and his thighs were leaner, enshrouded by skin that clung tightly to muscle. After studying the latest changes in the mirror, Gordon nodded and smiled to himself.

As he dressed, Gordon thought about the upcoming day. Instead of a long hike, he would spend most of the morning in the car. There might be a short hike in the afternoon, possibly up to Emerald Lake on the park's east side, but only if the weather cooperated. The plan then called for the Three Amigos to drive Ben's Mercedes to Estes Park, where they intended to get a couple of rooms at the Ridgeline Hotel.

Spending two nights in Estes Park had been Gabby's idea. Ever since they'd invited her to join their Longs Peak expedition, she'd provided helpful advice to make their mission safer and less demanding. Most people who climbed the massive mountain in a single day commenced their hike around two in the morning. Therefore, Gabby suggested that a comfortable hotel located only a short drive from the trailhead would offer a restful shuteye before beginning their grueling journey. They planned to eat an early dinner and be in bed by nine.

While Gordon gathered the clothing and gear he would need over the next two days, his cell broadcasted the Budweiser theme song. Seeing it was Jim, he answered immediately and turned on the speaker function to continue packing.

"Hey, Buddy!" the voice called over the tiny speaker. "How's it going out there?"

"Hi, Jim," Gordon replied. "Overall, it's going very well. Have you been receiving my texts with the pictures?"

"Yes, they're *wonderful*. Grand Lake looks gorgeous, and you've got a good eye. *Man*, the scenery and wildlife out there are awesome. And by the way . . ." he added almost as an afterthought, "I barely recognize *you* in those pictures. It looks like you've lost some serious weight, huh?"

Gordon smiled but feigned modesty. "It's amazing how many pounds you can shed with a little photoshopping."

"Well, I have to admit, Gordon, I'm pretty envious. I've never been west of Kansas City. I'm going with my folks to their cabin on the Lake of the Ozarks after summer school ends, but I doubt it'll be much cooler there than it's been here all summer." After some hesitation, Jim added, "You know, I was originally so excited to move into administration. It meant more money, and frankly, more prestige. And when I took the position, I knew there'd be greater responsibilities and less freedom. It just seemed like the natural path. But now . . ." Jim's voice trailed off, and for a few seconds, the phone went silent.

"Jim. You still there?"

"Yeah, sorry Gordon, I'm still here. I was just thinking about the reasons why I decided to go into administration."

"Hmm, I suppose that's the big question we all end up asking ourselves."

Gordon knew this wasn't the time to get into such a serious discussion. He purposefully changed the subject. "Otherwise, you're doing okay?"

"Yeah, things are fine," Jim responded. "I've seen a lot more of Amy lately. I don't blame you if you're skeptical, but this time, I think it may be for real. This past weekend, we had the *talk*. As of now, we're officially exclusive. A big step, *huh*?

"Yeah, that's *terrific*. I'll look forward to meeting Amy."

"I'd like you to meet her. I was just wondering . . ."

There was a pause, and once again, Gordon thought he might have lost the connection since the signal in Grand Lake was notoriously unreliable. Finally, Jim resumed asking his question.

"Any idea when you'll be back so we can schedule some time for all of us to go out? Also, do you think it'll be a double date, that is, if you catch my drift?"

"Well, today we're driving over to Estes on the east side of the park so we can get an early start on tomorrow morning's hike up Longs Peak. It's a huge undertaking, so I haven't given much thought to anything beyond tomorrow. I originally intended to be back in St. Louis by the end of July, so I guess that's still the plan."

"You *guess*?" Jim probed. "If you don't mind me asking, Gordon, how are you doing with those other issues?"

"I'm getting there," Gordon responded. "Physically, I'm already in better shape—no more cigarettes and only one or two beers a week. I've cut out most junk food, and I've been taking long hikes every day. I look better, and I *feel* better."

"That's a good start," Jim replied tentatively. "And you're planning on returning, right? I mean, you're not tempted to stay out there, are you?"

Gordon squeezed in another long-sleeve T-shirt, buckled the flap at the top of his backpack, and then slowly eased down onto the edge of his bed. For a moment, he stared at the phone and tried to think of an answer. He knew Jim couldn't see him, but any extended silence would give him away. Gordon had to make a quick decision.

"No, of *course* not. Don't worry, Jim, I'll be back within a couple of weeks. Regardless of what happens with Elaine, there's still David, Annie, and my job."

Gordon turned away from the phone while he spoke. Lying was easier if he didn't have to look directly at the source of Jim's voice.

"That's good," Jim replied. "And what's this about Longs Peak? You did that back in college, right? Didn't you say it was kind of dangerous?"

"It's more of a long hike. Sixteen miles round trip, and there's some climbing. But it's not technical, and you don't need equipment. I wouldn't say it's dangerous. It's more like running a marathon. It's the big goal we set for ourselves this summer, and we just want to see if we can do it again."

More silence. Gordon suspected Jim didn't necessarily believe everything he'd just said. Finally, in a more subdued voice, Jim added, "Okay then, be safe, Gordon, and remember to send more pictures."

"Yeah, sure. Hey, Jim, I should probably get going. We're leaving in a few minutes, and it's almost a half-day drive through the park. *Oh*, I almost forgot. Real quick, any word about my little buddy, Andre? How's he been doing this summer?"

"Andre? As you know, Gordon, that kid is *damn* smart." After a brief pause, Jim added, "Unfortunately, we had to kick him out of summer school."

"What? *Why?*"

"Well, the kid has a temper. He got into a fight last week. I don't think he started it, but you know the policy; there's no wiggle room in summer school. He'll be back in August, but I'd say he's hit a fork in the road. Andre will need a lot of TLC this fall. I heard you had him switched into your AP class. I think that's *great*. You could do a lot of good with that kid."

Gordon glanced up and peered out through his bedroom window. Tiny hummingbirds darted around a plastic feeder dangling from the eave above, but Gordon didn't notice. His mind was hundreds of miles away.

Finally, he responded. "That's a shame; Andre's a good kid. You're right, Jim. There's no limit to how far he can go. I guess that'll get decided this year." After a brief pause, he added, "Well, *brother*, thanks for the call. I'll send you pictures from the top of Longs Peak."

"Sounds good," replied Jim. "And hey, I know what you said a few minutes ago, but remember, if you *did* make any decision that might affect your employment status this fall, be sure to let me know ASAP. I'm sure you know this already, but any violation of the contract you signed last spring could mean no more teaching in the state of Missouri."

"Yeah, I get it. Thanks, Jim. You're a good friend, and I appreciate how you're always looking out for me."

Gordon was baffled by how well his old friend knew him. He immediately pictured the pros and cons list he'd formulated and made a mental note to add "missing Jim" under the cons list for remaining in Colorado.

Ten minutes later, as Gordon carried his pack to the car, the phone dinged in his pocket. He pulled it out and saw it was a text from Elaine.

> Gordon, a little bird just texted me and confirmed something I've been suspecting. Are you going up Longs Peak tomorrow? When you described that trek back in college, it sounded dangerous. Now you're planning to do it again? For now, DON'T answer that question. I don't want to know. Just be sure you call tomorrow night after it's over, okay? I'll be waiting, so DON'T FORGET!

Climbing into the backseat, Gordon had to decide how to respond. One option would be to ignore the text, but that would be wrong. On the other hand, there wouldn't be enough time for a fuller response since he'd lose his signal shortly after climbing into the mountains. Gordon quickly pecked out "I promise to call" and then added a thumbs-up emoji. On an impulse, he also threw in the visual image of a heart. He then tapped the send button.

Four hours later, the Three Amigos arrived at Bear Lake. They were lucky to find a parking place since this was the staging area for several trails blanketing the park's eastern side. Their destination was one of the most iconic spots in the area, Emerald Lake. It was a relatively easy hike, under four miles roundtrip and less than seven hundred feet of climbing. The trek also had the bonus of passing two other lakes, each unique in its appearance. Gordon and Ben had fond memories of this trail from their days in college, and Gabby said she never missed a chance to complete this hike whenever she was in the area.

Twenty minutes after starting, low clouds moved in, and it began to rain. It was only a chilly drizzle, but it was enough to force them to pull out rain ponchos from their packs. A gray mist obscured the higher peaks, and although no one saw lightning, a deep rumble echoed from the lower canyons. At times, Gordon couldn't tell if the growling was thunder or if it came from commercial aircraft flying above the blanket of clouds. Summer afternoon rain fell in the Rockies like clockwork, but the duration was anyone's guess. This was one of the longer showers.

Raindrops bounced off the lily pads on the surface of Nymph Lake, making a steady patter like a drum. When the Three Amigos arrived at Dream Lake, the second stepping stone on their journey, concentric circles on the water's surface formed by the rain concealed the lake trout lurking below. The weather still hadn't improved much when they reached Emerald Lake. The murky sky above had drowned the water's green color, making the lake's name less apropos. Hallett Peak and Flattop Mountain, the two giants that stood guard above the lake, were invisible, hidden above the steely mist.

On the way back down, the drizzle finally subsided. Somewhere between Dream Lake and Nymph Lake, shafts of sunlight broke out between parting clouds, and the Three Amigos stopped to remove their ponchos and wring out their socks. Gordon happily took his time with this chore, hoping that every extra moment on the trail might finally reveal some of the scenery he'd remembered from the past. His reward came a few minutes later. Gordon watched in awe as an electric blue pushed away the stubborn gray in the south, revealing the granite crest of Longs Peak. It was truly magnificent. On one side was a mantle of leaden white snow; on the other, an aperture, like a gap between teeth.

Realizing this was tomorrow's quest, Gordon pulled out his phone and opened the camera app. Since they were several miles away, this spot provided a broader view. If Gordon cnlargcd one of these pictures, he could display it like a trophy. Although Gabby and Ben typically deferred to Gordon when taking pictures, they couldn't pass this opportunity. As the three pointed, zoomed, and shot their photographs, the western edge of the clouds parted to reveal the afternoon sun and a brilliant rainbow. The Three Amigos faced each other, and their smiles turned into laughter. Was this an omen? Vivid colors soon arched from Longs Peak at one end to Hallett Peak at the other.

The remainder of the day was a blur. After checking into the hotel, the threesome shared a pizza and a pitcher of beer at Cousin Pat's Pub and Grill. As planned, they were in their rooms by eight o'clock and in bed by nine. Gordon was unconscious for four dreamless hours and then brusquely woken by the alarm on his phone. It was one o'clock in the morning. The Three Amigos had given themselves an hour to wake up, dress, and drive to the trailhead.

Gordon squeezed in a few extra minutes for coffee. While life slowly flowed through his veins and arteries, he found himself feeling resentful towards the summer weather patterns in the Rocky Mountains. Daily afternoon showers with the potential for deadly lightning meant Longs Peak had to be summited by eleven in the morning. Any later and the hikers above the tree line would become walking lightning rods. Gordon knew that even at two in the morning, trekkers like himself would be crowding the trailhead.

Back in college, Ben and Gordon had taken two days to hike to the summit. This plan meant climbing thousands of feet in elevation with cumbersome bundles on their backs so they could camp overnight just below the Keyhole. It was a tradeoff. Two days were available to complete the sixteen-mile hike, but backpacking and sleeping in claustrophobic tents was the price. Now, seventeen years later, the Three Amigos decided to forgo the backpacking experience and opt instead for one exceptionally long day.

There were no open spaces left in the parking lot by the time they arrived at the trailhead. Therefore, they drove back down the road and took the first available spot. Ben parked his Mercedes about a quartermile from the trailhead, and while this seemed like a trivial distance, it would feel much longer twelve hours later. The Three Amigos silently made their last-minute preparations next to the car's open trunk. They put on hiking boots, slapped suntan lotion on their faces and necks, and carefully positioned battery-powered lamps on their heads. Since this was a moonless night, the headlamps would be the difference between a successful hike for the first four hours and a painful spill caused by a rock or an exposed root on the trail.

Gabby took the lead, Ben followed, and Gordon was happy to bring up the rear. A temperature in the mid-thirties meant each breath clouded the light cast by their headlamps. The Three Amigos each wore cargo slacks they could later transform into shorts by zipping off the lower half. They sported nylon clothing next to their skin to wick away the sweat, topped by waterproof fleece jackets. They also wore warm hats and gloves, although these would disappear as their steady climbing generated more body heat.

About twenty minutes into the hike, Gordon noticed his two partners had temporarily disappeared around a curve. Realizing he'd entered a clearing, Gordon paused, shut off his headlamp, and looked straight up. The sky was a billion effervescent bubbles swirling like Van Gogh's "Starry Night." It was the Fourth of July in every corner of the sky. Jagged shadows of the surrounding mountains framed the expansive canvas. The only sound came from a light breeze whistling through the pine needles.

Two hours later, Gordon noticed they were nearing the tree line. As the shrubbery shrank, the vistas grew. Looking up, Gordon saw dots of light slowly zigzagging up the switchbacks he would soon traverse. Looking back, he could make out more of the same. These were all hikers like himself, wearing or carrying their battery-powered illumination.

It reminded Gordon of *Fantasia*, the old Disney film he watched as a kid. In the *Night on Bald Mountain* segment, the villagers finally return after a terrifying night, bearing torches in a single file. The scene, set to the musical composition by Mussorgsky, shows the slow progression of flames appearing to usher in the approaching dawn. Gordon knew each beam he saw represented one of the dozens who attempted this trudge up Longs Peak every morning in the summer. At this moment, the line of climbers provided an awe-inspiring sight.

The trail turned south at Granite Pass. The sun hadn't risen yet, but a rosy glow came from the east, radiating enough light to bring Mt. Lady Washington into full view. It was a massive monster, one that would have to be overtaken by the wayfarers on their predawn pilgrimage. Beyond this thirteen-thousand-foot behemoth awaited Longs Peak. By now, the Three Amigos had been hiking uphill for almost four hours. They found a flat boulder on which to sit and rest.

As they munched trail mix washed down by water from their camel packs, Gordon, Ben, and Gabby quietly gazed at the expanse in front of them. Breathing was more challenging, not only because of the strenuous climbing but also due to the declining level of oxygen. Even now, they only whispered a few words. The Three Amigos were happy with the steady progress they'd made, but no one shared aloud their anxieties over what was coming next.

Ahead of them lay the Boulder Field. The regular trail was about to end, and from this point on, they would have to scramble for almost a mile over an enormous expanse of rocks and stones, slowly making their way upward. The Keyhole, a giant fissure in the granite wall that formed the northern edge of the mountain, was the target guiding each step. It didn't look notable from a distance, but when Gordon used the zoom on his phone's camera to take its picture, he was shocked by the tiny dots resting at its base. These were people.

Gordon was the first to reach the Keyhole. Looking back, he could see the tents belonging to the backpackers who'd begun their journey the day before. Their occupants would soon be joining them for the final three-hour ascent. Gordon also observed the Agnes Vaille Hut, a beehive-shaped stone shelter named after a woman climber who'd died there back in the 1920s. Gordon found a flat perch to sit and wait. Shortly afterward, Ben and Gabby joined him, one on each side. No one spoke as they struggled to catch their breath.

They needed a rest. The Three Amigos had just completed an arduous climb above thirteen thousand feet through a rock-strewn moonscape. Some of the boulders were larger than semi-trailers. Fifteen minutes of snacking, drinking, and sitting should do the trick.

After emptying a bag of beef jerky, Ben admitted his vision was a little blurry. Gabby and Gordon exchanged looks, but Ben refused when they offered to turn back. Instead, he laid back using his pack as a pillow and closed his eyes. Seeing they still had a few more minutes before continuing the climb, Gordon glanced over at Gabby.

"I meant to ask you something, Gabby. It goes back to your story about why you never had kids."

Gabby smiled, nodded, and looked down while continuing to munch her trail mix.

"Did you and Peter ever consider a surrogate?"

"No," Gabby replied. "We never really got past the initial fight. When Peter blamed me for having the abortion, that pretty much ended the conversation. Looking back, I think that secret is what poisoned our marriage. Anyhow, we never really got around to exploring other options."

Gabby looked up and, after a pause, added, "How about you, Gordon? I know you've got two kids, but you've never said much about them."

Gordon glanced over where Ben was still lying flat on his back, frozen like a statue. His eyes were closed, but Gordon knew he was listening.

"They're great, Gabby. I love them to death. David and Annie aren't perfect, but overall, they're delightful kids." After a brief pause, he added, "But I do have something to confess."

Gordon observed that Ben's eyes had opened, and he was turning to join the conversation. Owning up to a confession always drew attention. Gordon realized it was too late to turn back now, so with some trepidation, he continued.

"I haven't *always* been the best father. When they were babies, I thought something was wrong with me because I didn't gush over them like the fathers of most newborns."

Gabby nodded to indicate Gordon should continue.

"I mean, I did the basics. I changed their poopy diapers, I played with them sometimes, and I occasionally read to them before they'd go to sleep. It just seemed hard to establish a bond. Then last December, I left and moved in with my Dad. Elaine and I aren't divorced, but when it comes to the kids, for the last few months, I've been doing the divorced dad routine."

For a moment, there was nothing but silence. Gabby was a master listener, and she patiently waited for Gordon to collect his thoughts. Finally, Gordon looked up and grimaced.

"Gabby, not a day goes by when I don't think about David and Annie. It may have taken a while, but recently, those two kids have gotten under my skin."

He smiled at the thought and picked up a tiny polished rock between his feet to examine. After tossing it aside, Gordon turned to face Ben.

"That said, I'm still not sure about the future. I think a lot about Elaine too, but at the same time, I'm not looking forward to the drive back to St. Louis. Do you think it's possible to be a good father after a divorce?"

Gabby's eyes enlarged, and she sucked in a deep breath. Then she turned to face Gordon directly and slowly nodded.

"Even from far away?"

This time, she hesitated. "Yes," she finally answered, "but it's harder. It requires a lot of travel and a lot of phone calls. That said," she added in a more hopeful tone, "the kids will probably be better off with a happy father who lives out of town than a miserable one that lives under their roof."

Before Gordon could respond, Ben rose while slinging his pack over his shoulders. Then he glanced down at Gabby and Gordon.

"You know, Gabby, that's a *good* way to frame the issue. But it also raises the obvious question. I mean, this isn't a hypothetical scenario, is it? Gordon, in *your* case, would you be happy enough in Colorado to be a better father to David and Annie than you'd be if you remained in St. Louis?"

Gordon and Gabby rose and secured their packs. All three were speaking with greater ease now and appeared ready to continue the next stage of their climb. Before stepping through the Keyhole, Gordon momentarily froze to address his friends. He felt the need for closure, at least for the time being.

"I agree. Gabby raised an excellent question. At this point, I'm still not sure about the *answer*. Also, even if I wanted to remain here in Colorado, I'd have to find a teaching job, and high school social studies positions don't exactly grow on trees."

Hearing that final point, Gabby and Ben exchanged looks. Behind Gordon's back, Ben shook his head, and Gabby faintly nodded to acknowledge the unspoken message. Then Ben took the lead and advanced through the Keyhole like he was stepping into a mirror.

Immediately, a stiff breeze greeted the Three Amigos. Despite the pale blue sky on the other side, Gordon noticed the gust included tiny snowflakes. Traversing through the Keyhole was like falling into the Rabbit Hole. The western side of the mountain was a different world. For starters, there was no trail, at least not in the conventional sense. Although the mountain's peak was less than a mile away, the remaining distance would turn the hikers into Class 3 rock scramblers, and for most, it would take approximately three hours to reach the summit. The only way to determine the safest route was to spot round painted markers on specific boulders. They looked like targets, yellow balls encircled by red frames. Once they reached the rock with a painted circle, they would locate the next one.

The remainder of the hike included the "Ledges," the "Trough," and the "Narrows." Each involved dangerous, exposed areas with drop-offs of up to two thousand vertical feet. Hikers now needed at least three points of contact with the mountain at all times. They had to negotiate the climb behind dozens of other hikers, some of who would turn back before making it to the top. Over the years, sixty people had died attempting to follow the Keyhole route to the apex of Longs Peak.

Gordon, Ben, and Gabby continued to climb steadily. Except for pointing out the markers, there was no conversation. Talking was almost impossible because breathing was almost impossible. That wasn't the only factor behind their silence. Each step required intense concentration. In the few level spots, they relaxed just long enough to catch their breath or study the route that lay ahead.

Gordon had done this before. He was younger, lighter, and in better shape back then. It also helped that there wasn't a family back in St. Louis dependent upon him seventeen years ago. Nevertheless, he'd made it this far, and in an hour or two, he'd be standing on the flat peak looking down at the rest of the world. One step at a time, one reach at a time. Ignore the drop-offs. Gordon knew he wasn't afraid of heights, but still, there was no point peering over the edges that lurked only a few feet away.

Finally, the Three Amigos reached the base of the Homestretch. At this point, it was only three hundred feet to the top, but it would be a *long* three hundred feet. The Homestretch was a broad expanse of flat granite, angled so steeply it required vertical climbing, hand-and-foot, all the way to the summit. Because of the location of the hand and footholds, it was best to do this diagonally in a single file. One line of climbers sluggishly snaked its way up while another traveled downward, many on their rear ends, like crabs scurrying across a beach.

Gordon once again took the lead. He patiently waited in the queue while other hikers in front crawled upwards, like angels climbing Jacob's

Ladder. With one final surge, Gordon scrambled over a slippery ledge of slate and, for the first time in more than an hour, stood up without holding on to anything with his hands. Seconds later, Gabby and Ben joined him.

For a moment, they pivoted back and forth, smiling at each other in disbelief. Then Gordon bent forward with his hands planted on his thighs, attempting to breathe. Ben turned to Gabby, and they embraced. After pulling apart, he then reached up, cupped her cheeks in his palms, tilted her head for greater access, and planted a kiss on her lips as though they were just pronounced husband and wife. Around them, other hikers swarmed onto the flat summit while another group lined up, waiting to begin their descent.

After catching their breath, the Three Amigos commenced a tour of the crest. Unlike many mountains, the summit of Longs Peak was relatively flat, encompassing several rocky acres. Strolling the outer perimeter, they took photographs, some of the distant horizon and several of each other. They also took the requisite number of selfies, both individual and group. With his gray hair flowing from under his woolen cap, an older man seated nearby volunteered to take their group photo, patiently doing so with all three of their phones. The sky was a clear, cobalt blue, with only a hint of clouds on the western skyline. The wind that had gusted through the Keyhole a few hours earlier had settled down into gentle puffs of air.

In the northwest corner of the summit, the threesome settled onto a rocky bench, unpacked their remaining trail mix and jerky for lunch, and took long swigs from the plastic tubes linked to their camel packs. It was time for a lengthy, well-deserved break. Ben sat on one end of the stone bench and reminisced to Gabby about the Longs Peak climb they'd made back in college. Gordon listened, silently grazing on some granola and staring off into the distance.

In his description, Ben casually mentioned a name that Gordon had developed the habit of avoiding. He'd trained himself to dodge even thinking about this person. In the world of behavioral psychology, this name was the stimulus to a gut-wrenching response. As Ben continued his narrative, the name came up several more times. The more Gordon heard it repeated, the more difficult it was to repress his reaction.

Suddenly, tears started to stream down Gordon's cheeks. He buried his face in his palms and turned away, hoping to regain control and go unnoticed. But, hearing Ben's description about their trek seventeen years earlier had unleashed a torrent of emotion, and just like with a water main break, there was no holding back the deluge. Gabby, sitting in the middle, turned towards Gordon and gently placed a hand on his shoulder. His abrupt transformation mystified her, but for now, all she could think to do was to rub the upper portion of Gordon's back in a circular motion.

Ben was also confused about the cause behind Gordon's breakdown. He stood up, glanced about to see if others had noticed, and then skirted around to confront his friend directly. Ben knelt down and compassionately gripped Gordon's shoulder. Then he slowly placed a hand up behind his friend's neck, gently squeezing in sync with the rhythmic sobs. For a moment, the only sound was the soft whimpering that came from beneath Gordon's folded arms where he'd buried his face. In the distance came laughter from other hikers picnicking on top of the massive summit, oblivious to the scene among the Three Amigos.

Finally, Gabby placed a hand on one of Ben's extended arms, quietly beckoning for information. Seeing the alarm on her face, Ben nodded faintly, indicating he'd break the silence.

"Hey, buddy. You okay?"

Gordon looked up like a turtle peering from his shell, wet lines streaming down his grizzled cheeks. He nodded, indicating he was all right, but his sallow expression said otherwise.

"You were listening to my story about how we came up here seventeen years ago, huh?"

Gordon nodded again, then reburied his face in the cradle of his crossed arms. The bawling resumed, this time with more force. The upper portion of his body quivered in unison with his heavy breathing.

"Was it something I said?"

Ben paused to give Gordon a chance to calm down. He continued rubbing the back of Gordon's sweaty neck. Gabby alternated between massaging Gordon's shoulder and looking over at Ben with a puzzled expression on her face. Gradually, the trembling subsided, and Gordon slowed his breathing. Finally, he looked up. There was still moisture beneath his eyes, but the crying ceased. Gordon used the sleeve of his shirt to wipe beneath his nose, but when this wasn't enough, he smiled awkwardly, held up a finger, and turned away long enough to blow his nose into his armpit.

"I'm sorry," he breathed. "Pretty disgusting, huh?"

"*No*," Ben replied laughing, "not under the circumstances. You okay?"

"Yeah," Gordon replied. "It was the story you were telling, but you had no idea it would upset me."

"I'm sorry, Gordon," Ben whispered the words so quietly Gabby couldn't hear them. "Whatever I said certainly wasn't intended to hurt you."

"I know," Gordon replied. "You couldn't have known. But, uh . . ."

Gordon turned to stare off at the western sky. Seeing the jagged horizon, brilliantly illuminated by the mid-morning sunshine, gave him the fortitude to collect his thoughts. Finally, he wiped his eyes, clenched his jaw, and turned to face Ben.

"Maybe it's time I *finally* talked about Ryan."

CHAPTER

16

Gordon stood up. Without uttering a word, he held up a hand indicating he needed a moment, placed the sunglasses and hat back onto his head, and wandered over to a precipice about twenty feet away. Standing on the edge, Gordon looked down. If he took a step, he imagined several seconds of floating as his body fell through the void and crashed onto the unseen boulders below. The fall would be as exhilarating as the first downhill of a roller coaster. What followed would be ugly to witness, but the experience would be over in a blazing flash. Gordon inched forward. He glanced over his shoulder and saw looks of concern on the faces of his two friends. They still sat on their granite bench, respecting his need for privacy and introspection. Then he turned back and closed his eyes.

Instantly, a parade of images streamed through his brain. Gordon visualized Annie's appreciative face as he placed Big Bird back into her small outreached hands. Then he envisioned David walking by his side, talking about the latest Cardinals' game. Next, Gordon saw his father, the agony on his dad's face reflecting the pain he'd harbored for the last two and a half years. Finally, he saw Elaine. Not the recent image, with the pleading look on her face imploring Gordon to "come home the man she'd married." No, this was the younger Elaine, the coed with the wavy golden hair he'd met in college. She was *so* beautiful.

About halfway through their junior year, Gordon, by luck, had sat next to Elaine at a Mizzou basketball game. Her eyes sparkled every time the Tigers scored, and there was magnetism in her smile. They were in St. Louis because this was the neutral site where Mizzou held its annual "Braggin' Rights" grudge match against the University of Illinois. The

Tigers lost, but it didn't matter. By the end of the game, Gordon and Elaine were more interested in each other than the game's final score. They ditched their friends that night and went to a nearby sports bar to prolong the magic. Later, Gordon drove Elaine back to Columbia, arriving shortly before dawn.

Hardly a day passed after the game when Gordon didn't see Elaine. They were an instant item, and no one was surprised to see her sporting an engagement ring shortly before their college graduation. Both were on a parallel arc aimed at teaching careers in the western suburbs of St. Louis. Everything fell into place as though they followed the steps in a how-to-live-your-life instruction manual. Securing teaching jobs came after their engagement, buying a house followed their wedding, and having children came after the improvements made to their home.

Gordon stepped back. Ultimately, he wasn't any more inclined to leap into the abyss than he'd been to drive through the interstate barrier on the way to school. Something inside might give him a little shove during the darker moments, but sunny memories from the past always rose in time to grab his shoulders and yank him back.

Gordon took off his cap and sunglasses to wipe away the remaining moisture beneath his eyes. Glancing at his reflection in the tinted lens, he couldn't help but grin at the despondent image staring back. His eyes were red and swollen, and sweaty tufts of hair randomly stuck up as though his head had exploded. Gordon quickly patted down his hair and replaced the cap on his head. He kept his sunglasses off, preferring to let them dangle from the collar of his shirt.

Before turning back, Gordon surveyed the rugged landscape. While he fixed his eyes on the sundrenched horizon in northern Colorado, his mind drifted back to a dark evening in St. Louis. Whenever he thought about that night, something always snapped inside his head like the jaws of a trap. It was just too painful. Gordon assumed this was some kind of defense mechanism, a psychological security alarm designed to guard his psyche against the hurt, the guilt, and the despair that would explode if he spent too much time reconstructing the events of that evening. As a result, he never shared anything about that night with Ben, including what happened to his older brother.

Gordon had studied enough psychology back in college to know it wasn't healthy to repress something too deeply into the subconscious. For the last two and a half years, he'd been doing just that, but it was a decision made on a conscious level. His sleep was restless, but blood-curdling dreams had never haunted him at night. He figured with enough time, the memory of that evening would gradually fade the way dark evaporates before the first flicker of dawn. Gordon's recent breakdown, however, indicated this plan hadn't worked. Perhaps he should employ a new approach. It was time to open up about Ryan.

He looked over at Gabby and Ben. They smiled back with expressions of sympathy. This moment was the best time and place to dismantle the barriers fortifying the past. The low clouds in the west indicated they didn't need to be in a rush to begin their hike down the mountain. They could probably spend up to an hour or so talking before it would become necessary to start their descent. Ben had been Gordon's friend for twenty years, and what's more, he'd known Ryan. Gabby was a new comrade, but she was kind and open-hearted, and she might offer a more objective view. Yes, this was the time, the place, and unquestionably the right people.

Gordon slowly walked back to his friends. As he approached, Gabby and Ben slid apart. They turned towards Gordon as he unceremoniously plopped down between them. Gordon drew in a deep breath, scanning to his left and right.

"You guys up to hearing this story?" he asked.

"Yeah," Ben responded. "I've been curious about Ryan, but it's been clear from the start you didn't want to talk about him. Gordon, I've known you long enough to understand when I should avoid a sensitive subject." After a pause, he added, "I just assumed you two had a blowup or something and that you weren't speaking."

Silence.

"Is that it? Am I close?" Ben inquired.

More silence. This time, Ben was determined to wait him out. Finally, Gordon responded.

"No, that's not what happened . . ." Gordon's voice trailed off. Then he added, "Look, Ben, this might be easier if I just start from the beginning. Okay?"

"Sure, Gordon. I'm just happy you're ready to talk. I mean, what's there to lose? We may not be able to offer a magical tonic, but getting this off your chest will probably help, right?"

"Well, let's start with a simple question," Gabby stated. "Who's Ryan?"

Gordon nodded. "Here goes . . ."

Ryan's my older brother, my only sibling. We're about two and a half years apart in age, although he was three years ahead of me in school. When I was younger, I always looked up to him. He could do no wrong. There were times when he blew me off, like when his friends would come over, but he seemed to enjoy the older brother role most of the time. I remember once when we were sitting in the outfield at a Cardinals game, Vince Coleman hit a homerun in our direction. Ryan scrambled beneath the seats and fought off an older kid to get the ball. Then without any hesitation, he handed it to me. He knew Coleman was my favorite Cardinals player mainly because he always stole so many bases. I was about eight years old at the time, and Ryan was eleven. What eleven-year-old gives up a home run ball to his kid brother?

When I started high school, Ryan entered his senior year. Ordinarily, two brothers at that point might become rivals, but in our case, there was enough distance between us to keep that from happening. By this point, I was the better student, but Ryan never seemed to notice. He was always proud of his kid brother. Ryan continued to be my role model, guardian, and mentor throughout my freshman year.

I didn't look up to him literally because I passed him up in height somewhere in the eighth grade. But he didn't care about that either. Maybe that's because, in high school, Ryan was lean and athletic, with blondish hair and boyish charm. He was incredibly popular, too, especially with the girls. Back then, Ryan seemed to have more charisma in his little finger than most people had in their entire bodies.

What's more, despite earning average grades, he was *brilliant*. Ryan knew everything there was to know about baseball statistics. He was a good chess player, and he saw every movie, including the old classics.

Among his friends, most of whom ran cross country or swam on the swimming team with him, he was the leader. When Ryan decided to go to Mizzou, several followed his lead.

Ryan's grades picked up some in his senior year of high school, so he planned to double major in chemistry and biology and use it as a launching pad into medical school when he started college. This plan delighted my father, of course, since he was a high school biology teacher. Both my parents were awe-struck by Ryan's academic turnaround. I remember how much they beamed at his high school graduation. When he left for Mizzou, he was the golden kid, and we all believed he could do no wrong. That's why a stupid, *stupid* decision he made in his junior year of college came as such a shock.

Ryan took an organic chemistry class with a professor known to be one of the bigger assholes on the Mizzou campus. This guy was the sort that liked to brag about all the students he'd fail. He saw himself as an early gatekeeper for those who wanted to become doctors. Only those who mastered his impossibly high standards would be able to move on to medical school.

It didn't help that Ryan couldn't stand the guy, and apparently, the feelings were mutual. They butted heads once after class, and the professor got under his skin. He once joked in front of all the students that someone with Ryan's good looks didn't have the brains to get into medical school. The situation took a toll, and Ryan worried about passing the class. When my brother came home for a weekend visit in early October, he didn't look good.

Ryan told us all about this professor and his class. He confessed it had become a daily struggle. Dad offered to help with the content, but one glance at the hefty textbook scared him off. At that point, Dad told Ryan that he *had* to talk to the professor. Ryan said he didn't feel comfortable asking for his help. Another factor adding to the stress was that there were no significant grades in this class until the midterm exam. As a result, Ryan had no idea how well he was doing.

That whole weekend, Ryan talked about nothing but the upcoming exam. He was visibly obsessed. As we talked over the situation, Ryan came up with the idea of seeking help from some of the seniors who'd already taken the class, thinking one might be able to help. Unfortunately, he approached the *wrong* one.

The midterm had two hundred and fifty questions, and it took a memory like Einstein's to recall all the material. Troy, the senior that Ryan approached, told him the professor gave the same exam each year and that he *had* a copy. There were no smartphones then, but this guy snuck in a small digital camera and managed to take a picture of each page. As it turned out, Troy barely passed the exam, but now he had a copy of it, and for the right price, he'd pass it on to future generations.

The price was five hundred bucks. Out of desperation, Ryan came up with the cash. He dipped into his account, figuring he'd cut some corners later in the semester. A few other students may have also purchased copies of the exam from Troy, but nothing was ever proven. Ryan spent most of his time looking up the answers to each question and then memorizing them. In the end, he "earned" his A.

When Ryan saw the posted grade, he went out with friends that night to celebrate. The following day, the professor publicly acknowledged that Ryan earned the highest marks in the class. I'm guessing it was a bittersweet victory. Still, he felt like the circumstances justified his action. Two days later, his excitement evaporated when he received an email from the Student Conduct Committee describing some vague concerns and requesting his presence at a hearing the following afternoon. Ryan didn't sleep much that night.

When he walked into the hearing the next day, three students from his class passed him in the foyer outside the committee's chambers. According to Ryan, they glared at him, and none spoke. Inside, the wood-paneled room looked like an informal courtroom. There were two long tables arranged in a "T" shape. Some administrators told Ryan to sit at the end of one to face the panel seated alongside the other. The professor sat at one end, and according to Ryan, if looks could kill, he would've been dead the moment he entered the room. At the other end was an empty chair.

After the committee head reviewed the charges, they asked Ryan to respond. Feeling like a cornered animal, he instinctively denied the accusation. The committee then read written summaries submitted by the three students from Ryan's class. Each repeated the same account of what they saw the day before the exam.

As it turned out, on that day, the three were part of a study group who'd been in the library preparing for the same midterm. Ryan had foolishly gone to the library to review his purchased exam copy in a private study carrel. He'd wanted to escape the distractions in his dorm room. As the three were walking out, they happened to notice Ryan, and one peeked over his shoulder. When he realized that Ryan was looking over an old copy of the exam rather than studying class notes or text materials, he called over the other two.

For a few minutes, they watched as Ryan prepared for the exam. Walking out, they fumed over what they'd seen. When Ryan later received the accolades in front of the whole class for earning the highest grade, they decided this was grossly unfair to themselves and all the other students who had worked harder and received a lower mark. The three decided to report the infraction.

After hearing the three statements, Ryan finally owned up to how he'd cheated on the midterm. He never told us much about that part of the hearing, but I suspect he broke down and cried. Then he did something I still question. The professor was determined to know how Ryan acquired his copy of the exam, so the committee offered him a deal. If he'd give up Troy's name as the source of the stolen copy of the exam, he'd receive a lighter penalty. He'd still fail the class, and they would suspend him for the rest of the semester, but he could avoid expulsion. Ryan didn't hesitate. He stood up, apologized for cheating, and then walked out of the room. I guess he thought this was the honorable thing to do, and at the time, he most likely didn't foresee all the long-term consequences. A few hours after exiting the hearing, Ryan packed his belongings and drove home.

From that point on, Ryan was never the same. He told us what happened but struggled with the disgrace. My parents encouraged him to transfer to a different university or enroll at the local junior college. He refused; Ryan was *done* with school. The desire to take his education seriously that began in his final year of high school wholly faded. He got a job at Walmart and then moved into an apartment. For a while, we thought there was a chance he might rise in management, but without a college degree, there were limits.

Even worse, Ryan started to drink. *Heavily.* He'd consumed his fair share of beer at keggers and fraternity parties, but that was mostly on weekends. Now, it became a daily routine. He'd come into work late, and a few times, he didn't make it at all. Ryan lost his job at Walmart. He moved from one place of employment to another as often as the seasons changed. Depending on the employer, Ryan stocked shelves, bussed tables, and did simple construction work. He didn't care too much about the job if he earned enough to pay rent and keep his fridge stocked with beer.

Ryan's physical appearance also reflected his descent. He stopped exercising and put on some weight. He added tobacco and marijuana to his alcohol addiction. Bags gathered beneath his eyes as if he hadn't slept, and these soon became a permanent feature. Ryan's hair was usually unkempt, his clothes were untidy, and his hygiene plunged to the point where I could barely sit next to him. My parents were sick with worry.

On the surface, Ryan still acted like everything was okay. He'd always been close to my mother, so he tried to reduce her anxiety. For example, Ryan would come over Sunday nights, relatively sober, and happily let her cook and serve him dinner. I was off at college by this point, but I heard he'd do his laundry at the house while watching Sunday Night Football. Then he'd take home the leftovers from dinner, which probably was the only decent food he'd eat until the following Sunday.

For a while, Ryan tried to maintain our relationship. Like I said before, he'd been like a god in my eyes until the cheating scandal, and even that did little to impact my feelings. I figured everyone's capable of screwing up, and part of me took a little comfort knowing my big brother wasn't Superman. When I started college, though, everything changed. Granted, it probably didn't help that I chose the university that had expelled him, but like Ryan, I wanted to join my friends at the same school they were attending.

It wasn't like we had a falling out. Ryan just went out of his way to avoid me. As soon as I began college, Ryan shifted his Sunday night routine to Monday night. He claimed there was a conflict of some kind and that football on Monday was just as fun to watch as football on Sunday.

In reality, I don't think he wanted to be around if I came home for a weekend visit. More and more, our paths ceased to cross, and when they did, the talk was superficial. Ryan wouldn't share anything meaningful about his life, and he asked less about mine. He always avoided talking about Mizzou. If I mentioned how things were going at school, he'd change the subject, end our phone conversation, or leave the room.

During my four years of college, Ryan and I drifted further apart. The only exception came one summer, right here in Colorado. It was hard, but I convinced Ryan to drive out and join Ben and me in the Rockies. He came out for a week, and Ben was kind enough to host him at his parent's cabin in Grand Lake. We attempted the Longs Peak climb on his second-to-last day to give Ryan enough time to adjust to the altitude. He lagged behind most of the way, but I'll give him credit—Ryan never complained.

I can't speak for Ben or Ryan, but reaching the top of this mountain was the highlight of my life up to that point. Remember how we felt? We laughed and hugged, and I think my hands were sore from all the high-fiving. Ryan seemed as excited as the two of us. For a little while, it was like we were kids again, and it made me think Ryan had turned a corner. That was a special moment I'll *never* forget. Unfortunately, when I saw him back home a month later, he'd gone right back to his old ways.

It's a remarkable feature of human nature that, given enough time, people seem to adapt to almost anything. For Ryan, leaving a pre-med program and descending into a life of perpetual inebriation and constant job-hopping was a *deep* plunge. Still, he gradually adjusted. Somehow, Ryan managed to meet women, and some turned into relationships that might last a few months. I only met a couple of his girlfriends, and none brought out his better angels, but at least he settled into a manageable life.

Once I graduated from college and married Elaine, we agreed on a peace settlement. Ryan feigned interest in my teaching, he got along well with Elaine, and he attempted to do the respectable uncle thing with David. In return, we'd have him over to the house for barbecues and parties. For a little while, we even established a routine where he'd come over to watch college football on Saturday afternoons, provided Mizzou wasn't playing. As my parents aged, we hosted the Sunday night family dinners, and Ryan joined us most of the time.

By his thirties, it appeared that Ryan had finally grown up. He cut back on the bad habits, and his appearance gradually improved. Jill, his latest girlfriend, was around for a while, and there was even talk about a proposal and marriage. Ryan might never live up to his pre-scandal potential, but at least he'd found some inner peace. In many respects, it was like we'd reversed roles. I was now the older brother, but that was okay. It was just wonderful to *have* a brother again.

Then came the diagnosis. Dad had us over one Saturday afternoon, ostensibly to watch a college football game. Mom was out visiting with a friend. He told us that our mother had been diagnosed with stage IV leukemia. We were both in shock, and there were plenty of tears. The only good thing was that Mom didn't linger long, so she didn't suffer a painful decline. Six months later, we attended her funeral.

As you might guess, it was tough on all of us, particularly Dad. It took about a year for him to bounce back, but he gradually returned to the real world. Life goes on, as they say, and he and I slowly found ways to adjust. Ryan, on the other hand, reverted to his old habits. He was *so* close to Mom, and I guess her loss pushed him in the wrong direction.

The first victim was Jill. I think he dumped her almost like a mercy killing since he didn't want to subject her to what was coming. Then the drinking resumed. One time, I was dropping something off at Ryan's apartment on trash day and happened to get a peek inside his waste can. It was nothing but empty beer and liquor bottles. The merry-go-round with employment also restarted. He might go weeks or even months unemployed. Dad floated him some loans, and I slipped him some cash on more than one occasion. What else could we do?

The months following Mom's death dragged into years. Ryan gradually settled into his familiar, self-destructive lifestyle. Even when he had a job, it was only a matter of time before he'd quit or get fired. Once again, Ryan and I drifted apart. At Thanksgiving dinners and Fourth of July barbecues, I'd sometimes catch him glaring at me resentfully. He stopped taking an interest in Elaine and the kids, and if I brought them up, he'd find a way to change the subject. Once again, we *never* had a big flare-up.

That may happen with other brothers, but in our case, we'd repress our feelings rather than share them aloud.

About three years ago, the situation unexpectedly improved when Ryan met Lisa. We didn't know it at the time, but they'd been bar buddies for years. When their friendship blossomed into a romance, our hopes rose. He introduced us to Lisa at a Sunday night dinner, and we all thought she might be the one to settle him down. She had a talent for making good first impressions. On the surface, Lisa was attractive, with dark hair and even darker eyes. She was also intelligent. Lisa had a degree in finance from Missouri State and held down a regular job.

Unfortunately, we later learned Lisa suffered from a critical opioid addiction. She got hooked on pain medication after a simple appendectomy. That's all it took. Once Ryan moved into her apartment, she shared her pills with him.

We knew there was a problem, but when Dad and I tried to confront Ryan in something like an intervention, he stormed out of the room. Elaine and I then met with Dad to discuss the options. Ryan was still family, so we decided to provide him with the most extensive safety net possible. We also agreed to set some limits. For example, to keep him from being homeless, we'd pay his rent, but only if one of us wrote the check directly to his landlord. We also agreed to buy his groceries, but never by giving him cash since there was no telling where the money would go.

Looking back several years, I still believe the real turning point in Ryan's life was that *stupid* decision to cheat on a college exam. Up until then, he was happy and headed in the right direction. That moment when he exercised horrible judgment haunted him for the rest of his life. Ryan never really recovered from that hearing. For him, the next twenty years were a series of up and down climbs. There were some peaks, but there were also some deep valleys. Shortly after meeting her, Lisa dragged Ryan into his deepest canyon yet.

It was right before the holidays, and David's class was preparing to present a play they'd written for their parents. David only had a minor role, but he helped write most of the script. He was *so* proud. It would mean the world to him if everyone in the family came to see his little play in the school gymnasium. I tried to explain this to Ryan, so maybe he and Lisa would attend. Just because the distance between brothers had grown didn't mean Uncle Ryan had to turn away from his nephew. David was sweet and forgiving by nature. He didn't know about Ryan's problems. He just wanted his uncle to see his play.

They scheduled the production to begin at half-past seven in the evening. All afternoon, David fretted over the weather. As it turned out, the temperature remained high enough to keep the misty rain from turning into ice or snow. Dad met us in the hallway outside the gymnasium, but there was no sign of Ryan. We didn't know it, but apparently, other classes were also putting on plays, and the schedule called for David's to go last. I guess they did this to build up the size of the audience. This schedule seemed like good news at the time since it meant that even if he was running late, Uncle Ryan might still catch David's play.

About an hour after the plays began, they took a little break. When my cell phone vibrated, I stepped outside to take the call. I still remember this conversation like it was yesterday. The rain had stopped, but the blacktop outside the school gym was saturated. A foggy mist floated out of my mouth every time I exhaled. Inside, bright lights and boisterous noises flooded through the narrow space where a trash can served as a doorstop. On the other side of the basketball court, a couple of dads braved the damp cold for a quick smoke.

Somehow, even before looking at my phone, I knew Ryan was the caller. From the sound of his voice, I'd guess he and Lisa had already popped a few pills before heading to a bar somewhere in Valley Park. He seemed flustered when I asked if he was coming to David's play. For a moment, I only heard country music playing in the background, along with some laughter and distant conversation. Finally, Ryan replied.

"Gordon, I'm *sorry* about the play. I'm not going to lie. I completely forgot about it. My mind just isn't what it used to be. Please apologize to the little dude, all right?"

"So," I responded, "If you forgot about the play, why'd you call?"

Once again, Ryan hesitated to respond. I could hear what sounded like whispering. I think his hand partially covered the phone while he spoke to Lisa. I was still holding out hope they'd try to make it to David's play.

"Look, Gordon," he finally mumbled, "I was calling to ask a favor. I forgot you'd be at the play."

Once again, Ryan was silent. More music, more bar noise.

"Yeah? So, what's the favor?"

I started to get irritated, especially after he mentioned needing a favor. Lately, the only time I ever heard from Ryan was when he needed a favor. I had my phone set up so his picture popped up whenever he called. Like Pavlov's dog, I'd become negatively conditioned to groan whenever that picture appeared on my phone's screen. Finally, after more indecipherable whispering, Ryan came back on the phone.

"Well, Gordon, to be honest, Lisa and I are pretty wasted. We shouldn't be driving. I'm not looking for an award or anything. I just figured you'd rather me call for a ride rather than get behind the wheel."

I was ready to go ballistic. Instead, I covered my mouth so words wouldn't come out that I would later regret. I spun around and peeked inside the gym. Looking through the crowd, I saw Elaine waving to me. The play was about to begin, and she wanted me to return to my seat. David was standing next to her with a look on his face like he'd just seen his first horror movie.

"Gordon? *Gordon?* You still there?"

"Yeah, Ryan, I'm still here. Look, why don't you two stay put for a little while? I can probably be there in an hour, two at the most."

I knew he'd say no. Over the last few years, he'd lost any semblance of patience. When Ryan was ready to go, he definitely wouldn't hang around. I was stalling, trying to think of a better solution.

"No, I don't think so. *Hey, man,* don't worry about it. We'll be okay. Lisa's in pretty bad shape, but I'm all right." After a pause, Ryan added, "We'll be *fine.*"

"*Oh,* I know what you can do," I responded eagerly. "The last time this happened, I put the Uber app on your phone, remember?"

"Yeah, but I've never used it. I don't think I even know how. Besides, I don't have the money to pay for Uber." He stretched out the first syllable of Uber to accentuate the "U."

"Well, buddy, maybe this is a good time to learn. Just touch the app and type in the address where you want to go. Uber will already know where you are, and it will even tell you how long it'll take for your ride to show up. I'm sure it won't be more than a few minutes. Also, I used my credit card account when I signed you up, so you don't need to worry about the money."

Silence. I looked inside again, and the crowd had cleared. Elaine and David were still there, but everyone else had returned to their seats. I could see Elaine's face. She was staring in my direction with widening eyes, beckoning me to come back inside. After a few seconds, she glanced down at David, gave him a little nudge, and together, they walked back into the gym.

"*Look,* Gordon, no offense, man, but it's just a little grade school play. There'll be plenty of others. Besides, if you come to pick us up now, we can all party together." At that point, I heard laughter in the background.

"*Look,* Ryan, no offense, *man*, but I don't want to leave David's play." After a pause, I added, "It may not mean much to you, but it's important to him. I need to get going. Ryan, *take the damn Uber.*"

Then I hung up. That was it. Those were the last words I ever said to my brother. I made it back to my open spot in the bleachers just before David's play began. Thirty minutes later, it was over, and the family rejoiced as though we'd just seen the premiere of *Hamilton.* I have to admit it was a pretty entertaining play.

An hour later, while we celebrated with ice cream at Oberweis Dairy, Dad's cell phone rang. I'll never forget the look on his face about thirty seconds into that call. Dad's smile, which had been there since the end of the play, suddenly shattered into a hundred pieces like a delicate piece of porcelain hitting the floor. It was the state police.

Ryan never called Uber. Instead, he'd decided to drive. We're not sure where he and Lisa were going, but it certainly wasn't home. They were on I-64, and when they took the exit north onto 270, they crashed right through the barrier and fell at least thirty feet into a parking lot.

Since Dad had registered the car in his name, the police could trace the license plate back to him. Where were they going? I've given this a *lot* of thought. There's no way to say for sure, but I think they were headed to the school to catch the end of David's play.

That's it, that's the whole story. After the funerals, Dad became a recluse. I certainly don't blame him, but he was hardly around when I needed him badly. Gradually, after about a year, Dad returned to the light of day. He kept saying there'd been so much agony in Ryan's life that maybe the accident was God's way to grant him relief. He also liked to say that Ryan died quickly, so there was no pain. Dad managed to talk his way into dealing with two major tragedies. In both cases, however, he never had to wrestle with any guilt.

I never told Dad or Elaine about the phone conversation with Ryan that night shortly before the accident. Today is the first time I've shared this with *anyone*. That evening has haunted me for the last two and a half years. Not a day goes by when I don't think about that phone call. I keep remembering how I hung up on my brother. I'd give anything if I could go back in time, miss that one little grade school play, and have Ryan with us right now. That one night poisoned everything in my life.

Gordon inhaled a deep breath. Throughout the story, he kept waiting for an implosion, but tears never came. He slowly turned left and then glanced right, looking at the matching expressions on Gabby's and Ben's faces. The corners of his mouth turned up, and then his head went down. For a little while, he studied the dust caked on his hiking boots. Together, they sat motionless and silent, like three statues. Finally, Gordon felt a tender hand on his left shoulder. Then another on his right. Slowly and without uttering a word, the Three Amigos stood up and moved into a human knot.

The weeping slowly began. It started like the trickle of a small stream fed by the snowmelt near the top of a mountain. It was Gabby who softly sniffled first. The stream grew into a small river as Ben accompanied her with a few muffled sobs of his own. Gordon turned the river into a deluge. Hearing and feeling the response of his two friends toppled the levee. Gordon lurched and heaved and wailed. This wasn't normal crying; this was the catharsis that only comes when a demon is exorcised.

CHAPTER

17

It was a bizarre experience. The Three Amigos were on the summit of a magnificent mountain standing in line behind a dozen other people as though they were waiting to pay for groceries. There was only one safe way down, and a traffic jam currently tied up the route on the Homestretch. From a distance, it looked like a line of ants crawling down a large rock. The only option available now was patience.

Since Gordon was still regaining his composure, he purposefully positioned himself at the end of the queue. This spot enabled him to blow his nose and relax his breathing without attracting attention. There was nervous chatter ahead among those about to step over the ledge; otherwise, the only sound came from the gentle breeze blowing below.

Gordon glanced up and over his shoulder. While he saw thin strands of cirrus clouds painted in the sky above, heavier gray smudges gathered in the west. For now, they were still primarily anchored to the far horizon. Based on his previous experience in the Rockies, Gordon knew there should still be enough time to get below the taller trees before the storms arrived. In all likelihood, he'd be wearing a poncho on the final stretch of the hike.

As he stepped toward the threshold, Gordon gulped in a mouthful of air. Despite the elevation, he found it easier to breathe. It felt like his lungs had grown more elastic, capable of expanding beyond normal limits to take in additional oxygen. Gordon wondered if this was a physiological response to his recent outburst or more psychological, the sense that he no longer carried an emotional burden on his shoulders. Either way, it felt *good*.

While Ben swung a leg down like he was stepping onto an attic ladder, Gordon glanced back to examine the top of the peak one last time. He was alone. Seven and a half billion people on the planet, and at this moment, Gordon was the only one who occupied the top of this eminent mountain. In all likelihood, he'd never be back. He wiped the moisture from beneath his nose and smiled. Gordon had spent a relatively brief period on these few acres twice in his life. It had become sacred ground. Ryan had been with him the first time, and on the second, he still felt his brother's presence.

What had taken three hours coming up from the Keyhole took only half that amount of time going down. Still, it was hardly a relaxing experience. Every step was carefully measured so as not to fall. Scooting down the Homestretch on their backsides proved more manageable than it looked coming up. It was like using your hands, feet, and rear end to scamper down backward on a playground slide. In this case, though, the drop was fourteen thousand feet above sea level.

From the apex of the mountain to the Keyhole, the Three Amigos didn't say a word. Their descent required intense concentration. In addition, the absence of a trail meant they couldn't hike side-by-side. This stretch allowed Gordon to mentally process what had happened on top of the mountain. His first thought was a total sense of embarrassment. How many people witnessed his breakdown? Then he remembered the questions he always asked when trying to quell the humiliation of others. Will you ever see these people again? Why should you care what they think?

Next, Gordon felt a surge of pride. For two and half years, he carried a heavy load. Many knew about his brother's tragic accident, but *no one* was aware of the phone call that had taken place between Gordon and Ryan only an hour before. Gordon knew the next step towards his salvation would be sharing this information with Elaine and Dad. This morning's mountaintop confession would make this easier.

When she asked about the call, Gordon told Elaine it was from a distraught parent, *not* Ryan. He thought he was shielding his brother from adding more weight to his wife's resentment. From that night on, Gordon entombed the memory of his brother's phone call. He didn't even want to think about his final conversation with Ryan. Its memory was lodged deep inside his mind, like a town covered by an avalanche. At times, even Gordon questioned whether or not it had taken place.

Within sight of the Keyhole, Gordon's thought process hit a logjam. *Guilt.* Explaining to others how he'd responded to Ryan's call was not the same as receiving absolution. Wasn't that the impediment for most people dealing with sins from the past? Whenever someone commits an action that harms another, intentional or not, how do they get past the feelings of responsibility? It may not be a problem for a sociopath, but assuming one has a conscience, there's no trail map to steer a person around guilt. What's more, this emotion is toxic. It slowly poisons the soul.

Gordon could confess about hanging up the phone on his brother that night to everyone he knew. Hell, he could scream it from a mountaintop. But as every good Catholic knows, confessing sin to a priest is only the *first* step. Next comes penance, an action that will absolve sinners of their sin, clearing the way for absolution and, eventually, salvation. But what could Gordon do? There were no good works that would bring his brother back to life.

Gordon's thoughts were interrupted when the Three Amigos stopped once again at the Keyhole for another break. As they munched down the last of the trail mix and jerky, they mostly talked about how they wanted to celebrate later that night. There was an unspoken agreement to avoid what took place earlier on top of the mountain.

Once they had scrambled through the Boulder Field and relocated a visible trail, Gordon quietly breathed a sigh of relief. By this point, every step became painful. Most people who hike the mountains know downhill can be just as challenging as going up. The heart and lungs get a break, but the knees and lower back take a beating. With every step on a steep decline, ligaments and tendons act as shock absorbers, cushioning the body's weight. After a while, the strain on this soft tissue sends emergency signals to the brain. Gordon experienced the pain on earlier downhill hikes, and he knew it would pass in a day or two. At this moment, though, they still had several miles of downhill left to go.

During this stretch, Gordon purposefully hung back. He could tell from their animated hand gestures that Ben and Gabby were engaged in earnest conversation, and he wanted to respect their privacy. Even though the trail was still narrow in places, Ben and Gabby managed to squeeze in together and walk side-by-side. For a moment, Gordon speculated on what they were discussing. Ben was also wrestling with some significant issues about the future. What role, if any, would Gabby play?

Up ahead, Gordon saw the first miniature trees, weather-beaten by brutal Rocky Mountain blizzards. At this higher elevation, especially on the dry, exposed slopes, the white pines were the only vegetation capable of survival. Most were only two or three feet tall despite their advanced age since the growing season was short. Many had branches extending only to the east since the icy gales usually blew from the west. As Gordon passed these saplings, many looking like discarded Christmas trees, he heard the low rumble of thunder.

Up ahead, they could see a spruce-fir forest. Without saying a word, the Three Amigos accelerated their pace, appreciating the need to reach the shelter of the more towering trees. It poured just as the olive-colored branches embraced them. Without stopping, they pulled off their packs, yanked out their ponchos, and whipped the waterproof wraps over their heads. Gabby took the lead and set a swifter pace from this point on. For the next twenty minutes, a chilly shower bathed the Three Amigos. Ordinarily, Gordon might have been annoyed, but now the water was rejuvenating, almost baptismal.

As heavy droplets devolved into a more delicate mist, Ben dropped back from Gabby and pulled up next to Gordon. Beneath the hood of his poncho, Gordon could see Ben's furrowed brow. There was something on his mind.

"Hey, I wanted to talk a little more about what you shared up on the mountain. Is that okay?" Ben asked hesitantly.

"Sure," Gordon replied. "What's on your mind?"

"Well, first, I wanted to pass on my condolences about Ryan. I *never* knew he'd passed away. I'm still in shock. Had I known, you would've heard from me a long time ago."

"That's all right," replied Gordon. "How could you have known? It's not like I told you."

"Yeah, but if I had done more over the past few years to maintain our friendship, you would've told me."

"I *don't* accept that, Ben. We were busy living our lives two thousand miles away from each other. We'd drifted apart. That happens, and it was as much my fault as it was yours. Besides," Gordon added after a brief pause, "you're the one who reached out to *me*. If you hadn't called last month, we wouldn't be having this conversation right now."

"Fair enough," replied Ben. "Let's move on to the main thing I wanted to talk about."

For a moment, there was silence as the two friends walked side-by-side just out of Gabby's hearing. Gordon observed the mist coalescing into sizeable drops on their ponchos and running down the waterproof plastic to soak the double socks inside their hiking boots. He heard squishing noises coming from each step. Finally, Ben continued.

"I'm no psychologist, Gordon, but I think when someone has an experience as you did up on the mountain, that person probably feels a huge surge of relief. However, that doesn't mean their guilt is gone. When you think back to the night of Ryan's accident, do you still feel guilty?"

Silence. Gordon deliberately kept his face concealed beneath his poncho's orange hood.

"Gordon?"

"Yeah, I heard," Gordon finally responded. "You pretty much hit the bullseye. It was bad enough losing my brother, but what still bothers me was that damn phone call. Ben, I told Ryan to take an Uber when I knew he wouldn't. And then what did I do? I *hung up* on him."

"I get it," Ben replied. "And for the last two and half years, you've been replaying that call inside your head, right?"

"Yeah," whispered Gordon. Ben didn't hear the answer, but he could see the poncho's hood nodding up and down.

"Well, this is the point where I feed you the standard lines. You probably know what I'm about to say. Just because they sound like platitudes, though, doesn't mean they aren't true. So, I want you to do me a favor, all right? I just want you to *listen* to them."

Gordon didn't verbalize a response, but Ben could see him faintly nodding his head again.

"No, I *mean* it, Gordon. I want you to listen. Okay?"

This time, Gordon turned enough to make eye contact. He cleared his throat and responded with more conviction. "Okay, I'll listen. I *promise*."

"*Good*. Okay, I've given this some thought, Gordon, and I have three points to make. The first is Ryan *chose* to drive that night when he knew he shouldn't. That means if it's necessary to assign fault, it belongs to him, *not* you. Got it?"

Gordon started to speak, but Ben quickly cut him off. "Whoa, wait a minute. You promised to listen, remember? That means no talking. You'll have your chance."

Other than the soft patter of raindrops on their hoods, there was nothing but silence.

"Second," Ben continued, "you're not clairvoyant, so there was no way to predict what was going to happen after you hung up the phone. It's always easy to look back at the past with twenty-twenty hindsight, but at that moment, there was *no way* to predict what was going to happen. Okay?"

This time, Gordon remained silent.

"And here's my third point. Maybe choosing to do *right* by David was better at that time than bailing on his play to pick up your brother who *should've* been at the play."

After a pause, Gordon replied, "You're right. That all makes sense, and I've already given it plenty of thought. Your points sound reasonable to any objective person, but guilt isn't something you cure through logic."

"Good point," Ben replied. "I kind of expected you to say that. That's why I want to try a different approach."

Suddenly, Ben looked up the trail, cupped his mouth, and hollered out to Gabby, who was at least twenty yards ahead.

"Hey, Gabby!" Ben shouted. When she turned around, he continued, "Take a break up ahead when you find a good spot to rest and then wait for us. There's something I want to discuss with Gordon."

Gabby waved to acknowledge the plan and then turned back around. Seeing this, Ben halted in his tracks and put out a hand to stop Gordon. He turned to face his old college roommate, placed both hands squarely on Gordon's shoulders, and looked him directly in the eye. From a distance, they appeared as two hooded monks facing each other in the fog. They were utterly alone after Gabby curved around a bend, obscured by the alpine mist. Behind them, a distant ray of sunlight peeked from over a jagged ridge.

"Look, Gordon, it's simple. Unless you know something about time travel, you can't go back into the past, and you *cannot* change the past. *Period.* That leaves you two choices. *One*, you can spend the rest of your life beating yourself up about a questionable decision you had to make in a rush. That's the option you chose two and a half years ago. How's it been working out for you? I get the impression that after you picked self-flagellation, you and everyone around you has been forced to suffer. Am I right?"

Up to this point, Gordon looked unflinchingly at Ben. With this last question, his gaze turned downward, once again concealing his expression beneath the poncho's hood.

"Now, let's look at your second option," Ben continued. "You can just say, '*fuck the past.*' You can't change the past, and nothing in the world will ever bring Ryan back to life. But Gordon, what about your *future*? Man, you'll need to dig deep to have a future, but you can do it. Here's an analogy. Think of your guilt like it's chronic pain, something no doctor can cure. We both know plenty of people who live with back pain that never goes away or arthritis that screams every time they move. They learn to live with it, don't they? They buck up, keep it to themselves, and don't subject it to others. Gordon, you're *just* as tough. It may never completely go away, but you can learn to live with your guilt. You don't want to keep subjecting your wife, your kids, your students, and everyone else around you to the pain you're experiencing, *do* you?"

Gordon looked up and, for a moment, locked eyes with Ben. He clenched his lips together while inhaling deeply through his nose.

Ben continued. "Look, I'm probably not supposed to say this. I'm no therapist, and I realize that I'm in way over my head, but this is the hard logic of an accountant. Gordon, you're not living on a deserted island. Whether you go back to St. Louis or not, there'll always be people around you. If you continue holding on to your guilt, you'll end up driving them away. Gordon, find the strength to *survive* your guilt."

Slowly, Gordon nodded. Because Ben was six inches shorter than his old friend, he had to tilt his head up a little to maintain eye contact. For a moment, they stared at each other. Then, without saying a word, Gordon reached out, and the two men embraced.

"I get it," Gordon stated when drawing back. "What you're saying makes a lot of sense. That said, I still can't promise that after two and a half years of—what did you call it? Self-flagellation? I'm going to be able to get over my guilt just because of one little pep talk."

"Yeah, but you've got to admit," Ben replied with a smile creasing his face, "it was one *hell* of a pep talk, wasn't it? And how about that word, self-flagellation? Impressive, huh?"

Gordon returned the smile and then broke out laughing. "Nothing's changed," he quipped. "You're still an asshole."

"Be that as it may," Ben replied while glancing over to face the mountain, "we still *did* it today, didn't we? For the second time in our lives, we climbed Longs *fucking* Peak! And let's face it, the first time was a *whole* lot easier."

"Yeah, that's true," Gordon replied while gazing admirably at the mountain. "Back then, we were younger, in better shape, and a whole lot dumber."

"Despite the handicaps, though, we still did it," Ben responded. "For that, we should be proud. If we can accomplish that feat in one day, we should be up to dealing with anything else. Now, let's go catch up with my girlfriend."

When Gordon nodded, Ben spun around and headed down the trail. Gordon remained motionless for a few seconds. He wanted a little more time on his own. Noting the rain had ceased, he shed his poncho, and from this point on, was determined to enjoy what remained of the hike. True, he was physically exhausted and the pain in his right knee sharpened with every step. The best thing he could do now was distract himself by focusing on other thoughts. Besides, he *was* tough. He could live with the pain.

The sun glowed stronger over his right shoulder, making the remainder of the afternoon more pleasant. The air was crisper after the daily rainstorm. From what Gordon could see, all of today's climbers were in front of him, and he was utterly alone. What's more, even though there were still a few miles left to go, it was all downhill. This stretch was a good time for a little more reflection.

Weeks earlier, he'd decided to focus on *two* issues. The first involved getting over a past that had grown impossible to contemplate but was still sullying the present. Pride had kept Gordon from discussing his history with a professional, but with close friends this morning, it had spewed out like Mount Saint Helens. If he could finally open up to Ben and Gabby, he could do the same with others.

Gordon next considered the conversation he just had with Ben. It was a lot more than a pep talk. The analogy between guilt and chronic pain stuck with him more than anything else. Ben had made a *good* point. Millions of people suffer from pain every day and still manage to live their lives. The important thing was to be careful about the medication. Gordon had treated his guilt with cigarettes, beer, and self-pity for two and a half years. It was high time to put aside his inner demons. He always took pride in his toughness, both physical and mental. Gordon *could* learn to live with his guilt.

Gordon then moved on to the second issue, which was still unresolved. What about his *future*? Despite physical exhaustion, Gordon had gained a second wind and found his mind surprisingly lucid. He divided the question about this future into two parts. The first involved his career options. Regardless of where he decided to live, Gordon now understood one thing with firm conviction. He *loved* teaching history and had no desire to do anything else.

It had been almost two months since Gordon taught his last history class, and with each passing day, he realized how much he missed the classroom. His interest in history had waned in recent years, but he had surprisingly rediscovered it this past summer. A simple conversation at Wounded Knee, a hike up to a ghost town called Lulu City, and an hour exploring the Grand Lake Cemetery all helped rekindle an old passion. It was like someone had lit a torch to illuminate unseen treasures right in front of him.

Gordon recalled the incredible thrill of getting a classroom excited about history and guiding the students to connect the past with their present. He considered how these experiences even infiltrated his sleep. For the past several weeks, there had been at least one dream each night, usually right before he woke up, where a historical discussion or debate was going on in his classroom. These dreams usually left a smile imprinted on his face to start the day.

Gordon also understood that he'd have to make some fundamental changes whether he returned to his old classroom in the St. Louis suburbs or a new one in the Rocky Mountains. He would have to spice up his units with more creative lessons to hook and hold the students' attention. What's more, the classroom spotlight needed to shine brighter on the students. Gordon needed to talk less and encourage his students to talk more.

The key would be returning to his younger days when he'd mainly focused on student engagement. In the long run, it wasn't important how many historical details the students put to memory. They would soon forget most of them. What mattered was whether or not he had adequately prepared the students to be active participants in a democratic society—this required guidance and experience with making decisions. Gordon found himself thinking about a new approach where he'd ditch the textbook and the traditional timeline. Instead, he'd guide students to ask questions about their world and then teach them how to mine the past to find the answers.

Gordon felt increasingly excited as he pondered the possibilities. He'd resumed walking towards the trailhead, and with each new idea about teaching history, his pace quickened. Gordon planned to later jot down details back at the cabin in Grand Lake, but for now, an image of what his teaching might look like in the fall came into focus. On top of everything else he'd confronted today, this resolution to revitalize his teaching was invigorating.

That left just one more question, but it was the most important. *Where* should Gordon teach? It wasn't just a question of geography. Beneath the Missouri versus Colorado question was the deeper issue of family versus freedom. Should Gordon continue to teach in St. Louis with his wife and kids? Or should he start over up here in the mountains where he might flourish in his newfound freedom? As each summer day passed, this question became increasingly urgent.

Had this summer just been a fun interlude, a memorable vacation? If so, then pretty soon, Gordon should be loading up the Corolla and heading back to Missouri. There, he still had a wife he loved but who was permanently rooted in St. Louis. Gordon also had two incredible kids, but by now, they had probably grown accustomed to having a father who was hundreds of miles away. And as much as he wanted to continue to teach, he'd been at Beachwood North High School for a *long* time, and the situation there had grown somewhat stale. Sure, he had Jim and a few other friends back at North High, but maybe it would be nice to make some new friends in a new school. A change of scenery would be *so* welcome.

On the other hand, out here, Gordon, at this moment, didn't even have a teaching job. His experience would be an asset, and hopefully, he'd find something, but there were no guarantees. Even if he did land a teaching position up here in the mountains, his only current friends were up ahead on the trail, and he was uncertain if Ben planned to stick around. Most of all, even though Gabby and Ben were ideal friends, they *weren't* family. In Colorado, Gordon could enjoy unfettered freedom, but his only family would be eight hundred and fifty miles away.

Suddenly, Gordon stopped. He knew Gabby and Ben would soon be looking for him, but right now, they were probably so lost in their conversation, they wouldn't miss him for a little while. All around him were the sounds of the forest: wind whistling through the pines, ground squirrels rustling through a pile of crispy aspen leaves, a babbling brook off in the distance. Gordon took a few steps, curious to see what lay beyond the next thicket of pines.

To Gordon's delight, one more panoramic view of the mountain came into view. Looking up, he took in the full sight of Longs Peak and its renowned two-thousand-foot diamond. Gordon snapped more pictures, swelling with pride over the knowledge he'd just been up there a few hours ago.

After putting away his phone, Gordon closed his eyes and inhaled the fresh, pine-scented air. For a moment, he visualized his life in these mountains. Winters would be frigid, and the snow would be bottomless. What's more, Gordon was never a fan of skiing. Still, he didn't mind the cold, and he'd always wanted to try hiking in snowshoes. There was something wholesome and honest about these snow-covered peaks. Gordon considered that he'd spent some of the best times of his life out here in the west.

Gordon had already made enough progress for one day and decided this last question would have to wait. He opened his eyes, looked up the path, and picked up the pace to catch Ben and Gabby. Since the next stretch of trail was relatively flat, he even jogged part of the way. It only took a few minutes. The pain in his knee temporarily subsided, and Gordon was smiling when he caught up with his friends.

CHAPTER

18

A few hours later, the Three Amigos were back at the Ridgeline Hotel, where they planned to spend a second night. Gordon was alone in his room, and his priority was to launch a FaceTime call to the kids. He had already sent them the Longs Peak pictures, but when he asked David and Annie for their reaction, they were surprisingly unmoved. Spectacular scenery bathed in the early morning light didn't have the same appeal as furry marmots or a family of black bears. After he finished his conversation with the children, Gordon asked for a little "private time to talk with Mommy." When Elaine's face came into view, he cleared his throat and unknowingly reached up to caress his chin.

"Honey, there's something you should know about today." Gordon could see her nodding to indicate she wanted him to continue. "I don't know if you remember this, but one of my best memories with Ryan was on top of Longs Peak. I told you about that, right?"

"Yeah, you said he went out to Colorado for a week and joined you and Ben to climb Longs Peak."

"Right," Gordon continued. "Well, today, when we were back on top of the mountain, that memory came flashing back. Actually, it came *flooding* back."

"What do you mean?"

"Okay," Gordon replied, "to begin with, getting to the peak was a *lot* harder than the first time, but we still made it by ten thirty or so without any hang-ups. Once we were on top, we did the usual stuff, you know, we celebrated, took some pictures, and then finally sat down to rest and have a little lunch. Everything was fine up to that point."

Gordon paused and looked away from his phone. Elaine could see his chest swell as he drew in a deep breath. She waited for him to proceed.

"We'd found a quiet place to sit and relax," Gordon finally continued. "While I ate, Ben told Gabby the story about how we climbed Longs Peak back in college. Naturally, he mentioned Ryan."

"Uh oh," Elaine interrupted. "I think I can see where this is going."

"Yeah, but there are some things you don't know." After another brief pause, Gordon added, "like up until that moment, I hadn't even told Ben about Ryan's death."

"*Really*? Why not?"

"I don't know," Gordon replied. "Since leaving St. Louis, I haven't told anyone. I guess I figured if I didn't talk about Ryan, it would be easier to avoid thinking about him."

"I see. What happened next?"

"I tried to ignore Ben's story for a little while, but then something happened. It was kind of like that feeling you get when you have to throw up, but in this case, it wasn't coming from my stomach. Elaine, this has never happened to me before, and at first, it was pretty scary. I guess it was some kind of emotional meltdown. I started to cry—*hard*—and I couldn't stop."

"*Oh*," Elaine replied in a voice that conveyed growing concern.

"The good news is that after I finally calmed down, I started to talk. It was like one of those epiphany moments people supposedly have with their therapists. You know, it was like you see in the movies. Remember that scene between Judd Hirsch and Timothy Hutton in *Ordinary People*? Or how about that one near the end of *Good Will Hunting* between Robin Williams and Matt Damon? Anyhow, I told Ben and Gabby the whole story. *Everything* came out."

"Oh yeah?"

"Elaine, I don't mean to say it cured me." Gordon held up his fingers so she could see air quotes. "I mean, one breakthrough doesn't fix everything. But I do know I felt a *lot* better when it was over."

"That's great to hear," Elaine responded. There was a buoyant tone in her voice now.

"Wait," Gordon added. "That's not all. I told them something today I've never told *you*. In fact, before today, I've never told anyone."

Gordon could see Elaine's eyes enlarge on the small screen of his smartphone.

"Elaine, on the night of Ryan's death, when we were at David's play, do you remember how I got a phone call right before the play was about to begin?"

"Yeah, vaguely. It's been a while. Didn't you say it was from an angry parent?"

"Yes, that's what I said, but it wasn't the truth."

Gordon paused again. This time, he looked like a child who needed to confess something to soothe a guilty conscience.

"It was Ryan who called. I knew you weren't too pleased with him back in those days, and I didn't want to get you even more upset with him. Ryan said he wanted a ride. He said he and Lisa were too wasted to drive. I told him to take an Uber because I didn't want to miss David's play. When he started to argue, I *hung up* on him."

Moisture collected beneath Gordon's eyes. Determined not to repeat his explosive eruption from earlier that day, he clenched his lips together and briefly glanced away. Seeing this, Elaine attempted to come to his rescue.

"You mean to tell me you've been keeping this inside you for over two years? You've never told *anyone* about that call?"

Still looking away from the pinhole camera lens on his phone, Gordon slowly shook his head.

"*Wow! Holy Jesus!* Gordon, you should've told me this a *long* time ago. I would've understood. I'm your *wife*. I could've helped."

Elaine hesitated to gather her thoughts. Then she continued under a new head of steam.

"What you did that night is what most men in your situation would've done. Ryan knew about David's play. He should've been there. Ryan had no right to expect you to miss your son's play. As for hanging up on him, that's not a big deal. I was rushing you to come back inside before the play started. You only hung up on him because you didn't want to waste any more time arguing. That's all it was. It's not like you knew at the time what Ryan was going to do next. You've got *nothing* to feel bad about."

At this point, Gordon glanced up and forced a smile.

"Look," Elaine added, "I need some time to process what you've just told me. *Wow*! This explains *so* much."

"All right," responded Gordon. "I should probably get going. We're headed out for dinner pretty soon to celebrate today's victory. You and I can talk some more over the next few days."

Gordon could see his wife squint a little, and her face grew larger as she appeared to examine his image on her iPad carefully. Then he saw a soft smile.

"Yeah, that sounds good. Hey, Gordon, before you go, there's one more thing. I'm not sure why, but I'm trying to figure out why you *look* different. Maybe it's my imagination, and of course, I can only see you on this little screen, but you look, I don't know, *younger*."

"Is that a compliment?" Gordon inquired.

"Yes, of course, it is, but that's not what I'm saying. Look, you've lost a lot of weight, and I know you're in better physical condition. But there's something different about your *face*."

Elaine paused again and bit down on her lower lip as her smile brightened.

"Gordon, you resemble that college kid I first met seventeen years ago at a Mizzou basketball game." After another brief pause, she added, "You understand what I'm saying?"

Gordon's lips pressed together, and the corners of his mouth turned up. He didn't say anything; instead, he slowly reached up and touched his wife's image on the phone's screen. Elaine did the same.

After ending the call, Gordon showered, dressed, and met Gabby and Ben in the hotel lobby. The Three Amigos headed out for a hearty dinner at the Twin Owls Steakhouse, looking clean and surprisingly invigorated. This establishment was one of the pricier restaurants in Estes Park, but since Ben had vehemently insisted on treating to celebrate some news he wanted to share, Gordon finally relented. Still, he was determined to look for the least expensive steak on the menu and confine his drinking to diet soda.

The evening was a sheer delight. All three of the Amigos were in boisterous moods, and they took turns toasting the morning's triumph and everything related to their successful ascent. Once the waiter served the main course, the conversation curved in a more serious direction. Ben kicked it off.

"As I told you guys earlier, I have some news."

Gordon and Gabby promptly turned to face him.

"I've already told you about my divorce. That was the *first* domino, and now the others have recently fallen into place. So, tighten your seatbelts, ladies and gentlemen, because I've got a *lot* more to say."

Gordan and Gabby exchanged glances and simultaneously raised their eyebrows.

"For starters," Ben continued, "I received a text today on the mountain from my business partners. I'd been exchanging phone calls and emails with them for the past week, and as of today, it's become official. I've sold them my firm in L.A. I'm *so* done with living in that smoggy, congested hellhole. Now I'll have the cash to make the other two purchases I've been negotiating in Grand Lake."

Ben paused to catch his breath. Then he slowly sipped his red wine, using the silence to build the tension.

"The first is my parents' cabin. I knew they were planning to sell it pretty soon. They only kept it as a vacation home, and now that Mom and Dad are getting older, they're using it less and less. For me, it'll be my *permanent* residence. I told them they're still welcome to use it for vacations whenever they want. They were happy with this arrangement, especially when they realized we'd see each other more often. You could call it a win-win for all of us."

Then came another pause and another sip of wine.

"Oh, and one other thing," Ben finally added. "Before I go on and tell you about the second purchase, I have an important question to ask."

Ben turned to face Gabby directly. She clasped her hands on the table and looked up at him, her eyes glowing. The candlelight added a golden tinge to her smile.

"Gabby, you've pretty much moved in with me already. Can we make it permanent? I'll help you pack, and we can bring your stuff over to *our* new cabin. What do you say?"

"Whoa!" Gordon interjected. "Should I excuse myself to the bathroom or something? It looks like you guys could use some privacy."

"That's not necessary," Ben replied, winking at Gabby. "You're one of the Three Amigos. I don't think Gabby will mind. Besides, this isn't a marriage proposal. At least, not yet."

"No, but it's a step in that direction, right?" Gabby added, this time winking at Gordon. "Hey, I told you when we first met I needed a better filter."

Everyone laughed. Then Ben and Gordon turned expectantly towards Gabby. She gazed squarely back into Ben's eyes, reached out to take his hand, and nodded vigorously. A smile burst across Ben's face as he stood, walked around the table, helped Gabby to her feet, and passionately kissed her on the lips. Other diners took notice, and some even applauded and whistled. After a moment, Ben returned to his seat, tossed a napkin back into his lap, and looked up to indicate he was ready to proceed.

"As I said before," Ben continued, "the dominoes are all falling into place. Here's another. If I'm going to live in Grand Lake permanently, I'll need *something* to do, you know? Something to fill my time, preferably something that'll be more rewarding than doing rich people's taxes."

"Yeah?" Gordon asked. "So, what's this '*something*?'"

"You have *no* idea? What kind of friend are you? I bet Gabby knows."

Gabby kept silent but enthusiastically nodded her head.

"Well, *good* for Gabby," Gordon replied mockingly. "How about you inform your old dim buddy from college."

"Okay, I'll spell it out for you. I made a call earlier this evening after getting out of the shower. It was to Shannon over in Grand Lake. You know, the owner of the bookstore? I don't know if you've noticed, Gordon, but I've been hanging out there a lot lately."

"I noticed," replied Gordon defensively. "I was starting to wonder if Gabby had a reason to be jealous."

"Yeah, that's funny. Gordon, you might remember Shannon's been trying to sell her store? Since I've known for a while that I might make Grand Lake my home, I've thought this could be another win-win situation."

Ben once more stopped to amplify the tension. This time, he swallowed the last of his wine and then refilled his glass along with Gabby's.

"It's pretty simple," Ben finally continued. "Shannon wants out, I want in, and this area still needs a good bookstore. I'd made her an offer a while ago, but she knew it was contingent on the sale of my accounting firm. Since that happened today, I called Shannon, renewing my offer, and she promptly accepted. Guys, you're looking at the new owner of the Rocky Mountain Books!"

Silence. The Three Amigos looked back and forth at each other, grinning madly. Then Gordon raised his half-empty glass of Diet Coke and offered a toast.

"To Ben, the man who lined up his dominoes and made them all fall into the right place. I'm impressed, buddy. Good for you. *Good* for both of you!"

Ben glowed while lifting his glass of wine. Gordon observed that he quietly reached over with his empty hand and embraced Gabby's shoulder. It was a special moment for the two of them. It occurred to Gordon that tonight was probably a turning point in their lives. They'd each hit a fork in the road and had decided to travel the same path together. Gordon was impressed by the joy he saw reflected in the faces of these two special people.

"Well," Gordon added in an intentionally solemn tone, "I hate to steer us away from all the wonderful news, but I don't want the evening to pass without me saying something that needs to be said."

He paused and cleared his throat, replacing his grin with a more somber expression. After a moment, when it was clear he had their attention, Gordon continued.

"Guys, from the bottom of my heart, I want to *thank you,* and I also want to apologize. The time spent on top of a fourteener is supposed to be a special moment, a celebration. I'm sure the last thing you wanted to do today was to spend that moment consoling a blubbering baby."

"Whoa, wait a minute!" Ben interrupted. "You may have done a little blubbering this morning, but at that moment, you simply needed the support of friends. I'm just glad we could be there for you today. "

Gabby nodded emphatically. "Besides," she added, "Ben's told me you're a great teacher, Gordon, and today I witnessed it first-hand. You know how to tell a compelling story. More important, after today, I feel like we've become life-long friends."

Ben glanced at Gabby and then added, "I think I can speak for both of us when I say we're happy to accept your gratitude, Gordon, but the apology isn't necessary."

This time, it was Gordon who reached out and gripped the hands of his two friends. Since he was momentarily at a loss for words, he just smiled and quietly nodded.

Finally, Gordon broke the silence. "Well, I still feel it's important that I express my gratitude. And you've got no idea how *good* I've been feeling since this morning. It's like a huge weight was lifted off my shoulders. Coming down the mountain this afternoon, I spent a lot of time going over some things in my head. And Ben, that includes your little pep talk this afternoon. I know there's still a ways to go, and I've got some more things left to figure out, but today *helped*. Thank you guys *so* much. I'll always be grateful to you for being there to support me this morning on top of Longs Peak."

"Gordon, when you say you still have some things to figure out," Ben asked, "I assume you're talking about the future?" As he said this, he was looking at Gabby. "I mean, you just heard about my dominoes falling into place. What about *yours*?"

"I've made some decisions about how to revive my teaching this fall. But I'm still pretty uncertain about *where* I want to teach. And that means . . ." Gordon stopped, uncertain how to proceed. "And that means I still don't know about my marriage. I guess that domino isn't ready to fall yet."

Gabby returned Ben's gaze, lifted her eyebrows, and winked in his direction. "Because . . ." she said, drawing out the last syllable. "I also received a text this afternoon. It was from an old college friend." Turning to face Gordon directly, she continued. "He's now the principal of Middle Park High School. Gordon, have you ever heard of it?"

Gordon glanced back and forth between Gabby and Ben. He was starting to realize they had planned this part of the conversation.

"No," he replied. "Why? What are you guys up to?"

"Gordon, the principal's name is Bryan LeBeau. We've remained good friends over the years, especially after I moved up to Grand Lake. I spoke to him a few days ago—*about you*. I hope you don't mind. I told him about your current situation."

Gabby paused. She peeked over at Ben and then returned her gaze to Gordon. A smile erupted across her face.

"Gordon, they have a social studies opening in their high school, and Bryan's *very* excited about talking to you. He thinks that with your experience, you might be the perfect person to fill the position. The school is in Granby, just fifteen miles down the road from Grand Lake. Gordon, it's a *good* school. Middle Park has just under four hundred students. It's where all the kids from Grand Lake and the surrounding towns attend. I think they only have three or four history teachers, so openings like this are rare."

Gabby bent forward, planted her elbows on the table, and slowly lowered her chin into the cradle of her clasped hands. She looked up with a mischievous smile. At the same time, Ben scooted his chair back far enough to fold one leg over the other. A similar grin appeared on his face.

"Look," she added, "I'm not saying . . ." and then glancing at Ben, she corrected herself. "*We're* not saying you should leave St. Louis and move out here. That's something only *you* can decide."

Then Ben added, "That said, though, if you *were* leaning towards a move to Grand Lake, and I've gotten the impression you were, then this domino should make it a whole lot easier."

Gordon looked up at the ceiling. He was overwhelmed by this news and didn't know how to respond. He drew in a deep breath and then dropped his head down to gaze at his feet. At the moment, Gordon wanted to avoid eye contact. If he looked up at Gabby or Ben right now, he might break down again.

A chance to teach history in Granby would be the ideal path towards creating a new life for himself. It probably would pay less than his current job, but so what? Living on his own in the mountains, he could undeniably keep his costs down. A school located in the heart of the Rockies. *Wow!* Gabby and Ben would live nearby, and he'd soon make new friends. His kids? They'd love it up here in the mountains. Gordon was confident Elaine would be willing to send them out every summer, and maybe during the extended school breaks.

Then there was Elaine. What were the chances of saving their marriage? The FaceTime conversation a little while ago was encouraging, but there was *no way* she'd relocate to Colorado. It wouldn't be fair to ask. Elaine was born and raised in St. Louis. Her family all lived there, and she had deep roots in Missouri. Elaine had made it clear in the past she had no desire to live anywhere else. If there were any hope of saving their marriage, Gordon would have to return to St. Louis.

It was all happening too fast, and at the moment, Gordon was too exhausted to absorb everything he'd just heard. He'd been awake since one in the morning, hiked one of the most challenging mountains in the Rockies, and experienced an emotional earthquake on top followed by seismic tremors that had yet to subside. Then came the conversation with Elaine, followed by Ben's news. Now *this*?

It was overwhelming. Gordon needed time to process everything. Talking about Ryan's death twice in one day unearthed a decomposing skeleton. It would take time and reflection to give it a proper burial. Then there was the question about his future. It wasn't as simple as interviewing for a teaching position in a new school. This decision involved his wife, his kids, his family. It was a life-changing decision that would hugely impact the lives of several people.

Finally, Gordon looked up. Gabby and Ben waited patiently with identical expressions on their faces. They both understood that it helps to have the best options available when facing a tough decision.

"I don't know what to say," Gordon finally responded. "I guess there's not much time to think this over, is there?"

Gabby shook her head. "No, Gordon, I'm sorry. School starts back up in less than a month, and Bryan has a position to fill. That was the one condition he made clear. He'd like you to call him to set up an interview, and *the sooner, the better.*"

Gordon woke early. He'd forgotten to close the drapes in his hotel room the night before, and now the rising sun hurled light beams directly into his face. In the past, this would've been like rousing a hibernating bear. Gordon had *never* been a morning person. Until black coffee flowed through his veins, he was sluggish and ill-tempered. This morning felt different.

Then he stood up. His muscles screamed to be left alone, especially in his upper thighs. As Gordon stepped towards the bathroom, his knees ached from the pounding they'd taken coming down from the mountain the day before. Mentally, he was alert and ready to begin his day. Physically, his body needed more time to recuperate. Gordon was grateful that his biggest challenge that day would be sitting in the backseat as the Three Amigos drove back across the park to Grand Lake. He was looking forward to some quiet time as he took in the scenery and wrestled with the biggest dilemma of his life.

When the Three Amigos returned from dinner the night before, Gordon had brushed his teeth, climbed into bed, and descended into a coma for the next eight hours. From ten that evening to six in the morning, he slept without stirring. Most of his bed still looked made up from the day before. This image put a smile on his face. It had been a long time since he had such a good night's sleep.

Catching his reflection in the bathroom mirror put another grin on his face. It was like he'd spent the last six weeks at an adult weight loss camp. Most of the fat that had hugged his torso for so long was gone, replaced by leaner muscle. Gordon had hiked hundreds of miles. He had substituted diet drinks and water for beer and whiskey, clean mountain air for tobacco smoke, and low-fat chicken for hotdogs and pizza. He guessed his weight loss at this point was between forty and fifty pounds.

Gordon felt like a new man. Several factors could explain this phenomenon, most of them obvious, but then Gordon remembered the person who'd set off this chain of events. He took a picture of his reflection wearing only a pair of cargo shorts and a sleeveless T-shirt. Then he sent the picture to his dad. Beneath the photo, he added the following caption:

> Dad, I feel even better than I look. I'll call you tonight to catch up on the last few days, but for now, I just want to thank you. You're the one who made this all possible. I'm lucky to have you as my father. – G

An hour later, Gordon reclined in the rear seat of Ben's Mercedes as they drove west through the national park on their way back to Grand Lake. He studied the landscape as though seeing it for the first time. The thought of living in these mountains year-round was electrifying. He couldn't wait till he had a steady signal on his phone to call Bryan LeBeau about scheduling an interview.

The music blasting out of the car's speakers accompanied the stunning vistas and the cool breeze streaming through the open windows. Ben's taste in music was similar to Gordon's, with a heavy emphasis on Classic Rock. At the moment, they were listening to Bob Seger. Gordon found himself mindlessly singing along, but then he took note of the lyrics of one of his favorite songs, "Beautiful Loser:"

> He wants to dream like a young man
> With the wisdom of an old man
> He wants his home and security
> He wants to live like a sailor at sea
> Beautiful loser, where you gonna fall?
> You realize you just can't have it all

For Gordon, the last line touched a nerve. He'd been living what seemed like an idyllic life back in St. Louis, one that included a wife, two kids, and a rewarding job. Then came that tragic night two and half years ago. It was bad enough to lose his only sibling, but the accompanying guilt had festered like a debilitating disease.

Now he had a chance to start over in Colorado. Gordon had two fantastic friends sitting in the front seat, an inspiring landscape everywhere he looked, and a chance to get a fresh start teaching in a new high school. What should he do? It always came back to the same competing values, family versus freedom. *You realize you just can't have it all.*

Later in the afternoon, the Three Amigos set off in three different directions. They dropped Gabby off at her cabin to pack her things. Ben left to nail down some details regarding the purchase of his bookstore. Gordon headed out to the deck to make a phone call. A few minutes later, he scheduled an interview at Middle Park High School. It would take place the following Monday.

For now, Gordon took in the view of Shadow Mountain, mirrored on the surface of Grand Lake. The afternoon thunderstorms failed to make their daily appearance, so the additional sunlight warmed the temperature and acted as a sedative. Gordon was out to the world for the next two hours. Despite his early morning vitality, the day before had drained him, both physically and emotionally.

When he woke for the second time that day, Gordon realized he was still alone. Ben was supposed to buy some salmon for the outdoor grill, and Gabby planned to bring over a carload of her stuff. For the time being, neither had returned, and the sun was now lodged just above the serrated mountain peaks. Gordon looked down at the lake in the distance. The sun's angled rays illuminated the clouds above, turning them into fluffs of cotton candy. Golden contrails from jets headed west radiated a puffy grid of parallel lines.

Gordon thought about the thousands of people in those narrow tubes racing to the west at almost six hundred miles per hour. They'd soon be landing in places like Phoenix, San Francisco, and Seattle. Some might be returning home from business trips, others possibly starting late-summer vacations. Were any moving to the West? Gordon thought about the Turner Thesis. Migrating west was a common thread running throughout America's history. According to Frederick Jackson Turner, it'd helped define who we are as a people. Most of the time, the pioneers traveling west sought greater freedom and a new life.

It was now the twenty-first century, but Gordon still felt a kinship with those nineteenth-century voyagers. In the back of his mind, coming west to Colorado this summer gave him the option of starting a new life. Gordon knew he still had a family back in St. Louis. Ordinarily, leaving them would never have crossed his mind. The past two and half years had changed everything, though, and now he faced the hardest decision of his life.

A thought suddenly struck Gordon like a bolt of lightning. He grabbed his phone and opened up the list of contacts. Was it there? Gordon couldn't remember. Yes, there it was. He touched the name and number and, since he was still alone, set it to speakerphone. After three rings, a gravelly voice answered.

"Dylan?"

"Yes," the voice replied in a slow, steady cadence. "Who's this?"

"It's Gordon. We hiked together several weeks ago in the Dakotas, remember?"

After a brief pause, a chuckle streamed through the phone's speaker. "Oh yeah, of *course*. You're the guy that's always wearing that damn Cardinals hat. I wasn't sure I'd hear from you. How're things going?"

"They're good, thanks," Gordon replied. "Since we parted, I made it down to Colorado as planned, and I've been here since. The hiking's been amazing, and yesterday, we climbed Longs Peak. I told you how we did that back in college, right?"

"Yes, I believe you did. That sounded like a harrowing experience. Did it go okay?"

"Yeah, it was fine. I did it with a couple of friends, and there were no problems." Deliberately pausing, Gordon added, "How about you and Phil? Where are you guys right now?"

"We're in Cannon Beach on the Oregon coast. I'm sitting on a lounge chair right now, staring out at the Pacific Ocean. Phil's lying here next to my feet. I wish you could see this place, Gordon. It's not far from where

Lewis and Clark first came across the Pacific Ocean. Cannon Beach is one of the most *beautiful* places I've ever seen. I'm looking up at this huge monolith right now called Haystack Rock. It's right on the beach, and it sticks up more than two hundred and thirty feet. Phil and I walk around its base at low tide, exploring the tidepools. The starfish are everywhere."

Gordon inhaled a deep breath and closed his eyes. Visualizing the image, Gordon made a mental note to add Cannon Beach to his bucket list. He also regretted not calling via FaceTime to see what Dylan was describing.

"*Man*, that sounds nice," Gordon stated. "I can visualize you wearing that damn Cubs hat while poking around on the beach."

Dylan snickered. "Well, you're right about that. The blue cap never leaves my head. I have to admit, though, it's been a while since I've seen the standings."

"Yeah? Well, I don't blame you. If I were a Cubs fan, I'd avoid checking the standings too."

"There's that Cardinals arrogance again."

Gordon and Dylan both laughed. Silence followed as each waited for the other to speak. Finally, Dylan said, "Hey, Gordon, I'm happy to catch up all day if you want, but I'm guessing there's a reason you called. Am I right?"

After another pause, Gordon replied, "Yeah, you're right. I'll get to the point. Let me start by saying that the time we spent together in the Dakotas was a special period for me. I enjoyed your company on our hikes, and I appreciated all the fatherly advice. But there was something else, Dylan. The more I got to know you, the more it seemed like I was staring at my future in a crystal ball."

Gordon assumed Dylan's silence meant he should continue. "I hope this makes sense. It's just that you and I seem to have a lot in common."

"Except baseball teams," Dylan replied with a chuckle.

"Well, that's true. We don't like the same teams. But we're still avid fans of the game, right? We both like to travel and hike. And when you described your family, it reminded me a lot of my own."

Gordon paused but, hearing only silence, decided to continue.

"And then, Dylan, you told me about your *dream*. I still recall your words. You said, and I quote, 'I've always wanted to hitch a camper to my car and take a road trip. It's been a dream for as long as I can remember.' Then you said, 'Just go wherever the spirit takes me. Absolute, *total* freedom.'"

"That's all true," replied Dylan. "It's what I'm doing right now. Me and my little buddy here. *Huh,* Phil?"

Gordon could envision Dylan reaching down at that moment to scratch behind the Irish Setter's ears.

"Okay, so, this brings me to the question I wanted to ask. Dylan, did you *ever* have any regrets about not doing this sooner? By waiting, there was no guarantee your dream would come true. And no offense, but taking this trip at your current age means you probably can't do as much now as you might've when you were younger."

Gordon stopped to wait for a reaction. He figured Dylan had failed to understand his point, or he was trying to think of a good response.

Finally, Dylan spoke, but his tone grew somber. "I get it, Gordon. You've been having the time of your life in Colorado, and now you're wondering if you should go back home when the summer's over. Is that about it?"

"The short answer is yes, but it's not that simple. Yes, I *love* these mountains and would be happy to spend the rest of my life out here. But it's isn't just the scenery. It's all the freedom. Out here, I can do pretty much whatever I want."

Gordon again hesitated, trying to figure out what to say next. He decided to be more specific.

"Look, Dylan, I have an interview on Monday for a teaching position that would enable me to move here for good. But I also have to think about my situation back in St. Louis. I told you before that my wife and I have lived apart since December. If I want to make this move to Colorado, *now* would be the time."

"So, in your view, this is not just a midlife crisis, huh?"

"No, I don't think so. It's more like I've hit a fork in the road, and I want to be sure I pick the right path. Dylan, this is where you come in. Whatever I decide, I don't want to feel any regrets about the choice I made once I'm in my eighties. It would help me a great deal to know if you have any regrets now. "

"I see. Well, Gordon, since you're the one who'll have to live with this decision, no one can tell you what to do. But that's just the legal disclaimer of an old, retired lawyer. I realize what you want to know is what I'd do in your shoes. Right?"

"*Yeah*, pretty much. The interview's coming up in a few days, and I think there's a good chance they'll offer me the position. By that point, I need to know for sure what I want to do."

"All right. First, let me start by saying that Emma and I didn't always see eye to eye over the years. Like most couples, we hit a few bumps in the road. And once or twice, I may have *briefly* considered taking off. If I had, I'm sure it would've been in a westward direction. But something always held me back."

"What was that?" Gordon asked, realizing the eagerness in his voice.

"Let's call it instinct, something inside my gut. No one can predict the future, but something told me I should stick it out with Emma. Whatever problems we were experiencing at the time would pass, and afterward, I'd have the perfect partner with whom to share my life. You see, Gordon, in the *long run*, what matters the most isn't *where* you travel; it's who you travel *with*."

This time, Gordon remained quiet, and Dylan took the silence as a sign to continue.

"If I could be with Emma right now, I'd immediately drop everything and drive nonstop back to Chicago. I miss that woman *so* much. She's in my thoughts every moment of the day."

There was another pause. Gordon could visualize his friend staring out at the ocean while wiping away tears streaking down his unshaven cheeks.

"You see, freedom sounds great, but for me, it was the consolation prize that came near the end of my life. In the end, it's the *people* that mattered the most, *not* the places."

After more silence, Dylan asked, "Gordon? Are you still there?"

"Yeah, I'm sorry," Gordon finally answered. "I was thinking about what you just said."

"Look, Gordon, I don't know your wife, but I do know you've been married to her for over fifteen years, right? And you've also got yourself a couple of young kids? Ask yourself, will you find another family like them in Colorado? If you do, will they make you as happy as the one you left behind? And, if you don't, will the pretty scenery and all the freedom be enough to make up for their loss?"

"*Jesus,* Dylan, you must have been like Clarence Darrow in the courtroom."

Sensing he was on a roll, Dylan decided to continue. "Look, Gordon, I told you I'm eighty-four, right? If I could go back to being a younger man like yourself, I wouldn't do *anything* different. When I look back today, you know what brings me the greatest joy? It isn't my career, and it's not the places I've traveled. It's not even the friends I've made. It's my marriage and my family. That's what enriched my life the most. But now, I've lost my Emma, and the kids are grown. The freedom I have now, the freedom you covet so badly, that's all I have left. It's not much of a consolation. Tonight, Gordon, I'll be alone in my trailer with Phil and a good book. Ask yourself, would you *really* want to trade places with me?"

"Hmm. That's a lot to consider. I wanted a straight answer, Dylan, and you gave me one. I don't know what I'm going to do yet, but I greatly appreciate the advice."

For a moment, there was silence. Finally, Gordon sensed the need to lighten things up a bit and shifted the conversation back to familiar territory. "Hey, Dylan, on a different note, I have one more question."

"Sure, go ahead," Dylan replied. "Although I may start charging for these pearls of wisdom."

"Do you think you could maintain a long-term friendship with a Cardinals fan?"

Dylan chuckled and then replied, "It'll be tough, but I'll try. I tell you what. Next spring, when it's time for me to head back east, I'll probably pass through Colorado and then St. Louis. How about I give *you* a call? Maybe we can catch a game at Coors Field or god forbid, Busch Stadium."

"That sounds good. I'd really like that. Let's be sure to stay in touch, all right?"

"You got it, buddy."

After hanging up, Gordon realized he had received a text from his dad thanking him for this morning's message. Then he opened his email. The subject heading of Elaine's note immediately caught his attention— "Annie had an accident, but no need to worry."

Dear Gordon,

I took Annie to Stacy Park this morning to play with Scott. While climbing the ladder to go down a slide, she slipped and fell. You know what a klutz she can be. Anyhow, Annie hit one of the ladder's rungs on the way down and opened up a nasty cut under her chin. She cried like it was the end of the world, especially when she saw all the red and realized the blood was hers.

I took her to St. Luke's ER for what turned out to be six stitches. Annie basked in all the attention from the medical staff. Your daughter especially hammed it up when Scott's mother, who'd come with us to the ER, made such a big fuss over her "bravery."

When it was time to take Annie into the backroom to get her stitches, she was once again terrified. She cried and carried on like she was about to be tortured during the Spanish Inquisition (like my historical reference?). They wanted to take her by herself, but I insisted on going along.

As Annie stood to walk into the backroom, she looked at me with tears streaming down her cheeks and said something you should appreciate. At least, I hope you will since it didn't do much to boost my spirits. Annie screamed, "I want Daddy!"

Frankly, I was shocked. No offense, but it's not like you've been around much this summer. In all fairness, you've done an excellent job texting your pictures and FaceTiming with the kids. But come on! "I want Daddy!" Really? When she knew you were hundreds of miles away?

That said, I'm coming to understand how she feels. Last night before going to bed, I looked over the Longs Peak pictures one more time. My favorite is the one with you on top of the mountain with your fists raised. You look terrific. More important, there's an expression on your face I haven't seen in years.

I may be setting myself up for pain and embarrassment by writing this, Gordon, but I miss you. I miss us. I don't want to find someone else to be a stepdad for the kids. I want to be married to you. I love you, Gordon. Please come home.

Gordon abruptly woke from a dream. It wasn't a nightmare; in fact, it left a pleasant feeling, almost like the delicious aftertaste that sometimes follows a tasty meal. Since the details of his dreams would quickly evaporate after he woke, Gordon made a concerted effort to review the particulars from this one before they could disappear.

In the dream, Gordon remembered taking roll in his class and noting that Andre was absent. Then Andre walked into the classroom beaming from ear to ear. He was tardy again but was noticeably excited to be in Mr. G's class. Gordon stood and began his lesson by asking the students to brainstorm how history might explain why white supremacists and Neo-Nazis still plagued American society. Hands immediately flew up, including Andre's.

Gordon remembered smiling when he realized that Andre restrained himself from blurting out a response without raising his hand. He was about to reward Andre by calling on him when he noticed Elaine in the rear of the classroom. David stood next to her, looking predictably anxious. On the other side, Elaine held Annie's hand. His daughter smiled faintly, and a bandage was under her chin. Elaine was smiling and waving with her free hand. Gordon wished he could fall back to sleep to discover how the dream would end.

He glanced over at the clock next to his bed. It was only a quarter after five, at least half an hour before sunrise. Still, Gordon was wide awake. He rose, threw on some shorts and a long-sleeve T-shirt, and headed into the kitchen to make coffee. While waiting, Gordon pulled out an open box of high-fiber cereal and munched on it like popcorn in a movie theater. Then he pulled out his phone and reread Elaine's email from the day before. "I love you, Gordon. Please come home." Just seven words, but they were crystal clear.

After closing the email, Gordon noted the date on the screen's upper corner—July 23. There were still about three weeks before teachers would have to report back to school, but in reality, Gordon knew his summer was almost over. Now that Ben found his compass, he'd be preoccupied with launching a new business in Grand Lake. What's more, with Gabby moving in, they'd want some privacy to let their relationship blossom. Gordon would just be in the way. It was time to choose a path and begin his journey.

The first glimmers of light filtered in through the sliding glass door next to the fireplace. After pouring coffee, Gordon grabbed a blanket folded on the leather couch and moved his breakfast out to the deck. Since he was facing west, there was no spectacular sunrise to anticipate. As the light coming over his shoulder intensified, it cast a spell on the lake a hundred feet below. The pastel colors—blue, green, and pink—blended into a Monet painting. As Gordon watched, the luminosity brightened, turning the lake's surface into a smooth mirror. He could see delicate clouds in the reflection, framed by the encircling peaks.

Suddenly, movement below snared Gordon's attention. He sprang up from his Adirondack chair and saw the same black bears he'd seen weeks before. The cubs that flanked the mama bear were slightly larger. Gordon reached for his phone to take more pictures. When he looked up, he saw the family had grown. Now, an even heftier bear was behind the cubs, uninterested in the berries they were eating. Instead, the papa bear stood up on his hind legs, pointed his snout into the air, and sniffed for unseen dangers.

Over the next few minutes, Gordon took his best wildlife photos of the summer. The kids would go ballistic. After arriving home, Gordon would buy the most immense stuffed bear he could afford for Annie, and he'd take David back to see the bear dens at the zoo. The symbolism of what he'd just seen wasn't lost on him either. Now there was a papa bear?

Sensing his time in Grand Lake was running low, Gordon dashed back to his room, strapped on his hiking boots, and bolted out the front door. Today, he'd take a short hike on his own. Moving swiftly, he skirted around the northern side of the lake and made his way to the East Inlet Trailhead. From there, it was less than a half-mile hike to Adams Falls. He'd already been to the falls earlier in the summer, but it was with Ben, and he'd only remained there long enough to snap a few pictures. Now, he wanted some time alone.

Adams Falls was spectacular. The water from the East Inlet Creek that fed into Grand Lake fell more than fifty feet in a series of steps through a narrow rock gorge. What Gordon craved this morning was the sound. He knew the echoing thunder from the water as it cascaded onto the granite boulders would drown out everything else, removing distractions that might hamper serious reflection.

Gordon examined the immediate area, found a flat boulder that looked comfortable, and sat down. By now, there was enough sunlight peering through the mist to create a blurry rainbow. Gordon glanced around, satisfied he was utterly alone. There would be no diversions. He finally felt ready to chart his future.

Gordon's first thought immediately put a smile on his face. It'd only been a couple of days, but so far, his recent experience on the summit of Longs Peak continued to exert a healing effect. For the last two and a half years, Gordon had lived under a dark cloud. Most of the time, he was too preoccupied to think about Ryan's death consciously, but that didn't nullify its controlling influence. His brother's accident had transformed him into a different man, one he didn't respect. The memory of that night was like a magnet applying a powerful but invisible force.

Gordon had told Elaine that he'd be willing to see a professional if necessary. That was still an option, but for now, Ben and Gabby had done an excellent job filling that role. Over the last two days, Gordon felt like a new man. He knew Ryan's accident would always be a painful memory, but it had lost its firm grip over his life. Just an hour spent on top of a mountain combined with some insightful advice had already produced a minor miracle.

Gordon was regaining control over his life. Since starting the summer trip, he'd found the strength to exercise his free will. Gordon could finally admire his reflection in the mirror. Even before the Longs Peak climb, he'd given up smoking, improved his diet, begun a rigorous exercise program, cut back to drinking only an occasional beer, and lost a significant amount of weight. Even Elaine had commented on his physical appearance, which was just from the small image she saw on her iPad screen. She had also indicated that Gordon had transformed himself back into the man she had first married. He smiled to himself and reached over his shoulder to pat himself on the back.

Even more important was the impact of the psychological experience on the summit of Longs Peak. Gordon may never fully understand what had happened, but in his gut, he knew that the man who came down from the mountain was different from the one who went up. He was no longer the tanked-up dad who'd ignored his kids on a family picnic or smacked his son over spilled grape juice. It may have been only a couple of days since his emotional reawakening, but Gordon was sure it would last. The wedge that had driven him from his wife and kids was gone.

The situation was now less complicated. It was no longer a matter of whether Gordon *could* resume his former role as a husband and father. Now the only question was whether he wanted to. Elaine's last email asked him to come home. Is this what *he* wanted? Should he head back to his old life in St. Louis, or should he prepare for a new one in the Colorado Rockies?

For weeks, Gordon had analyzed this issue. He'd broken it down into two competing values: family versus freedom. Now there were details to bring greater clarity. Gordon had his interview scheduled for Monday if he wanted to begin a new life in Colorado. Assuming they offered him the job, he would need to give notice to Jim, find a place to live in or near Grand Lake, and prepare for his move. On the other hand, if he wanted to reunite with his family in St. Louis, he could simply cancel the interview, pack his belongings, and start the long drive home.

Gordon had spent the last several weeks listing and evaluating the pros and cons of both options. Now it was time to make a decision. Maybe this was not a choice to make by weighing the pros and cons. Perhaps he should try a different approach.

Gordon stared blankly at the foaming water beneath the falls as it twisted and twirled, finding its way around smaller rocks and larger boulders. While the icy stream seldom followed a straight path, Gordon observed a consistency to its movement. The guiding force was gravity. No matter the obstacles, water from the mountain's snowmelt consistently flowed from the higher elevations to the lower. Energized by this natural law of the universe, the water, clouded with its effervescent bubbles, frantically scrambled down the steep incline and would soon settle in the tranquil depths of Grand Lake.

Suddenly, Gordon realized the answer was metaphorically in front of him. Just as the physical law of gravity forced water to seek the lowest elevation, there were natural laws that guided the human quest for inner peace. Many people never gave much thought to these laws, and as a result, they futilely struggled against them. These were the people who ended their lives full of regret. Since Gordon knew he didn't want to feel remorse as an older man on his deathbed, he would no longer resist these laws.

It was like a breeze had suddenly blown away the haze, revealing a great truth. Gravity pulled the water down from the mountains to settle into serene lakes or turbulent oceans. What held that same sway over humans? What force would guide people towards true happiness? The answer? As corny as it might sound, it was love. The love of a spouse, the love for a child or a parent. The love between a master teacher and his students. The love between good friends.

Gordon recalled Dylan's words. "It's the *people* in your life that matter the most, *not* the places." Gordon knew he'd have friends and students in Colorado, and over time, there might even be a second wife. But she wouldn't be Elaine. And there was no replacing David and Annie. Gordon loved the mountains, but they would always be here, and he could visit them whenever he wanted. Hell, as a teacher, he could even spend entire summers in Grand Lake. It wouldn't be hard.

Where Gordon chose to live wasn't essential. What mattered most was that he should be with his family. Elaine was his wife, and she wanted him to come home. Ever since that college basketball game in St. Louis, they'd been a couple, each bringing out the best in the other. Tragedy had severely tested their love, but in the end, it had survived. What's more, their love had spawned the creation of two remarkable people.

And what about their children? David and Annie were both sweet and gentle. They were bright, and their potential was infinite. Until now, Gordon had played only a limited role in shaping their humanity. Would it not be wondrously rewarding to help mold and shape their futures? Most important, they were *his* kids. Annie had his smile; David's eyes reflected his own. Gordon yanked out his phone and touched the photo app. He skipped the hundreds of recent pictures from Colorado and raced to the photograph he'd taken of his children that day at the zoo. They stared back at him, David with his arm slung over Annie's shoulder, Annie affectionately hugging her Big Bird puppet. Their smiles begged him to come home.

Gordon realized that since leaving St. Louis, he'd not looked at any pictures of his children. Not once. Sure, he saw their images during their FaceTime calls, and he thought about them when he was weighing his decisions about the future. Otherwise, Gordon had purposely avoided thinking about his children. He'd become good at repressing memories he didn't want to face. Gordon had done this with his brother, and now, he was practicing the same mental gymnastics with his children.

As he stared at their faces on the screen of his phone, memories came flooding back. Some were distant, like midnight feedings and pig-gybacked rides. Others were more recent. Gordon used his thumb and index finger to enlarge their images on the screen. For a moment, he hypnotically gazed at their beaming faces.

Why had he repressed these memories? Gordon glanced to his right and realized that the further the brook's waters traveled from the falls, the easier it became to see the creek's rocky bottom. Suddenly, Gordon knew the answer to his question. David and Annie represented his murky past in Missouri, not his visible future in Colorado. For a time, he'd been on this quixotic quest to be free, to be able to travel throughout the west like Dylan in his Coleman camper. But what was he thinking? Ben and Gabby provided good company, but that was temporary. Their future lay with each other, and pretty soon, Gordon would have to be on his own. In the long run, could he find happiness in Colorado?

Gordon momentarily closed his eyes and thought back to the past. He recalled that up until the night of his brother's death, he'd been happy.

Everything abruptly changed with the news of Ryan's death. During the period that followed, particularly since moving out of his house, Gordon's happiness had shriveled up like a dried grape. Now that he'd shared his past and his shame with others, he was ready to face the future. And thanks to their help and advice, Gordon was finally ready to go home.

His home was in St. Louis. That's where he had a teaching job with friends like Jim and students like Andre. That's where his father, who'd made this trip possible, was awaiting his return. And in the western suburbs of St. Louis, he had a home with two delightful children. Most important, Elaine was in St. Louis. True, the Missouri Ozarks paled in comparison to these majestic mountains, but that didn't matter. Gordon was drawn towards the love of these people by the same laws of nature that attracted these tumbling waters towards the tranquility of Grand Lake.

Gordon glanced at the time posted on his phone. It was still only seven o'clock. If he rushed, he could be back at the cabin in thirty minutes and on the road an hour later. Ben and Gabby would just be waking up and having their coffee. He could quickly explain, and they'd understand. Once on the road, Gordon would think of a nice gift he could send to show his appreciation. Otherwise, there was no reason to delay. It was time to go.

"*It's—time—to—go*," Gordon said loud enough to be heard above the raging falls. He glanced around, smiling in embarrassment when he realized what he'd done. There was still no one in sight. Gordon jumped up and sprinted down the trail. Then one final thought forced him to slam the brakes. He wouldn't bother with an email this time, just a quick text:

Elaine, I'll be home by midnight.

Most of the route was downhill, and Gordon managed to jog the entire way in about twenty minutes. He was out of breath when he reached Ben's cabin, so he stopped for a moment at the front door. That's when he heard the ding coming from his pocket. It was Elaine's reply:

I'll be waiting.

The rest of the morning was a blur. Gabby and Ben had just finished their coffee, and when Gordon explained his decision, they were
delighted. Ben was adamant he should come back next summer and every
summer afterward. Gabby stressed their cabin was his home away from
home and that he should bring the whole family. The Three Amigos! One
might spend ten months of the year in St. Louis, but they should reunite
every summer.

Gordon then raced to pack his belongings and load the car. As he
prepared to leave, he yanked out his phone and called Bryan LeBeau to
cancel the job interview. It was only eight o'clock, but principals were
busy this time of year getting ready for the opening of school, so Gordon
wasn't surprised when Bryan answered after the first ring. It only took
Gordon a minute to explain, and Bryan responded that he completely
understood. He seemed like a good man.

Gabby and Ben walked Gordon out to his car. They each hugged
him tight for an extended period. Gabby had tears in her eyes when they
pulled apart. Then Gordon started up the old Corolla. He'd spent little
time in it over the past several weeks, and after tooling around in Ben's
Mercedes, driving the old Toyota was like riding in a buggy pulled by an
aging horse. Gordon opened the car window, gave a wave, and turned
towards Highway 34. Ben and Gabby waved back while embracing each
other.

An hour later, Gordon linked up with I-70, the interstate that blasted
its way through the Rockies. It was a roller coaster ride as he navigated
his way up and down the steep inclines and through a mammoth tunnel.
Next came the steep descent into Denver. It was mid-morning, so most
of the rush hour traffic had subsided. Up to this point, Gordon had been
rocking through Springsteen's greatest hits. As the city's skyline came into
view, with its sweeping prairies in the background, Gordon shut off the
CD player and switched to the radio.

Once again, the music gods must have been smiling. The first rock
station he found was playing "Home" by Phillip Phillips. Feeling like this
song was a bit sappy, he searched for a different station and came upon
John Denver singing "Back Home Again." Was this just a coincidence?

John Denver was understandably popular in Colorado, and while Gordon liked some of his music, this song reeked of even more schmaltz, so he searched again for another station. He half-expected to stumble across "Homeward Bound" by Simon and Garfunkel. Instead, he landed on a classic rock station where Graham Nash crooned "Our House."

Gordon laughed out loud. This series of songs was just too bizarre. He understood that when something rises to the surface of your brain, it seems to appear everywhere. Gordon was anxious to get home, and now everything reminded him of his destination. Pretty soon, he'd be soaring across the emptiness of Kansas, and that reminded him of that final scene from *The Wizard of Oz*. Dorothy looks around at her loving family and friends in their Kansas farmhouse, smiles, and declares, "There's no place like home!"

As Gordon approached the bedroom community of Aurora in Denver's eastern suburbs, he glanced into his side mirror. He saw a reflection of the Rocky Mountains slowly receding into the far-off horizon. Gordon sucked in a deep breath, slowly exhaled, and then pressed his lips together into a smile. He knew he'd be back next summer, and this time, he'd bring the whole family.

Turning his attention next to the road in front of him, Gordon knew he was in for a *long* day. It would be almost six hundred miles of open prairie between Denver and Kansas City, with at least four more hours to cross his home state after that. The best scenery he could hope to see would be the rippling fields of sunflowers that might grace the landscape of western Kansas. Otherwise, there would just be time to think. He assembled a mental checklist to contemplate—how to continue healthy living habits, regain his mojo in the classroom, and be a better husband and father.

Gordon started this process by focusing on the recent past. In less than two months, his life had turned around. He'd renewed a tight bond with an old college roommate and found a new friend in Gabby. He'd improved his physical health. There was still a pale scar on the side of his face, but in this instance, it was a wound he wore with pride. Gordon had encountered other people, like Hanska and Dylan, who shared life-altering words of advice. All of this would serve him well as he faced his future. But most important, Gordon left his demons behind on the summit of Longs Peak.

About the Author

JOE REGENBOGEN taught high school history for 40 years. He began teaching in the Ninth Ward of New Orleans in 1979 where two years later, he was named runner-up for New Orleans teacher-of-the-year. After moving to St. Louis in 1984, he continued to teach for the Parkway School District in the western suburbs of St. Louis. In the final years of his teaching career, Joe taught in a special program for the exceptionally gifted where his students ended their eighth grade year by taking the AP exam in American History.

As Joe approached his retirement from teaching, he took up writing as a second career. To date, he has published four books, all non-fiction. The first two, *Questioning History* and *Relearning History*, were intended to deepen his students' understanding of the past beyond the classroom. Joe's third book, *The Boys of Brookdale*, told the stories of World War Two veterans who all lived their final years in the same senior living facility where Joe's father resided. His most recent book, *Making a Difference*, recounted the story of Irl Solomon and his 38-year teaching career in East St. Louis, Illinois, one of the toughest school districts in the nation.

Joe currently lives with Dana, his wife of 42 years in the same home where they raised their two children, both of whom grew up to become attorneys. At the present, Joe continues to write, tutor and travel. Joe and Dana are preparing to provide full-time daycare for Ava, their first grandchild.

www.ingramcontent.com/pod-product-compliance
Lightning Source LLC
Chambersburg PA
CBHW022207030726
47494CB00021B/2016